Truth in Cinders

a Kingdom of Xol novel

Denise B. Tanaka

Sasoriza Books

San Jose

I0561111

Truth in Cinders

Denise Tanaka

Published by Sasoriza Books, 2017.

for Laura

"Help me!" huffed a hoarse male voice. A man thrust his head and half his body in through the open window.

Condrie dropped the bellows that she had been using to revive the kitchen's fire for supper. Wooden handles clattered on the stone floor.

The man glanced backward at the town's streets behind him. Evening made the shadows dim. Insects continued droning their summer song undisturbed. He appeared to calm down one notch from total panic.

Surprisingly nimble for a man so tall, he tucked up his long legs to roll over the windowsill. He slammed the shutters and dropped the bolt to seal them. Though he moved quickly, she caught the twinkle of jeweled buttons in a blur of elegant colors. Never had she seen such intense purple, indigo, clover, and scarlet except in a field of wild flowers. *A gentleman . . . on this side of town?*

Crouching alongside her at the hearth, he looked up with vivid blue eyes. "Help me, girl. They want to kill me."

Coin-pinchers are getting more bold and violent these days. Condrie flapped her hand to draw him toward the center of the room.

The gentleman helped her slide the heavy table aside. She plucked up an iron ring in the floor's hatch. He didn't balk at the dark pit. He didn't hesitate to plunge blindly into the root cellar with the barley stalks, juniper berries, cardamom pods, and radishes. Enough of a glow came from the smoldering fireplace to see the top of his head. Shaggy, pale hair was like fronds of wheat crouching among the bitter vegetables.

Condrie let the hatch fall. The table was too heavy to drag back into place by herself, so she adjusted the stools and then dropped a sack full of lemons over the hatch's iron ring.

Someone knocked on the back door.

Condrie swallowed her heart back down into her chest.

"Open in the name of King Davarche of Xol," demanded an angry voice. Several others muttered outside.

She frowned to wonder why agents of the kingdom to the south had ventured so far from their domain. Briefly she wished for the courage to shout at them, *Go away, your hornets! You have no business here!*

Condrie slid aside the plank that bolted the door.

Knights of Xol entered the kitchen—tall, muscled beings clothed in the dark wool of foreign rams. Metallic chips were riveted to the shoulder pads of their coats and the bracers on their forearms. Crescent gorgets hung over their chests. Their heavy boots pounded on the hard floor. Seven of them—seven soldiers and seven swords—entered to poke around. One stayed outside to watch the street.

One beardless knight spoke in a strong, clear voice. "We're looking for a gentleman. Have you seen or heard someone of quality run by?"

A woman! In the identical stiff uniform as the others, and with the mannerisms of a cavalryman, Condrie had not recognized this knight's sex until she spoke.

Condrie shook her head to answer. She continued gawking, not only because a woman bore arms in service of the southern king, but she had the exotic look of a foreigner. She had wide-set pale eyes, a blunt nose, caramel-toned skin, and auburn hair that she had chopped short to the collar like the other knights.

"Is your mother at home, girl?"

My mother is dead. I'm an orphan. I just work in the kitchen here. Too many words, too much explanation clogged up at the back of her tongue. Again, she shook her head to answer.

The woman knight stepped in closer to stare down at Condrie's upraised eyes. "Are you a mute?"

"N-n-n-n-no . . . I-I-I-I. . . ." She balled her fists, silently cursing her stubborn tongue. Of all the times for it to fail! Why could the words never make the journey smoothly from her mind to her mouth? *Especially at a time like this. They'll think I'm nervous; they'll think I'm hiding something.*

The other knights checked the window shutter, seeing it was bolted from inside. They poked their leather gloves into barrels of flour and pickles, knocked the skillets and pans at their hooks, and even picked through the stack of logs by the smoldering hearth. One of them took a ripe peach from the basket and gnawed into its sweetness. *Put that down! It doesn't belong to you!* Yet she did not dare to scold him.

"Do you have a husband?"

Condrie shook her head. "N-n-n-no husband."

"Surely you don't live alone in this grand house? You look too young to be the mistress, so where is your master?"

Condrie's tongue gagged in the back of her throat. She wanted to cry out, *Don't you know where you are? Didn't you see the sign on the street?*

"Answer me, wench," the woman knight snapped.

The knight from outside put one foot in the door. "Captain? There's a placard over the door. This isn't a home, it's a brewery."

"No, we're a dis-. . . dis-. . ." Condrie stammered and gritted her teeth. The correct word, *distillery*—such a simple word—refused to come out of her mouth.

"A brewery?" The woman knight snickered to her companions. "We're wasting time here. He must have gone the other way."

With a rattle of scabbards, the seven of them filed out the door. The vacant kitchen suddenly seemed enormous when she was alone.

Condrie carefully bolted the door shut. She pressed her ear to a gap in the planks and listened to the whistle of outside air. She waited until she was sure that their heavy boots had tromped the cobblestones farther down the street.

When she raised the heavy trap door, her arms trembled. She wasn't sure if it was from nervousness or the exertion.

"Are they gone?" the man whispered from deep down in the hole.

Condrie nodded.

After a hesitation, he slowly emerged from the root cellar. Condrie's eyes opened wide as she took her first long study of him. He was a tall foreign man, as the knights were, but slender so he didn't seem overwhelmingly large. Coppery blond hair extended past his shoulders in the flamboyant fashion of lords in the southern kingdom. He had recently shaved; only a day's worth of stubble made a fuzz at his chin. Such clothes! He dressed better than any land baron she knew. The velvets were as soft as a brushed cat. Buttons made a row of jewels down his jerkin's breast line. Brass buckles die-cast as bulls' horns clipped his cape together. His belt was narrow, and he carried no weapons. His boots were soft-soled suede not meant for traveling.

The man slouched wearily as he sat by the hearth bricks. Condrie expected that his rush of fear would take some time to drain away.

Condrie asked, "Have you done something terrible, sir?"

"I have offended my king." He had a deep, melodic voice like a singer talking. A cultured, foreign accent gave a sense of importance to even the simplest of words. "My departure from court was, shall I say, disruptive."

"Knights," she repeated. The sound of his voice warmed her to the core like a hot toddy on a bitter winter's morning. "Knights! I never thought I would see the King of Xol's legions harassing people in our territory. . . ."

Condrie took a breath of surprise at how easily the words flowed off her tongue. *Perhaps it's the excitement.*

"They have a right to harass me." He stared into the growing fire. "I am a citizen of Xol with a warrant for my apprehension."

"Appre- . . . I don't know that word."

He smiled at that. Condrie gasped at the flash of white teeth, for it only made him more handsome. Such men they bred in the southern lands! His features had the perfectly measured proportions of a storyteller's mask, almost too perfect to have been born by chance.

"It means the king wants me back. He wants me very much."

"You need to get out of here, sir." Condrie gestured at the window with a sweep of her arm. "I thought, when I first saw you, that highway bandits were after you. But knights! If knights are after a gentleman like you, sir, then you must be a poet or a philosopher or some kind of trouble-maker."

"Quaintly put," he said. "I'm sorry to cause you trouble, miss. Believe me, the less you know, the safer you'll be."

The man went to the window, opened the shutter slightly, and listened to the air. Pigeons cooed as they settled into their nests on the roof. Farther away was the murmur of conversation, too faint to hear the words, but the inflection and tone of a foreign language were unmistakable.

Condrie asked, "Are they still out there?"

"Yes, they are."

"I need to tell Mama. It may be she'll have an idea of how you can blend in with our customers. It's almost evening. The customers come around after sunset."

He surveyed his elegant clothes with a rueful smirk. "I think I'll have a hard time blending in with your customers on this side of town."

"True, but Mama has clothes you can buy." Condrie shaped three loaves of risen dough onto a wooden paddle and slid it into the hob in the fireplace.

"In my size?"

"Any size, sir."

"Is your mother a seamstress?"

"No, sir."

He tilted one of his neatly plucked eyebrows. It made his blue eye gleam in the lamplight like a fine gem. "And yet, there is a selection of men's clothes?"

"Oh yes, sir." Condrie fanned the growing flames and stirred the chunks of bacon into the pea soup. "Sometimes, the customers spill on their own or they don't wish to go home smelling like they've been here."

"Smelling like they've been here, you say? What sort of place is this?"

"Don't you know where you are, sir?"

"Clearly, I do not."

"You are in the Goldenwood Bough Tavern," she told him with pride. "We are the finest quality gin distillery west of the Clement River."

"A gin distillery?" He smiled again. "That's perfect. They certainly won't look for me here."

"Oh? Why?"

"I don't drink liquor," he said firmly.

A man who doesn't drink gin? How odd, she thought, but the first rule of the house was not to ask questions.

"What's your name, girl?"

"Condrie. Who are you, sir?"

At his flinch of hesitation, she regretted asking. But it was too late. "You may call me . . . uh, Wegdell."

"Take off your shirt, sir." She eyed the measurements of his long torso that surpassed the height of most townsmen, boatmen, and farmers in the area. "I'll need to search upstairs for something big enough to fit you."

Wegdell shook his head. "I would rather you not see me unclothed. I'm . . . I'm, uh, shy."

"As you say, sir." Condrie headed for the curtained partition that separated the kitchen from the tasting room. Her blue clay bell, on a beaded thong around her neck, thok-thokked as she walked.

He pointed and remarked, "That's a charm from the Clichard valleys, isn't it?"

"Yes, sir." She turned with a pause to let him view the bell hanging on her flat chest. "The priestesses mix clay with sacred mountain spring water. Its sound keeps away angry ghosts and evil spirits, I heard."

"Keeps away ghosts, eh? Do you have an extra one for me?"

"No, sir. Sorry."

*

As soon as she started rummaging about in the upstairs hall closet, Condrie heard women's voices through the floorboards beneath her feet.

"Who's up there?"

"What's that noise?"

Condrie chose a large shirt woven of local hyssk linen and a pair of burlap trousers that she hoped would be long enough. After digging out a wool cloak from beneath a stack of clean towels, she started down the creaky stairs to the ground floor.

Ma Kielsing emerged at the base of the stairs, waiting for her to descend. Juniper and cardamom pulp stained her apron in blotches of black and green. Her gray-streaked black hair was half-tucked into a linen cap that made her cheeks seem to be rounder than they were.

"Condy, why aren't you putting supper on the table? What are you doing with those clothes?"

The room behind Ma Kielsing gurgled and hissed with the vapors swirling through the Goldenwood Bough. The copper vats shined with lantern light as a sunny afternoon boxed up in brick walls. Women's voices murmured at their work, talking amongst themselves. *Talking*, she thought with a pang in her chest. *Always so easily and so happily talking.*

"Uh . . . uh . . . a m-m-m-man . . . came."

"Condy, I'm surprised at you, serving a customer by yourself and before we've opened our doors for the evening."

"He's not . . . not . . ."

"Not a customer?" Ma Kielsing finished for her.

Condrie nodded and then shook her head.

"Is he one of our vendors? A coppersmith? A troubadour? Or is he a beggar?"

Condrie continued shaking her head.

The exasperated grunt from her mother propelled Condrie forward. Leading the way, she hurried along the narrow hallway that connected the distillery room to the kitchen. Back-to-back fireplaces shared a wall; smoke from both hearths went up a common chimney. Ma Kielsing followed on her heels.

Niarr, one of the tavern's barmaids, emerged from the distillery room. In a bushel basket, she carried slender glass bottles full of the precious golden liquid. Niarr was a hardy younger version of Ma Kielsing; she walked smoothly even with a dozen bottles weighed against her hip.

"What's the bustle?" Niarr asked.

Ma Kielsing answered, "Take that batch to the bar. We'll be along."

Niarr trailed behind them instead, bottles clink-clink-clinking with her every step. "Something's up in the kitchen, is it? I saw knights of Xol go around on the porch earlier. What did they want with us?"

"The knights?" other voices asked from the distillery room. "Are they in here?"

By the time they reached the kitchen's curtain, Condrie had several women in aprons trailing behind her.

The man rose politely to his feet at the sight of them. "Good afternoon, ladies. So sorry for the inconvenience. Condrie told me you were yet closed for business, but I. . . ."

As weary as they were from the hours of watching fruit pulp turn to steam, the women turned on their best smiles and pumped up their buxom chests. In moments, Wegdell had gentle hands stroking his shoulders and arms, pressing him back down to the stool where he had been sitting. Niarr plowed her fingers into that lengthy mop of wheat-colored hair. "Oh, he's a walking work of art," she remarked to the other women.

Condrie frowned more deeply than she'd thought herself capable of frowning. *He's mine*, she wanted to say. *He asked me for help, not you.*

Ma Kielsing came forward, snatching the clothes out of Condrie's arms on the way. "I charge one copper coin for each article of clothing. Unless you want to trade in these foppish linens for an open tab at the bar—redeemable at a later date, when you're not in whatever trouble you're in that I don't want to know about?"

Wegdell bent his head forward to avoid the hands ruffling his long hair. It was odd, Condrie thought, the way he wasn't responding to them. She had never known a man who could just sit there, not even the Lord High Sheriff who had a mournful difficulty in becoming aroused. Stranger still, this man's lack of reaction eased the tense knot in the center of her chest. *He's different from every other man I've seen. We don't need to slap his hands away.*

"I actually, uh. . . . Could you stop making tangles? Actually, I just need the change of clothes. I don't drink liquor, so I'll have no use for an open tab, thank you just the same. Keep my garments as my gift—no, my apology for distressing you, madam."

Condrie's mother nodded to accept the deal.

Another woman, Lienya, bent forward to his cheek and inspected the dark roots of his hair. "You're not a blond. You dye it, don't you?"

"Yes, I do," he said.

Niarr sniffed loudly at his scalp. "Smells like marigolds and apple cider. It's a beautiful color. Professional job. How much did it cost? Where did you get it done?"

"I, uh, did it myself." Wegdell squirmed away and stood up to escape them.

"Yourself?" Niarr repeated. "What sort of man dyes his own hair?"

"A man who would like a change of clothes," he said.

Condrie rolled her eyes to survey his wardrobe once more, from his pleated batiste collar down to his soft suede boots. *Are those really his clothes, or did he steal them? Is he really a gentleman at all?*

Ma Kielsing put the plain clothes on the butcher-block table. "Hurry up and change. The sooner we get those damned velvets stashed away in the attic, the sooner we can slip you out the back door. No questions."

Niarr snaked her arm around his and pressed close against him. "Oh, Mama, must we send him away?"

Ma Kielsing said, "Get back to work, all of you! Doors open for business soon. There's glasses to be filled and spills to be wiped and drunkards to be consoled."

Niarr led the way out of the kitchen. The other women, passing through the curtain, murmured to each other, "I'll be seeing that face on every face I serve tonight . . ." and "A feast for the eyes, he was . . ." and "What a waste that lil' Condy saw him first. . . ."

Ma Kielsing said to him sternly, "My tavern is known for its discretion as a sanctuary for all. We repeat no secrets spilled under this roof. We ask no questions. On the other hand, I trust you not to bring calamity and woe to my doorstep."

"I understand," he said.

Ma Kielsing tapped Condrie on the shoulder. "You should've fetched me."

"Yes, Mama. I'm sorry."

"No harm done." One more severe scowl over her shoulder at Wegdell, and Condrie's mother left.

*

Condrie left him privacy in the kitchen to change his clothes. After all, she had her usual chores to do—the same chores as every night. Outside in the street, she pushed open the striped canvas awnings that had covered the shuttered windows during the day. With a flickering oil cup in her palm, she lit the wicks of red lantern hanging over the front door. She straightened the placard—the painted sign of a naked woman surrounded by juniper blossoms. In the pause, she thought of the knights violating her kitchen, taking liberties where they did not belong. *Let him go. Give up your pursuit. Go back to the southern lands where you came from.*

Upon returning to the kitchen's back door, she discovered a pug-faced orphan boy in dirty clothes sitting on the step.

"Hey, Kin," she said.

He had the scruffy look of a caterpillar curled up in a gutter, sleeping off the day as townsfolk stepped over and around him.

"Hey, Condy," he replied in that drawling street accent of his. Kin was a coarse boy who frightened most people—for good reason. He was a pick-pocket and a burglar, but he was always kind to her. Condrie knew that he'd be hanged for his crimes before he reached the age of manhood, but he acted as if he were immortal.

"Heard the buzz?"

"No," she said. "What?"

"There's a murderer on the loose!" He showed his brown teeth with an excited, happy grin. "The King of Xol's knights are hunting him in every shack and silo and gully for twenty leagues around."

Condrie clutched her flickering oil pot more tightly. Hot ceramic almost burned her palm, but she barely felt it.

"A murderer?" she asked. "Who did he murder?"

"Ain't seen him, have you? A foreigner on the run? He broke into Tailor Marlen's shop earlier today and stole a gentleman's suit of clothes."

Condrie ducked back into kitchen. She headed for the fireplace to take the freshly baked baguettes out of the hob.

Kin followed her inside. He always kept in motion, pacing in front of the hearth, as if afraid to sit down and get caught by the knights himself. "They say he poisoned four people in the castle of the king. Or he drowned them. Or he went on a rampage and set 'em on fire. I'm hearing lots of versions. Some say his own brother were among them. Circle of blood, to murder his own brother!"

"I can't believe it," she softly said. "Who could do such a thing?"

Wegdell strolled into the kitchen from the water closet. He wore the common clothes now, and with his long hair unbrushed, he looked less handsome than he had an hour before. As if he were in his own home, he reached for a wedge of cheese. Then he thought better and stopped. "May I?"

She nodded permission. Wegdell chose a bit of cheese and an apple, and then he tore off the end from one of the baguettes.

Condrie stirred the pea soup that was gradually getting warmer over the low-smoldering fire. Soon the women finishing their day's labor at the still would come to gobble supper before the customers arrived.

"You know what else I heard?" Kin went on, leaning close to her to whisper the secret. "They say the murderer might be a Sagewyn."

Condrie looked up just then and saw Wegdell's hand tremble as he poured tea from the copper kettle. He raised his head and saw that she saw. *A Sagewyn, here?* Condrie shrank back a step, wondering if he had a goat's horns beneath all that shaggy hair, suddenly more afraid than she had ever felt in her life.

"Rumors have a way of exaggerating things," Wegdell said in as gentle a voice as she had ever heard from a man. "I wouldn't be afraid of shadows, if I were you."

"Lot you know," Kin snapped back. "The king's knights don't chase just nobody overland for three full weeks of days an' nights. This murderer is one crafty shrew. But we'll see him in bindings by dawn, mark my words."

Wegdell inhaled a bit. "Say, don't you have some coin purses to go pinch?"

"Hey, shun you," Kin cursed in the language of outerland nomads. The consonants were harsh, and one had to bite and spit to pronounce the words well. Kin, like most gutter rats, was multi-lingual and could give full force to the oath.

Wegdell didn't answer. He calmly chewed into his apple with those perfectly white teeth of his. Condrie glanced to him sideways, trying to see if his side-teeth were fangs.

"I'll be around, Condy," Kin said over his shoulder as he made his exit.

"Yeah. Bye, Kin."

The rear door slapped shut. The kitchen fell into silence.

Condrie went to work with the hand-held peppermill, grinding a few black flakes into the green pea soup, just so she wouldn't have to stare at him. *A Sagewyn!* Her mind buzzed with the idea, replaying every puppet show and troubadour's tale she had heard since childhood. *The zeter-bear, the zeter-bear, will come at night to eat your hair.* She had always avoided drawing water from forest ponds for fear that a nymph's hands would grab her wrists and drag her underwater. The blue clay bell dangling from her throat was supposed to repel ghosts and wraiths; apparently it did not repel him.

"I won't hurt you," he said. "Please believe me."

"I do."

"An explanation is certainly in order, but I don't know where to begin. I don't know if you could ever understand."

"You heard Mama. We don't ask questions."

"You saved my life when you didn't have to hide a stranger. And I saw the way you looked at me when the others were pawing through my hair. Women look at me that way quite often, but I feel awkward when they're as young as you. What are you, fourteen? Fifteen?"

"I'm not so young as that." She looked up at him and wondered what sort of men were bred in the Kingdom of Xol, who felt awkward at indulging younger girls. "I'm in my seventeenth year."

"Seventeen, eh? If you were a cicada, you'd be ready to emerge and spread your wings." He furrowed his brow and stared at her more intensely. "But you're not a cicada."

Condrie bit on her smile. "No, silly, I'm a girl."

"A girl?" He drew in a slow breath. "Of course you are."

Condrie set out five bowls on the butcher-block table with five soup spoons and five chunks of cheese. In the center, she placed one loaf of bread on a paddle with a serrated knife.

"Where's your supper?" he asked.

"I eat mine after they eat. The bar maids need their strength to stand up pouring drinks all night. I just clean up the kitchen."

"Mmm," he murmured thoughtfully while chewing his bread and cheese. "Do you ever think you could be more than what you are . . . more than the little girl who feeds the tavern wenches?"

"What more could I hope to be?" she said. "I'm an orphan with no family and no name. The lowliest class of wagoner or riverman is above me. If not for Mama, I'd be a starving rat in the streets like my friend Kin. She gave me a warm bed and a job when I had nowhere else to go."

"I understand," he said. "Though I would caution you against mistaking sanctuary for servitude. It's a mistake that I've made in accepting the generosity of those in a position to bestow favors . . . part of the reason why King Davarche's knights are pursuing me across half the world."

Condrie stiffened her back. "Mama's trusting you, that you're not bringing danger to our door. Are you a murderer?"

"No," he assured her, fixing his blue eyes into hers to push his sincerity.

"Are you a Sagewyn?"

He lowered his eyes as he loosened the drawstring neckline of his coarse shirt. Slowly, he pulled the fabric away from his collarbone. On his left breast was the tattoo of a sunburst: a perfect circle with dozens of triangles jutting outward from it.

Condrie shuddered at the indelible mark of the King of Xol. A real Sagewyn sat here, in her kitchen. *Is he doing something to me with his magic?*

Can he see the thoughts inside my mind? Is this why I don't stutter when he's in the room?

"What sort of beast are you?" she asked. No wonder he hadn't responded to the women's attentions. Sagewyn were magical creatures who only pretended to be people: shadow wraiths, water nymphs, firebirds, dream-walkers, ghost eaters, and snake men . . . and those were just the ones she knew of.

"It isn't important that you know what I really am when I'm not in human skin. In fact, it's probably safer if you don't." Wegdell tightened the drawstring of his shirt and covered up the mark on his chest. "I swear by God, I won't harm you or any of your barmaids, and I won't allow the king's knights to cause any more distress than they already have. I'll leave as soon as the street is clear."

*

The women gobbled their soup and bread. Under the mother's watchful eye, they spoke no more to the man loitering on the hearth stones. He sipped brown tea from a tankard meant for ale. He watched the flames dance over the logs while Condrie took bar towels from the shelf.

Customers started strolling into the main door by nightfall, and Condrie didn't have a chance to talk to the Sagewyn anymore. She ate her own supper off to the side while standing at a basin quickly filling with drinking glasses to be wiped. In addition to their usual customers—the shopkeepers and tradesmen and artisans of the town—a convoy of river boats had docked ashore with their cargo for the night. While the boatmen were idle, there was plenty of gin and bitter waters to drink.

All the while, the man calling himself Wegdell paced the kitchen's stone floor. He helped Condrie put away the clean soup bowls on a high shelf so she did not need to hop onto the step-stool. He checked out the back window from time to time, and each time shook his head; a glint of silvery armor caught his eye.

"Why won't they go away?" she whispered under her breath.

"I'm too much of a prize. The foot soldier who bags me will be promoted to first lieutenant on the spot."

"Well, can't you do something . . . how shall I say . . ." Condrie let go of wiping a drinking glass to flap her hand meaningfully in the air, ". . . do something unusual to get away?"

He shook his head. "At the moment, I am in human skin."

"I've heard that wraiths rape women in their sleep."

"I am certainly *not* a wraith." He showed his hands. "See? No grimy fingernails."

"Then just tell me," she begged. "What sort of Sagewyn are you?"

"I'd rather not say." He leaned against the fireplace mantle to watch the smoldering logs sputter and spark. He looked at the orange in a strange way, as if it meant something more to him than warmth.

A pounding commotion came from the front tasting room. Glassware crashed to the floor. Ma Kielsing called out in protest. The angry voices of the king's knights were unmistakable.

Condrie clutched her apron, paralyzed with fear. Now, the trays full of clean drinking glasses weighed down the butcher-block table. The table covered the hatch to the root cellar. There was no time to move it.

Wegdell ran for the back door, opened it a crack and peeped outside. "There are still three of them in the alleyway. I'm too tall to blend in with the boatmen, damnit."

"Do the knights know your face?"

"No."

"Are you sure?"

"Yes, I'm very sure, and I've bleached my hair. But this," Wegdell tapped at his left breast where the mark of the king lay beneath his shirt, "this I can't erase."

"Maybe you can." Condrie dove for the larder and pulled out another box. It had a leather buckle that, in her haste, her fumbling fingers almost couldn't get open. Wegdell came beside her, curious to see what was inside.

A dozen or more ceramic jars of medicinal salves were packed neatly in songbird nests. Condrie popped the lids, searching for a cream that would match his skin tone. His cheeks and neck were toasted by the sun but his chest was as pale as a plucked quail. Condrie plunged her fingers into the lightest shade she could find.

"A taverness and an apothecary?" he remarked.

"This is an asafoetida paste for customers with a bad cough. Sorry about the smell."

"Smells don't bother me."

Wegdell cooperatively opened the drawstring neckline of his shirt. He had a few slivers of hair on his breastbone that were as dark as coal. Condrie realized that was his true hair color, not blond. She smeared the cream over the tattoo, stroking repeatedly to blend it into his skin. *So soft*, she thought with amazement. She never imagined a man could feel like this.

"There." Wiping her fingers clean on her apron, Condrie hastily packed the jars back into the box.

Wegdell dashed to the hearth and got himself another cup of tea. Just as he sat down, a pair of knights thrust the curtain aside and entered. It was a squad of only men this time, with similarly exotic faces as the ones from before.

"We're looking for a fugitive criminal," said one of them. "He has a scar on his chest. Take off your shirt."

"Sure." Wegdell took one more sip of his tea, deliberately casual, and set the cup aside. Grabbing fistfuls of his shirt at the back of his neck, he yanked the fabric off his head. The fire was behind him, but enough moonlight came from the open window to illuminate the broad canvas of his chest.

The knights looked at him. Then they turned to leave. Condrie leaned to the window sill to listen for their boots clump-clumping away.

Wegdell hooted out a long stream of breath. "I owe you my life a second time," he said. "How can I ever repay you?"

Condrie kept staring at the muscles of his shoulders and arms and the articulation of his abdomen. His body had sleek lines—strong but smooth—not at all like the brawny boatmen at the river's docks. She remembered the softness of his skin and couldn't look away.

As he picked up his mug, he said, "You're doing it again, Condy. Do you mind if I call you 'Condy' like your street rat friend?"

When he put his shirt back on, she kept looking, remembering the form that was beneath. "I'm doing what?"

"Come now, is it really so spectacular for me to take my shirt off?"

His penetrating eyes caused her heart to pulse an extra beat. Condrie turned away in embarrassment. Some stories said that Sagewyn could walk into dreams and know the secrets of one's innermost soul. Other stories said that Sagewyn could fly beyond the hours of the day and see things have not yet happened. Could he predict her future? Would she spend the rest of her life baking bread in this kitchen? How could she ask, and would he grace her with an answer if he knew?

"This is a mask, remember? This is not my face. You should keep in mind that you and I are two very different creatures."

From outside, Condrie heard something rattle. Curious, she went to the back door and looked to the alleyway. The knights were gone. It seemed safe, yet she had an odd feeling that something wasn't right.

Down by the doorstep was the core of a honey peach. The shreds of fruit clinging to the pit were still white, a sign that it hadn't been discarded for long. A honey peach would quickly turn brown in the open air. She told herself that any passerby could have tossed it there, but she knew—with a sickening feeling—that her pickpocket friend Kin loved this fruit. If he had been listening at the window. . . . If he had peeped in and seen her cover the tattoo with cream. . . .

Ma Kielsing came into the kitchen, unusually distressed and dabbing at her forehead with a handkerchief. She told Wegdell, "I should have smuggled you out sooner."

Wegdell nodded with the humility of a boy being scolded.

"Now, a foreign king's knights have violated the tranquility of this establishment. They humiliated my customers. They damaged my inventory. Such a thing should never have happened."

"I'm sorry," he said. "I regret that I've stayed too long. I apologize for the inconvenience. Good evening to you, madam."

Wegdell went to fetch his woolen cloak from a hook near the door.

Condrie stepped closer to her mother. "Mama, I have a problem."

"Wait until he's out of here, sweetie."

"But Mama. . . ."

Again, the front door slammed open, and steel armor clattered in the outer room. Condrie heard the knights yelling, "Bring him forth. Stop hiding him! We know he's here."

Ma Kielsing sighed with exasperation as she turned to duck through the curtain. "Now they're back again."

Wegdell rushed for the back door and gasped out, "Thanks, love," over his shoulder. Not even checking if someone was in the alleyway, he burst out the back door and was gone.

Something large cracked apart in the front room, the sound of a drunkard falling to crush a bar stool. Ma Kielsing got an angry frown at that, and she called out, "Here, now, have a care for the furniture!"

Kin. A fury that she'd never known hurled Condrie out the back door. Her hands balled into fists.

She ran through the narrow alleyways and ducked the awnings of the traders' shops. All of Kin's favorite hangouts were closed for the night: the fruit stand, the fishmonger, the pigeon coops. She wasn't even sure what she'd do when she caught him. He was only a boy, and she was old enough to be his mother. *Yes*, she thought with satisfaction, *I'll spank that naughty little brat.*

"Fire!" someone called.

Condrie stopped in the middle of the street. Like everyone else, she turned to look for the source. Gray smoke floated over the rooftops from behind the soapmaker's shop.

Wait, she thought as she got her bearings. Behind the soapmaker's shop was . . . *home!*

The blacksmith and his apprentice grabbed buckets and ran for the well at the center of town. More shopkeepers hopped out of their beds and rushed into the street. Wearing only nightshirts, they carried shovels, axes and buckets. Condrie was nearly trampled going the opposite way. She ran with the crowd and turned the corner.

Thunder boomed indoors. The Goldenwood Bough—the copper vats of the still at the heart of the tavern—hissed a cloud of fragrant smoke from the open windows. A swathe of black vapors gushed underneath the eaves. It looked like a pot of pea soup bubbling over upside-down. Women screamed in chorus with the howling drunkards.

The blacksmith arrived first and threw a bucket of water at the plaster walls. It splashed weakly.

Ma Kielsing emerged from the kitchen door, clutching several women in her arms. Their hair was singed. Their cheeks were black with soot. They coughed into their hands.

The king's knights maneuvered to surround them. Not to help. Some gripped bottles of gin. One knight shoved Ma Kielsing hard in the chest.

"Where is he?" the knight demanded. "Tell us now!"

"I don't know," Ma Kielsing cried, still more defiant than fearful. "He left already."

The knight slapped her cheek.

Condrie recoiled as if she'd been hit herself. The people in the crowd also gasped with shock, but no one dared come forth to defend her.

"Has anyone seen him?" the knight called out to the crowd. "He is a murderer and a fugitive from the justice of King Davarche of Xol. Those who give him to us shall be rewarded. Those who harbor and hide him shall suffer the same fate as these gin whores!"

Condrie took a step forward.

A strong hand grabbed her arm, halting her. He pulled her aside to the shadows. Condrie rolled into his chest, snuggling under the protective—or restraining—arm of the man named Wegdell.

"Help them," she whispered into his collar. "Do something magical."

"I can't do anything in human skin. If I step out there, they'll arrest me."

"But the tavern . . . the still. . . ."

"I'm sorry, Condy, I really am. I'm sorry about the damage. I should have left hours ago."

"Why didn't you keep running?" she asked.

Wegdell gulped his nervousness and the crone's knot in his throat bobbed up and down. "I, uh, got lost."

"But, you're a Sagewyn. Aren't you all-knowing and all-seeing?"

Wegdell rolled his eyes upward. "If only I were. Truth is, I've got a lousy sense of direction on foot. Could you help me get out of town?"

Condrie gawked at him. "Why should I? I'm in enough trouble already."

"Yes, and I apologize, but the sooner I draw my pursuers away from you and your home, the sooner your life can return to normal."

Condrie sighed through the uncomfortable silence that lingered between them. "There's a caravan of merchants," she said. "They just left town yesterday. Good customers, honest men. They're journeying northwest to the Pine Mountains, and for now they're camped by the river's bend. I can take you there. Maybe you can travel with them."

"Thank you, love. I owe you my life again."

*

The last of the town's familiar buildings dropped away behind their footprints. Condrie clung near to his side like a moth following a lantern. Together they ventured step by tentative step off the wagon road and into the wide-open meadowlands. By moonlight, all colors were gray. Thistles and wildflowers and juniper bushes covered the slopes with an herbal-scented fur. Too dark for the butterflies and honeybees; only mosquitoes and crickets were awake at this hour.

"Will you tell me now?" she asked. "What sort of Sagewyn are you?"

"I'm what is known as a firebird."

A firebird! She tried to hold onto the appearance of calm, not letting the Sagewyn at her side know that her throat went dry and her heart palpitated in her chest. "Is that so? Are you really? Can you sprout wings of flame and a fiery tail?"

"Yes."

"Show me."

"I can't," he said. "So long as King Davarche holds . . . well, he holds me bound by magical means. I cannot transform into a firebird except at the king's bidding."

"Oh, that's why you're on foot."

"Yes, clearly. Otherwise I would have sprouted fiery wings and soared to the highest mountains where his legions of knights could not follow me. You see, even though I've run away from the king's court, I am not truly free. I am shackled in human skin."

"That's a shame."

"Yes, it is." An owl glided silently overhead. Wegdell looked up at the bird in flight. His eyes widened with a long, mournful stare.

They walked on for a while. His boots and her flat house shoes plodded side by side through the fragrant weeds.

"Let me ask you a question, Condy, if I may. Were you truly content to spend your entire life growing up in a gin tavern's kitchen? Did you ever wish to be . . . well, somewhere else? Have you ever dreamed of being someone other than this little girl in an apron?"

"I was married once," she said, shrugging away the distracting idea of wishes and dreams.

"How's that again?"

"I'm a widow."

"A widow at seventeen? I'm so sorry for your loss."

Condrie shook her head to shrug away his sympathy even as the wild flowers in the meadow reminded her of a funeral wreath. "I carry no grief. I have finished my mourning years ago."

"Years?" he repeated, curiously.

"I was given into marriage when I was eleven."

Wegdell stopped walking. "How could you be married when were only a child?"

"My late father owed a debt to our landlord and had no means to pay. So he paid with me." Condrie went on a few steps before she noticed that he had stopped several paces behind her. She stood still, facing the crickets chirping in the moonlit thistles. "My husband was an old man and not robust. Our marriage only lasted three years before his heart gave out. They blamed me, calling me a husband-killer. Since I had not managed to bear any children, I had no right to stay in the household. His brothers inherited . . . no, they took everything. So at fourteen, I was a childless widow, shunned, nameless, and homeless. My maidenhood was gone so I had no value for another marriage. My family did not have the means to take me back as my father had piled up more debts. That winter he died of a chill. I found sanctuary working in the tavern's kitchen."

"Sanctuary," he repeated.

"For the first time in my life, I am treated fairly as a sister or a daughter should be treated. In these last few years, I've never been happier."

"Truly, are you happy?" he asked.

She turned in surprise. "What? I just told you."

"No, you've told me that you're content to hide away in a kitchen. You refer to your employer as 'mother' because you had nowhere else to go. When you speak of your father's death, there is no grief in your voice. So I'll ask again. Can you truly say you're happy in this cocoon you've spun around yourself?"

Her heart thumped. Words choked up in her throat. All she could manage was a bittersweet smile.

*

The merchants had flatbed covered wagons aligned on the banks of the river. Huge white oxen with long horns and bony rumps reclined nearby, chewing their cuds. Come the morning, they would be strapped into their yokes and called upon to haul the loads.

Condrie wasn't sure when to stop, when to say goodbye, when to let Wegdell go on by himself. So she kept walking with him through a swarm of fireflies that tickled her cheeks. They went right up to the first wagon. A man sat on a barrel smoking a pipe.

It was hard to judge the merchant's age since his whole body and head were shrouded in a brown linen veil typical of a caravanner's customary garb. Only his fingertips and toes protruded from the voluminous cloth. He didn't look up from his pipe's bowl as they came near.

"Got somethin' to trade?" the merchant asked.

"Work, for passage west," Wegdell said.

"What sort of work can you do?"

The Sagewyn hesitated, and Condrie regretted not thinking this through. Of course, he had never been called on to do manual labor. His only skills were to transform into a fiery bird and do the bidding of King Davarche of Xol. Now, trapped in the form of a man, there was nothing useful he could do.

"I can sing," Wegdell told him.

The merchant looked up, squinting to regard the tall man with the blond hair. "You're a balladeer?"

"I know some ballads, yes."

"Where's your lute, or harp, or drum? Is she your flute?"

"No, she's my little sister. She came to say goodbye, but she's leaving now." Wegdell turned to her and, with the casual intimacy of a brother, he put his arms around her. Condrie sank into his chest and squeezed him back. "Don't worry about me, Condy," he murmured onto the top of her head. "I'll be fine."

"Take care of yourself." When she stepped back, the air was cold without him.

Condrie turned away from him and started the long walk back to town. She left behind the faint conversation of the Sagewyn firebird and the caravan merchant. The low mooing of the drowsy oxen blurred into the rustling of the dry weeds, and soon she was alone with the swarming gnats of the night.

The town was farther away than she had thought, a glimmering cluster of faintly lit windows on the horizon. She had never seen the town from this distance in the dark. How small it seemed; how large the emptiness of the world around it.

His question lingered in the stillness of her mind. *Are you truly happy in this cocoon you've spun around yourself?* Her feet grew sluggish plodding over the brambles and pebbles. After a few steps, she started to cry, and her eyes remained wet all the way back to town.

*

Kin loitered by the basket weaver's shop. It wasn't really a surprise for Condrie to see him there in the dark waiting for dawn. People who went to buy baskets usually needed them to carry things, and people who had that many things were good targets for a pickpocket. Kin sat at the edge of the awning, eating a honey peach.

When Condrie saw him, she rushed right at him and started screeching. "You pox-carrying, lice-ridden, sniveling gutter runt! You conniving, garbage-eating mother-raper!"

"Hey, what'd I do?"

She slapped the top of his head.

"Ow!"

Condrie looked down at the bag on his belt, which looked considerably fatter and heavier than it had an hour ago. "How much blood money did they pay you?"

"Shh." Kin grabbed her arm and pulled her aside to the shadowy place by a stack of barrels. Condrie resisted a little, but she sensed his urgency. "Keep your voice down. You're in enough trouble already."

"Me?" she asked.

"You shouldn't even be here. They're looking for you."

"Who is?"

"The king's knights," Kin whispered. "Somebody remembered there was 'a plain kitchen wench' who wasn't there when they raided the place. They think you helped him get away. They think you know where he is."

Condrie hugged herself.

"Great circle of holy blood, what if they nab you this far from home? What's 'the plain kitchen wench' doing over at this end of town?"

"Are you going to turn me in, too?"

"No, I'd never do that to you, Condy. But they're up and down these streets poking into every barrel and shed. I'm sitting in the open 'cause it's less risky than hiding in my usual places. They'll overlook a filthy street rat like me. They won't overlook you with them clean teeth and whole fingernails."

"So? I'm not afraid."

"They'll grill you."

"So? I won't tell."

"They'll make you tell. They'll . . . they'll. . . ." He stammered as badly as she often did. For a moment, he really did look like the boy that he was. "They'll hurt you, Condy. I don't want to see you hurt."

"Mmm-hmm." She frowned at his coin purse. "You should've thought of that before you squealed to a squad of knights."

Kin said, "I never thought they'd set fire to the tavern. Really, who would blow up a still full of gin? That's just plain evil, that is."

Condrie sighed. She couldn't stay mad at him when he looked so miserable and contrite. "What should I do?"

"Get out of town. There's a passel of refugees out of Xol's borders. They're heading to the baron's mill to harvest the wheat fields. Maybe you could hide out with them."

"Refugees from Xol?" Condrie tugged at her limp, dark hair. Too dark and thin to be the cinnamon locks of that woman knight.

"They call themselves Athel—y'know, from the islands in the Great Northern Bay. You could pass for one of those."

Condrie bit her lip, thinking of her situation. Until the last few hours, her greatest concern in life was putting a hearty meal on the table. "At least say you're sorry for ruining my life."

"Me, ruin your life? No, it was that murderer, the Sagewyn who dazzled and seduced you."

"He did not seduce me," Condrie objected. "I helped him get away because the knights of Xol are thugs and brutes. It's plain to see he's innocent."

Kin cackled like a crow. Blood leaked over his brownish teeth from his malnourished gums. "I can smell guilt on a man, and I smelled it tonight on him in your kitchen. Plain as the stink of garlic, it is, what weighs on his heart. Whatever they say he did? Whatever he says he didn't do? Oh, he done it."

"You're wrong."

"Believe you me, Condy, he done it. He murdered them all, just like they say he did, as sure as I'm standing here. Stay clear from him or he'll murder you, too."

Chuckling at his own wit, Kin slipped away into the shadows.

*

At dawn's first light, Condrie found the Athel refugees easily enough. About two dozen of them, barefoot and empty-handed, walked the gravelly banks of the river. In the past year or two, more of this sort had fled the Kingdom of Xol by over-crowding leaky river boats or walking over land until they dropped from exhaustion. Some said the Athel were driven from their islands by the King Davarche's ruthless troops. Others said it was a famine from a blight that destroyed their staple grain. It had not mattered to Condrie until now why they came westward; she had seen these sorts of refugees starving in the streets of the town; she had given crusts of day-old bread when she could; she had given spare socks and blankets and coats to the street beggars, but it never seemed to be enough. More and more refugees had shuffled into the meadowlands this year, so many that Condrie wondered what a dreadful miserable place the Kingdom of Xol might be. *And now even the king's Sagewyn are running away from him.*

The Athel people dressed strangely, men and women alike, in a single veil of bleached linen swaddled tightly around their bodies. Strips of rags wrapped their forearms and calves, what at first Condrie thought to be bandages except they were wound in an artful crisscross pattern. Perfumed oil slicked their hair flat and made it a shade darker than it probably was by nature. Athel were an odd folk who kept close to themselves, apart from others, and never came into town for a drink at the tavern. Condrie didn't even know what their language might sound like.

Fighting the twinge of nervousness, she hopped through purple weeds to catch up to them. Condrie fell in with the pace of the person in the rear and walked.

For a while, no one noticed her.

They followed the river road to Falls Bridge and, after a pause, started across. Condrie stayed with them. Her town shoes with flat hard soles made clip-clop sounds on the black, weathered planks. The others, barefoot, silently traversed the span. They kept their heads slightly bowed as they walked, their eyes concentrated on the way ahead.

Condrie looked sideways past the railing at the white waters of the Clement River roiling violently beneath her, surging over boulders, curdling and frothing in the hollows. This was the mighty river that flowed down from the snow-capped mountains in the North. These waters passed through and kept going southward to faraway places that she had only heard of in tales told by drunken men, to the larger towns and busy trading posts, to the Kingdom of Xol, to the shores of the Southern Sea. She had never even ventured to the far side of Falls Bridge before.

To her slight disappointment, the wild weeds looked just the same on the other side. Spindly thistles had bright purple stalks and magenta blossoms framed in lace. Butterflies flitted about, their vivid colors like cinders blowing off a campfire.

She followed the Athel people for the better part of the morning. Eventually, they came to the fields of golden wheat that seemed to be the fur of an enormous, sleeping beast. A thin line of reapers were hacking with scythes and sickles at a corner of the field. Condrie smiled, feeling her anxieties lessen. There was plenty of work for itinerant laborers like herself.

The Athel people suddenly stopped, though no one had given an audible signal. All together, they dropped to the ground and sat with their legs in triangles. From cords on their backs, they took out packets of dry crackers and water pouches.

Condrie sat down too, but she had nothing to eat or drink. Having never run for her life before, she regretted not thinking that far ahead.

A motherly woman passed along her water pouch, a scuffed-up animal skin. Condrie eagerly slurped from its spout.

"Thank . . . thank you."

She expected a conversation to start then and waited for the woman to ask her questions about who she was or why she was following them. Condrie waited some more, and some more, until she realized that no one was going to say a thing.

One young girl, about her age, came forward. Like the others, she had a narrow face with a long nose and close-set black eyes. Her olive-toned skin darkened in the sun. Her brown hair dripped perfumed oil, and Condrie saw smudges of it on the shoulders of her knotted-rag clothing.

The girl pointed to the clay bell hanging around Condrie's neck. "Tenmarkian blue."

"Yes." Condrie wanted to explain that the bell was crafted by the people of the Clichard valleys on the other side of the oak hills. The holy ones were known as People of the Bells who made charms by mixing mountain spring water into the clay. When Condrie had bought it off a merchant's pushcart for a quarter of a copper coin, she was told that the bell would keep away angry ghosts and evil spirits. So much to explain, Condrie thought, as the words clogged up in her mind. All she could do was smile in an offer of friendship to a girl not much younger than herself.

"Tenmarkian blue," the girl repeated before sitting down again.

"Do you . . . do you like it?" Condrie fondled the bell to have something to do with her hands. Twiddling her fingers sometimes helped untangle her tongue. "I could . . . could trade it for food."

The matronly woman said, "Keep your bell. Tenmarkian blue."

Several people offered up stale crackers and dried figs. Condrie took them. She sat down by the young girl to eat, and asked, "Why . . . why . . . this blue?"

"Tenmarkian blue means friendship and unity," the girl replied.

"Oh?"

A fatherly man, sitting on the other side of the girl, remarked, "She's so white."

Condrie furrowed her brows in confusion, knowing that her hair, eyes, and skin were varying shades of brown. Nothing about her appearance—not even her soiled apron—came close to being white. She looked to the girl for the answer.

"White means you're blank, empty, and ready to be painted."

"White," murmured the people around her. "Very white."

"I'm so-so-sorry I don't under- . . . understand. White? B-b-blue?"

"When we talk," said the matronly woman who had given her water. "We must use foreign words because our own language is too beautiful for you foreigners to understand. We speak in color."

"How?"

"In our own way."

Condrie looked around expectantly, but no one explained further. So she fell silent, afraid to pester them or they might become angry and chase her away. It was enough that they had shared food with her. When she moved again, the bell around her neck made a dull clicking noise, and it comforted her. Because of it, she'd been accepted. Perhaps it was a lucky charm after all.

*

The reeve in charge of the field workers was a portly man in an ill-fitting tunic. His outer layers were dyed in turmeric to a bright shade of yellowish orange, deeper than chamomile flowers and brighter than madder rouge. The color displayed his master's wealth in the foreign spice trade. He carried an ox horn suspended on a brass chain.

He told the arriving group that every field hand got three pewter coins a week, but only if they worked every day. Anyone who didn't pull their share would be chased off the baron's land.

"Yes, sir," said the eldest woman of the Athel who spoke for them all. "We understand, sir. Thank you for allowing us to work for His Lordship, sir."

Condrie went to work in the fields with the rest of them. Though she had never worked a harvest before, the task was not so hard. She followed behind a row of young men swinging long-handled scythes. When they cut the stalks of wheat and stepped forward, she bent over to gather them into neat piles. Condrie took pride in aligning the stalks with the kernels pointed upward, creating perfect cylinders of sweet-smelling gold to be threshed and winnowed later.

At night, they rested in the common yard amid the haystacks. The matron of the chow wagon set up a cauldron and made enough lentil-onion soup for everyone. Condrie drained her bowl and wanted more but didn't dare ask.

The young Athel girl tapped Condrie's arm. "We're going to sing. Come watch."

Condrie followed her to a patch of bare ground where harvesters had stripped everything down to the soil. On the dirt in the open field, enthroned on an idle plough, there sat the eldest white-haired woman in the group alongside an even older wizened man. The two dozen Athel people gathered in a crescent circle around their feet. Condrie sensed their respect for the two elders, and it gave her a tingle of anticipation for seeing something new. Her eyes got dry because she didn't want to blink. Every detail of their movement, she etched into her mind so that she could remember it always.

The older woman had a tray on her lap. On it were frizzle nut shells, dozens of them, each containing a bit of pigment. Condrie couldn't tell, at a distance, if it was powder or paint.

In unison, the woman and man unwrapped the linen strips that were tightly wound about their arms. They exposed their flesh as high as the elbows and let the rags dangle. Because they'd been covered, their arms were not as dark as their faces.

The woman started. She dipped her smallest finger in pink and dabbed it near her wrist. The old man went next, drawing a streak of blue at his wrist. In turn, they painted streaks of various colors up their arms. The woman kept with the warm shades of burgundy, tangerine, honeysuckle, and magenta. The man used aquamarine, teal, azure blue, and purple.

When she dipped into lime green, the crowd of spectators gasped, "Ahhh."

The old man made a spot of red near the hollow of his elbow. At that, the spectators burst out crying and groaning with despair. Condrie squinted, straining to learn what meaning they gleaned from those colors.

Together, the woman and man dipped their thumbs into a cup of white chalk. They smeared broad streaks of colorlessness across the multi-hued stripes, with dramatic motions of their arms. All that work to paint the dozens of neat lines, Condrie thought, was ruined.

Condrie shook her head, unable to understand. The young girl next to her spoke, softly, so she wouldn't break the spell in the air. "It's the song of our people's struggle that the children must never forget. We are the blue. Each shade represents a different island in the Northern Bay. The Kingdom of Xol is the red, the color of blood and death and fire. The red traveled north as the Xol conquered more land. When they reached high enough, they turned green with envy for our beautiful islands."

Condrie looked again to the green spot at the peak of the red patterns.

"The continuity of our blue was cut by the red."

Turning to the man, again, Condrie now understood why the people had wept when he topped his blue bands with a spot of crimson.

"The king of the South is white with ignorance," the girl said. "It covers everything. His blankness smothers all colors like snow."

That's why they left their home. Condrie blinked, and a tear trickled down her cheek.

*

Condrie worked the fields for days upon days until her legs and back ached from bending over for more hours than she stood straight. Her palms developed yellow blisters from gripping the wheat stalks and the twine that bound the sheaves. Yet she voiced no complaint. The Athel people to the left and right of her, doing the same labors, wrapped strips of rags around the bleeding blisters on their palms and kept working.

Each evening, as sunset approached, the Athel people took a moment for themselves. Condrie did not see or hear any signal. No whispers. No hand gestures. Yet they acted all as one in laying down their sickles and scythes at the same time. They closed their eyes as they straightened up tall. They faced the setting sun and its brilliant ruddy hues. Their sun-toasted skin turned to the color of finely dyed silks and glazed porcelain. They held the pose for a few moments—only a few short moments—until the last shining lip of the sun's disk dropped behind the distant hills.

Red, she thought. *It's the color of death because it's the end of each day.*

"I didn't blow my horn yet!" the reeve shouted. "I've warned you before about stopping work too early. Do it again tomorrow, and I dock all your wages half a day's worth. You hear me?"

"They . . . they hear you." Condrie's small voice carried in the stillness.

The reeve turned to look at her. Backlit by the sunset's glory, his orange tunic radiated all the brighter.

"Say, girl, what's your name? Have I seen you in town? You look familiar."

"I've . . . uh, done some odd jobs in town," Condrie said.

"Uh-huh."

Condrie lowered her head in a feeble attempt to hide her face in the growing dim of evening. If he had been a customer at the tavern, he might have spied her going in and out of the kitchen with clean glasses and refilling the salted crackers at the bar. She hoped he wouldn't remember her too keenly. After all, no one ever took much notice of the kitchen wench.

The sun had finished setting and the sky began to fade to gray. The Athel people all as one bent over to gather their tools for the night. The reeve shouted at their hunched backs, "I'm warning you one more time! I'd better not see this lolly-nannying again tomorrow. Don't make me speak to the baron about this. Bear in mind there's more wastrels and malcontents stragglin' out of Xol's borders every day. Don't think I won't advise His Lordship to send the lot of you packing down the road. We can replace you in a day. In a day, I said!"

Condrie took a tentative step closer to the reeve. "It's . . . it's . . . it's im-im-important to them. It's ju-ju-just a little m-m-moment. P-p-please?"

The reeve cocked an eyebrow to gaze at her. "You speak boldly but in whispers. You're an odd little thing. You never did tell me your name."

"It's Co-Co-Co...."

"Blank," said the Athel girl coming to Condrie's side. "Her name is Blank, but our language is too difficult for outsiders to speak. You should call her by the same word in your own tongue."

"So she's one of you, is she?"

"Yes," said the Athel girl.

"Then how's come she's wearing town clothes?"

"She was lost. Now she is found."

"Lost, eh?" The reeve took a pipe off his belt. He pinched some dry weeds out of a pouch and gingerly poked them into the pipe's bowl. "Seems that's going around these days. Did you hear what happened in town last week? Some rogue Sagewyn was on the loose. Story is he went flippin' mad and murdered four other Sagewyn in the court of King Davarche. There's a bounty of a hundred silver coins if he's captured alive and a flogging due to anyone who helps him."

Condrie held still.

The reeve snapped the needle of a small tinder box and lit the weeds of his pipe. For a brief moment, a fiery orange moth fluttered in his palm.

"Sagewyn do not tread lightly in the world," said the Athel girl, a bitterness darkening her voice. "He is one violet orchid in a field of yellow buttercups. The blackcoats will find him."

"They haven't yet." The reeve puffed his pipe. "Y'know, if either of you sees him and tips me off, I'd consider cutting you in on the reward."

"How... how...?" Condrie gulped at the pounding heart in her throat.

"How would you know him if he's hiding in the skin of a man? Because they all have the same tattoo on their chests. A mark of honor, it is, the Seal of the King of Xol. Now, it'll condemn him. He can't hide under a shirt in this summer heat."

Condrie squeezed her hands together. Sweat moistened her palms and the blisters stung.

"If I see a Sagewyn," said the Athel girl. "I will deliver him to you. I don't need a reward."

"Oh yeah, yeah, I get it. You folk got no love for the Sagewyn kind."

"They are poison and destruction," the girl said hoarsely.

"Oh yeah, tell that to the good wenches at Ma Kielsing's house. What a shame that was, and all because the Sagewyn tried hiding out there . . . in the kitchen, they say."

Condrie held her breath. *Does he remember me? Is he going to turn me into the Lord High Sheriff to collect the reward?*

He continued, "The knights of Xol blew up the still. Took off half the roof. What a tragedy. Best gin joint this side of the Clement River Valley, and the house is shingled with ashes."

Condrie sniffled and hurriedly wiped her nose. *Because of me . . . because I helped a man running from foreign thugs.* She hoped he would assume his pipe smoke bothered her.

"But this'll warm your heart: I've heard the community is setting up a fund to help Ma Kielsing rebuild her roof. Now there's the kind of cooperative village spirit you don't see too often these days. Everyone feels sorry for what the blackcoats did to them. It's clear they felt no sympathy for the Sagewyn. Those good-hearted wenches were all deceived by that wily creature in disguise."

"Yes," said the Athel girl. "They are chameleons who change colors to hide from the sight of honest eyes. Sagewyn are creatures of lies."

Condrie lowered her eyes and in the deepening twilight could not see her own feet. *I am lying too. When could I ever tell them? Would they shun me if they knew?*

The reeve strolled away. When he had gone out of earshot, Condrie had the chance to ask the girl, "What . . . what's your name?"

"Amber," she said. "The stone of a color like a drop of honey seen in the sunlight."

"That's b-b-beautiful." Condrie fell silent with awe. Too many emotions rose up, becoming a thunderstorm pounding within her chest. Too many words filled her mind. Again, she lowered her eyes, and in the dim of evening, her own hands were gray.

*

"Come," said Amber, taking her by the hand. The girl led Condrie to the gathering circle at the feet of the gray-haired man and silver-haired woman.

As before, the elders unwrapped the strips of rags from around their arms. They held a tray of frizzle nut shells between them. Their wrinkled hands moved wearily in the aches of the day's labors. Each turn of the wrist and each swipe of a fingertip into colored paste was deliberate and important.

The storytellers dabbed spots of colors slowly up and down their forearms. The mineral pigments were vivid colors that even firelight could not distort. Amber, sitting next to her, whispered a translation for Condrie's ears alone.

"In the time of long ago, when people were few and rare, there was a wise old woman who lived by herself on an island in the Great Northern Bay. She was alone because her husband had died. Her parents had died. Her friends and her neighbors had died. She stayed at home after her children and her children's children had made boats to travel across the waters to larger and larger islands. On those islands, some people made farms of barley or *komiioc* beans. Some hunted wild game and gathered tree nuts. Each island had different features—some were grassy, some were rocky, some had waterfalls, and some were all dry sand. The people of each island kept to themselves and did not trade with each other. Years passed. The children of her children's children on each island came to use different words, until such a time came that the people of the islands could not speak to each other in a way they could understand."

So the Northern Bay island people have different dialects among themselves, Condrie thought. *Surely they all know this. How is this a story?*

Amber continued translating the splotches and stripes that the elderly couple smeared across their forearms. Their movements were like musicians playing flutes.

"One day, the old woman of the first island became very sad that the children of her children's children could not speak to each other. 'I need to teach them new words to be shared,' she said to face of the setting sun. 'I will show them a diamond. It is a pure crystal of no color itself that breaks apart the sunshine into all the colors of the rainbow. It is a language we can all see; it is a language we can all know. Though the words of humankind may slur and change, the colors of the sun's light will never change.' And so she chose a diamond from the caves of the island where she dwelt alone."

Condrie furrowed her brow in wondering how the same woman could stay alive so long as to fret over the state of her descendants. *Oh well,* she thought. *It's only a story. Impossible things are supposed to happen in stories.*

"The old woman did not have boat and had no means to carry her message of unity to the people of the many islands. So she asked the great blue water snake, 'Will you carry this diamond to my children's children and tell them my message of how to speak in the colors of the rainbow?' Snake agreed and took the diamond in his mouth. Snake swam the waters of the Great Northern Bay and came to the shore of the next island, but by carrying the diamond in his mouth he could not help but swallow it. The people saw only a snake, and were afraid, and chased Snake back into the sea."

At that point, the elderly woman and gray-haired man paused to wipe their forearms clean. One of the mowers, a strong man with broad shoulders, put a log on the open fire to keep the flames high and bright.

"Next, the old woman asked Seal, 'Will you carry this diamond to my children's children and tell them my message of how to speak in the colors of the rainbow?' Seal agreed and took the diamond in his paw. Seal jumped into the waters of the Great Northern Bay but in swimming he opened his paw and dropped the diamond to sink into the deep of the deep waters. Seal was too embarrassed at his own failure, so he kept on swimming without ever coming to shore. There is where you will find Seal to this day, swimming and swimming in the open waters."

Condrie had seen fur trappers at the tavern bringing seal pelts for sale, and she had sometimes tried to imagine what odd sort of creatures they had been while they were alive.

"Finally, the old woman asked the Roc bird, 'Will you carry this diamond to my children's children and tell them my message of how to speak in the colors of the rainbow?' Roc agreed and took the diamond in his talons. He flew high over the gray waters of the Great Northern Bay and soared easily to the other islands. Roc soared in circles above the people. Sunlight flashed into the diamond that Roc held in his talons. The diamond broke sunshine into all the colors of the rainbow, and all the different people of all the different islands saw the same colors in the same way. And so it was that we learned to look to the sky to teach us that we are the same. Though we come from different islands and survive in different ways, the sky above our heads is always the same kind of blue."

Condrie crossed her sore arms over the aching muscles of her gut. The blue clay bell at her throat dangled and clicked. *I don't understand*, she thought. *What is this story teaching them? What is it teaching me?*

*

The next day, Condrie's hands did the usual labors while her mind floated ahead to worry about the upcoming nightfall. *What if they do it again?* she kept thinking in an echo that rang endlessly in her head. If the Athel continued their practice of standing to revere the setting sun, the reeve would have them flogged before he ordered them dismissed from the fields. She had seen whipped men visiting the tavern; she knew the look of broken hands and shattered noses.

All day the reeve patrolled the fields with a watchful eye and carried a long stick on his shoulder. He looked hard for slackers and found none.

At midday, he blew a toot on his ox-horn to signal a time when they were allowed to rest for a meal. From the chow wagon, the reeve's crew handed out wrapped bundles of lentil paste and flatbread. He nodded satisfaction to observe the Athel people kept up their work after his horn sounded and did not stop until each hand received their flatbread roll. *But what if they do it again?* They had already come so far; the elderly woman and the older man had missing toenails and scars of blisters on their feet. *What if they do it again?* She could not bear to imagine the kindly storyteller with a battered swollen eye. Her stomach twisted into a hard lump and she felt no appetite for her flatbread.

After the lunch break, they resumed their work in the fields. Condrie maneuvered herself alongside the Athel girl who seemed close to her own age.

"Here." She offered her half-eaten flatbread roll. "I c-c-c-can't finish it."

"Maple-leaf green," said Amber while tucking the roll into the neckline of her raggy bodice. "I mean, thank you."

"Is that . . . that how you say th-thanks?"

"Yes, because the maple leaves drink in the sunshine that is freely given from the sky."

Condrie said, "That's b-beautiful."

Amber nodded humbly. "Not everyone thinks so."

"I do. I . . . I. . . ." Condrie glanced over her shoulder to be sure the reeve was out of earshot. His back was turned, his orange tunic stark against the backdrop of the blue sky. "I'm worried about s-s-sunset. What if they do it again?"

"Do what?" The girl bobbed up and down, bending and straightening as she gathered the stalks of wheat cut by the able-bodied men with scythes.

Condrie followed along at her side. "Sunset."

"We must."

"Why?"

"It is our way."

"Why?"

"When the sun sets, all colors are gone from the world. Yellow turns white. Red and green turn black. Blue turns to gray."

"Yes, but—"

"Voices are silent in the gray of night. Flowers close their petals. Hummingbirds go to nest."

"Yes, but—"

"It is a time when we must rely on firelight to see, and the color of flame is not the color of the sun. Flame is not true."

Condrie looked back over her shoulder to the reeve. He strutted with his back stiff and fingered the shaft of the stick he carried, waiting for the chance to strike someone for being lazy.

"He'll b-b-beat you. He'll d-d-dismiss you."

"Then we must endure it."

"Why? Why c-c-can't you just . . . just *not*?"

Amber looked up at her. Sunlight flashing across her dark eyes gave her irises a tint of lighter brown. "Not?"

"Not s-s-stop work until he . . . he blows his horn."

"We must show reverence for the passing of the sun. We must show the skin of our faces to the sunlight in the same way the maple tree shows its leaves. We must show gratitude and pray for the sun to return in the morning, to bring back color to the world."

"Yes, but . . ." Condrie saw the reeve's shadow lengthening toward them and she lowered her already quiet voice. "C-c-can't you just show rev- . . . rev- . . . *that*, and keep working too? Show . . . show your faces but k-k-keep your hands moving."

The girl bent and picked up wheat stalks. She bent and picked up more, and more, and added them to the bundle in her arms.

"The sun can see your faces," Condrie whispered urgently. "Don't . . . don't let *him* see."

"You're asking us to lie."

"No."

"You're asking us to put away who we are. We have lost our homes to the king of the South. We have lost children and parents, sisters and brothers. Our brown skin is stained red with blood. King Davarche has taken everything, but he cannot erase the colors from the world. Only the setting sun can do that; the setting sun is a greater king than he will ever be."

Condrie blinked at the tears bubbling up to her eyes. *They're going to do it again. They're going to do it again.*

"He'll b-b-beat you. Elders, too."

"Yes."

"Where will you g-g-go next? No one in town will give . . . give you a job if the b-b-baron chucks you. This . . . this is the last . . . the last estate before the b-b-boundary of the West. It's nothing . . . nothing but grasslands and sands after this."

The girl wrapped twine around her bundle of sheaves. She set it on the ground and then starting collecting more stalks in her arms. She stayed silent for a long time, working side by side with Condrie doing the same.

Condrie gathered up several bundles of wheat stalks, setting them upright with the precious beads of grain as a furry mushroom top. She looked ahead to the reapers swinging their scythes farther and farther down the field. Strong young men flexed their shoulders with each sideways stroke of their hooked blades. Brothers and fathers. Honest men chased out of their homes. Bruised men willing to be bruised again.

"Listen to me, p-p-p-please, Amber. I don't want . . . want to see you hurt. Talk to the others. Talk to your elders. Tell them . . . d-don't. Honor the sun with your faces, but . . . just . . . please! D-d-d-don't stop work with your hands until the reeve blows his horn."

"I will try," Amber said. "I will try."

*

As sunset approached, Condrie's gut twisted into knots. She eyed the descent of that bright ruddy disk, all too soon sinking into the smoky clouds above the hills. *Please, please,* she thought. *Please be smart. Please don't do it again.*

She maneuvered nearer to the matronly woman who had given her water on the first day they met. This woman's task was to push a long wheelbarrow, carrying the bundles of wheat sheaves back to the mill's yard for the threshers. Also hooked onto the prow of the wheelbarrow were kegs of drinking water.

Condrie scooped up sheaves and put them on the wheelbarrow.

The woman said, "My kegs are empty. If you're thirsty, I have no drink to give."

Shaking her head and shrugging, she conveyed the idea that it was not water she wanted. Condrie licked her dry lips. "Wha- . . . what's your name?"

"Violet," the woman said.

Glancing nervously over her shoulder at the setting sun, Condrie asked, "Did . . . did Amber talk to you?"

"Yes."

"Will they d-d-do it?"

"Blank, you might be an open stretch of sands uncluttered by the driftwood and washed-up weeds of the sea. You could also be white as the powder snows which cover the crevasses in the rocks and hide dangers from our sight. I have not yet decided which one you are."

"I . . . I could also b-b-be the white wool cloak that keeps you warm," Condrie suggested.

Violet raised her chin, using her face to point ahead at the rows of men mowing a path ahead of them.

"See that man there? At the left side of that group of three?"

Condrie recognized the broad-shouldered fellow who had stoked the storytellers' campfire the night before. He was one of the strongest mowers among them; he and his scythe danced smoothly through the wheat.

"He is my brother," Violet said. "His name is Indigo-in-Water. Our family owns . . . that is, it used to own a field of flowering shrubs in a warm valley sheltered from the sea's winds. Summer is the time of harvesting the blue flowers and soaking them in water to make the precious blue ink. Our family was something like your baron here. We paid wages to workers in the field. We lived in a house with floors and windows. We bottled the blue ink and bartered with the merchants who traveled to our islands from faraway lands. Indigo is one of the many rare treasures of our islands. It is one reason why King Davarche desired to possess our homes and our fields."

"The king's g-g-greed is not your fault," Condrie said.

Violet smiled broadly. "Of course it isn't."

Turning her wheelbarrow toward the setting sun, Violet stopped in place. She let go of the handles. Ahead and to either side of them, the scythe-wielding mowers and the bare-handed gatherers came to a halt. They stood tall and faced the shimmering red crescent slowly sinking into the hills. Their long shadows turned to the color of wine stains as the smoky sky radiated a brilliant shade of scarlet silk. Wheat stalks seemed to be skeins of blood-soaked wool.

The reeve raised his stick high as an extension of his arm. "No stopping work until I blow my horn! I told you!"

"We . . . we aren't s-s-stopping," Condrie squeaked.

The reeve looked at her sharply. "Not moving is what I call stopping, you stupid girl. I warned you, and now I have to—"

Condrie bobbed to the ground and picked up another bundle of wheat. Violet, though she faced the setting sun with eyes closed, pushed her wheelbarrow forward one step. The mowers all as one, like dancers with maypole sticks, swung their scythes from right to left.

"See? See? We . . . we're still w-w-working."

"Ugh, I guess you are," the reeve grumbled as he settled the stick onto his shoulder. By then, the sun had set behind the hills. Gray twilight blanketed the sky overhead. Only a tinge of pinkish orange lingered on the undersides of distant clouds.

He blew his ox horn.

The workers turned away from their labors. They started the hike back to the clearing of hay bales and rain barrels where they would sleep in blanket rolls on the ground until sunrise the next day. Condrie exhaled a long sigh of relief.

She walked alongside Violet and her wheelbarrow. Though her muscles ached and her throat was parched, she could not stop smiling. *We did it. We did it. We got through it without being punished.*

Violet said, "Some of us think we have lost a little of ourselves today."

Her smile faded. "What d-d-do you think?"

"I think the maple tree's leaves change color with the seasons and yet it is still a maple tree. It is the way of things to change when the time comes."

Condrie's smile returned. "Then it . . . it was a good thing?"

Violet nodded. "I think so. But you should know, not all of us do. You are no longer Blank after today. You have a spot. You are Speckled."

The matron of the chow wagon served a pumpkin and white bean stew along with rye crackers. *A mixture of orange and white things,* Condrie thought, *and black chips as spoons. Do they see a special meaning in tonight's meal, as I do? Isn't it odd that I, the blank white one, suggested a compromise with the reeve who wears orange, and tonight we're eating pumpkin mixed with beans? What does it mean? What do they think of me? Have I advised them to do the right thing, or have I convinced them to give up something precious? Will they thank me or resent me for saving them all from a beating?*

*

On pay day at the end of the week, the reeve set up a makeshift table in the mill's yard. Two barrels supported a plank. Behind it, he straddled a high-legged stool so that he was at eye level with those standing before him. The various groups of field laborers approached single-file to receive their wages: vagabond Clichard herbalists, the outcasts from the evergreen forests, and the Athel people who spoke with color.

A wooden basket at his side was full of coins. Some were copper circles stamped with the bull's head emblem of King Davarche the First of Xol. Some were pewter bearing the garlands of the Clichard valleys' goddess trinity. Each land baron of the free territories, each seafaring mogul, and each nobleman of Xol minted their own unique coins; some were square, some were round, and some had a hole cut in the middle. It seemed to Condrie that the whole of the known world was contained in that basket.

The reeve extracted handfuls of coins at a time. He marked an exact account in a leather-bound ledger. Then he used the edge of the stylus to scrape the coins into neat piles.

Condrie noticed that he carefully avoided physical contact with the workers. Their hands were roughly calloused and dirty. Their blunt fingertips resembled slugs. The reeve used his stylus to slide exactly three coins forward. Retracting his own caramel-brown fingers was the man's signal to take his pay.

Each of the men bowed and said something like, "Thank you for your generosity, sir."

When it came Condrie's turn, instead of sliding the coins forward, the reeve looked up at her. "Step aside, girl."

"But . . . but . . . but . . . my coins?"

From behind, she heard a rattle—a very familiar rattle, like pots and pans walking. Condrie shivered in spite of the late afternoon heat. Restraining an urge to run for her life, she turned around.

There stood the woman knight with the cinnamon-colored hair who had come into the kitchen that first night. Afternoon sun shined across her. The steel breastplate gleamed on the underside of her chin, making her seem like a luminous being.

"Come here, girl."

Upon sizing up the broadsword at the woman knight's hip, Condrie cooperatively approached. A gauntlet grabbed her arm, squeezing her with steel fingers that hardly seemed like a living thing.

The knight led her aside. Behind her, Condrie felt the curious stares of the laborers all around.

"Where is he?"

"I . . . I . . . I don't know," Condrie answered in a small voice. "Who . . . who?"

"You're the kitchen wench from the tavern—don't deny it. I remember your face. You saw him, the fugitive Sagewyn."

"Yes. He . . . he left."

"Why are you hiding out here in the fields instead of in town where you belong?"

"Because," Condrie gripped her apron, "you b-b-b-b-burned it. I was af-f-f-fraid."

The knight grabbed Condrie by both shoulders and shook her hard. "Stop lying. You're in a great deal of trouble, girl."

Condrie burst out sobbing. Tears dribbled down her cheeks. With the knight gripping her arms, she couldn't even raise her hands to her face.

"Hey, let her go," said the loud bass voice of Indigo-in-Water. "You black cloud covering the yellow sun."

"I must say," the reeve piped up in agreement, "I didn't think you'd get rough on the poor little girl. Now you've got her so scared she can't remember her own name."

"Quiet, all of you," the woman knight blasted. "She's under arrest for assisting a fugitive, a murderer, a traitor to the king. Now, do any of you still want to defend her?"

Condrie looked back over her shoulder at the crowd. The Athel people had been chased out of their beautiful islands by knights such as this. The reapers held scythes. The threshers carried flails. As much as Condrie wanted them all to rush forth and save her, she didn't want to see anyone else suffer for her mistake. Not like the women at the tavern; not again.

"I confess," Condrie blurted. "Yes, I helped him out of town. He's heading—" the least she could do was lie "—n-n-n-north to hide in the high mountain caves."

The woman knight released her grip. "That's the first smart thing you've done, girl."

A pair of horses approached. So bright was the gleam off the knight's gorget that Condrie couldn't clearly see the riders. She heard the voice of a man, and it was like no one she had ever heard before. His words were as smooth as hot syrup, softly articulated, in the lilting singsong that she assumed was the inflection of High Formal Xol.

"Whatever, all, and everything this wench has said to you is a lie," the man said. "Utter falsities. She is not afraid of you—not as much as she should be."

Condrie squinted to try and see who sat upon the large stallion. All she could see was the color of his clothes—bright purple, crimson, and princely green—in bold stripes and parti-colored patterns. The Athel were wise to speak in color; colors told a lot about a person.

A lady beside him, mounted on a spotted gray horse, twittered a haughty laugh. "She's such a pathetic looking, dirty little thing. Must we go near her, or can you do it from here, darling?"

Do what? Condrie wondered.

"Bring her to the reeve's tent," the mounted man said. "I'll not display my magic in front of a common audience."

Magic? It's another Sagewyn.

*

The woman knight brought Condrie into the reeve's field tent. From the outside, it was beige tarp; from the inside, the sunlight turned the canvas to a radiant amber-orange. It gave warmth to the dull colors of the blankets on the reeve's cot. It turned to gold the straw mats that created something of a floor. It brightened the brassy shine of jugs and ewers that the reeve used for washing. It turned his oak table into cherrywood.

Forced into a rickety wooden chair, Condrie sat with her knees clamped together. She wondered if the knight would tie her up or put her in iron chains. Yet nothing happened, as if they didn't think she was a threat just sitting there. Morosely, Condrie realized that they were right.

"Don't resist," the knight advised her. "It'll go better for you if you surrender to him."

Through the canvas, Condrie heard the rattle of armor surrounding her. Horses nickered from several directions. Her heartbeat thundered inside her narrow ribs. *What are they going to do? Surely they aren't going to ravage and brutalize me, are they? No . . . no, they wouldn't. The mood isn't right. The lord is not enraged. It's too cold . . . too calm. He wouldn't hurt me while he's calm, would he?*

The tent flap parted for the two Sagewyn to enter. Condrie took her first good look at the pair. The lord had the fleshy face of someone who ate sumptuous feasts on a regular basis but strained to keep himself from ballooning beyond hope. The lady beside him was as slender as a starving woman, which surprised Condrie for someone of such rank. She had white-blonde hair colored with streaks of indigo ink. Her gown had a low scooping neckline that displayed part of the tattoo on her left breast. Like Wegdell, she thought, marked by the king.

The lord came forward, smiling slightly in an effort to put her at ease. It failed. "Don't be a-feared of me. You'll be free to go on about your day, if you tell me the truth."

"I have told the truth already. I haven't seen him since the night that he dropped into the back window of my kitchen. I helped him escape the town and elude your squad of knights, and that's all I've done. He went northward, last I saw of him, heading for the caves in the high mountains. I don't know where he is now."

Condrie took a breath. As it had been with Wegdell, it was easy to speak quickly without stammering in the presence of a Sagewyn.

The man pursed his sensuous lips and made a funny, clicking noise with his tongue. "No, you're lying. Your words and your heart's pulse are like chimes and cow bells clashing. Why do you protect him? You only met him briefly. He is nothing to you. He is alone, so he has no power to influence you ... as I do."

Condrie tried to swallow, but her throat was too dry. That man's eyes became increasingly compelling. She couldn't look away. Such a color she'd never seen—grayish hazel, but with flecks of other colors in the irises that were fascinating. The longer she looked, the more myriad colors she discovered.

The woman beside him laughed again. The shrill twitter broke Condrie's concentration, and she could look up at the woman with a bit more composure.

"Oh, darling," the woman said. "Isn't it obvious? She's at that zestful age. She has never felt the stirrings of passion before, and Wegsemze is utterly gorgeous. If she only knew how futile her awakening lusts truly are."

Wegsemze? Is that his real name?

The man snapped around to face her. "Whatever do you mean to imply by that statement, darling? 'He's utterly gorgeous'? Dare you speak thusly of another man in my presence?"

A couple of quick kisses to the corner of his pouting mouth cooled the man's anger. "Darling, don't be jealous," the woman said. "I'm forever and always yours and no other's, as it must be."

"Don't distract me again," the man said, raising a scolding finger.

His eyes returned. Condrie shrank against the back of the wooden chair but couldn't escape. She began to feel dizzy. The room spun about and there was nothing to hold onto—nothing but his eyes.

"So, you desire him? Give into these new feelings, little girl. Dream of him. Lust for him. Imagine his skin as soft and warm in your hands."

Condrie's eyelids fluttered as her eyes rolled up into her head. She felt herself fly away from the tent. Guided only by a whispery voice that spoke, not in words, but in soothing cool colors—it urged her to go to him, to find him, to rush into his arms.

Fluttering between grayish-brown wings, her sights soared eastward over fields of purple weeds and clusters of cat-fur trees in jagged gulleys. Finally, she swooped into the chain of dray wagons plodding across toward the border of the outerlands where the rolling grassy meadows flattened into barren netherwastes.

The air chilled her because she flew so fast. The oxen moaned low as she zipped between their horns. Down along the ribbed spines of the oxen she glided, past the harness straps and up to the driver's seat.

Wegdell sat on a bench seat with his back to the driver. She only had a moment to glimpse his surprise as she hurtled into his face.

She perched on the tip of his nose. Her feet and hands were spindly and small enough to straddle between his nostrils. She gazed up at his frowning eyebrows.

Wegdell crossed his eyes to look at her. "Condy? Oh my God, no, they've found you!"

Uh-mmm-mmmm, she buzzed while rolling and un-rolling her long moth-like tongue.

"Go back, go back," he shouted into her tiny face. "You're a girl, remember? Say his name. His name is Gerrawgon. Say it, Condy. Say it quickly, and he won't be able to hurt you anymore."

This doesn't hurt, she thought while stroking his nose with her antenna.

"Say it, Condy, if you can. Speak in human words. Say *Gerrawgon*."

"Ge- . . . Ge-. . . ." Her moth-like mandible flexed and clicked with the effort. Her tongue rolled up like a wet noodle against the roof of her mouth.

Wegdell smiled in an enticing way. His voice became low and soothing. "You're doing fine. Just take the word one piece at a time. Start with the first sound, *Ger-*. . . . You can do it."

Condrie whimpered her frustration. Her furry brown wings flexed up and down. "G-G-Ger- . . . raw- . . ."

". . . gon," he helped her finish.

"Gerrawgon," Condrie repeated once more. Her mandible flexed open, smiling in anticipation of his praise.

A strong breeze blew her sideways. She fell off the tip of his nose and went swirling, spinning wildly in the air.

Condrie blinked and shook the sparkles out of her vision. Someone jostled her, and she realized that she was not a moth anymore. She was back in the reeve's tent, sitting in the chair. The woman knight's leather gloves had a firm grip of her shoulders. "Pox'ed whore! Why do you protect him?"

The Sagewyn man crouched forward, clutching his own head with both hands. "That was very foolish," he cried in the voice of pain.

"What happened?" Condrie licked her lips, surprised to feel they were soft again and that her tongue was so small.

"I'll enjoy watching him suffer!" the man cried. Under his wife's tender caresses, he regained his posture. "Lord Wegsemze is traveling west with a caravan of merchants. He has dyed his hair blond and he wears a common man's clothes. Oh, and he's covered his chest tattoo with a salve paste."

"Probably her idea," the noblewoman said. "She is a gin whore, after all."

"Even so," the lord continued, "it shouldn't be hard to recognize him: a tall, blond, 'gorgeous' man."

The woman knight nodded before heading outside to shout orders to the other armored men. They mobilized with a thunderous rattle of steel plates and horse flesh.

Condrie shivered where she sat. In spite of the summer heat, she couldn't stop quivering. "What just happened?"

"I have seen him in your eyes," the man explained. It seemed he was feeling better now, and he had the composure to gloat. "Like a moth to the flame, the heat of your lust clings to the tail of the firebird. He's a pretty peacock but not very smart. He cannot elude me—a *hikalusta*, an eternal shining being who has already walked this world for a thousand years. Yes, I have not aged in a thousand years! Know that I will continue to walk in this world for centuries yet to come, long after you. . . ." He displayed an expression similar to someone who had stepped in ox dung. "You will age and pass away in the blink of my immortal eye. Let that be a lesson to you, little larva. Knowing my name will not be enough to break my concentration and save you."

"Well said, darling!"

To celebrate, the two of them wrapped their arms around each other and kissed, sloppily and badly. He missed the woman's upper lip altogether. Condrie cringed at the sight. Could he really kill her without ever laying a hand upon her, or was he lying to try and frighten her, the way Kin often bragged of his superhuman accomplishments? Long ago, Condrie had stopped believing that her orphan friend had stolen half the treasure he'd claimed to have in a secret horde. She clung to that skepticism now. It was her one chance to avoid total panic.

*

Condrie emerged from the reeve's tent and blinked at the setting sun low to the horizon and glaring straight into her eyes. She lingered behind the trailing skirts of the lady. The lord's cloak picked up dust and burrs on his way to mount his horse.

Am I not under arrest?

The two mounted up—the lord with more of a grunting effort than the winnowy lady—and they set off at an ambling stroll. Horses side by side swished their long tails. They headed up the wagon road that would eventually take them to the baron's manor house.

Condrie stood alone. By now, the harvesters had quit their field work for the day. The threshers had left the mill's yard. No one was within sight. She stood in between one place and another place. Footpaths led off in several directions. A slight breeze rustled in the dry golden stalks.

She clenched her empty fist, realizing that she had not been paid her wages for the week's labor. *Do I still have a job? Should I find the reeve and ask for my coins? Or now that the ruse is exposed, should I return to the tavern and work the kitchen as I did before this all happened? Is the tavern repaired and open for business yet? Where should I go? What should I do?*

She gazed out at the open grasslands before the harvested fields. Rouge grasses spread to the horizon with sparse tufts of pale green shrubs to break the monotony. She wondered how far the merchant's caravan had traveled in the past week. Having spent all her life in one kitchen or another, she had no knowledge of how quickly ox wagons could make up ground. She recalled the lanky shoulders of the draft animals, their knobby knees and their woody hooves. They were no match for an ordinary horse, much less the grand black stallions of King Davarche's legions.

The knights and the lords have no more use for me. I've betrayed him. . . . I've revealed where he is hiding. In spite of my best efforts to give sanctuary to an innocent fugitive, I've failed. They will have him in chains very soon. . . . But how soon?

Condrie gripped her long skirt in the place where her apron would be, if she were still wearing one. *How much time does Wegdell have?* she wondered. Not that she could do anything to help, but she needed to know.

Legs heavy with despair, she turned for the wagon road leading up to the baron's manor house.

Before long, she came to the lone shack that served as a smokehouse. The stench of meat and fire wafted out of its shingles. A pair of foresters swung their axes, chopping more firewood. They wore only trousers. Shirtless, their skin was toasted to a rich deep brown in the sun. Condrie paused to watch them swing their arms. Logs cracked in half. *Surely they have experience with ox wagons hauling lumber of the forest. They would know how far the merchant's caravan would have gotten by now. I could stroll up, say hello, and ask them all about it. We could have a fine conversation. Then I would offer to refill their water jugs as my way of saying thanks.* Condrie licked her dry lips. *It should be so easy to go over and talk to them . . . so, so easy.*

Condrie turned from the smokehouse and continued up the road.

Why can't I talk to people? She gritted her teeth around her twisted tongue. It had been this way for as long as she could remember. As a child, her happiest days were spent in solitude doing tasks about her father's house. A day when she was not compelled to speak a single word was the best day she could hope for. Later, in her brief marriage, her husband had preferred it when she did not speak. In the tavern, Ma Kielsing had patience—most days—to wait for Condrie to choke out a few words.

Her inability to speak smoothly had never bothered her until now, until she'd had a taste of how it felt to let words tumble freely out of her mouth. *Sagewyn are creatures of lies, Amber said. They are monsters of shadows wearing human skin. But they are also the keys that unlock my jaw. Dreadful things though they may have done in this world, perhaps Sagewyn have the ability to do some good as well. If Wegdell is running away from the king, then he is not like these other two. Doesn't he deserve a chance to be something better than what he is?*

Condrie arrived at the carriage house and the stables. A few of the baron's trotters were at leisure in a fenced corral. She leaned on a post and studied their sleek profiles, their slender necks, their spindly crane-like legs. *I could ask one of the wranglers. How fast can a horse with a single rider gallop compared to the plodding pace of an ox drawing a wagon? How far can they go before they need to rest? How quickly can the king's knights cover ground in pursuit of him? It should be so easy to strike up a conversation with one of the stable boys who are about my same age . . . so, so easy.*

A bucket of water splashed to the ground nearby. "Ho, there, don't you fidget!"

Condrie perked up at the twangy accent of a king's knight. *Have they not all galloped away in pursuit of him? Are there more?*

She hurried around the fence line. Behind the stables was a pasture of dry, trampled grass. One grand stallion of the king's legions was tethered to an oak tree. No bridle. No saddle. One lone knight used a paddle-sized brush to scrub the horse's dark hair. He had removed his uniform's jacket down to a linen shirt with the sleeves rolled up to the elbows. The sword belt hung from a branch nearby. He was a soldier only below the waist, wearing black wool trousers and knee-high riding boots.

Her feet plugged to a halt. The knight's back was turned to her as he worked to scrub and groom the horse. She hoped that he had not seen her approach.

Compared to the baron's trotters, the stallion was a bullish beast. The knight standing was eye level with its shoulder. He reached high and far to scrub up to its backbone. He walked five paces from its neck to its haunches. The legs were as thick as fence posts. The hooves were like iron skillets turned over. Its neck seemed as broad as a rain barrel, and its wavy tail was luxurious enough to curtain a doorway.

Heaviness sank deep into her gut at the sight of such a beast. She had no doubt that such horses could overtake the merchant's caravan in a day. *It's no wonder that the king's legions are bullying the world if they are mounted upon such horses as these.*

*

Dark had come by the time Condrie returned to the stillness of the field workers' encampment. The fire pit had died down to a smoldering pallet of charred logs. *I missed the telling of stories,* she thought with a pang of regret. People were already settled into their bedrolls on the ground, for without sunlight or firelight there was not much else to do but sleep. They did not have proper tents as the reeve did. Five ragged tarps were draped over slanted poles as a crude half-tent without walls. Six to eight people snuggled under each. It was not the season for rain, and it had little effect on repelling the swarms of gnats and mosquitoes; it served only to block their view of the starry sky.

Condrie tiptoed into her place in the middle of two rows of bedrolls. She could not name any of the gray shadowy heads all around her feet, but it did not matter. In the moonlit dark—as the Athel would say—all people were the same blue.

She curled herself into the scratchy wool blanket. She lay down on the prickly straw mat and rested her head on a burlap pillow stuffed with chaff. She closed her eyes but sleep did not come. The eyes of the Sagewyn lord haunted her, looming in her thoughts as clearly as if he stood over her again. *What did he do to me? How did he spin my thoughts . . . my spirit . . . my soul? Did he truly see through my eyes . . . through my heart? Do the king's legions really know how to find him at the merchant's caravan?*

Someone's bedroll shifted. Someone crawled over the ground, in between the gaps, and dragged along their own straw mat and blanket. By the scent of eucalyptus oil in the girl's hair, Condrie knew who it was in spite of the darkness.

"Am-... Amber?" she whispered to be sure.

"Yes." The girl settled next to her in the narrow space between Condrie and the next person. "I was worried for you when they took you to the reeve's tent."

Condrie sighed, wanting to say so much more, but all that she could utter was a single word: "Thanks."

"So, you sheltered someone who they are chasing?"

"Yes... he..."

"Don't tell me any more about him," Amber interrupted. "You should not speak of him or think of him, if you can. The Sagewyn lord will smell it inside you. If the knights don't catch him soon, they might hurt you. I've seen them hurt people when they don't get what they want. I don't want to see you hurt."

The woman next to Amber whispered, "Neither do I."

"Nor I," murmured a man with a deep bass voice.

Condrie blinked at the darkness. "Thanks... I mean, maple-leaf green."

*

In her sleep, Condrie dreamed of being a moth.

Her moth's wings were a mousey brown. Her long twisted tongue unwound. The anxious knots in her gut untangled. What had been clogged inside of her for so long burst free. Silk strands flowed smoothly out of her core and spun a cocoon. She wagged her fuzzy body in the thrill of release. When it was done, she settled down to rest within a dome shimmering a silver hue.

Too long have I dreamed of being a human girl, with only two legs and no wings. I could not fly in that dream. I could not spin strands of silk out of myself. I had skin that oozed sweat and burned in the sunshine. I had no antennae but hair that served no purpose. At last, I am awake! I am myself again!

Condrie jolted awake. Stiff canvas lay across her face, not the silk of a cocoon. It was heavy with field dirt and damp with morning dew.

"By the blackness!" the bass-voiced man nearby swore loudly, straining to sit up.

Amber pushed her arms straight overhead and created a pocket canopy. "What happened?"

"The poles collapsed," said a gravelly voice, perhaps the old storyteller or perhaps someone who did not sound his best in the morning. Condrie could not see anyone's faces in the tangle of canvas and sticks, only the shuffling of people crawling out from under the tarp.

Condrie sat upright but did not make an effort to get to her feet. The fallen tarp weighed down her legs. She looked at her own hands and felt a wave of disappointment that she was not a moth after all but a human girl. *It felt so real . . . the dream . . . like what Lord Gerrawgon did to me. Is he still doing something to me with his Sagewyn magic? Is he corrupting my thoughts while I sleep?*

A few others from outside came to help roll back the fallen tarp. Condrie squinted at the morning sunshine. She looked up at Indigo-in-Water, his sister Violet, and a couple of lanky fellows from the Brown family.

"Poles snapped," said the younger one of the Browns. "Old wood. Rotten to the core."

Amber stood up. She held fragments of broken tent poles for all to see. "There's festering mold-green and mold-blue in the wood. It can't be fixed."

Violet put both fists against her hips. "Skinflint! When I paid wages to field workers, I gave them huts as shelter and cots to sleep on. What are we, dogs?"

The storyteller woman grunted loudly as she raised herself off the ground. Standing with knees bent and shoulders hunched, Silver wagged a scolding finger at the mess of collapsed canvas. "The baron is another color."

"We can fix it ourselves," said Indigo-in-Water with a sideways glance to his sister, as if asking for her permission or approval.

The reeve's horn tooted twice from the mill's yard. All heads turned in that direction. Soon the morning's porridge would be ladled out of a bucket, and soon after that they would all report to the day's labor in the field.

"We'll deal with it tonight," said Violet in a loud, decisive voice.

Her brother opened his mouth as if to say something, but then he stopped and bowed his head. He followed his sister strolling away toward the mill yard. Others joined in file behind those two, and others joined them, until all of the two dozen Athel people shuffled uphill to receive their breakfast.

Condrie lingered, standing at the fallen tarp with Amber. "We . . . we c-c-could—"

"She's right," said the girl. "Let it go. We'll shift our bedrolls around and let the elders be sheltered. I don't need a canvas over my head."

"But. . . ."

Amber briefly squeezed Condrie's hand. "Let it go." The girl turned away and followed in the dusty footprints of the others.

Condrie sighed, hugging herself, feeling the knots and tangles curdle up in the core of her guts once more. She recalled how she had felt in the dream, to spread her wings and spew forth beautiful strands of silk in the ecstasy of abandon. The waking world was dirty and stinky. Her limbs felt heavy. Her mouth was dry. Her skin was caked with the dusty sweat of the previous day. *If we let the baron treat us like dogs, then we really will be no better than animals sleeping on the open ground.*

Determined to do something about it, Condrie set off walking to a path that diverged from the wagon road leading up to the mill's yard. Her empty stomach gurgled hunger as the scent of barley porridge wafted over the warm morning breeze. No time to eat. She forced her feet to hurry over the hard, dry ground.

Someone trotted up behind her. One of the young men from the Brown family. "Hey, where are you going?"

"I know . . . um, by the s-s-smokehouse . . . there's long sticks in the, uh, wood pile."

His mouth twitched a smile. "I'll help."

"No . . . I—"

"I'll help," he said again, and Condrie had no will to refuse him.

*

The smokehouse was cold and abandoned. Perhaps the workers had gone to the river to catch more fish, she thought, or perhaps they were busy with other chores. It made things easier if she did not have to explain why she and this fellow were not down at the wheat fields.

"My name is Taupe," he said as they approached the wood pile.

"Ta- . . . Taupe?" she repeated. "Isn't that, uh, a gray?"

"Taupe is the color of a ground squeaker. Its fur could be gray or brown or something in between, but in our family, it's got to be brown. We are called the Browns because my family is all wood carvers. My brother Tawny and my sister Sienna are makers of fine chairs and boxes and oaken chests. We're known for knowing about different types of brown."

"Oh." His voice sounded odd and new to her ears; she had never heard him talk before, not even among the field workers.

He circled behind the awning that sheltered chopped logs stacked higher than a tall man could reach. Between the wood pile and the grass was a jumble of half-dried branches for kindling. Taupe bent over them in search of anything that could serve as a tent pole. Condrie joined him, side by side, bobbing and picking at the pile of sticks.

"Brown," he repeated.

Condrie looked to him curiously.

No longer moving, he had taken hold of a mulberry branch with leaves dry and curled like crumpled paper. No older than twenty-five, his sloped shoulders drooped like an aged man. His neck craned forward in the way of clerks or tradesmen who worked with their hands and rarely got to their feet. Clearly he had never done field labor until this summer.

"If I tell you a secret about myself, I trust you won't tell another person." He spoke in a flat monotone; it was not a question.

She nodded a promise.

"There's something wrong with my eyes." He looked aside with shame. "I can't see the difference between the colors of red or green. To me, they both look the same shade of brown."

Condrie took a step back. "How . . . how did that happen? Were you, uh, sick?"

"I don't know. It's been this way as long as I can remember. As a child, I quickly learned to pretend that I could see what everyone else sees. When the storytellers sing, I nod along as if I understand, but I don't. I don't know most of our people's stories. I've been hearing them for the first time in my life when I hear Amber translate for you."

"I don't un-...understand."

"My eyes work fine otherwise. Everything is clear. It's just the colors...I don't see the colors."

"Oh." She sighed heavily to imagine what a life among the Athel would be. *It's like he's a blind man.*

"My father knew." Taupe hesitated, and in that moment of silence, Condrie understood his father was dead. "He helped me. He kept it secret. Even my mother never knew. Tawny and Sienna don't know. Nobody knows."

"T-t-tell them," she said. "They're your family."

Taupe wagged his head furiously. "They have no affection for me. They're disappointed in me for being such a failure in my life. If they knew I've been lying to them, they'd be angry. They'd reject me. They'd shun me."

Condrie drew in a shuddering breath and wished that it were not true. After losing their homeland and clinging together by a thread in a foreign land, would his brother and sister toss aside a blood relative? Yet she had to admit to herself that she did not understand their customs.

"My father wanted me to be a priest like my uncle Ecru, and I wanted it too."

"You have p-p-priests?" she asked.

He shrugged. "They're not like your bell tollers and chanters over the dead. No, the priests of our islands sing with the living spirits of the land and sky. A priest will spend all of the day's hours in sitting—just sitting—to watch the sunshine pass through the veins of a maple leaf. I tried, but I couldn't. They tell me that maple trees change color from green to red in the autumn, and I can't see the difference. I know fifty-seven words for the color red, but they are all the same hue of brown to me. I couldn't ever be a priest . . . I couldn't. . . . "

When he choked up, she reached out to his shoulder. He flinched from her gentle touch and stepped away farther.

"I couldn't explain to Uncle Ecru why I didn't follow his lessons, why I turned away, why I misbehaved, or why I tossed his tray of colored powders into the sea."

"Oh, you did?"

He wiped his forearm across his nose while sniffling loudly. The artfully wrapped bandages that covered the span from his wrist to his elbow came away with a dusty brown smudge.

"It's too late to explain to Uncle Ecru now," he said. "Tawny and Sienna judge me to be black-hearted. You'd call it wicked. They've tolerated me only because my father stepped in and begged Uncle Ecru to forgive me. I was only eight years old. 'Only a boy,' my father said. I haven't done anything naughty since then, but I feel them watching me. One more misdeed, one more black spot, and I'll no longer be in the Brown family."

"Don't . . . don't be afraid," Condrie said. "Your secret is safe with me."

At last he turned to look at her with eyes wide and unblinking. "Thanks."

*

The row of reapers stopped swinging their scythes. All as one, they jumped away from something on the ground.

A scarlet snake with light blue rings slithered between their legs.

Women and girls cried out in their native dialects. Condrie was not sure if the words meant *snake* or *help*, but the words did not matter. The women were terrified, holding hands in a circle, ready to run in whatever direction was opposite of the snake's path. *I need to tell them it's just a harmless mole-gobber, not a viper or a cobra. Travelers from a foreign land, they don't know the animals around here.*

Taupe brought his scythe blade around and took a stab. Too late, too slow, all he managed to stab was the dirt. The long snake wriggled into the uncut grasses. The golden stalks rippled, perhaps from the tepid breeze or perhaps from the snake's passing.

"It's . . . it's . . ." Condrie sang out a well-known children's rhyme—in the original version, not the drinking song it later became: "red and blue swallow mice, red and yellow are deadly bites."

Faces turned in her direction. Some of them were listening. Some of them still watched the beige grasses nervously.

Condrie locked her gaze with Taupe from afar. She held up one finger. "Red and . . ." she held up two fingers, ". . . blue . . . swallow mice." One finger again, meant just for him, to signify the first color. "Red and . . ." she held up three fingers, ". . . and yellow are deadly bites."

Taupe nodded understanding. It was not as elaborate as the subtle variations in hue that the storytellers' palette offered, but it was enough for now. Between the two of them, they shared a secret.

Amber joined in singing the rhyme yet again, "Red and blue swallow mice, red and yellow are deadly bites."

The singsong rhyme echoed in the other voices, repeating over and over, as the mowers and the gatherers returned to their monotonous labor. That group of men—Taupe, Slate, Auburn, and Raven—swung their scythes to the rhythm of the chant. The women and girls—Amber, Cherry, Magenta, Olive, and Coral—bowed and bent to pick up the sheared stalks.

"Hey, what's that slackin' off?" The reeve shouted from the far side of the fields. A larger group of mowers and gatherers were harvesting a line through the tall golden stalks.

Raven cupped his left hand around his mouth to holler. "So sorry, sir! We saw a snake!"

"You're bigger than they are!" the reeve called back. "If you see another one, just keep working. They'll get outta your way."

"Yes, sir!" Raven lowered his head and grumbled to his companions. "He's fainter than pale."

Taupe and Auburn chuckled. A few of the girls giggled. But the man known as Slate cautioned in a dry, hoarse growl, "Don't let Reeve hear you talk like that, or you'll be hauled off like *her* . . . or worse."

Condrie caught a glint of Slate's eye glancing at her sideways. She blushed in the heat of his scornful stare.

Taupe nudged Slate with his elbow. "She did nothing wrong."

"None of us did," said Slate. "Yet here we are, burned out of our homes, strangers in a foreign land, doing hard labor we've never done before, speaking to each other in *their* words, learning *their* songs. . . . It's hard enough to hold onto ourselves without sheltering someone who is being watched by the king's knights shining cold silver against the sun."

She looked down at her feet. *What is happening? Why are they arguing? Weren't we all happy a moment ago? I told them it was not a viper and we all shared a song. When did that become a bad thing?*

"If only we had a priest among us," Slate said. "We wouldn't be losing our way."

"Yeah, well, we don't. . . ." Taupe turned his back and resumed swinging his scythe.

I'm sorry for everything you've been through, she wanted to say, but the words did not come out of her tangled tongue. In silence, she bent over to gather the freshly sheared stalks.

*

After the day's work and after the evening meal, darkness settled all around. The only light in all the world came from the flames dancing over the fire pit's logs. Condrie sat cross-legged on the ground. Amber and the other girls sat nearby, knees touching. The men flexed their weary shoulders or slumped over their legs. No one spoke in anticipation of the stories to be told. But for the popping of knots in the fiery logs and the buzzing of summer insects in the grass, all the world was respectfully silent.

The old woman and the old man snuggled up next to each other, as always, with the broad tray of pigment-filled nut shells spread across their laps. She dipped her wrinkled fingertips into the brightly colored powders. The old man unwrapped the strips of cloth from his forearm.

When the old woman held forth her palm to display a different color on each fingertip, the crowd murmured in surprise and appreciation. Amber leaned closer to Condrie and translated, "Tonight they will tell the story of the girl born in a special kind of seashell. It is one of our sacred stories."

From nearby, Taupe said, "Abalone. . . . Their word for it is abalone."

"Abalone," Condrie repeated. "I think I've heard of it as a jewelry bead. I didn't know it came from a seashell."

"The inside of abalone shell is not plain white, like oysters," Taupe said in monotone. "It's like an opal stone full of random, beautiful colors."

"I see." Condrie shared the direct gaze of his eyes for just a moment, knowing his secret that he could not fully appreciate the beauty of the thing he described. He knew the words, but his faulty eyes could not see it for himself.

Taupe quickly averted his gaze as the storytellers began painting the tale with colored stripes spreading across their arms.

"There was a day in the days of long ago," Amber translated softly, "when a man lived alone on an island. He had no wife. He had no children. He had spent his life collecting many rare and beautiful things that he received from travelers who came to his island's harbor. He had built a large home with many rooms to offer hospitality to visitors. But though many travelers enjoyed his meals and the comforts of his guest beds, no one stayed for long. As the years went on, he became lonely. He prayed to the spirits of the water for someone to inherit all the beautiful things he had collected and to continue offering hospitality to the visitors who docked their boats in his island's harbor. So, one day, a traveler arrived with a boatload of abalone...."

Servants of the baron's household burst into the circle. A chambermaid swept up fiery embers with her long aprons and skirts. A man in work boots carried a large flannel shawl.

"I saw it go this way!" the maid cried.

"Dumb girl," the workman grunted. "It wouldn't run into a group of people."

"But I saw it!" she insisted.

The Athel people sitting on the ground held still. Even the storytellers did not move. Wide-eyed, they watched the baron's servants dashing about the rim of the fire pit in search of something.

Out of the darkness piped a shrill voice in the cultured accent of the gentry. "Have you found Vanilla yet? Did I hear someone say they've seen her?"

"No, Miss Osette," the workman said. "It musta gone the other way."

The baron's daughter Osette was a wispy willow stick of a girl. A few years younger than Condrie—at fourteen—she wore a dark velvet house gown suited for a much older woman. The cord that belted her waist formed pleats over her belly that gave her the look of bearing a child, though clearly it was all fabric and no substance. A wool nightcap supported a silk veil draped like a cowl around her head and shoulders. In profile, Condrie saw nothing of Lady Osette's face but the tip of her bone-white nose.

"You must find her! What if she's been eaten by a snake?" Osette gushed out warbling sobs. She balled her silk-gloved hands into fists the size of rosebuds.

"We're tryin' to, miss," said the workman as he bowed to her.

"You must! You must! Don't you understand, you stupid clod? She is a gift of Baron Pegamodi, my betrothed. Whatever am I going to do next year when I come of age to go take my place as his wife? How can I explain that I was so careless with the *cavie* he gifted to me?"

"We could get you another one, miss," suggested the maid, wringing her hands on her apron. "They sell *cavies* in the marketplace in town."

Condrie bit her lip with worry for the maid's sake. *Yes, they sell them for stew meat along with caged rabbits and pigeons.*

Miss Osette swung her full arm and slapped the maid's shoulder, as she was not yet tall enough to reach the maid's cheek. "Stupid girl! Stupid, stupid, worthless girl! Each *cavie* has its own distinct coloring on its fur. Do you know what distinct means? Listen, it means that Vanilla has a spot of ginger brown over her left eye and a mixed patch of auburn and burnt umber brown on her right shoulder. No other *cavie* in all the world has ever had—nor ever will have—that particular pattern of coloring. Baron Pegamodi will certainly know if I try to replace Vanilla with some other little rodent, and he will be outraged at my attempt to deceive, and he will surely revoke the betrothal. My father will be ashamed forever. The alliance of our households will be broken. I will be a ruined divorcée at the age of fifteen, and it will be all your fault for leaving my bedroom door open while Vanilla was playing out of her cage!"

The maid genuflected on one knee. "Forgive me, Miss Osette."

"I don't forgive you. I will never forgive you!" The baron's daughter slapped her cheek now, but as she wore silk gloves, it did not seem to have much effect.

Condrie looked aside, no longer able to stomach the spectacle.

"Let's keep looking," the workman said. "I'm sure it wasn't eaten by a snake. Don't you worry, Miss Osette—a snake would have to be monstrous huge to eat a plump squeaker like that."

A pale spot in the grass caught her eye. Condrie squinted to focus away from the brightness of the firelight. Indeed, it was a small furry animal with stunted legs. Golden brown fur surrounded the dark spot of its eye. It was utterly still—a living rock.

Poor little frightened thing, Condrie thought.

The animal emerged from the grass. It scurried on its tiny legs making straight for where Condrie sat on the ground. When it came within arm's reach, it sprang into her lap.

"Oh!" Condrie cupped her hands around the warm, furry body. The *cavie* purred quietly like a kitten.

"She found it," Amber said incredulously.

Taupe called out, "Look, is that the animal you lost?"

"Praises be!" The workman reached her in three quick strides.

"Are you sure?" asked the baron's daughter.

"Sure is, Miss Osette, yeah. That's the one, all right."

Condrie offered the *cavie* upward to be received into the flannel shawl that the man held. She felt the tiny heartbeat rapidly pattering on the palms of her hands.

"Be careful! Don't drop it!" The baron's daughter turned her back on them all. She hoisted the long, trailing hem of her velvet gown and walked away.

"Should be in a stew pot," the workman grumbled as he gently cradled the swaddling into his chest.

Poor little thing, Condrie thought. *It'll spend the rest of its short life in a cage. It just wanted to be free to eat the grass.*

She looked up to the dark starry sky and thought of Wegdell, the firebird who wanted to fly free of King Davarche's cage. In the privacy of her mind, she whispered a secret prayer to the spirits of the air and sky. If they watched over Sagewyn creatures as well as people, she hoped they would help him elude the king's knights. *He deserves to fly free. Every living thing deserves to be free.*

*

Condrie stood upright to wipe a kerchief over her sweat-drenched brow. This afternoon in the wheat fields was hotter than the day before. *Shouldn't the autumn be getting cooler?* she thought. It would be hours until the relief of sunset and six weeks until the first moon of winter.

"Need a drink?" Violet called to her from the wheelbarrow.

"Thanks." Condrie brought over a bundle of warm sheaves. She lingered by the oak keg and gratefully accepted a ladle from Violet's hands. The water was tepid and tasted of dirt, but it was the best she could hope for.

"Another week at most, I figure," Violet said. "We're making quick work of these fields."

"Where—?" Condrie choked on dust. She dipped the ladle into the keg again.

"Will we go after the harvest is done?" Violet finished.

Condrie nodded.

"I don't know. These days—it feels strange—the group can't agree on a direction. Some of us want to stay, if the baron will give us work through the winter. Some of us want to go into the town. Some of us want to keep moving westward, farther from the reach of the king. They're unnerved that the knights have come this far into the meadowlands, that a Sagewyn lord is the guest of the baron, and that they...."

Condrie looked away in shame for thinking of the trouble she had brought to these serene fields of grain. *They questioned me not far from where we stand. The knights of a foreign land harassed a citizen of the town, and the baron let it happen on his own land. Nowhere is safe. Nowhere is free.*

"Oh," said Violet. "Speak of the ghost."

A black horse galloped up the wagon road. The rider's silvery shoulder pads, throat and breast plates, and sword belt glistened brightly in the sun. A second rider straddled the broad rump, and his gangly body was entirely wrapped in the tea-brown draped veil of a caravan merchant.

Condrie's heart thumped down into her gut. *They found him.*

The lone horse drew nearer, passing from right to left across Condrie's field of vision. The rider leaned forward to the mane. The second rider held on tightly, albeit willingly. *Not him,* she thought with a rush of relief. *Then who? Why?*

She looked back farther to the distant lowlands beyond the wheat fields. Several other black horses ambled up the wagon road, approaching at a less hurried pace.

"Now they just scoop people up randomly from the countryside," Violet said with a fist against her hip. "What'll they want with that poor wagoner?"

Condrie recalled the piercing eyes of the Sagewyn lord. Once again, her mind felt lighter than air and filled with cobwebs. *They'll question the merchant just as they did to me. They'll keep questioning people until they find someone who knows where he is hiding. Perhaps this merchant already does!*

"Co-co-cover for me?"

Violet sighed disapproval even as she nodded to agree. "Here, take an empty keg. I'll say you went to the mill's sluice for more water."

Condrie tucked an oak keg under her arm. She smiled a thanks.

"Don't thank me," Violet said. "Just don't get caught spying."

She darted over the bare ground, her flat shoes crunching into the stubble of sheared dry grasses, stirring up the dust of sunbaked earth as she ran parallel to the wagon road. The horse quickly streaked ahead of her, but she did not worry; she knew their destination. Condrie scurried into the thickets of juniper bushes and breathed the pungent odor of inedible berries. She streaked behind the tool sheds and the smokehouse.

The horse galloped the longer circular course of the wagon road around the mill pond. Condrie sprinted in a straight line underneath the support posts of the sluice that dribbled water onto the mighty wheel. The mill's stone was turning, groaning and grinding wheat kernels into flour. The noise muffled the patter of the horse's hooves crossing the stone bridge. When Condrie emerged on the other side of the mill's shadow, she had lost sight of the horse. Her heart lurched up to her throat. *Faster! I must be faster!*

Condrie set down the empty keg. Both arms free, she pumped her elbows in line with her ribs. She forced her legs to pedal faster, ever faster, up the grassy incline toward the baron's manor house. She dodged the servants' quarters that were a miniature village of thatched cottages. The wagon road led to the carriage house and the stables, but she doubted that the knight would go there first. No, the first duty would be to report to the Sagewyn lord.

Condrie stayed on course for the open veranda at the rear of the manor house. If the baron followed the usual customs of the gentry, he would be taking his afternoon tea in the open air. She expected that the Sagewyn lord, as his guest, would be indulging in the hospitality. Her ankles burned by the time she reached the hedges of geraniums and hydrangeas, but she did not slow down. She leaped over the flower beds and startled a spray of butterflies into flight.

The manor house was an imposing two-story block with a shingled roof higher than the oak and chestnut trees that shaded its glass-paned windows. Bricks of grayish and bluish clay formed the walls, and dark, creeping vines clung to the crevasses.

As she predicted, the knight's horse had stopped at the base of the granite steps. The baron's valet had come to the edge of the veranda and was having a dialogue with the knight.

Condrie crouched into the blocks of granite forming the base of the veranda. She peered through the gaps in the railing's balustrade.

The baron remained seated at the wrought-iron patio table. He stared down into his teacup and gave no sign of acknowledging the knight's arrival.

"It's not him," said the lady with the watery-blue hair.

"Clearly," the Sagewyn lord remarked as he dabbed his piggish lips with a napkin.

The dismounted knight dragged the merchant by his hair. "Ow! Ow! I'm coming willingly! You don't have to be so rough!"

"Quiet," scolded the knight in a hoarse but unmistakable female voice. "Show respect for your betters."

The merchant dropped to his knees, or perhaps the female captain shoved him to the patio tiles. His voluminous body veil fell off his head and created loops of fabric around his shoulders.

"Sir," he cried as the Sagewyn lord strolled toward him. "Have mercy. We did nothing wrong. We did not know the man was a fugitive from Your Most August Majesty."

"You need not prostrate yourself before me," Gerrawgon said, though he didn't sound displeased at this display. "Please, get up so that I may look at you directly."

The young merchant rose to his feet but kept his head bowed.

Condrie shivered with fear and anticipation, peeking through the stone railing at what the Sagewyn was about to do.

Gerrawgon stroked the merchant's chin to raise his face to the sunlight. "When did you last see him?"

"Five . . . no, six days ago. In the middle of the night, for no reason, he awoke from a bad dream. He stole a horse and galloped away as if the Four-Horned One himself were after him."

"I see."

"We want to help you capture him, sir. We want our stolen horse back!"

Gerrawgon tilted his head left and right, gazing into the young man's eyes from all angles. "Have you heard him sing?"

"Yes, sir. For a lying, back-biting horse thief, he sang well."

"Did you enjoy hearing him sing?"

"Yes, sir. At the time, he made us all laugh. He knew lots of drinking songs and bawdy ballads."

"Indeed." With a sigh, the Sagewyn turned away and reported to the captain, "I can't use this one. Weg didn't bond with him. Tell me, boy, did he have any friends among you?"

"We were all his friends, in a way. He seemed like a nice fellow until he stole a horse. I'm surprised to learn that he was a murderer."

The Sagewyn's wife ducked behind her paper fan. Condrie could see, in her slight gesture, that the word murderer hurt her. A smile of satisfaction tightened the girl's cheeks. She knew, with utter certainty, that it was true. Wegdell was innocent. Condrie began to wonder if this gaudily dressed man weren't the one who slaughtered four people and let Wegdell be blamed for it. He certainly seemed more like the type to be so ruthless.

Just as she was thinking that, Gerrawgon revolved in place. He peered through the balustrade and spotted her. Their gazes locked. "You! You've been spying on us, little larva."

"Yes, sir, I came to draw more water from the well, and voices carry, and I got curious when I saw the knight's horse. I couldn't help it. I'm sorry."

The Sagewyn's long cloak swelled behind his legs as he strolled across the width of the veranda. He came to rest an arm casually on the granite railing. All it took was one chance encounter with his eyes, and she couldn't make herself look away. "I should tell you, for you might be interested to know, you being such a curious girl . . . Lord Wegsemze is a very skilled equestrian. He enjoys it. He used to remark that riding at the gallop was the nearest thing to flying that he could feel in human form. Why, I can just imagine him on that blue spotted draft horse. Have you ever seen a horse of that type?"

"Yes, sir," she whispered. They were popular among merchants, because they were heavy and long-legged. Such horses could haul large wagons for weeks at a time without becoming fatigued, and yet they were as graceful as the knight's black stallion.

"Can you imagine for me what Weg would look like on a horse of that type? His long legs astride that saddle, gracefully leaning over the neck, in perfect union with his mount—it could gallop and he would seem to float above its back."

Condrie began to feel dizzy and sick. She closed her eyes. There was the sensation of floating, or flying, of being as weightless as a moth fluttering toward a lantern in the night. Purple grass streaked beneath her. A dim voice from far away reminded her of what Wegdell's long blond hair might look like if it were flapping alongside the gray mane of his horse. The two of them would be like parts of one beast.

In this state of half-dream, half-imagination, she saw Wegdell again. He was galloping across dry fields of grasses as pale blond as his bleached hair. Condrie sensed that someone, somewhere, wanted to know where he was going. A bolt of fear gave her the ability to form words in her mind again. The triplet patters of horse hooves in her imagination became a throbbing in her head. Louder and louder, it smothered everything . . . but for one word.

"Gerrawgon," she said aloud.

Someone slapped her cheek hard enough to give her the taste of blood in her mouth. Condrie squeaked from surprise and pain and started to cry.

"You stupid gin-whore," the lord shrieked in her face. He leaned over, his belly on the railing, his face looming close to her own. "You think that's an amusing trick, don't you?"

"Oh, take it easy on the girl, Gerrie," his wife coaxed, coming over to stroke his shoulder. "Have some dignity. Look, you've dirtied your hand with her."

Condrie gasped up a few deep breaths to get control of her sobbing. With her apron, she wiped her wet cheeks, and then ran her tongue inside her cheek to find the tender spot.

"How close did she get to him?" the lady asked.

"Not very close at all, actually. I couldn't even see which direction he's going. East or northeast. It's been almost a week since he parted company with the merchants. He could be anywhere."

The lady rubbed her husband's forehead and temples with her fingers. He closed his eyes to give in to her soothing touch. "You see?" she said. "This wench is already useless. Their bond is weakening. Now that she knows your name, she'll use it out of reflex every time you touch her. You'll just hurt yourself, darling, smacking your head against this stone."

Condrie sniffled and wiped her nose. She felt a tinge of indignation to realize that "this stone" referred to her. "I want to go back to work, sir," she whimpered. "Please, let me go."

Slowly, he opened his lashes, and his gaze seemed far less captivating than it had before. The Sagewyn seemed weary like a drunken customer who had spent all night reveling at the tavern. "Very well," he said in a dreamy slur. "Go."

*

Water sparkled from the creek feeding into the mill's sluice. Thirst made Condrie's tongue feel like a fuzzy caterpillar in her mouth. She staggered toward the trickling water, trampling through hyssk reeds and fern grasses. Wading into the shallows, she dropped to all fours. Her tender knees bumped on the melon-sized pebbles beneath the rushing current. She scooped cool water with her hands and splashed it to her dusty face.

Am I free? she wondered. *Will they stop harassing me? The lady said that my bond with Wegdell is weakening. Perhaps I am no longer useful to them. Perhaps I can return to my normal life after the harvest is done. Is that what I wish to do?*

Condrie lay down to rest in the grass. She slept and, in her ordinary dream, she experienced again her husband's funeral. Dressed in mourning veils, hungry from days of fasting, she sat vigil by the old man's corpse. She wept into her hands, not for love or loss, but for fear of her own fate. As soon as the funeral ended, her late husband's family would strip her of her clothes and cast her out of the house; she knew it would happen again as it already had happened. In this dream, a man tumbled through the open window. He was a tall, blond man dressed in the sumptuous velvet clothes of a lord. *Help me*, he cried. *They want to kill me.*

A man's voice startled her into wakefulness. "Ow! Char! Ouch, ouch, ouch."

Condrie sat up and peeked through the marsh reeds. A man staggered into the creek, splashing loudly, and crouched over to pat at his knees. He wore brown trousers and a dark wool cloak. His hair was a shaggy mop of bright copper.

No, she thought. *It can't be.*

He staggered to the opposite shore and collapsed onto his back. Face up, but eyes closed, Wegdell moaned at the sky. Condrie saw the knees of his trousers were badly torn, hanging in shreds, and the flesh beneath was red with fresh blood.

Condrie rose to her feet.

When she splashed loudly through the creek, Wegdell lurched up from where he lay. They saw each other, and he laughed. The melodious sound of his voice sent a rush of pleasure tickling through her core. She surprised herself by how much she had forgotten: how white his teeth were, how perfectly straight his nose was, how sparkling his blue eyes.

"What happened to you?" she asked.

"I was crossing a gully that I thought was full of grass. It had briar thorns, too. Just my luck, eh?"

Condrie looked down at the scratches on his knees. "You need a jar of clover honey to clean this so you won't get the black-flesh."

"I know. Got any on you, love?"

"No. Sorry."

"I think washing myself in the stream here might be the next best thing. What other choice does a fugitive have?" He touched her cheek, on impulse, and immediately retracted his hand. "Condy, what in hell's bells are you doing here?"

"Well, I was afraid to go back to the tavern after they burned it and in case they might come looking for you there. I came here to work the harvest."

"Good idea."

"They found me anyway. I was questioned, but since I really didn't know where you were, they let me go."

"I'm glad. I'm sorry for the trouble I've caused you. Are you on your way home now?"

Condrie shrugged, looking aside. "I'm not sure where I'd like to go. It's not so bad working the harvest. It's no worse than working in the tavern's kitchen."

"I see."

Condrie asked, "Where's your horse?"

"I set it free when I felt you coming again."

"Again?" Condrie took a deep breath, recalling the light-headed feeling of being aloft on a moth's wings. "Then it really did happen?"

"Yes, love, you really did come to me at his bidding . . . twice." Wegdell licked his lips, becoming serious now. "I'm proud of you, remembering to use his name the second time. That's why he let you go today. Gerrie knows he can't use you anymore without hurting himself."

Condrie nodded, remembering the Sagewyn lady had said the same thing.

"Go home, Condy. The longer you're away from me, the weaker the bond will be, and the safer you'll be from the king's lackeys."

"I don't understand what's going on," she said in a wavering voice that threatened to dissolve into sobs. She fixated on the tip of his long straight nose and remembered being perched there, licking his skin with her retractable moth-like tongue. "What did he do to me? How did he use me to find you?"

"Don't be afraid of him. He bluffs a good game, but he is not omniscient."

She crinkled her brows. "I don't know that word."

"I mean to say, he does not know everything. He does not see everything. He is very old in years and he does not age, but otherwise he is very much an ordinary man. His powers of perception are limited to the passions of those around him. Passions—like fear, hate, jealousy, or patriotism—bind people together. You feel compassion for those who you see as being victimized. You also feel for me a strong . . . uh, let's call it an attraction."

Condrie's cheeks flushed warm. She hoped that working in the fields had tanned her cheeks and he would not notice her blush.

"Gerrie used those feelings. He walked the threads of your strong emotions the way a spider walks across its web."

"He's so evil."

Wegdell sighed from a sadness that seemed to come from the depths of his soul. "Don't judge him too harshly, love. His only fault is being loyal to the king. That isn't supposed to be a crime."

Condrie had a wicked thought: *Maybe the king is evil.* Even though she sat by the side of a fugitive and a traitor, she wasn't brave enough to say it aloud.

"Where are you going to go now?" she asked.

"I don't know."

Condrie looked at him, and she knew how he felt: lost and all alone, weary and afraid, and weary of being afraid. Tired of running. He had come so far, and he wondered if he had the strength to go any farther.

"Perhaps I could hide in the hayloft."

"No," she said. "Your king's knights have their horses in the stables."

"Well, then perhaps I could hide in the rafters of the mill."

"No," she said. "The grindstone is turning every day. Millers are up and down the ladders every hour. Threshers and winnowers are all around. Wagons come and go from every direction. Someone will spot you."

He gazed away to the distance in the direction of the wheat fields. "You say you're working the harvest? How much more reaping is yet to be done?"

"Another week . . . or two, at most."

"Who makes up the field crew?" he asked.

Condrie clutched her skirts. "Oh, you can't think of slipping in!"

"Why not? If they already searched for me so close to town, they won't look in the same place twice. They'll assume I'm running as far away from Gerrie as possible. They won't imagine I'm so brazen as to sneak up under his nose."

Condrie looked back over her shoulder. "They hauled in one of the caravan merchants for questioning. He's here! If he sees you—"

"Did they deem him useless and let him go?"

"Yes."

Wegdell smiled. "Then he'll be plodding along the road to go rejoin his companions. Why would he stick around here?"

Condrie frowned at her hands in her lap. "That makes sense, actually."

"Tell me about the work crews. Are they meadowlanders or foresters? Please tell me it's the latter. I do a fair impression of a woodcutter's dialect."

A terrible thought occurred to her. "Your tattoo!"

"Shouldn't be a problem. My shirt covers it. Field workers don't bathe."

"No, no, no. The reeve—he . . . he. . . ." Condrie stammered in her sudden attack of nervousness. "He makes all his new field hands take off their shirts to check for the fugitive."

Wegdell lowered his head "Oh God."

"I could get you more of a mustard salve. Stay here and wait for me. I'll run back to the town and . . . oh, I could get you some honey salve for your scraped knees, too. Hide in the ferns. Don't move until I return."

"No, no, Condy," he said with a sad smile. "I've asked too much of you already. I'll wait for darkness and then run . . . somewhere."

"Where will you go?"

"I don't know," he said.

Hot tears bubbled up to her eyes. "It's not fair that you're forced to be so . . . so speckled."

"Speckled?" he repeated, tilting his head curiously.

"Like a very small fish with speckles that blend into the rocks so that bigger fish can't see it."

Condrie used her apron to wipe the tears from her face. She sniffled and sucked up several deep breaths to get control of her urge to break down weeping. *That greedy king in the South! His knights gallop into the free meadowlands and bully whomever they please. His legions chase gentle people out of their homes and set magical creatures to flight. When will it be enough?*

He asked, "Tell me, what other sorts of people are in the field crews?"

"The Athel," she said, gulping down tears. "You know, the Northern Bay Islanders?"

"I know who the Athel are." His ever-present smile dropped away and its absence changed the contours of his face. His eyes grew larger and his mouth grew thin.

Condrie brightened, thinking of the friends she had recently made. "They've been so kind and welcoming to me. I've been learning their stories and some of their words. It's beautiful the way they use paints and colors to—"

Wegdell raised his hand in a restraining gesture. For a moment, it frightened her because the other Sagewyn had made the identical movement when ordering the knights about.

"May I borrow your knife?"

"Why?" she asked.

He pointed to the black roots of his copper-blond hair. "If I shed my plumage, I could pass for one of their lot."

"Are you sure? Do you know them well enough to speak as one of their own?"

"Each of the islands has a distinct language. That's why they use colors to communicate. Out here, it's easier for them to speak to each other in the common tongue of the meadowlands. Even so, there's a risk of claiming to be from such-and-such island that no one of your group would know."

"Exactly," she said. "They're a mixed group from several different islands."

"I figured as much. Refugee groups are often a mixed bunch." He pointed to the small knife sheathed on her belt. "May I?"

Condrie offered her meal knife that was no longer than her hand.

"Say goodbye to the hair." He leaned sideways to embrace the volumes of wheat-colored stalks. In a few hard strokes, he sliced it all away, leaving a dark stubble close to the scalp. The back of his slender neck was pale compared to his sun-tanned cheeks.

Condrie scrutinized what remained. "It's not evenly trimmed. I wish I had a good pair of scissors."

The shorn pieces he tucked in the roots of a marsh berry bush. "For the birds' nests," he quipped.

"What about your tattoo?"

"I have an idea for that." Wegdell paused, eyeing her sideways. "I've got to warn you now, the shirt's coming off."

At that, Condrie giggled. "Do you think I'll swoon?"

"Well, you do look at me."

"Sure I do. What's wrong with looking?"

Wegdell made a thoughtful *hmmph* and answered, "Nothing, I guess."

In one swift, decisive motion, he yanked the coarse shirt up over his head. Once again, Condrie was treated to a view of his broad, smooth chest. Slivers of dark hair made a faint line down the center of his contoured abdomen.

He said, "Do me the favor of shredding the shirt into bandage strips. I expect you understand what I need."

Condrie used her knife to jab into the linen threads. She tore it apart into the narrow strips that the Athel customarily wrapped around their forearms. "But what about your tattoo?"

He plunged his hand into the slick greenish mud at the creek's edge. Fingers spread wide open, he stamped the shape of his palm against his chest. "It should dry quick in this heat."

"Why did you do that?" she asked.

Wegdell looked down in concentration at wrapping the linen strips around his forearms. He pinched the strands with meticulous care, as a bird weaving its nest, turning the twists in that particularly style that the Athel used. "You see, love, I do know them. The king provided a thorough education in the customs of subjugated people."

Condrie sat back in her skirts to watch him complete the transformation.

"When you introduce me to the group," he said, "you can tell them that you encountered me on the road and I've apparently been wandering alone for quite some time. In a way of omitting the most important details, that is essentially true. I won't ask you to lie. I've asked enough of you already. I only ask you to keep my secret."

"But you'll be lying," she said softly.

"Yes," he said without mirth. "Though I won't speak a word from this moment forth. You see, I'll be under a vow of silence. I shall play the role of an itinerant pilgrim—thus, the mark on my chest."

"A pilgrim?" she repeated.

"It's a holy man who goes alone on a meditative quest," he told her. "In other words, a priest."

*

Condrie led him along the footpath that passed behind the mill's slowly turning wheel. They strolled together over the serene fields of coarse dirt littered with scraps of wheat grasses. Nerves tightened the closer they approached the people who bobbed and bent to gather stalks of wheat from the ground. *What if they don't believe the deception? What if they call him out as an intruder and bring that squad of knights galloping down upon us all?*

"Don't worry," he whispered. "I'm yellow."

"Yellow?" she repeated. "What does that mean?"

He tilted his head in a calm, reassuring expression but was unable to speak the answer as they drew nearer to the others.

Silver, the storyteller, saw him first. She dropped the sheaves out of her hands. Golden fronds fluttered softly to the dusty ground. "Look!"

Violet let go of the handles of her wheelbarrow. With the back of her hand, she wiped a long strand of dark hair away from her eye. "Who is he?"

Olive, Magenta, and Coral responded as a group moving together to encircle him. Wegdell stood straight in their midst, his backbone long and his chin held high, flattening the canvas of his chest to display the hand print. By now, the creek's mud had dried to a whitish-green paste like tarnish on a copper kettle.

"I found him out on the road," Condrie said.

"A wanderer," Violet exclaimed.

"A seer and thinker," said Magenta.

The oldest woman squinted her wrinkled eyes. "A priest."

Men in the group ahead stopped swinging their scythes. Taupe, Slate, and Cyan exchanged quick stares of surprise and then dropped their tools in the grass. The men bounded over the dirt to join the circle.

"Where did you come from?" Slate asked breathlessly.

A roll of the eyes and a shrug was the only answer Wegdell gave.

Taupe elbowed his friend in the ribs. "He's under a vow of silence, you browned head. What a stupid question to ask! Why does it matter which island he's from? He's one of us."

"One of us," said Olive in a tender girlish tone.

"Blue," said the oldest woman as she strained to reach a hand up to his face. Her aged hunched-over shoulders made her too short, so Wegdell bowed forward. Her wrinkled hand with its swollen knuckles came to rest against his cheek. He closed his eyes to receive her silent blessing.

Condrie smiled with relief that his plan was working—for now. He had found a place to be safe until the king's knights gave up the search and moved elsewhere.

The reeve's harsh voice broke the tranquility of the scene. "Here now, what's all this lolling about on the job?"

His cap's brim shielded the sunlight and made the reeve's face a mask of half-darkness. The orange tunic was as vivid as poppies contrasting the beige fields all around. He brandished the ox horn as if threatening to blow the alarm.

"A wanderer," said Violet boldly. "He's just arrived."

"I'm not hiring anymore," the reeve told him. "You should move along to the town. . . ."

Slate spoke up, "I'll take a pay cut."

"I will too," added Cyan.

Taupe remained silent.

The storyteller Silver explained, "He is a priest. It means he's a holy man—"

"I know what a priest is." The reeve tilted his head to survey Wegdell's physique. "Your back looks strong. No calluses on your hands. Do you think you could do this sort of work?"

"He won't speak," Cyan said. "He's taken a vow of silence while he's on a pilgrimage."

The reeve cackled with mercenary glee. "A vow of silence, you say? Then he won't waste time talking on the job? You're hired for whatever is left. It's a fortnight at most until the end of harvest. A bonus of three copper coins for you, Mister Priest, if you inspire these lazy dogs to mow it all out to the fence line in under ten days."

Wegdell dropped to his knees. He respectfully touched the toes of the reeve's dark leather boots.

"And he's got manners!" The reeve puffed up his chest. "That's a refreshing turn from the bunch of you rude ingrates. But say . . . what's that mud slapped on his chest?"

"It is a holy sign," said Slate.

"What . . . holy sign? A circle-in-a-square is a holy symbol. This is a sloppy hand print. Wash it off!"

Condrie took a breath. *What to do? What to say?* If the reeve forced him to wash away the hand print, the tattoo would be revealed. Everyone would know it; no one but the wanted fugitive bore the sunburst mark of the king. Even if Wegdell ran, the reeve could blow the alarm on his horn and bring all the knights galloping on his heels.

"Please, sir, don't ask him to wash it off." Condrie gasped in surprise at the words blurting out of her mouth, but once started, it was too late to stop. "It won't slow down his work to keep it, don't you think? Show him compassion and he will adore you. He will work swiftly and cheerfully to do your every bidding. But if you force him to erase the thing that he values as holy, then he will be dispirited. Of course, he will still obey your orders, but there will be a heaviness in his heart and a heaviness in his feet."

"Huh." The reeve tapped his fingers on the curve of his ox horn. "So, little girl, you *do* know how to talk without stammering."

Condrie looked to the back of Wegdell's long neck and the bristles of dark hair that capped his scalp. "When it's, uh, important."

"A smear of mud on a man's chest is important?" the reeve asked.

"Yes," she said.

The reeve laughed loudly from his open throat. He clutched his jiggling belly. He rocked back and forth in the rhythm of his hearty guffaws.

Violet traded a sour glance with the group of men. Condrie sensed the woman's displeasure; it was the same expression she often saw on the faces of the barmaids at the tavern. Drunken men assumed they were brilliant while making nonsensical conversation. *You're just an illiterate gin-whore*, the finely dressed gentlemen used to say, slobbering into their cups. *You're too stupid to understand what I'm telling you.*

When he finally got up his breath again, the reeve raised his ox horn to his mouth. A mournful blast rang out over the fields. "Back to work," he cried, "or I'll cut today's wages in half for everyone . . . including your priest!"

*

That afternoon, they gave him a sickle—a crescent hook with a handle no longer than a soup ladle—because he had never before handled a full-length scythe. While the other men stayed on their feet swinging the long bladed poles, Wegdell bent over. He joined the old storytelling man, side by side, hunched and bobbing over the wheat stalks. Together they followed in the wide swath cut by the mowers. Together they grasped whatever brittle stalks remained standing and with a flick of the wrist cut them free of the ground.

Condrie and the other women labored behind the men, gathering the sheaves. They tied the bundles with twine and stacked them like tufts of shaggy mushrooms. Until this day, Condrie had never looked up from her own hands doing the same monotonous chore. This was her first chance to observe the Sagewyn at a distance. A firebird masquerading in the form of a man, she wondered how he would be among other ordinary people. Would he move differently—more like a bird than a man?

For hours she admired the muscles of his shoulders flexing to each stroke of the sickle. His skin became drenched with sweat in the heat of the full sun. He huffed when he bent over. He licked his thirsty lips. By the end of the day, her apprehensions faded; if she did not know his secret, she would not have guessed he was anything but an ordinary man.

As sunset stained the blue sky to a palette of orange and crimson, and as the bright fiery orb sank into the smoky gray horizon, only Wegdell paused in his work. He put down his sickle. He stood tall, facing the west, and closed his eyes to let the scarlet glow wash his cheeks. He was the only one.

The others faced west but only half-closed their eyes. They slowed their movements but did not stand still. Scythe blades tilted from right to left without actually cutting anything. It was how each day had ended—until now.

Someone should have told him! I should have told him! Why didn't I think that he knew their customs so well? Condrie looked around, and just as she feared, the reverence for the sunset had not gone unnoticed.

The reeve strolled closer and closer, his horn in his left hand and a whip in the other. "First day on the job, Priest? I'll let you have this one, but do it again tomorrow and I'll dock your pay."

With eyes downcast, Wegdell turned to face him. He gave the reeve a humble nod to show that he understood.

"No back-talk?" The reeve smiled, and in the sunset's colors, his teeth were as orange as his tunic. "I like this vow of silence. By th' powers, I'm of a mind to let you indulge in watching the sun set. Just you, Priest! Just you."

Wegdell lowered his nod into a proper bow. Then he winced and laid a hand to his lower back. Condrie bit down to hide her smile. *He does well pretending to be an ordinary man.*

Reeve blew his horn signaling the end of the day.

"Come, come," said the old storytelling man. Others gathered around him, scythes in hand, and escorted Wegdell across the harvested fields to where the chow wagon was parked. They did not speak amongst themselves. Condrie had expected them to be more talkative than usual in asking questions of the newly arrived priest. *Where are you from? Where are you going? What have you learned on your journey?* Instead, they only guided him to partake from the basket full of flatbread patties, the vat of fish-and-onion chowder, and the tray of sliced carrots and radishes.

They gathered in the usual place to sit on the ground, near the tarps on poles that served as their homes in the fields, sitting on the dusty, dry ground, quietly dipping their flatbreads into the soup and crunching on the carrot sticks. Wegdell had a peculiar manner of raising his chin before dropping each morsel of food into his mouth—the only hint of his birdlike nature—but he did it gracefully and not so noticeably.

Condrie dared not sit near him. To avoid suspicion, she took a place at the rear of the women's group.

Amber snuggled close beside her. "Isn't it exciting?" she whispered. "A priest . . . a real priest here among us!"

"I'm sure he just, uh, wishes you would treat him as you would treat any other man."

"How can I?" Amber hugged herself. "The king forbade them. His blackcoats imprisoned them and whipped them. There are so few of them left, scattered to the winds."

Condrie looked aside to the man named Taupe and wondered what thoughts lurked behind those dark eyes. She recalled what he had told her in confidence: *I know fifty-seven words for the color red, but they are all the same hue of brown to me. I couldn't ever be a priest.* If anyone could detect the slightest mistake in Wegdell's disguise, it would be this man.

"Please sit with us," said the old storytelling woman as she took her place on the stump.

"Yes, come." The old man brought the tray of frizzle nut shells and the powdery pastes of all colors.

Slate used a tinderbox that he kept hanging on a cord around his waist. Every night it was his appointed task to use flint and steel to make light in the darkness. He struck up sparks to the kindling around a stack of logs. He waved a straw fan, and the flames grew.

"Tell us a story," the old woman invited. Murmurs of "yes, yes" rippled around the seated group.

Wegdell's slender legs bent at sharp angles as he sat by the tray. Six rows of seven frizzle nut shells, in halves, contained every color imaginable. Condrie watched his gentle hands with fascination. He had long, graceful fingers that dabbed at the console of color spots, unerringly choosing burgundy instead of crimson and turquoise over teal. He drew dots and stripes and sweeping curls of rainbows on the tender inside skin of his left arm.

The entire group voiced a hushed *ahhh* as they all visibly stiffened. Slate lowered his head as if ashamed. Taupe gritted his teeth hard enough for the muscle of his jaw to pulse.

Condrie looked to the girl at her side. "What is it?"

"He asks, 'Why do we tell our stories by firelight?' He means, 'The colors are not the same as they are by the light of day.'"

The old man explained, "It is the only time we are allowed to do as we wish. By daylight, we must perform labor."

Wegdell wiped his arm clean in one bold stroke across the rags wrapped around his opposite forearm. He used all five fingers at once to paint a short streak of rainbow, then quickly crossed over it with a thick stripe of blackish brown.

Amber translated, "He says, 'I can't tell stories in the dark.'"

What is he doing? Is this part of his masquerade? Surely if he knows their customs and their language of colors, he must know their stories?

"He's right," said Taupe. "We've compromised enough for them and their ways. What say you all, tomorrow at midday when we break for a repast, he tells us a story then?"

"Yes," said Slate while prodding the fire logs and growing the flames.

"Yes, yes," said the other men in deep, rumbling voices.

Condrie met his steady gaze from across the distance. She wanted to cry out, *Is this part of your plan? How long can you keep fooling them?*

*

That night, she slept near him on hyssk reed mats slapped on the ground. He fidgeted long after the others had drifted into slumber. Condrie's body ached down to the marrow of her bones; she felt like a slug, unable to move. Each time she started to doze off, he flipped his long torso to the other side and startled her awake. Each time he kicked the threadbare blanket off his slender legs, she pulled it back over him. "You'll be eaten alive by mosquitoes if you sleep uncovered," she whispered. When he finally settled down to sleep, like a bird, he tucked his face into the bend of his arm.

Condrie lay awake for hours, unable to quell the worries crying out in her mind. *The fields will be harvested in ten days . . . a fortnight at most. Threshing and winnowing must be done before the first rains. What will the Athel people do then? Shall we stay for the harrowing and seeding of winter wheat? And what will he do? How long can he maintain this charade?*

*

The next day began with a lightness of mood and clear blue skies. Taupe, Slate, and Cyan made good progress across the field, each man's scythe sweeping in an elegant dance. They sheared off more golden grasses from the earth than they had ever done in one morning. The women hummed among themselves in melodies that Condrie did not know; she had never heard them sing before. *Can it be that having a priest among them has meant so much?* she wondered.

Reeve tooted his horn in one short burst. He hollered out a single word, but from a distance Condrie could not understand. She did not need to hear it; she knew, and everyone on the crew knew, the horn's toot meant one thing. *Lunch*.

Violet parked her wheelbarrow. The laborers all gathered around, taking turns with dipping a soup ladle into the keg of tepid, dusty water. Stale flatbread, pickled cucumbers, and handfuls of carrot sticks got passed around.

"For you," said Amber, handing an extra carrot to Wegdell.

He nodded thanks.

The old storyteller man lifted a kerchief off the tray of pigments that Violet had carried on her wheelbarrow with the basket of pickles and bread. "It will have to be a quick story. The lunch break is not much time."

Wegdell opened his hands as a silent request. The old man hesitated, standing there with the tray as if unsure of what to do.

Amber asked, "Are you offering to hold the tray while Willow Leaf paints us a story?" When he shook his head, she asked, "Are you requesting permission to use Willow Leaf's pigments to paint a story of your own?"

He smiled.

"My arms are too sore to hold it for long," said the old man. Condrie recalled that he usually sat on the ground with the tray on his lap. Here there was no time to recline on the ground, not with the reeve watching from the comfort of his field chair.

Amber offered, "May I hold it for you?"

"Yes, thank you." The elder handed off the broad palette. Amber had stronger arms, but her shoulders were only half as wide, and she had to extend her arms to balance the tray against her belly.

The people formed a semi-circle around him in a triple layer of rows, about seven or eight people in each row, crunching on their carrots, sucking on their pickles, and all facing toward him to watch what colors he would dab on his arm.

Wegdell carefully unwrapped the pleated knots of the rags that wound about his left forearm. He dipped his fingertips in the colors. He painted streaks and dots and swirls from the crook of his elbow down to his wrist, and held it out for all to see.

Amber translated, for Condrie's benefit, "'On my travels, I saw a bird in a cage.'"

Wegdell wiped away only half of the design, and close to his wrist he dabbed a dark green, a lighter green, and a whiteish green, then circled it with a grayish blue.

"'On my travels, I saw a frog in a well.'"

Again, he wiped away only the second half. Then he painted on a double-stroke smear of orangish red, pumpkin brown, and scarlet and circled it with a bluish white.

"'On my travels, I saw a moth in a . . . a. . . .' I'm sorry, I don't know the word."

"Cocoon," said Condrie.

Wegdell wiped his entire forearm clean. Then he dabbed on a fresh spattering of colors in hues of bluish purple, shades of yellowish green, and pinkish crimson.

"'The bird sang, the frog croaked, and the moth dreamed.'"

With that, he wiped his skin clean and began rewrapping the intricate pleated twists of the rags around his forearm.

"That's it?" Slate asked, slurred with a cheek full of bread. "What sort of story is that? What does it mean?"

Taupe looked down at the ground, the brown dirt between his bare feet. "It's the kind of story that priests tell. It's not supposed to have a meaning."

His brother Tawny nudged him in the ribs. "Like *you* would know what stories priests tell."

Condrie held her breath at the belligerent tone in the brother's voice, and she braced herself for what might happen next. Even if they weren't in the tavern and filling their heads with gin, she knew the look of men itching to break out into a fight.

Instead, Taupe just slumped and withdrew. He slinked back through the rows and went to the rear and picked up his scythe off the ground. Just in time for Reeve to toot his horn and holler a command.

Lunch was over.

*

Days followed in a routine cycle of beige monotony of cutting the wheat, gathering the wheat, eating, drinking, and sleeping, and each morning, the cycle began anew. A cloudless sky was always the same shade of blue. A mild breeze was neither too hot nor too brisk. Day by day, the wheat stalks fell to the flattened fields as the lines of mowers progressed nearer the stacked stones at the edge. Reeve strolled the square edges of the fields, watching and measuring their progress. At mid-morning, at midday, and at the hour before sunset, he marked a small board with chalk for how many rows they finished.

Only Wegdell's lunchtime parables broke the monotony. Condrie wondered if they were well known among the Athel people or if he was composing them where he stood. "A green bug on a green leaf avoids the hungry bat" and "the plum blossoms must wither and drop to make way for the tasty fruit" left Condrie wondering.

Horses ambled onto the flattened fields one day as the people were gathered around Violet's wheelbarrow for a lunch break. Wegdell was the last to see them. The two riders in gleaming steel gorgets that flashed in the sun—the female captain with the cinnamon hair and a man, the guy with ginger curls that Condrie saw washing his horse a few weeks back—rode side by side on those broad-shouldered black steeds. The people standing in a semi-circle facing the wheelbarrow to watch the priest smear colors on his arm saw them first, and as a group, visibly stiffened and took a step back.

Wegdell inclined his head to glance over his shoulder, but otherwise did not move.

Both riders came from the baron's manor house, the horses facing in the direction of the river, perhaps heading toward the town. They detoured onto the fields and approached the group. As the reeve noticed them, he hopped out of his chair to sprint the distance.

"Is there a problem, Captain?" the reeve called.

She reined in her horse near the wheelbarrow piled high with sheaves, and her companion did the same. The black horses flared their nostrils, sniffing the hay, and yet with their riders' tight grip on the reins, the horses did not indulge their nature, did not dip their snouts into the wheelbarrow as if it were a manger in the barn.

"The steward reports you hired one more man onto the crew last week," the captain said. From high in her saddle, she held her chin aloof and only lowered her eyes to speak to the man standing by her stirrup.

Her companion, the man with ginger curls, narrowed his eyes and scanned over the group. Condrie's heart thumped at the keen gaze passing over them. *They're here looking for him! What to do? What to do? He can't outrun horses.*

"Yes," the reeve said. "Him . . . that one."

"Face me," she commanded.

Wegdell stepped around the wheelbarrow slowly, with halting steps that showed the ache in his legs and hunched shoulders from bending over a sickle for a week of days without rest. Unshaved stubble dirtied his jawline. Dirt soiled his cheeks. Gone was the waist-length mane of bleached locks, and his chest tattoo was concealed with the palm print of white paste. Condrie wondered if it would be enough; would the king's knights still recognize him?

"Lieutenant?" she prompted the ginger curls next to her.

"I regret to say, Captain, I can't be sure. He's got the right body, but there's a half dozen more standing here with the same height and lanky limbs."

"What's that mark on his chest?"

Reeve answered, "They tell me it's a sacred sign. He's a pilgrim priest."

"A priest?" she snorted.

The ginger curls nodded along. "Yes, Captain. I've seen this sort of thing before. It's a dying custom . . ."

Taupe whispered under his breath, "Dying because of you lot."

". . . but not so great a surprise to see a straggler wandering about. He may find other ways to cause a disruption, but for today, I'd say it's not him. Definitely, Captain—it can't be him."

"Why not, Jeree? Why are you so sure it's not *him*?" She maneuvered her horse one step closer to loom a large black shadow over the tall man.

"Very simply, Captain, it's because a pilgrim priest takes a holy vow of silence. For as long as he's on his quest for knowledge of the world's spirits, or some such nonsense, he will not utter a single word. Can you imagine Lord Wegsemze holding back his tongue for so much as an hour?"

The captain shared a smile with her lieutenant. "A most insightful observation, Jeree. That pompous peacock would go utterly mad to restrain his clucking, even if his very life depended on it! Clearly we're wasting our time here."

Condrie exhaled the breath she had been holding. *They don't know his face!* She felt a little dizzy and sick, but held her poise until the horses ambled away at an easygoing stroll, the long black tails swinging back and forth.

Slate murmured, "I kept thinking, one quick sweep of my scythe. . . ."

"Then what?" Indigo-in-Water challenged him. "Bring the whole squad galloping downhill to butcher us all? Don't be stupid. We've been stupid before, and look where we are now."

Cyan added, "It's the green bug on a green leaf that avoids the hungry bat."

"I know," Slate said with downcast eyes. "I know."

*

"It's nothing, it's nothing," said the old storyteller man. That night, he lay on the straw mat beneath the tarp. He raised his knees as if sitting in a chair while flat to the ground.

Olive knelt beside him. "Don't tell me it's nothing, Elder, when I've seen you hobbling on your sore knees for days. The strain of these labors is too much for you."

"It's nothing, I say."

Olive's face warped with concern. "If only we were at home, I could make you a poultice. I don't know any of the herbs in this foreign place."

Condrie stood at the edge of the tarp's frame, looking down on them, watching, and feeling so helpless. *If only the reeve would excuse me one day from work, I could walk into the town and ask Ma Kielsing for some of her medicinal powders. Hangover aches and stomach aches, fist fights and wench's ankles—she has a cure for them all in her pantry.*

"Stop fussing," the old man insisted. "I've walked across half the world by now. I can stand a few more days until the mowers reach the end of the field."

Wegdell tapped Condrie on the shoulder from behind. As she started to turn, he put a scrap of rag into her palm. By the time she fully turned, he was already strolling away.

She untangled the fabric scrap. Simple letters were scratched into the linen with a charred stick: *wintergreen, millwheel,* and *meet me.*

His lanky legs made broad strides away from the tarp, away from the camp's fire pit. He was soon lost to the darkness.

Condrie turned back to Olive, intending to say, *I've heard somewhere that a poultice of wintergreen leaves can soothe aching muscles. I remember there's a spread of wintergreen growing around the mill's wheel. Wait here for me. I'll run up there and be right back.*

What came out of her mouth was, "Wi-wi-wi-winter . . . green. . . . Wait here!"

She dashed away into the darkness. Her eyes soon adjusted to the pale light of stars and a half moon. The footpath was a lighter hue of gray than the smoky hues of the soil all around. Hurrying as best she could, she was breathless by the time she reached the black timbers of the millhouse.

Wintergreen, peppermint, rosemary, lavender, and geranium blasted their combined aromas into her senses. Condrie muffled a sneeze with her hand.

"Over here," he whispered from the shadows beneath the majestic wheel.

Condrie ducked around the stone trough at the base of the wheel. She crouched with him in the dim cubby between a stack of buckets and an idle wheelbarrow. Their knees touched, and he didn't move away.

"I've never heard of using wintergreen," she said softly. "Ma Kielsing's pantry has silver birch and willow bark."

"Wintergreen leaves are quicker and easier to obtain than traipsing off to the river bank to strip the bark off of trees. Hurry, pick the leaves before we're gone too long and they start rumors about us. God, I was lucky today that Leera and Jeree didn't recognize me. If they hear you're starting up a coziness with the newly arrived priest . . . well, maybe they'll come back and get a second look at me. Maybe they'll insist I wash off my holy hand stamp to check if I have a tattoo on my chest, and then. . . ."

At the pause, Condrie squinted at his face in the darkness. His voice was more hoarse and husky than she remembered. "What?"

"My God, listen to me. What's happened to my voice? I sound like a honking goose."

"You haven't used your voice for anything but snoring for a week. It's only natural that—"

"I do not snore."

"Yes, you do."

"I do not."

Condrie shrugged and continued gathering wintergreen stalks into her apron.

"Ugh," he groaned. "Jeree was right in what he said today. Has it only been a week? I don't know how I can endure one more day of not being able to talk!"

"You're only staying with them until your king's knights stop looking for you around here, right? It shouldn't be much longer."

"I had hoped, but it seems they are not giving up the chase so easily." Wegdell paused to clear his throat.

"How much longer can you keep up this disguise?"

"For as long as I must."

"Aren't you worried that you'll make a mistake? One of them will spot you as a pretender?"

He lowered his face deeper into the shadows. "No."

"You're being cocky."

"No," he said. "I won't make any mistakes. I know them very well, Condy. Foreign languages were primary among my studies at the king's palace. Especially the foreign languages of people to be spied upon and targeted for colonization."

"Why so glum? You should be proud. It doesn't look easy to remember all those colors."

"I was proud—once. I was very, very proud. Those were the days when I was stupid and loyal to the king. Oh, Condy, you're so sweet and innocent. You have no idea what things I've done."

"Don't be silly." Condrie had collected quite a lap full of wintergreen by then. To keep her hands busy, she started shredding the leaves from the stalks. "I'm not stupid."

"Of course you're not."

"You were a Sagewyn in service to your king. You behaved like *him*."

Wegdell dropped his head forward. He could almost be meditating. But she knew he wasn't. They both were silent for a while, reflecting on the man in the multi-colored velvets and satins who rode upon a black stallion.

"Did you spy on the Athel people?"

"Yes," he whispered.

"You were nasty, and cruel, and wicked?"

"Yes, God help me, yes."

Condrie patted his knee with sisterly familiarity. "I can see you regret it now, and that's what matters to me. You're like a drunkard who smashed things. Now you've sobered up and you're ready to apologize."

"Stop. You don't know what you're saying."

"Just tell me, Weg. . . ." She paused, knowing it wasn't really his name. "Have you ever killed anyone, really?"

Wegdell licked his lips, his tongue searching for an invisible palette in the air to find the right colored words. "No, I never harmed anyone, not directly."

"You see?"

"But with my fiery wings soaring in flight and with a sweep of my flaming tail, I set ablaze their farm fields and their homes. I caused the devastation that allowed the king's troops to saunter in and claim the territory without the loss of a single spear carrier. Indirectly, I'm responsible for a great deal of misery. It's a debt I can never repay these people."

Condrie patted his knee again, more firmly. "You're repaying it every day that you labor side by side with them, that you teach them and inspire them. It wasn't your idea to raze their fields. It's that king in the South who desires to stick his flag in every corner of the world. The King of Xol owes the Athel people a greater debt than you."

Wegdell's blue eyes widened until she could see the entire circumference of his irises. "My God, Condy, be careful what you're saying."

"I remember you told me that your king has you shackled by some magical means. You cannot transform into a firebird except at the king's bidding, you said. How does he hold you bound?"

Wegdell looked aside. "He keeps one of my fiery tail feathers in an iron box. I cannot transform into my glory if the feather is kept away from me. So, he controls when I am a firebird and when I am a man."

"But your king is just a man?"

"Yes, he is nothing more than a flesh-and-blood man."

"Couldn't you figure some way to resist his will?"

Wegdell shook his head. "If the king were to simply quench my fiery tail feather in a bowl of water, it matters not where I am in this world, I would die. I am only alive thus far because he does not want my life extinguished; he wants me back in my cage."

"Then couldn't you find this hidden box and reclaim your tail feather? Would you be free of him then?"

Before she'd finished speaking, Wegdell popped onto his feet and started walking away. "What have I done to you?" he groaned.

Condrie arose, but carefully so she wouldn't spill the wintergreen leaves out of her apron. His long legs were faster than hers, and she had to hurry to catch him halfway down the wagon road. Running after him made her blood pump, and ire rose to pound in her temples.

"Say, you. You really are vain, aren't you?"

Wegdell was surprised enough to slow down when she said that. "Vain? Me?"

"Just because I like to look at you, because you're a nice thing to look at, you think I'm that . . . that. . . ." In her stammering, she couldn't think of a word, but something else came to mind. "Blank white? I'll tell you, I have my own colors. I'm full of colors. So what, if sometimes your colors and mine match? It doesn't mean that you've painted them onto me. I've disapproved of greedy King Davarche all by myself, before I ever met you."

Instead of getting angry in return, Wegdell grinned at her. He spread his arms wide and bowed as if she were a princess. "My apologies, dear lady. My vanity indeed knows no boundaries, if I could ever imagine that I could color your thoughts. Do you forgive me?"

"Oh, stop it." Condrie gave his shoulder an open-palm slap. He obeyed and stood straight.

They continued walking together, and the way back to the encampment felt longer than it had on the way up to the mill. The vow of silence was in effect once again.

*

The stone wall inched closer and closer. She raised her eyes from the work of her hands to check their progress. The swish-swish of the mowers' blades stirred dry flurries of beige dust. The axel of Violet's wheelbarrow creaked. The warmth of the day moved toward the west. Woolly wind clouds gathering at the southern hills sent cool breezes to their backs. Ahead, at the north edge of the field, the weathered old wall was a stack of flat river stones.

Knee-high and overgrown with grass from the other side, it was not so much a barrier as a line to mark the boundary of the baron's fallow fields. *We're almost done. We're almost there.*

Reeve strolled the top of the wall from right to left as squirrels scampered out of his way. He called to the workers' faces, "Don't slow down now! One more row . . . one more . . . ! Don't let me catch you slackin' off to cheat my master out of one more day's pay."

Scythe blades swung back and forth, back and forth. Wegdell and the elder man hunched over their sickles. The women bobbed down and up, down and up, gathering the cut sheaves in their wake. The wheelbarrow creaked forward. Shadows grew longer, and more of the wall's stones came into view.

"I'm done," said Cyan.

"Me too." Slate turned his scythe upright and held its shaft like a flagpole.

Down the row, each of the men came to a halt. Taupe plucked a kerchief from the waistband of his trousers and used it to wipe his forehead. Ruddy and Verdant clapped each other on the back. Indigo-in-Water turned his back to the wall and, with a weary smile, faced the rest of the group. The elder man settled into his crossed legs on the ground, and Olive brought him a ladle of water.

"Hey now, hey! I say when you're done!" Reeve cocked his head to be sure that every last sliver of wheat had been cut flat.

Condrie looked to Wegdell's bare back. His shoulders slumped with exhaustion. His head was downcast. *What is he thinking? Is he glad to be done? Is he worried about what to do next?*

Reeve blew into his horn—a long, loud blast that sang like a loon crooning over the dry fields. He broke out in a grin and hollered, "You're done!"

Yet the people did not share his grin. They did not whoop or holler or cry out cheers of glee. They simply stood in place. Slowly, slowly, following the lead of the storyteller woman, they turned to face west.

The blazing ball of sun sank into the blurry, dusty mist of the distant purple hills. The sky-blue hue deepened to a rich gold at the horizon. Every person's face, toasted brown in the weeks of laboring in the sun, took on a glaze of bronze-gold. Together they stood, not moving, not speaking, eyelids half closed to face the setting sun.

Condrie joined them in the unmoving silence, but she kept her eyes open. She watched the reeve for his reaction, ready to call out pleas of mercy if he should reach for his whip.

Reeve hooked a thumb in his leather belt. "By th' spirits, I guess you've earned it. Go ahead and stare at the sunset all you damned please. When you're ready to share in a keg o' cider, I'll be up at the mill yard."

Whistling a merry tune, the reeve strolled away. His hard-soled shoes crunched in the pebbly dirt, fading with his whistles farther and farther away. Condrie looked back over her shoulder to watch the pumpkin-colored tunic shrink smaller and smaller. By the time he reached the wagon road, Reeve was just a speck of color on the dividing line between the golden earth and the gray sky.

"All this for a handful of coins," Slate said softly.

Men propped the scythes' long handles against their shoulders. In pairs or threes, they walked over their own footprints in the dirt, back over the ground they had achingly covered slice by slice. *They don't sing,* Condrie noticed. *How can they not be singing to celebrate the reaping's end? Do these people not have any songs except the ballads they paint on their arms?*

Violet hoisted the wheelbarrow and pivoted in place. Women and girls assembled loosely into a group behind her. Olive, Amber, and Condrie straggled at the rear. The storyteller Silver leaned one hand on the wheelbarrow's frame for balance, grunting with every step and every creak of the axle. But for a few mumbles and murmurs, they were too weary to speak.

"Wait!" Taupe called out. He staggered in helping the old storyteller man to his feet.

"Let go of me. Let go, I say!" The elder man pushed Taupe's hands away. He wobbled and would have fallen backward to the ground if Wegdell did not swoop in to catch him.

"I can walk!" the old man insisted, even as he leaned into one leg and bent the other knee.

"Of course you can, Elder," said Taupe. "But I can carry you faster, if you let me. Just this once? Just this day?"

Wegdell flexed his brows encouragingly. Even from a distance, Condrie could see his jaw flex as he bit down against the vow of silence.

"Ugh," the old man grunted. "Very well. Just this once, just this day. I don't want to be the reason for keeping you from a keg of cider."

Taupe hunkered down, turning his back to the old man's chest. "Climb on." Wegdell helped to hoist him onto the younger man's frame and supported his weight until Taupe had his wrists locked behind himself, his forearms making a sling for the old man's hips.

Slate, Flint, and Tawny trotted away from their place at the front of the people. Broad hopping strides brought them to Wegdell's side.

Tawny suggested, "We can cross our scythes and make a sort of stretcher for him."

"I got him," Taupe said.

The four men resumed walking with the group's pace, and Wegdell lagged behind their heels.

"What if your arms give out?" Slate challenged.

"They won't. I'm fine."

Flint said, "You're exhausted. We all are."

"I'm fine." Taupe picked up his pace, pulling alongside the women, strolling more quickly as if he did not carry a burden, as if the old man's rag-wrapped arms were not around his neck, as if the old man's rag-wrapped legs did not dangle at his sides.

Tawny stayed with his brother, moving in an awkward sideways sort of stroll to keep up at his side. "What are you trying to show us, you fool? That you're better or stronger than any of the rest of us?"

"Ha!" Taupe grunted. "Is that what you think of me? That even doing a kindness is a show of vanity? By the light of all, Brother! Why don't you formally shun me and be done with it?"

"Shun you?"

"You've wanted to do it for years. Go ahead. Do it! Say the words. Pronounce me a blackness and a blight. Cast me out. I'll carry Willow Leaf as far as the mill yard, and then I'll be on my way."

Tawny slapped him across the head, dislodging a greasy black lock of Taupe's hair to lie as a limp spear across one eye. "You're my brother. Why would I cast you out?"

"For the mistakes I've made. For the crimes I've done."

Tawny lowered his head and walked at a halting rhythm. "Oh, Brother . . . brother of mine. If I had any intention to cast you out, don't you think I would have done so by now?"

Slate coughed a few chuckles. "You grate on our nerves, yeah, but that doesn't make you not one of us."

"This is a fine thing to tell me now!" Taupe hollered, turning his head left and right to shout at them all. "How long have I waited for the word . . . the sign . . . to know that I've atoned at last?"

"We thought you knew," his brother said.

Taupe laughed openmouthed as if to swallow the moon if it should drop from the sky. He quickened his pace, walking faster and faster as if the old man clinging to his back weighed no more than a sack of down feathers.

Condrie blinked at happy tears. *The best outcome to the best day. At harvest tide's end, all transgressions are forgiven.*

Then she looked up to Wegdell's height and saw his face as a mask of gloom in shadow. Eyes downcast, his lips were thin as he chomped into his own teeth.

"What's wrong?" she asked softly.

He shook his head, unable to answer. The two of them lingered farther and farther behind as the rest of the group moved on. Men's murmuring voices blended with the squeak of the wheelbarrow's axle, farther and farther, fainter and fainter up ahead.

Condrie forgot about her own feet in looking up at his face looming above her. Evening's pale glow shined through his irises. Those blue eyes of his were so intense, so clear, like expensive glass. Those eyes had pleaded with her the first night they met: *Help me.*

"What's got you so sad?" she asked.

"I miss it," Wegdell whispered.

"What—?"

"God, I wish I could flare! All these months of running away . . . I have been so long in human skin that it makes me itch. When I used to soar to the skies by day, I blazed more brilliantly than the sun. When I used to take to the night air, I was the brightest thing in the sky. The pale moon wept with envy. When I spread my fiery wings in all my glory, the rush of flame sounds like thunder."

Condrie let her mouth hang open. "That sounds wonderful. I wish I could see it."

The corner of Wegdell's mouth twitched. "Would you not be scared of me? Most people are . . . even the veteran knights who guarded me are afraid of me."

She shook her head. "I could never be scared of you."

Wegdell's mouth flattened into a flat line and threatened to dip into a frown. "Perhaps you should be, for all the terrible things I've done."

"You regret it now," she said. "I know you do."

"Spending time among the Athel, I've seen firsthand the damage that I've caused from high above." His voice cracked and became hoarse, either from emotion or because he wasn't used to talking after so much silence.

Condrie rested her palm against his upper arm. His flesh was warm, even as the evening's air turned cool. "I know you did not desire to do those horrible things of your own will. The king of the South holds you bound, so you had no choice but to follow his orders."

"Truth be told, I was not so brave or so self-righteous as my companions. I was content to be a songbird in a cage. The others objected and tried to oppose his authority—to no avail. "

"Others?" Condrie asked. "There were other firebirds in your king's court, like you?"

"Yes, there were five of us. We were a flock."

"They are the ones you're accused of murdering?" When he nodded briefly, she pressed on. "They say one of them was your brother. Is that true?"

"Yes," he whispered. "We hatched in the same clutch of eggs from the same pair of nestmates. We were fledglings together—that is, we shared a childhood. Together, we learned to soar higher than eagles. We were the same age, but I always felt that Yigs was older somehow."

The mill came into view, the hulk of dark wood like a box on the rise of the slope, with the dark glassy pond to one side and a majestic cluster of pine and chestnut trees to the other. Reeve was a speck no larger than a gnat waving his arms to welcome the hunched, weary, shuffling group of people.

"Yigs?" she repeated softly. "Was that your brother's name?"

"His name was Yigzemsei when he was in human form. You can't pronounce his real name—or mine—without snorting through a beak." Wegdell cleared his hoarse, dry throat. "He had such a pure sense of wrong and right, kindness and cruelty. Yigs was a better one than I am, in every way. He was the one who led the flock to resistance, saying that we should no longer be carrier pigeons in service to a ruthless king, that we should no longer use our powers to harm innocent people and destroy their homes. It was his idea to. . . ."

Wegdell dropped his head forward. Arms dangling at his side, shoulders drooped, it seemed that all the strength had drained out of him.

"His idea . . . to what?" she prompted.

He shifted his weight to keep his feet moving, but he did not answer.

"You never told me what really happened that night," she said. "How did they die? Why do they think you did it?"

Still he did not answer.

Condrie stopped in front of him. She planted her palms against his bare chest to force him to stop too. "Did your brother do some brave and compassionate act that got him in trouble with your king, something that got him killed?"

"Stop. Don't ask." His hushed voice was no louder than the crickets chirping in the dry grass.

"Did your king's knights slaughter him and your flock? Did they put the blame on you?"

He shook his head, but she could not hear if he said a word.

"Do you know who really did it?"

"No."

"Then why are you hiding and running for your life instead of seeking out the real killer?"

"Even if I discover the truth . . . how . . . why . . . who . . . it won't change what happened. My flock will still be dead. Yigs will still be gone." His voice broke; he choked on his own words. "God, I miss him."

"Of course you do." Condrie nodded in sympathy, even though his head was still bent forward and he could not see her.

Wegdell sniffed wet and loud. He wiped his cheeks with his hands. Then he stared into his own open palms with a gasp of amazement. "I'm weeping!"

Condrie folded in her arms to step closer to him. He backed away from her, shuffling up clouds of dust around his calves.

"I don't weep. I can't weep! I'm not a human."

"For now, you are," she said.

"No, no, no." He crossed his arms around himself. For such a tall man, he managed to make himself seem very small.

She said, "You've been on the run for months now. You haven't given yourself a time to grieve and mourn the loss of your brother. What sort of customs do you have among your kind? Would you like me to help you hold a funeral?"

"It is not our way to have funerals," he said in a smoky whisper. "We don't bury our dead in the ground. We are creatures of the air. They say that when firebirds die, we become stars in the night sky. I'd like to believe that my brother's spirit is . . . is. . . ."

"I'm sure he is." Tears filled her eyes, and she saw halos of rainbows around the rising moon.

In silence, they walked together up the wagon road to rejoin the group. Reeve had built a fire in a tin tub near where he uncorked a keg of cider. The faces of the Athel people—only their faces—shared in the rich golden glow. Embers floated on the smoke and swirled like a cluster of fiery gnats.

*

Condrie awoke to the sunshine on her eyelids. *Morning!* She lurched upright from her sleeping mat.

Everyone else was still facedown, asleep, breathing softly, dark hair blending into dark blankets in lumpy, rumpled piles. The tarp overhead, supported on poles, sheltered them from the chilling mists of the night and the cool dew of the morning and blocked her view of the autumn sky. Whether there were clouds or a clear sky, she did not know. Yet the sunrise penetrated from the open sides, shining a ruddy golden sheen across the rumpled, sleepy people.

The reaping is done, she reminded herself. *Reeve promised a day of rest from labors. He won't be blowing his horn or snapping his whip in the air.*

Eyes wide awake, Condrie no longer felt she could lie down and sleep a moment longer. Her heartbeat quickened at the prospect of an entire day with no obligations, no duties, no required labors in a field or in a kitchen. It was better than a holiday, for on seasonal occasions there would be even more work to do—special decorations, laundering the linens, and cooking extra food for guests. On this day, she was free to lie on the ground from morning until sunset and throughout the night until dawn came again.

She glanced aside to Wegdell's bedroll. It was empty.

Amber whispered out of her pillow, "He'll be back soon. He went to the water."

"So-...so-...sorry I woke you," Condrie whispered back.

Amber unfolded herself from the blanket, the thin single layer, and with a gesture of beckoning, she rose out of her bedroll, inviting Condrie to come with her. Condrie stood up carefully so as not to disturb Olive or Violet sleeping nearby. Her grimy single layer of skirt was stiffened with weeks of caked-in dirt. She kicked out the dusty creases and followed the girl garbed only in a wraparound drape.

Amber led her on a sideways course away from the campsite, away from the mill's yard and the mill pond. They made fresh footprints in the straggly weeds that clung to the dry, cold soil.

"Where...where are we g-g-g-going?" Condrie asked from behind.

"You'll see."

Stacked river stones formed a waist-high wall, higher than the stones that marked the edges of the baron's crop fields. Moss gave the blue and gray stones a dusting of vivid green; Condrie briefly wondered what meaning the people would see in that combination. She was about to ask, when Amber scampered over the wall and was lost to sight.

Condrie pressed her belly against the wall's cool stones. Her ankle-length skirt felt stiff and heavy on her legs. She was unsure of how to hoist herself over the barrier, so she stayed where she stood.

Beyond the wall, flowers bloomed in more varieties and more colors than she could name all at once. Geraniums in vivid scarlet, bluebells, coral bells, bright yellow honeysuckles and poppies, ruffled hedges of rosemary, and the low-lying, soft orange blossoms of calendula. Condrie inhaled deeply the sweet mix of perfumes on the cool morning air. She thought of Ma Kielsing who always kept a pouch full of potpourri in her garment drawers.

Three large crates were propped up on stilts, set up at the center within the field of flowers. *What are they? Too high off the ground for rabbit hutches. Too boarded-up for pigeon cages.* Condrie tilted her head curiously to observe Amber's cautious approach. In the silence, she became aware of a faint, steady humming sound.

Amber plucked a twig of rosemary. In one swift motion, a pinch of thumb and forefinger, she stripped away the herb's spindly leaves.

"What . . . what . . . ?" Condrie gritted her teeth around her tangled tongue. She had gotten used to Wegdell being nearby, and somehow the presence of the Sagewyn had greased the wheels of the words rolling out of her mouth.

"Hush." Amber approached the crates slowly, cautiously. In a stealthy, deliberate way, she poked the rosemary twig into a gap in the slats and very carefully extracted it. Once free, she scurried back to meet Condrie at the wall.

Honey glazed the tip of the rosemary twig. Condrie opened her smiling mouth to allow the twig to smear the sweet, sticky droplets onto her tongue.

"On my island, we don't keep them in cages like this," Amber said. "We go to the tree groves and seek out hollow logs where they have already built their hives."

"Thank you." Condrie wanted say so much more than a simple phrase. She yearned to invite the girl to describe her homeland, to paint in words the scenery of a verdant, lush island among many islands in the bountiful waters of the Great Northern Bay that lay halfway around the world from where they now stood. Words flooded her mind and jammed up at the back of her throat. Too many words. Too many thoughts, imagining how such a pleasant conversation of Amber's reminiscences would soon turn to darkness and grief. *Why did you leave your homeland? What happened to your community and your family of beekeepers?* Such questions would not be easy for the girl to answer. Even now, in licking the honey drops off the twig, Amber did not show any pleasure at the taste.

"Let's get back," Amber said. "Before the others wake up and wonder where we've gone."

*

Silver and Willow Leaf used the hours of the bright sunlit day to paint stories up and down their forearms. With Amber sitting nearby as a translator, Condrie learned about loyalty and friendship from "The Tale of the Fisherman and the Tortoise." She laughed along with the group at "The Otter Who Thought He Was a Seal," and she wept for the tragic ending of "The Moth Who Wished to Marry a Candle Flame."

By the time of the midday meal of bean paste, flatbread, and pickled spinach, Wegdell gestured to the old couple with a wave of his hand over the tray of colors that they should cease with the storytelling.

"With all respect," Willow Leaf replied, "please don't ask us to stop now. The stories need to be told so that the people will remember. Who knows where we will be tomorrow?"

Wegdell shook his head more insistently and pointed at the tray on the old woman's lap. Her wrinkled eyes were downcast, and she said nothing in reply.

Condrie asked, "Why do you want them to stop?"

The old woman said, "We are using up many of the colors. If we tell another long story like 'Why the Rabbit King of the Moon Learned to Make Cheese,' we will surely run out."

Indigo-in-Water stood up. "How did this happen? Why didn't you say something before?"

Wegdell raised his arms with palms open to the sky. He opened his mouth as if to speak, and by the flex of his jaw he almost broke his vow of silence. Condrie held her breath at the fierceness of his exasperated expression.

"You knew!" Slate got to his feet as well. "That's why you suggested telling brief parables on the lunch breaks. You were trying to conserve."

Violet used a calm tone to say, "We'll get more."

"From where?" Taupe grumbled. "Where? Sure, there's limestone nearby that'll do as well as the chalk cliffs at home, but where do we get the colors? We've walked halfway around the world searching for a place to settle, where we could have a home again and plant a garden of flowers and herbs and berries. Where is the seashore where we could get buckets full of squid to give us black ink? Where are the lapis lazuli mines that give us vivid blue? Where are the copper mines that give us green? This land is infested with crickets and slugs. Where are we to find the scarlet beetles?"

Condrie said, "Can't you make colors out of other things that you find here?"

Taupe shook his head. The others soon joined him in grumbling, a murmuring drone of chanting, *no, no, no.* "If you understood our feelings, you would not ask such a thing."

"Oh." She crossed her arms and was once again self-conscious that she wore a pleated skirt with a drawstring waistband—not a draped wrap. She wore a linen blouse with sleeves and kept her old kitchen apron among her meager belongings. Although she had labored side by side with them for weeks upon weeks, Taupe had just reminded her that she would always be an outsider.

Wegdell jabbed two fingers into the paint tray. He smeared lines of yellow and white across his palm and held it forth to Taupe.

Taupe looked up at him wide-eyed, and only Condrie understood why. *He can't see colors. I've been faithful in keeping his secret. He can't reply without knowing the question, and I can't help him without revealing it in front of everybody.*

Indigo-in-Water rested his hands on his hips. "Compromise, you say? Woad is as blue as indigo, and calendula or turmeric can be as yellow as saffron, I'll grant you that. The problem is, Friend Priest, that if we sing our stories with the colors made of things from this land, we are no longer singing with the things grown in the soil of our homeland. Don't you see how much we have already changed by speaking to each other in words not our own? How much longer before we start telling their stories and forgetting our own?"

Wegdell rolled his fingers into a closed fist.

She looked up at him standing in front of all of them, the fugitive in disguise playing the part of a priest giving wise counsel. She expected him to go on preaching the pragmatism that he himself had used to survive this far while being hunted by the knights of the king in the South. Change was the way of things. Trees changed colors in the autumn and spring, and they were still the same tree underneath. Yes, it would be a compromise to use geraniums instead of scarlet beetles, but would it be so terrible compared to losing the stories altogether?

Wegdell reached into the kerchief pouch tied to his waistband. He brought out a single pewter coin and held it up for the group to behold.

"What are you suggesting?" Taupe asked.

Condrie burst out with a smile. "Purchase the colors, I think he's saying. Surely the artisans and peddlers in the town will know where to find . . ."

". . . to find in bottles what they've taken from our homeland?" Violet finished. "Do you think we haven't thought of that too? The king who claimed our islands as his own domain has picked our flowers and crushed our gemstones and boiled our beetles for himself. Of course we know that they sell our colors to the dyers of cloth and the painters of walls."

Slate and a few of the other men likewise gripped their coin pouches in their fists. "Even if we pool all of our wages, is it enough to satisfy the greedy people of this land? Can all of us afford to buy even one bottle of purple?"

Condrie said, "I can go into town and ask about at the shops. I can make a list of the supplies and tally a sum of the price for each—"

"Or . . ." Taupe interrupted, and in the pause, all eyes turned to him, ". . . we could earn a large pile of coins by another means."

"How?" Slate asked.

"If we track down the fugitive that they're after."

Wegdell sniffed loudly. He clapped a hand over his own mouth.

Taupe, from where he sat on the ground, looked up at the tall man looming over him. "Yes, I know it's a challenge. He's a Sagewyn of some kind—a magical creature with powers beyond those of mortal men—but if he were so fearsome, the king would not send mere knights on horseback to hunt him. If they stand a chance of bagging the monster, why don't we?"

His brother Tawny picked up the thought, nodding along, and said, "The bounty poster says they're hunting a man, which says to me that the monster is stuck in human skin for some reason."

"Like a seal-*skie* walking on land and someone stole its pelt?" asked Olive with a nod to the storyteller couple.

"Exactly!" said Magenta, clapping her hands.

Taupe continued, "He's probably not used to being in human skin and walking about the land like an ordinary man. He's lost. He's confused. He's panicked, but he's gotten lucky so far that the knights haven't found him. Now the warm days are coming to an end. There's a frost in the air, and it'll be first snowfall before too long. He'll be looking for a place to hide that's warm and safe where he can huddle down and wait for the knights to give up and go home."

Condrie looked up to Wegdell, who still kept a hand clamped over his mouth. She said, "But what if he's innocent?"

"It doesn't matter what he's done or what he hasn't done," said Slate. "He's not one of us."

Violet used her deep, motherly tone to say, "If the knights of King Davarche are hunting him across the countryside, then he may as well be one of us."

Silver said, "There must be other ways to earn coins."

Willow Leaf added, "If new colors were purchased with the blood of another living thing, no matter if it's a Sagewyn or a man, I would not be able to sing with them."

Taupe folded his arms. "I admire your virtue, Elder, but I must remind you that it was a Sagewyn that got us burned out of our homes. Will you stand on principle, if the cost of preserving what little we have left of ourselves can be paid by putting a monster of destruction back into its cage?"

Slate turned to look at Wegdell. "What do you say, Priest?"

All eyes turned to him. Wegdell looked aside, meeting Condrie's steady gaze. A pause hung over the group, and for that moment, all of the world held its breath.

Wegdell made a gesture of inviting guests to exit from a door.

Taupe burst to his feet, grinning, and clapped him on the bare shoulder. "Will you come with us?"

Wegdell shook his head, frowning a refusal.

"As you say." Taupe rotated on his heels. "Slate! Tawny! Ruddy! Are you with me?"

"Yes, yes!" the men called out.

Olive popped to her feet. "Don't forget to bring me, too. How will you find your way in the woodlands without me?"

Condrie kept staring at Wegdell, ignoring the gleeful, busy activity of the others gathering their things into bundles and strapping sandals to their feet.

How can you let them do this foolish thing with no hope of success? she wanted to scream at him.

Wegdell turned his back on her. In the brief moment before he broke the connection, his cold blue eyes were fierce in a way she had never seen before.

*

Crisp air chilled her cheeks as Condrie awoke to a dim gray morning.

She looked first to the vacant gaps on the ground where the other bedrolls had been the day before and for so many days before. She thought of Taupe, Slate, Olive, Tawny, and Ruddy scouring the hills for someone they would never find. *They have no food, no weapons, no tracking skills, and nothing but sandals and cloaks and rags to wrap their hands. He encouraged them to trek off into the wilds knowing the first snowfall is only a few weeks away. Is he selfish? Is he desperate? Or does he trust they'll come to their senses at the first frost and come back to us?*

Morning dew glistened as icy crystals on her flannel blanket, yet the rest of her body felt warm. Condrie stretched out her legs and nudged into his. Overnight, in her sleep, she had cuddled up closer to the firebird in human form.

Wegdell slept on his belly with his face tucked into his arms. His body radiated the warmth of fireplace bricks. Others had also snuggled up against him overnight. Amber was squeezed between Magenta and Violet; the storyteller couple, Indigo-in-Water, and a quiet man named Saffron curled around them like puppies in a basket.

"The winters in this land are brutal." The reeve's voice nearby carried on the cool air. "When I was a boy, my father used to say that the god of frost waged a battle in the heavens with the god of the sun. Every year, the frost god always won, and people were the spoils of war—at his mercy for the whole winter—until the sun god rallied his troops and came back to conquer in the springtime. It's a nice story to justify the savagery of this mindless, heartless cold, isn't it?"

"Maybe it's not just a story." The second man spoke with a low, husky voice. His accent had the twang of the southern kingdom.

A knight of Xol! Won't they ever give up the chase and go back where they came from? Condrie tensed within the flimsy blanket. She gritted her teeth and hoped that Reeve and the knight would keep on walking.

"We mortal men, bound to the earth, how do we know what happens in the heavens above us? Who are we to say if there's not a god of frost stomping around your clouds? Though I must say, I'm glad he's up in these skies and not so much over the skies of my homeland."

"What is the winter like in the land of Xol?"

"Mild," the knight said. "The only feature of my king's domain that you'd call mild is the weather. Sure, it's cloudy and gloomy in the winter. It's chilly, but not deathly cold. It mostly rains. From time to time, in the deep of the winter holidays, a few snowflakes sprinkle into the treetops."

The scent of burnt floral herbs carried on the chilly air. The two men, puffing on their pipes, ambled at a leisurely pace.

Reeve said, "Your armor plates must feel damned cold this morning. I pity you, sir."

"A wool jerkin and two layers of undershirts," grunted the knight. "I'm fine."

"Will your lord be staying as our guest for much longer?"

"Not for me to know," said the knight. "Not for me to say."

Condrie shivered in her blanket—not from the cold; just to think of the Sagewyn lord and his piercing stare.

"I'm just a lieutenant. I follow the orders of my captain and my lord. I go where they tell me, and I do my duty. So if they tell me to tromp about in the snow looking for melted footprints, that's what I do."

"Melted footprints?" the reeve repeated. "What do you mean by that, sir?"

Condrie snuggled her legs against Wegdell's warm bare feet.

The voices became fainter, moving away more quickly. Yet the knight's gruff voice came through clearly in the stillness. "The fugitive has led a pampered, sheltered life. He's never been alone. He's never had to survive by his own wits. I'm fucked if I know how he's eluded us this long. His Majesty is not happy that we don't have the pigeon back in his cage. I don't envy my captain making her weekly lack-of-progress reports. I dread to imagine how the missives are being received back at court. Let's just say, my king is not a patient man."

"You'll catch him soon, sir. Murderers always trip themselves up."

He's not a murderer! He's innocent! Condrie gritted her teeth as she clutched the blanket. The men's voices faded into the distance. She held onto the hope that if Wegdell could manage to conceal himself until springtime, surely the knights would give up and go away for good. The knight's deep voice kept echoing in her mind: the King of Xol was not a patient man.

*

The chow wagon did not appear at breakfast time. The reeve did not blow his horn. "Surely they didn't forget about us," Violet said.

Condrie and a few others strolled up the footpath toward the mill yard.

A dozen swarthy men stood around a stack of cut wheat. They wielded flails—a pair of wooden rods connected by a short rope. Six by six, left and right, they took turns swooping their flails into the center of the circle. Flails beat the wheat kernels, nugget by nugget, off the stalks of dry hay. The men's breaths grunted a steady rhythm, "Ha . . . ho . . . ha . . . ho . . ." as flails thumped against the hard, cold ground.

"Who are they?" Magenta wondered aloud.

Condrie surveyed their rustic clothing, the twine that stitched the seams of their jerkins and trousers, the high cuffs of their oiled burlap boots. *River People.* These were the people who loitered by the shores of the flowing waters offering themselves for day labor. If boatmen needed cargo loaded or unloaded, these were the hands to do the job.

"They . . . th-th-they, uh. . . ." She swallowed back her tangled tongue before the others might think it odd. She had almost forgotten how difficult it was to get the words from her brain to her mouth if he was not around her. Wegdell had stayed behind at the campfire with the other men.

Nearby were a few of the River People's women in their tight-laced bodices and tucked-up skirts. They held winnowing baskets as broad as a holiday serving platters. The women shimmied their basket platters back and forth, back and forth. Bits of chaff and hay and beige dust scattered on the cool autumn breezes. Only the precious kernels of wheat were left captured.

Violet went ahead to the reeve. He stood leaning on a rain barrel and held a clipboard in his arm.

"Say there, Mister Reeve, who are these folks?"

"Threshers." He did not look up at her, wholly concentrated in marking the papers on his clipboard.

"I can see that," Violet said, hands on her hips. "I'm asking why you didn't blow your horn to call us for today's work."

"Half your men set off to the open road. I reckoned you was all packing it along."

Violet began to visibly shiver, though Condrie could not be sure if it was rage or the fact that she was barefoot and garbed only in lengths of linen wrapped artfully around her torso.

"You were mistaken," she said. "Only a few of us left. The rest of us. . . ."

Reeve shrugged. "Should've told me. It's not my job to go beg you stray dogs to come work for me. It's my job to get all this grain into the silos before the first snowfall. What complaints you got is no worry of mine. You've all got your pay for the week, plus a harvest bonus. What else do you want?"

Violet took a step back. Her breath's vapor was like smoke from her open mouth. Condrie and the other women gathered around her.

Threshers did not miss a beat in their rhythm, "Ha . . . ho . . . ha . . . ho . . ." smacking their flails into the wheat stalks on the ground.

"Let's go back and tell the others," said Amber.

Violet led the way back downhill in halting, painful steps, her arms hanging at her sides. "What'll we do? What'll we do? If not for the work, they don't need us anymore. Will the baron even let us stay on the land? Are we to continue sleeping in the open air under a feeble tarp as the snows begin to fall?"

"It . . . it . . . it. . . ." Condrie hugged herself.

The reeve called out to their backs, "Oh, and I expect you to return that tarp you're all sleeping under. It needs to cover the leaky shingles on the carriage shack where the work crews will be bedding down for the winter."

Condrie looked back to him, and for the first time in a long time she envied someone for gloves, a wool scarf, and a hooded cloak.

Ruddy's wife, Auburn, whose belly was starting to show the child she carried, raised her fists to punch at the air. "We've been eating dirt and beans and last year's pickles for weeks. If we don't work to earn food, will they not feed us at all? Will they stand by and let us starve?"

"Where else can we go?" Amber said, "If those folks are willing to take our jobs, then what jobs are left for us in this land?"

Condrie skipped ahead of the group. *I know a place where we can all go*, she wanted to say, but the words would not come. She hopped over the ruts and gouges in the footpath. She hurried to reach the clearing where the remaining dozen women and the few men had built a jolly fire in the pit of stones. The old storyteller couple sat nearest to the shimmying cones of flame.

Wegdell saw her first. His welcoming smile quickly dropped into a concerned frown. "Ah . . ." he started to say before he caught himself.

Indigo-in-Water stood up from the fireside. The pleated tail of his wraparound garment draped off his left hip. "What's wrong?"

"They hired a crew of River People to thresh and winnow the wheat," Condrie blurted. "When he saw the others leaving, the reeve assumed that we were all leaving. He gave our jobs to them. That's why the chow wagon didn't bring breakfast. "We're not going to be swapping our scythes for flails after all."

Violet came up behind her. "Why didn't the moldy-green ask us? We could've explained that a few of us went off on a quest but the rest of us are still here."

"Isn't it obvious?" Auburn stroked her pregnant belly. "My husband will come back to his family whether he finds that fugitive Sagewyn or not."

Amber went to kneel by the storyteller's tray of walnut shells. Hunched over her knees, she raised her face to look imploringly up at Wegdell. "Priest, what should we do?"

Faces all turned to look at him. Gaunt cheeks were weathered and tanned to dark brown from weeks of laboring in the open sun. Firelight shined pale in the gray open air.

Wegdell furrowed his brow, and Condrie recalled the knight's conversation that she had overheard. *The fugitive has led a pampered, sheltered life. He's never been alone. He's never had to survive by his own wits.* She saw him flex his shoulders and wondered at his frustrated urge to sprout fiery wings and soar away to the skies. For as long as the King of Xol kept Wegdell's tail feather in a box, he could not transform into a firebird.

"We could go to town," Condrie said.

Indigo-in-Water shared a knowing glance with his sister Violet. "No, we talked about that before. What skills we do have, in furniture making and fabric dyeing, are already taken by the artisan guilds. Don't you think we'd rather be doing what we know to do? Did we choose to be cutting wheat first? No, no, there's nothing in town for us."

Condrie said, "I could ask Ma Kielsing for a favor. She's been like a mother to me."

Wegdell lowered his face into his hands.

"It's our only choice," she added. "When people have nothing, no one, and nowhere else in all the world, Ma Kielsing's tavern is the place they go."

*

Tools tapped and clattered along cramped, narrow streets. Condrie led the group past the wagoner's and blacksmith's workshops. They passed the basket weavers, the cobblers, the tinkers, and the tailors. The candlemaker had a line of customers extending out the front door. Everyone had shawls and capes, scarves and gloves, for the air was cool even in the afternoon. The sky was slate gray and threatened to rain. This was the time for stocking up firewood and shaking the moths out of blankets. Soon would come the time of always being indoors.

Condrie led the group to the rear of the tavern, to the kitchen door, for only customers entered at the front. The door was partly open. A golden glow of firelight beckoned from within. The scent of yeast bread and buttery onion soup carried on the air.

"Hello?" Condrie stepped into the threshold.

Ma Kielsing herself stood at the hearth bricks. She bent toward the fire to stir the cauldron with a long-handled spoon. Condrie recognized the small, stout woman's body from behind, but she had rarely seen her dressed like a kitchen maid. A dark linen skirt was dusty at the hem from brushing a floor that no one had swept. A crinkled blouse had gauzy sleeves rolled up to the elbows. A canvas bodice had crisscrossing lacings up the front and sides that strained to support her buxom breasts. Her curly hair was bundled into a cap.

"Condy, my sweet girl!" Ma Kielsing dropped the spoon into the cauldron. She opened wide her inviting arms.

She ran into an embrace so tight that she could barely breathe. She sniveled into Ma Kielsing's curls and the ruffles of her cap. "I missed you so much."

"There there, be a brave girl. No tears." Ma Kielsing raised her apron's hem to wipe Condrie's face. "Tell me, who are all these people you've brought? Not . . . customers?"

Violet drew herself up tall, straightening her spine, and with a subtle tug she adjusted the wrap of the linen veils that swathed her body. "We are what few remain of the free people of the Northern Bay Islands. These are our elders, Willow Leaf and Silver. You may call me Violet. This is my brother Indigo-in-Water and my cousin Teal. This is Amber, Magenta, Auburn. . . ."

"Excuse me." Ma Kielsing held forth her palm. "How many of you are here?"

"Seventeen," said Violet.

Condrie, still embraced under the motherly arm, gazed around at the haggard group. They stood packed into the kitchen, shoulder to shoulder, filling all of the space from the pantry shelves to the window. The only gap was around the butcher-block table at the center of the room. Both elders sat down at the hearth stones with the orange-twinkling black logs to warm their backs. Wegdell kept himself at the rear of the group, his head bowed as if in humility so that Ma Kielsing would not see his face—only the black stubble of his closely cropped hair.

"Seventeen," Ma Kielsing repeated. "Seventeen of you come pouring into my kitchen expecting . . . what? I don't have enough bread for you all. By the looks of you, I doubt you've got enough money to pay for my soup."

Violet tugged out a small coin bag from the veils tightly wrapped around her belly. "I can pay for supper."

Condrie added, "We're looking for jobs, Ma, not charity. We'll do anything that needs doing, like chopping firewood or carrying packages or shoveling the snow away from the front door. Please, Ma, we've been working the wheat harvest, and now the baron's reeve hired a different crew of River People to do the threshing, so we've got nowhere else to go."

Ma Kielsing crinkled her brow. "You're not stuttering."

"Oh." Condrie glanced to Wegdell at the rear of the group.

Her warm, motherly hand rested on Condrie's cheek. "These people have been good for you?"

Condrie blinked at tears. "Yes."

"Well, truth be told, I could use some hands. Most of my girls ran off after those knights came stomping around. Niarr and Remmie are the only ones who stayed with me. The gin still's destroyed, and I don't have the funds to fix it. We've been serving what few bottles we had in the cellar, but they've almost run out. I've been fermenting some mead, but it's not ready to drink yet."

"Oh, Mama," Condrie said. "How did it get so bad?"

Ma Kielsing put a hand on her hip. "Can these strapping men climb up top and fix my burned roof?"

"Yes," said Teal and Cyan in unison.

"Didn't the townsfolk help?" Condrie asked. "That's what I heard."

"They did for a while, but then they got busy with getting their own homes ready for winter. They've got their own leaky shingles to patch. I've heard nothing but apologies as my upstairs rooms still reek of charcoal."

Magenta said, "We can scrub and clean the rooms. We know very well what a mess that king's knights leave behind."

Amber and several others lowered their heads, saying nothing.

"Well, there we have something in common," Ma Kielsing said. "I've not suffered as much as you lot, but I share your frustrated outrage for that tyrant in the South. We aren't even his subjects. This isn't his domain, and yet King Davarche can send his armored thugs into free territory and brutalize us while no one says a thing in protest about it. I didn't harbor that fugitive! I would've handed him over so fast his eyes would spin, but even so, I got my roof burned off! You wonder why our Lord High Sheriff cooperated with them instead of doing something brave about the injustice of it all."

"Careful what you say," said Silver. "They'll come back. They always come back."

"Yeah, yeah, I'm not scared. That fugitive is long and faraway gone by now, and good riddance to him." Ma Kielsing brushed her hand across the air. "Condy, on that first night when he dropped in to hide from those knights, where did you stash him? In the root cellar? I thought as much. He should have left immediately, but he stayed. He imposed on you for a change of clothes, a cup of tea, and preyed upon your sympathy. Surely you understand that desperate people will always need more than you can give."

"I believe he's innocent, Ma. He didn't murder those people."

"He took your assistance and pressed upon your kindness and then abandoned you. He put your life at risk and gave you nothing in return. For that, I will never forgive him. He had best hope his king's knights find him first, for I would not be lenient on an unholy creature who has abused one of my girls."

"But Mama—"

"If he were not so handsome or so charming, would you have helped him? Would you? If he were a portly, freckled, gray-whiskered man like your late husband was?"

Condrie's throat tightened against the words she yearned to blurt out. *He is right here, Ma. He's been with me all the time. The Sagewyn fugitive is disguised as a pilgrim priest, and I'm been helping to conceal him.*

Violet said softly, "What she's done is done. As you say, he's long gone by now.

Ma Kielsing drew her into another soft embrace. "Let's hope you've learned your lesson, Condy."

Condrie rested against the woman's broad bosom, hearing a mother's heart beating as deep and regular as the rhythm of the world beneath her feet.

"Say, uh, I'm a coppersmith," said Verdant, a lean fellow with a surprisingly low voice. "If you have tools, I can do my best to get your distiller pipes functioning. By the way, what is gin?"

Ma Kielsing's cheeks spread in a more welcoming smile. "Soup's on me tonight."

*

After a supper of hot soup and bread, Condrie ascended the narrow stairwell. The blackened paneling stank of charred wood and ashes. *Even after all these weeks, the house is not healed from its wounds,* she thought. Boards creaked beneath her feet. The stairs groaned more loudly below and beneath her at the Athel people coming up behind.

Part of the upstairs wall had been gutted down to the beams. Burlap tarps, like crude curtains, kept out most of the cold night air. Where there had once been glass windows, now there were only boarded-up frames. Condrie rolled her eyes from the ground level up to the roof, studying the column of chimney stones. When the still had been destroyed, it sent fire upward to the roof. The attic's floor was eaten away; the trusses and support beams were angular stumps; the shingles were gone. Looking up, Condrie could see through the black framework to the even blacker sky beyond.

"Is the floor safe?" asked Sienna, springing up and down on her heels to test the squeaky floorboards.

A hallway extended to the left. From behind one of the closed doors, a woman's voice hollered, "What's that noise? By the Ancients, can't a gal sleep around here?"

The door opened inward on wooden peg hinges. Remmie, one of the tavern's longest-serving barmaids, had curly hair as frothy as black meringue. She wore a gauzy linen shift with a broad neckline that threatened to slip off her shoulders any moment.

"Who are you?" Remmie asked. "Trespassers? Beggars?"

Inside the room, a second woman groaned facedown in a pillow. All that Condrie could see of Niarr, the other barmaid, were disheveled raven locks.

"Don't you know me?" Condrie said. "Sure, I've tanned in the sun, but. . . ."

Remmie rubbed her sleepy eyes with one hand. "Condy? Is that you?"

"It's good to see you again, Remmie. You too, Niarr."

Laughing, Remmie pulled her into a soft embrace. "By the Ancients, I didn't know you for not stammering!" She pushed Condrie off for another, longer look. "You're so damned thin."

"I've been working the harvest up at the baron's wheat fields, but he hired a crew of River People to do the threshing. My friends and I needed a place to go. I brought them here. They're going to help rebuild."

Remmie's large eyes scanned past Condrie's shoulder. "You're the Athel folk, ain't you?"

"Yes," said Violet with her chin tilted up.

"If that's pride in your tone, you'd best leave it outside." Remmie slouched against the door frame and thrust one hip forward.

"Believe me, I have," Violet said.

"Oh, you disapprove of me? Of us?" Remmie asked. "Of us serving gin and whiskey to men who are looking for a bit of happiness?"

"Excuse me," Violet said, "but I do not understand how you choose to profane yourself by making a sacred gift of life and joy into a business transaction."

Condrie, with her heart galloping, stepped in between them. "Please don't argue."

"I'm not arguing." Remmie withdrew from the door frame. "What's to argue? Crops fail from drought and blight. Riverboats sink and lose their cargo. Even land barons sometimes lose their fortunes. But men will always want a drink and a smile. I am providing what will never be out of supply or demand. They can burn the roof off my house, and I still have a job."

"Indeed you do." Violet looked down at the floorboards.

Remmie closed the door.

The group began to grumble and murmur among themselves. Condrie caught bits and pieces of words that bubbled up to the surface. "Mistake to come here. . . ." "Rather starve. . . ." "Rather freeze. . . ." "Last of our dignity. . . ."

"Please, please!" Condrie waved her hands overhead.

Amber, at Wegdell's shoulder, looked up to his height. "Priest, what do you say we should do? Shall we stay?"

Through the myriad of faces, he focused on Condrie's direct stare. Wegdell nodded. All the grumblings fell silent.

Condrie sighed a relieved smile. "Thank you."

She led the way along the shadowy hallway. One by one, she opened the next four doors in a row. "Before this was a tavern, it was a traveler's inn. Each room has two beds, but I suppose if we don't mind doubling up, we can put four or five of us to each."

Magenta leaned into one room. She jumped back, putting a hand over her mouth. "It smells awful."

Condrie inhaled old smoke, ashes, and the musty stench of a coat closet sealed for the winter. "Perhaps if we open a window and sweep. . . ."

"It's fire damage." Indigo-in-Water lowered his voice to a hushed, reverent tone. "That stink will never be clean."

"Those mattresses have got to be thrown out," Violet agreed.

Sienna added, "Along with the drapes and the rugs. It's all ruined by smoke. It's all got to go."

Condrie looked aside to the dark stairwell. "I'll need to ask Ma first, as a courtesy, but I'm sure she'll agree . . ."

"You can't ask a dog to sleep in this ash pit," Violet said.

". . . and then I'll go down the street and knock on the rugmaker's door. He's probably closed up shop for the night by now, but he's a regular patron. I'm sure he'll give me a good price on a bulk order of rugs and drapes and blankets."

One by one, the people tugged out bundled kerchiefs from the linens wrapped around their abdomens. They untied the knots and exposed handfuls of dull and tarnished coins. Condrie walked through their midst. She pinched a few coins out of each open palm, collecting the bits of metal into the pocket of her apron.

At the edge of the top step, she looked back over her shoulder to Wegdell. "Mister Priest, would you come with me? I'll need help carrying things."

Wegdell nodded his agreement.

"I'll come too," said Cyan.

"And I," said Sienna and Amber in unison.

Wegdell shook his head. He pointed back and forth to the several open doors.

Paper-White said wearily, "He's right. There's more work for us here, dragging out the mattresses and draperies and rugs. More hands make quick work."

Condrie slipped her slender hand into his broad palm. The hands of the firebird were always so warm.

*

"Brilliant," said Wegdell hoarsely as they left the tavern behind.

Only the glass box lantern in Condrie's hand lit the way. Shops were closed. Awnings were down. Windows were dark. The hard-packed dirt streets were vacant of all foot traffic. Even the rats and stray dogs had tucked themselves away in the shadows for the night. Together, they turned the corner of the cross street.

"I'm not so sure," Condrie said. "I got so nervous at Remmie and Violet arguing."

How much had changed in the short time she had been away. The barmaids had always been laughing with cheer and loudly joining the crowds of men in song. *Pour me one more, pour me one more, pour one more an' I'll be on the floor.* . . . Niarr and Remmie had always been so jolly despite the hardships of their prior lives; they had always been so happy to pour drinks in Ma Kielsing's place instead of starving alone in the dark streets. Condrie had never even seen them frown before this night.

"And," she continued, "Ma wasn't too happy about throwing out the mattresses, either."

When Condrie had asked permission to throw out the mattresses and drapes that were damaged by smoke, Ma Kielsing had snorted a grunting assent. A silent flip of her hand meant, *Do what you like.* Before this night, Ma had never been one to refrain from a lengthy scolding or giving out a hearty earful of common sense. Her tirades were legendary, as was her blasting voice that could be heard over the cacophony of clinking glasses and drunken men. Condrie had never even seen her in a quiet mood.

Shivers racked her bones underneath her borrowed cloak. The night's chill crept upward from her thin socks and flat shoes.

"You're cold." Wegdell put his arm around her. Though he only wore the wraparound linens that left his legs and shoulders bare, his skin was as warm as a mug full of tea. "So, what's the plan?"

"I've never haggled before. I'm hoping the rugmaker will give me a good price."

"No, no." He chuckled and his breath billowed as a cloud of vapor. "Where are we really going?"

"To the rugmaker's shop," she said. "I need you with me so I won't stammer."

He plugged to a halt. "Do you mean to tell me that this is not a ruse? We're not making a run for it? Not going to hop aboard a river raft paddling north?"

"No." She pried herself out of his warm embrace so she could look up at his quizzical expression. "Why did you think we'd be running away?"

"Surely I can't stay at the tavern."

"Why?"

"They know this face! One good look in my eye and your Ma will point me out to collect the bounty. Surely you're not naïve enough to imagine she would humor you and continue to hide me."

"Don't be worried about it." Condrie quickened her pace. "You cut all your hair. You're sprouting whiskers. They won't recognize you."

"They might."

"They won't! Trust me, Remmie and Niarr won't look twice at you if you're not a paying customer. Ma will be too busy overseeing the roof work to give much notice to you. Avoid them. Keep your head down."

"For how long?" he asked. "I don't know how much longer I can endure this so-called 'vow of silence.' Every day, it gets harder and harder to keep up this pretense."

"You're doing fine."

"It was only supposed to be a short time that I would hide among them. I never planned to settle in and live with these people. The longer I stay, the greater the risk of them exposing me as a fraud. If they find out who I really am, and what I've done. . . ." His voice trailed away unfinished.

Condrie reached the turned-down awning of the rugmaker's shop. The placard over the door had an illustration of a hoop filled with stitches.

"I'm tired and cold," she said. "Let's just get blankets and rugs for now and get a good night's sleep. We'll talk tomorrow about the future."

She knocked on the door.

Rob Cordwinder, a bearded, white-haired man, leaned out the upstairs window. "My shop's closed! Who is it?"

"I'm so sorry to disturb you at this hour, Mister Cordwinder, but I come from Ma Kielsing's house."

"Who are you? I don't know you."

"My name is Condrie, sir, and I work in the kitchen. Ma's hired on a crew of workers to fix the roof and walls. We've had to throw out the mattresses that were full of stale smoke. We've come to purchase floor rugs and blankets enough for seventeen people."

"Tonight?"

"Yes, sir," she said, craning her neck upward. "Tonight."

He withdrew from the window. "I'll be right down!"

Wegdell continued gazing upward beyond the roof of the rugmaker's shop. "I can't see the stars."

Dim, wispy clouds drifted on the chilly breeze. Smoke rose out of chimneys and infused the night's air with the scent of pinewood, oak, cedar, and cinnamon.

"There's a frost in the air," she said. "Not long until the first snowfall."

She recalled the townsfolk celebrating the autumn holidays of years before—the music drumming in the streets, the wheat ale and peach cider carried in large mugs by happy hands. These were supposed to be the busiest working days at Ma Kielsing's place. *It's not right that it's all so quiet.*

Rob Cordwinder slid aside the panel door. "Come in—hurry, hurry!"

Condrie followed the brush of the man's hands. She entered a musty, cramped room that smelled of wool and cedar. Skeins of twisted wool hung like sausages from the rafters. Rolls of rugs were stacked shoulder-high on all sides, leaving only a narrow space to walk.

The rugmaker peered outside to the streets, left and right, before he slid the panel door tightly shut. He clamped down the bolt. "Pesky little gutter rats always trying to sneak in and steal my blankets."

It's cold, she wanted to say on behalf of those forlorn children drifting from gutter to gutter like her orphaned friend Kin, but she held her tongue.

She said, "The floor rugs are for the four upstairs rooms. We'd appreciate your softest weave."

"If you've thrown out your mattresses, it sounds to me that you're wanting bed rolls on top of plush rugs," he said. "And thirty or forty blankets?"

"Oh no, sir, there's only seventeen people."

He squeezed past her in the narrow walkway between two stacks of rug rolls. Going to a glass lamp ensconced on the wall, he turned up the wick and heightened the golden flame. The lumpy shapes turned from gray to amber.

"You'll want more than one blanket per person, won't ya? There's a chill in the air. I'm sure you feel it."

"Yes, it is getting colder every day," she admitted.

The rugmaker squinted his bushy eyebrows in looking at the man. Wegdell turned his face aside and made pretense of studying the geometric designs woven into a rug. "Who is he?"

"He's, uh . . . he's one of the. . . ."

"Athel," said the rugmaker bluntly. "I see the way he's wrapped that gauze around his arms. I know their kind. They harass my dyers. They throw rocks at my caravans. Don't they understand that I'm surviving here too? It used to cost me a month's profit to get my fine quality blacks and purples and reds. Sure, I can stock my brown and blue rugs up to the roof, but it's the elegant colors that are in demand. Every master and landlord in the town comes to *me* to carpet their homes, and if I can't supply what they ask, they'll go elsewhere. Since the king of the South opened up the trade routes, I can afford to charge my customers more reasonable prices and still make a profit. This is the first year in my life that I'll be serving a whole roasted pig at my holiday supper! It's folks like *him* who don't want me to have meat on my table."

When he paused for a breath at last, Condrie seized her chance to jump in. "I'm ready to pay a fair price for your rugs and blankets, sir. We don't need your fancy wares. The browns and blues will do just fine. How much do you ask?"

"How much do you got?"

She covered her apron's bulging pocket with her hand. Her mind was spinning with numbers recalled from Ma Kielsing haggling with vendors at the kitchen's back door. "I'll offer you the measure of twenty-two *tolls* for the entire lot, that is, four brown rugs and seventeen wool blankets."

He coughed into his fist. "Go home to your mother, girl. You insult me."

"I don't mean to, sir."

"One hearth rug alone is worth twenty-five *tolls*, and you wish to carpet the floor of a room? Four rooms?"

As he turned away and headed for the stairwell, Condrie's jaw shivered and caused her to stammer. "I . . . I can't pay you that much. Is there any other way that we can come to an agreement? Could I have the rugs and blankets tonight, and pay you more coins later?"

"If it were just for Ma Kielsing and her girls, I would." The rugmaker lingered at the base of the stairwell. The glass lantern on the wall gloried a sickly yellow halo in his curly white hair.

She glanced aside to Wegdell garbed in the wraparound veil garments of a foreign people. "Are you aware, sir, of what the king of the South did to open the trade routes? He burned them out of their homes. They aren't wandering all the way over here by choice."

"It was none of my doing," said the rugmaker gruffly.

"Very true," she said. "And yet you make a profit from their misfortune. Please, sir, they aren't asking for pity. I'm asking on their behalf. I'll give you all the coins I have in my pocket, with the promise of more, if you'll let me have what I need tonight."

The rugmaker thoughtfully scratched his whiskers. "This fellow looks to have a strong back and good arms. My apprentice is a lazy and feeble lad. I could use someone to haul the rolls and push the delivery cart around town."

She patted Wegdell's shoulder. "He'll do it!"

Those fierce blue eyes sparkled in the lamplight. His jaw flexed in biting down against the vow of silence.

"I think we might be getting close to a deal," said the rugmaker, crossing his arms. "Pick whatever you'd like. Let me watch him and how he's able to load up the cart."

"Thank you, sir!" In her rush of euphoria, she turned a twirl on her heel. She made a quick survey of the stacks of rolled rugs and the square blankets folded into shelves on the wall. The shades of brown and gray were woolly in the dim. Her attention came back to the brightness of the lamp on the wall.

"Excuse me, sir, could you bring another lantern so I can better see the colors to choose?"

The rugmaker threw his arms out wide. "Another lantern, you say? Do you want me to risk setting fire to my entire inventory? No, no, my girl, you either pick what you'd like *now* or you come back in the morning."

Wegdell rested a warm, reassuring hand on her shoulder. The light pressure of his palm guided her to the rear of the shop, to the corner farthest from the awning that would open to the street. Although the shadows were as dim as anywhere else, the glass lantern's glow reflected on the pine walls. Condrie squinted her focus. The harder and longer she looked at the fibers, the more visible the colors became: chestnut brown, chamomile yellow, woad-flower blue, and onion red. She inhaled deeply and her nose tingled faintly of the lingering herbal scents. Going down on her knees, she stroked the plush weave of hooked rag scraps.

"This one," she said. "And this . . . and this one."

"Aw, by th' spirits in th' deep," the rugmaker grumbled. "You've been in my shop before?"

"No, sir."

"How'd you know to pick the very cheapest rugs I've got? The *very* cheapest!"

She stood up on wobbly knees, feeling light-headed in the way that she had when the lord had interrogated her. *Is it Weg? Is he doing something to me with his Sagewyn powers? Can firebirds see colors in the dark? Did he help me see in the dark too?*

Wegdell put his shoulder to the stack of rolled rugs. He hoisted them up by leaning against the upper few. He tugged in short, yanking bursts to draw out the rolled rugs that Condrie had selected.

"Do . . . do you agree to let him work off the difference?" she asked.

The rugmaker hummed thoughtfully. "He works for me until the solstice."

Condrie gasped. "That's almost five weeks away!"

"You drive a hard bargain for such a mousey little girl. All right, how about we shave off a fortnight and call it good?"

Wegdell nodded before she could answer. She wanted to keep haggling for less time and fewer coins. The rugs smelled aged, as if they had been waiting to sell for longer than any of the others in the shop. By the spread of the rugmaker's grin, as he reached out to shake Wegdell's hand, she knew they had reached a deal too quickly. *It doesn't matter in the end*, she consoled herself. *We got what we came for. The people will sleep warm tonight.*

*

Everything looked brighter in the morning. Condrie went outside with her broom, the knots in the coarse handle as familiar as her own knuckles. She swept the dirt and sand off the front door's steps in the same way as she had been doing for years before. The scratch of the broom's bristles on the granite block, the odor of mud on stone, and the crisp nip of cool air on her cheeks all made it feel as if nothing had changed after all.

Hammer taps echoed down the cramped street. Condrie paused at the corner of the tavern's shadow. She shaded her eyes with one hand, blinking straight at the rising sun, and gazed upward to the roof. Men straddled piles of shingles and buckets of nails on the slanted roof beams. Piece by piece, the scars of the fire were being covered by chips of weathered oak.

It's going to be better starting now, she told herself.

Condrie returned to the kitchen thinking she'd make herself a cup of tea. Amber was already there, poking at the darkly glowing logs beneath the cauldron of simmering oats. The girl looked thinner with a blanket draped across her shoulders like a cloak. Her wraparound garment exposed her twiggy calves and her lower back. From behind, Condrie saw Amber's spine as a row of lumps.

Oat gruel needs cinnamon, Condrie thought. She was not much taller than the girl, but over the years she had devised a few tricks for getting around this kitchen. She hooked her foot on the bottom shelf, flexed up to her tiptoes, and stretched her arm straight up. She used her fingertips in the basket's slats to pinch it off the top shelf.

"Thanks!" said Amber. "I could smell it up there but couldn't reach. The table is too heavy to move by myself."

Condrie meandered over to the hearth fire. A copper kettle was blowing a plume of steam. "Water's b-b-b-boiling."

"I don't know which box has the tea," Amber said.

All of the cedar and sandalwood boxes on the shelf wore labels of dried willow leaves, each neatly inked by Ma Kielsing herself in the common phonetic script. *Red tea . . . black tea . . . raw tea . . . lemon rinds . . . peppercorns . . . chrysanthemum blossoms . . . rose hips. . . .*

"You can't . . . c-can't . . ."

Amber looked up from the fire and stared at Condrie blushing. "What's wrong?"

"... c-c-can't read?"

"Do you feel unwell? Do you have a fever?"

Condrie shrugged a vague response. *How can I explain that I can only speak normally if Weg is in the room with me? Is he still sleeping upstairs? Will he come down for breakfast soon?*

Taking the kettle off the hearth, she measured out a spoonful of black leaves, dried chrysanthemum blossoms, and rose hips. She inhaled the flowery fragrance deeply as the dark leaves danced. Words tumbled about in her mind like the tea leaves that scrambled in the simmering waters. *I'm not stupid! Why do my words get mixed up between my head and my tongue? How did this happen to me? Did my parents drop me on my head?*

"C-c-cold," she said, pointing to the broom as an excuse.

"Oh, you were outside just now! I see. Come sit by the fire and warm yourself."

Instead she went to a basket full of teacups in various sizes and colors that Ma Kielsing had collected over the years. "No thanks. I'll ... I'll t-t-take the k-k-kettle up ... up...."

"Up to the elders who are still resting?" Amber suggested.

Condrie sighed a nod. It usually bothered her when people finished her sentences but she had a larger worry that pressed upon her mind. *How will I ever explain why my stammering comes and goes if Wegdell is in the room or not?* The lies continued to build and fester. The words she could not say choked at the back of her tongue.

She briskly ascended the stairwell. The hammering was louder on the second floor. At the first closed door, she wondered if Remmie and Niarr were still asleep despite the noise. No sounds of voices came from within, and Condrie did not dare knock to wish them a good morning.

Two of the next rooms were empty, the Athel people up with the sun and gone about their daily chores. They had folded up their blankets into neat square stacks against the wall. The floorboards and wall paneling still carried the lingering scent of charred wood, but it was muted by the wooly musk and the herbal fragrance of the blue and brown rugs.

The next-to-last door was partly ajar. Condrie leaned her head inside. "G-g-g-good . . . uh, morn."

Only the two elder storytellers were awake and upright, sitting cross-legged with the tray of clamshells and taking stock of what remained of their powdered pigments. "Good morning," said Silver.

Wegdell slept in the far corner of the room. In his sleep, he had kicked away his blanket and rolled onto his belly. Like a bird, he tucked his face into his bent arms. His long legs folded awkwardly beneath him, raising his hips up to round, firm buns.

"I b-b-brought. . . ." Condrie set down the kettle and two teacups. Her eyes strayed once more in his direction. *So if he is sleeping, I am still prone to stammering?* Her attention focused on the curve of his backside. The linens that draped him were so thin that she could see every detail in the contour of his hips and thighs, the youthful vigor, the tight, lean strength of him. Although the firebird's human form was only an illusion, he had crafted himself into a flawless ideal of a man.

The elder man waggled his finger at her, snapping her attention away. "As long as he is on pilgrimage, he is celibate."

"Celi- . . . celi- . . . what?" Condrie furrowed her brows at the unknown word.

"He will not seek a wife until after he finds the wisdom he seeks," he said. "And even then, of course, it can't ever be an outsider."

Condrie blinked in surprise at the tears welling up in her eyes. *Do I want to be anyone's wife again?*

Silver tilted the kettle and filled the cups. "Thank you for the tea. We are grateful for everything you've done to help us."

"I'm . . . g-gl- . . . glad to help." In standing up quickly, her legs tangled and she tripped over her long skirt. Condrie gripped the door frame for balance. Hammers pounded on the roof in rhythm with the pounding of her heart. For the first time, she understood Wegdell's yearning to break away, to leave behind the kindly Athel people and fly for the mountaintops. *If only I were a firebird like him, I could soar blazing to the skies!*

*

Condrie strolled to the market square to buy vegetables, sausages, river trout, and late-season fruits. She filled a handcart with radishes, carrots, onions, cabbages, and winter squash. The colors of dark pomegranates and orange persimmons made her mouth water. A sack of unmilled grain turned her thoughts to how she had spent the last few weeks. Though she had only returned a few days before, it felt as if she had never left the bustling noise of the town's marketplace. Each of the booth vendors was a familiar face. The scent of the crowd's musky clothing blended with the odor of vegetables, meat, and fish. Chilly morning air nipped her nose as Condrie waited in line for her turn to elbow up to the front and choose wares from the farmers' crates.

The town's message board was a free-standing plank shielded by a shingled cone. Among the usual tattered and faded prohibitions declared by the town's mayor, a different-colored parchment caught her eye.

Condrie stopped to study the bold strokes of black ink. On top were the abstract pictographs of High Formal Xol, the original words of the king to the South. Condrie recognized them for what they were but couldn't understand them. Nor, she knew, could anyone else in the town except the barons and the highest-ranking magistrates. Beneath that elegant script were the graceless phonetic syllables depicting words in her own language.

It read, "This is the word of His Most August Majesty Davarche the Peacemaker, the First King of Xol. A bounty of one hundred silver coins shall be paid to the one who delivers the fugitive murderer—alive—to the king's justice. He is a man, about thirty years old, two sticks and three-quarters tall, of agile body and handsome face. You will know him by a tattoo of a sunburst on his chest. He is fluent in several foreign languages and may pass for one of your own. He does not know a handy trade but he is skillful at the noble arts: riding, fencing, marksmanship, poetry, music, and dramatic performance."

Condrie smiled sadly when she read that. *Yes, he was skillful at playacting, all right.*

At the very bottom of the page, for the benefit of illiterate foresters and river people, was a simple illustration of a person holding a knife, a stack of dead bodies at his feet, and the sign of many royal coins.

"Your lover-boy better watch his back," teased a familiar voice.

Condrie whirled about to face Kin. The scruffy orphan looked a bit more wretched than she remembered. His face was gaunt as if he'd starved more often than he'd eaten. He wasn't dressed well for the coming winter in shirt sleeves and a frayed wool scarf that he clutched to his belly.

"Oh, so you have your eyes on that reward?" she countered, but she couldn't feel any anger for her old friend. Somehow, the stray orphan put her at ease. Aside from Wegdell, he was the only other person in the world who did not bring out her stammer.

"An 'undred silver coins? Yeah, that would set me up fine."

"Oh yes, you could build a manor house for yourself and become a landlord in your own right, if you can bear the burden of guilt for sending an innocent man to the gallows."

"Innocent?" Kin laughed, and his breath floated like a cloud in front of his dirty face. "Condy, Condy, you've got it bad."

"Oh, you're just a little boy. What do you understand of what you think I've got?"

"Prettiest man I ever saw. Not like your usual customers." Crouched over because of the cold, Kin seemed even smaller than she knew him to be.

She tossed him a pomegranate. When he caught it, the dark globe was almost too large for his scrawny, pale hands.

"Whether he's pleasant to look at or not," Condrie said, "it's not important. He's innocent. He didn't murder those people."

"Then who did?" Kin hugged the pomegranate to his chest. "Four of the king's Sagewyn got slaughtered in one night. If not him, who? Who else has the power to kill *them* kind?"

"I . . . I . . . I don't know. It doesn't matter."

"Sure, whatever you say."

She tugged the handle of her wheeled cart to get it moving again. She strolled into the open street and headed back for the tavern. "Come inside for some hot food. Ma's gone off to haggle for copper tubing. No one will mind."

Kin lagged behind. "No thanks, Condy. Don't wanna be there when *he* comes back from deliverin' carpets around town."

"Who?" Her puff of breath floated in front of her lips. Despite the chill of the morning, her heart's pounding brought up a flush of heat to her cheeks.

"Don't be scared of me turning him in again. I wouldn't do that to you twice. Reward be damned—I'll keep your secret. Just . . . be careful, Condy." The boy's voice faded away, word by word. "It's not me you should be scared of."

With her grip on the heavy grocery cart, she could not turn about quickly enough to see Kin slip away into the shadows.

*

Ma Kielsing herself fed twigs and branches to the fire. Flames grew and licked at the bottom of the copper keg. The keg's sides had dents from Verdant's work of hammering it back into shape. Where the lid attached to the base of the keg, the clamps showed scratches. *Let's hope they hold tight.* Condrie wrapped her arms around her stomach as she stood to watch. This was the moment upon which everyone's future depended—the testing of repairs to the gin still.

"You sure everything's screwed on tight?" Remmie, with a shawl draped over her wavy hair like a hood, stood at the firewood box. She hugged a split log to her chest.

"We'll find out soon," said Ma.

Behind them, the group of Athel women hopped up on and down from stools or got down on their knees. They continued to slather new plaster onto the walls of the room. Burn marks had been scrubbed away and now were being covered. Dip-scrape, dip-scrape—the sound was like walking in freshly fallen dry snow. Wearing shawls over their traditional wraparound linens, they paid no attention to the goings-on with the gin still.

Cold rain hissed in the town's streets, and until this moment, Condrie had been worried if the newly laid shingles would hold watertight. *We'll find out soon*, she thought. Overhead, the sounds of feet clumped back and forth on the second floor. Briefly, she imagined Cyan, Teal, and Indigo-in-Water at their labors, carrying boards of lumber up the stairs and passing buckets full of joiners' pegs between them. Nails were expensive, and what little funds Ma

Kielsing had in reserve went to supplies for repairing the gin still. The woman named Sienna had assured her it was not a problem; in their native islands, the Athel people did not use nails in their homes. Condrie had no doubt that the people would replace the charred walls and the shattered windows before the first snow. Little by little, the damage was being erased.

"It's starting." Ma Kielsing listened to the gurgling of water simmering up to boil inside the capped keg. She reached to the limits of her stout arms and stroked the copper pipes extending upward out of the keg's lid.

"What is supposed to happen?" Verdant, the copper-smith, stood in front of the whole contraption with an expression of curiosity and wonder. He wore a jacket-tunic unlaced and open at the chest. His fleece-lined boots were too large for him, but he had needed something to keep his bare feet warm on this room's flagstones as he worked on the pipes; they were no longer in the wheat fields, and the indoors were almost as cold as outside.

Ma Kielsing lightly touched the highest spot of the pipe where it extended into the cooling vat. "It boils here . . . and the steam cools here." The tone of her voice was low and lyrical.

Niarr, with her luxurious black hair tied back in a rag cap, entered from the back door. She toted a bucket of water from the town's nearest well. "Is it starting?"

"Yes, yes." Ma Kielsing cocked her ear against the oak barrel. The copper pipe extending out of the keg dipped like a swan's neck into the cooling vat. Condrie could not see it from where she stood, but she had seen it before. She already knew that the pipe curled a spiral around the inner walls of the oak barrel. The snake, Ma Kielsing called it.

"Do you need more water?" Niarr asked.

"Not just yet." Ma Kielsing dipped her hand into the oak barrel. Her small fingers swished the water in which the spiral of pipes bathed.

Condrie looked down to the spout at the bottom of the oak barrel. Before she saw the first quivering drop of liquid emerge, she smelled the odor of hot vinegar and tarnished steam.

Dark blue liquid dripped out of the spout. Ma Kielsing laughed with a wide-open mouth. Remmie and Niarr joined her in howling whoops of delight. Laughter, which used to be common in the tavern, was a rare music that Condrie had not heard for a long time.

Blue ink plunked drop by drop into the cup. Verdant frowned at it. "The pipes are clogged with tarnish."

"Tarnish be damned. It works! We've got a workin' still again. You've saved us!" Ma Kielsing seized the man's cheeks in both her hands. She pulled him down from his height and smeared a long open-mouth kiss full into his mouth.

Condrie smiled, amused at the fully grown man blushing like a small boy.

The women plastering the walls paused in their work. Trowels caked with white paste were suspended from their unmoving hands. Violet said, "So this is a good thing?"

"Yes, yes, thanks to you all and your brilliant lad," Ma Kielsing said.

Verdant stepped away and turned his back to the gin still. He glanced in the direction of Violet's disapproving stare and lowered his head. Condrie's amused smile faded as she wondered how deep the offense was, how serious the transgression was. *It was just a harmless kiss*, she wanted to say, but without Wegdell in the room, she knew the words would not come.

Ma Kielsing planted her fists against her hips. With a satisfied grin widening her plump cheeks, she watched the blue liquid dripping. "We'll run a few more cycles of vinegar to clear out the green poison, and then we'll start making good, drinkable poison. Remmie? It's time to put together a mash."

"Hurrah!" Remmie dropped the log she held. "Who wants to help me pick juniper berries?"

Condrie raised her hand. Berry picking gave her a reason to be outside and to blame her stammering on the chilly weather.

Ginger, Auburn, and Coral also put aside their plaster trowels. "We're almost done here," said Ginger wiping her hands on the borrowed apron. "If we go, can you finish this corner without us?"

"Yes, we're fine." Violet glanced left and right to Magenta, Scarlet, Amber, and Lilac as her remaining crew. "A bowl of sweet berries is going to be a treat—thanks."

Remmie giggled. "What are you saying? You don't eat juniper berries!"

"No?" Violet furrowed her thin dark brows. "I'm sorry, I don't know the names for berries in this land. If they're not for eating, then why pick them?"

Ma Kielsing extended her arm toward the gin still as if introducing a dear friend. "It's my secret recipe that I learned from alchemists on my travels in the eastern peninsula's swamp lands. It is liquid turned to steam and turned back to liquid again. It is fruit and fire, sweet and spice, both poison and cure. It is the magical beverage that makes equals of all men. Whether he is a servant or a baron, a knight or a king, a bottle of gin will strip him down to his true nature."

*

A burlap sack on her shoulder, Condrie strolled with the other women beyond the outskirts of the town. Remmie knew the way, where to find the best juniper bushes. Once they had left behind the last of the town's sheds and burlap awnings, the land opened up to a patchwork of square plots. Most of the farmers had already harvested their vegetables and now pecked at the bare soil with hoes to make furrows for planting again in spring. A few tended to their winter squash and snow peas, their pigeon coops and rabbit hutches, but soon all of this would be covered in snow.

Condrie felt a rush of excitement as she left behind the last of the farmers' plots and ventured into the fields of uncultured weeds. She rarely went on berry picking excursions; it was always the other tavern maids who went outside, laughing and chatting amongst themselves, while Condrie stayed in the kitchen.

The Athel women lagged to the rear. Despite the child she carried, growing larger by the day, Auburn set a pace ahead of Ginger and Coral as if the weight of her belly gave her a force to keep her steady on the uphill slope, like the cargo in a river barge that kept the hull on an even keel. *How must it feel to bear a child?* Condrie wondered briefly. She had been married too young and widowed too soon to bring forth a child of her own. *Has the chance passed me by? Will I ever marry again? Will I ever have a real family of my own?*

Condrie realized that she had slowed her pace, and Remmie had gone on ahead. She gripped her long skirt to sprint uphill and closed the gap. "Do-.. . d-d-do you think . . . if we get the gin still fixed . . . will they . . . they . . . ?"

"Will the other gals come back?" Remmie finished for her. Condrie nodded. "No, they're gone."

"D-d-d-did . . . did . . . did you . . . hear . . . ?"

Remmie quickened her pace and pulled ahead, looking forward to the shrubbery and the sparse trees. She walked as if she had not heard. Her strong calves and thighs chewed into the gravelly ground.

"Where . . . where did they go?"

"Niarr heard from a boatman that they went down the river to ask for jobs at the ale house and the traveler's inn." At Remmie's meaningful pause, Condrie could hear the tone of bitterness in her voice. *Our competitors.* "Not sure if they settled there or not. I haven't heard a peep from any of them since that night, and I don't expect to. That's what people do. They pass into your life and then go on their own way. Stop asking after them gals, Condy. They ain't asking about you. Stick with your new friends now. They seem a decent bunch of folk."

The group reached the cluster of shrub trees. The junipers' pale trunks were like oak trees stripped of bark. Twisted and lopsided, they grew at weird angles, bowing over the slope. Bristly spines thicker than pine needles covered every branch. Condrie inhaled the scent of leathery fruit and woodsy resin. A meaty sort of herbal musk caused her mouth to water and her stomach to growl. She knew in her head that juniper berries were not good for eating raw—and she did not ever drink the product of Ma Kielsing's gin still—and yet the sight of the shrubbery aroused her appetite.

Remmie instructed the other three women, "Pick only the dark purple ones or scoop 'em up from the ground. Don't bother with the green berries that aren't ripe yet. You may see both sprouting out of the same branch, so watch what you're doing."

Condrie reached into the green bristles. She picked the dark berries, carefully selecting each small ball to pluck from its branch. She dropped them one by one into the burlap sack on her shoulder. The afternoon's chilly air nipped at her cheeks as sharply as the juniper needles poking at her gloves.

Auburn squatted on her heels to scoop up the dark pellets that had fallen to the ground. Her knees spread wide, her round belly filling the gap. "So, uh, your name is Red Meat?"

"Remmie," she corrected.

"Red-mie, yes—sorry." Auburn paused to put a handful of berries into her burlap sack. "So, uh, that fugitive Sagewyn? Did you see him at all?"

"Yeah, I saw him, for a few words." Remmie stretched up on her toes to reach farther into the shrubbery. It was the best she could do without a step stool or ladder.

"Would you know his face if you saw him again?"

"Oh yeah." Remmie snorted. "Not a face I'll ever forget."

Condrie kept her head down, focused on her hands probing into the bristles. She saw a hungry caterpillar clinging sideways to a branch, so absorbed in eating a single green needle that it was unaware of its own vulnerability. Its furry body curved and flexed. *So helpless . . . so tiny . . . no one else but me is aware of its little insignificant life.*

Auburn said, "Some of our men left us to go track him for the bounty."

Remmie laughed briefly. "May they have clear skies and wind in their sails! I doubt they'll find him if all the king's men have failed so far. He's a wily bastard."

"Do you believe he's a murderer, like they say?"

"I don't care what they say he did," Remmie said. "I know what he did to us and to our sweet Condy here. He took advantage of her kindness and her inexperience with men. He used her as a shield to hide from a squad of armed knights. He flashed his handsome face and blinked his pretty blue eyes, and there was nothing she wouldn't do for him."

"N-n-no . . . no . . . that's not. . . ." Condrie choked up.

Ginger came alongside her. "He is a Sagewyn and no doubt beguiled her with his mystic powers."

"He's a . . . what?" Remmie squeaked.

"You didn't know? You couldn't tell?"

"No," said Remmie. "He looked like a man, like any man, when he was huddled by the fire and bargaining with Ma for a change of clothes. Whatever unnatural powers he's got, he didn't use them on the rest of us."

Condrie thought, *Because the king of the South holds him bound. His fiery tail feather is in a box. He is caged even though he is running free.*

Figures moved in the oak and white birch trees farther up the hill. At first, Condrie assumed them to be townsmen hunting for meat in the hills. As they drew closer through the trees, they revealed a stiff-armed gait, a restrained, foreign rhythm to their steps, a movement not like the customary broad-stepping strides of the townsmen. Bare calves, bare feet, no trousers, they wore only hooded cloaks in defense against the cold.

Coral hollered out, "It's our men!"

Auburn ducked through the juniper fronds. She met the group in a clearing between the arches of two sagging oak branches.

One man embraced her, bending forward over the swell of her belly to hug her tightly into his chest. Ruddy's hood snuggled into her shoulder.

The other men gathered around the pair. Taupe, his brother Tawny, Slate, and the woman named Olive stood wearily with shoulders hunched, looking down in a mood of shame and utter exhaustion. Ginger and Coral rushed up to join them.

"We looked for you at the wheat fields," Slate said, stammering slightly as his jaw shivered in the cold. "The reeve said you were gone. Just . . . gone."

Ginger said, "We've been welcomed to stay in town. It's a clover green place."

Remmie set a hand on her hip as she surveyed the ragged group. "So are these the would-be bounty hunters? Looks like they didn't get very far."

*

Back at the kitchen, Condrie served up bowls of hot peas porridge to the group. They sat on the rug in front of the blazing hearth fire. Amber pulled a loaf of bread out of the brick cubby as soon as the crust started to turn golden. The scent of toasted yeast aroused Condrie's appetite, but it was not her turn yet; the number one rule was to serve guests first.

Behind them, in the dim brown shadows, Niarr rummaged about the cupboards for the tins of coriander seeds, anise pods, and dried orris root. The juniper berries needed to marinate with yeast in water and whatever tail-end remnants that Ma had saved from the last distilling. As more and more of the Athel people poured into the kitchen, work on the upstairs came to a halt. Silence fell over the entire tavern from the rafters to the cellar. Work on plastering the walls of the distilling chamber had stopped as well, but Niarr did not scold them. She did not show disapproval for them leaving their chores undone. Niarr did not look at them, but focused on her own task.

"We talked with caravan merchants and hunters and farmers on the road," Taupe said, gulping hot porridge from the bowl cupped in his hands. "They told us what the knights said of the fugitive's crime. He slaughtered four of the king's Sagewyn councilors all in one night in a fit of rage—his own brother among them."

No, no, no, Condrie thought. *It's a mistake. It's wrong. He's innocent.*

"We figured that means he's not a soldier or a clever assassin. We figured if he killed in rage, then his rage would be gone. He'd be desperate. He'd be scared. He'd be sloppy. We searched abandoned sheds and gullies and caves for where he might be hiding. We got as far as the foothills of the Blue Mountains until we met up with a . . . a. . . ."

"A what?" Violet prompted.

Slate finished, "A tree goblin."

A hush settled over the room. Eyes widened and sparkled in the firelight. Condrie wrapped her arms around herself, thinking of the stories she had heard in her childhood. *Don't go into the woods at night. The tree goblins will play tricks on naughty children so they never find their way home.*

Niarr, with her arms full of spice tins, shouldered her way through the standing crowd and made her way to the connecting door. "I come from a family of foresters. Tree goblins are fairly harmless pests. Is that who stole your shoes?"

"Yes," Olive admitted when the four men were silent.

Niarr rolled her eyes to the ceiling. She squeezed out of the room as more Athel pressed their way inside, the older storytellers coming last to listen.

Olive continued, "It straddled a branch and laughed at us. It dangled our shoes on the highest leaves where we could never climb. It knew what we were doing out there in the forest. I guess it was watching us for a while and heard us talk."

Taupe added, "It mocked us, saying, 'Oh you're hunting the murderer firebird? What'll you do when you catch him?' And we thought. . . ."

His brother Tawny finished in a clear bass voice, "We took stock of our situation and got sensible. Clearly it was not a man we were hunting. If a feeble tree goblin could get the best of us, how would we ever bag a firebird?"

Violet leaned in closer, peering at Taupe's face as if to read the colors of the words he had spoken. "You're sure the tree goblin called the murderer a firebird?"

"Yes," said Taupe.

A hush silenced everyone sitting or standing in the kitchen. The soft purr of the flames ate into the dry logs.

The old storyteller man said hoarsely, "You were very wise to give up the chase and come back to us."

The old woman Silver agreed, "If it's common knowledge among the weird folk that it's a firebird type of Sagewyn that the king seeks . . ."

"He is a monster even among monsters," the old man finished.

Condrie started to tremble. She wanted to cry out that they shouldn't be afraid, that Wegdell was a tender soul who did not intend the harm that his fiery wings had done, that he was bound to follow the command of the wicked king of the South, that he was innocent of the murders they claimed he committed. *Goblins are tricksters and mischief-makers*, she thought. *Murderer firebird? No, no, it has to be wrong.*

Indigo-in-Water looked around, left and right, to every face gathered in the kitchen. "Say, where is our priest? What is his opinion of this?"

Cyan said, "He is out in the town, delivering rugs to the rugmaker's customers to work off the price of our blankets."

Taupe furrowed his brow. "How odd that he would agree to such work. Couldn't any one of you have taken that chore? When does he have time to reflect on larger questions and meditate on his place and ours in this world?"

Slate nodded along. "You speak wisely for all of us. We are losing ourselves here among the mainlanders. It was bad enough harvesting the wheat fields, but at least we were together. Now we are living in the town, wearing their clothes, eating their food, speaking in their words, and working for their benefit. We are forgetting who we are."

"Yes," said Violet. "We are forgetting our true colors."

The sunset turned the window panes to circles of bright crimson. All of the Athel people stood up on their feet. They faced the window, standing quietly and watching as the red hue washed over their faces. They bathed in the silence of the last light of day.

Condrie alone looked down at the fireplace, watching the flames rise off the logs like a bird flexing its wings. *No, no, it has to be wrong. It can't be true. He's not a monster. He's not a murderer.*

*

At dusk, Condrie ventured outside on the pretext of doing an errand. Her true purpose was to find him—Wegdell—at the end of his daily deliveries and before he returned to the crowded tavern. Their only chance to have a private conversation was outside in the open streets. She hurried from street corner to street corner. At the end of the day, the shopkeepers were pulling down their awnings and closing the bolts on their windows; the weaver's loom fell silent; the cobbler's tack hammer tapped no more; the cooper, the chandler, and the cobbler huddled in the amber glow of handheld lanterns to share a pack of dried weeds in their pipes. She ran past them, sprinting faster and faster in an ever-widening circle. Her mouth opened to breathe harder. She puffed white clouds as she scurried back and forth in the twisted branches of unmarked streets. Cold air chilled her tongue.

Her mind crystallized into two distinct parts like the sleeves of the Sagewyn lord's luxurious garments: the serene side was clover green, and the worried thoughts were fuchsia purple. What if the goblins' rumors were true? What if Wegdell truly was guilty of the murders after all, and he had been lying to save himself. There was so much about Sagewyn lore that she didn't understand. How could she be sure of his innocence?

She spotted him strolling by the breadmaker's shop. The dough man had long since battened down his awnings. He went to bed hours earlier to be ready to make the next day's batch of loaves before dawn.

"Weg?"

"Towel." His voice was thick and wet with the blood oozing from his nose. "Towel, towel."

"What happened?"

Condrie untied her own apron, for she had nothing else to offer his face. She recalled her friend Kin, who often got into street fights. Many was the morning she'd be coming back with a fresh pot of milk from the dairyman, and there would be Kin, slouched by the doorstep with a black eye or a bloody nose. He never would tell her how he'd gotten hurt or who he'd been fighting with. Whether it was from evading the law or competing with fellow street thieves, she never knew and learned never to ask.

"I came around a corner just as Potter dropped his awning. He yelled at me to be more careful, the uncouth clod."

"Sit down," she ordered, gesturing to the breadmaker's doorstep. "Put your head back. Press the side of your nose here. . . ."

"Ow, it hurts. Is it broken?"

"We'll see when the swelling goes down," she said.

"Swelling? Human noses can swell?"

"Bird beaks are easier, I suppose." Condrie pressed the apron wadded up against his nose. He licked his lips, and his tongue was tinged with red. Wegdell grimaced. She smelled it and could almost taste blood in her own mouth.

"The others came back," she said. "Taupe and Tawny and—"

"I know who you mean."

Condrie frowned standing over the seated man. *What kind of manners are these?* she wondered. No thanks for ruining her only apron.

"They encountered a tree goblin who stole their shoes."

Wegdell snorted, perhaps a muffled laugh or perhaps trying to clear the blood from his nose. She could not see his mood with his eyes closed. Dusk sapped the light from the sky. Shadows turned from brown to blue to indigo and gray.

The goblin called you a murderer. Is it true? Words choked up in her throat. Even if she were to ask him bluntly, she did not know how to be sure of his answer.

"If I didn't know better," he said, "I'd wonder if you put the goblin up to that little trick."

"Me?"

"As I expected." He cautiously peeled the blood-soaked apron away from his face. "You don't traffic with tree goblins . . . just the ones in town."

"Excuse me?"

"Oh, I've seen that little imp friend of yours tagging around behind me. I trust he's properly remorseful after what happened to you the last time he tattled on me?"

Condrie frowned so hard that her eyes squinted into slits. "Do you mean Kin?"

"Of course."

"Here now, he's in a pathetic situation by no fault of his own. That's no reason to call him a goblin. You . . . you should apologize for insulting him so."

"Insulting?" Wegdell dabbed the apron at his nose, testing to see if the blood had stopped. "Do you honestly not know what he is? Condy, my dear, your street friend really is a hobgoblin."

"Oh?"

"You didn't notice the ears?"

"He wears his hair long and shaggy," she said.

"The teeth . . . surely, the brown teeth. . . ."

"He lives in the streets and eats garbage."

Wegdell added, "Have you ever seen him beyond a stone's throw from your back door? You haven't, have you? Because he's a hobgoblin bound to forever lurk near the bricks of your tavern's chimney. I figure he's a century old—at least."

She took a step back and turned her head, scanning the shadows in hope—or in dread—of seeing Kin dart by. "Is that why I don't stammer around him? It's something to do with magical folk that stills the jitters in my tongue?"

"Yes."

"So he always knew who you were—what you were—from that very first moment he saw you in the kitchen?"

"Yes."

Kin's warnings echoed in her memory. *I can smell guilt on a man, and I smelled it tonight on him in your kitchen. Plain as the stink of garlic, it is, what weighs on his heart. Whatever they say he did? Whatever he says he didn't do? Oh, he done it. Believe you me, Condy, he done it. He murdered them all, just like they say he did, as sure as I'm standing here. Stay clear from him or he'll murder you, too.* Condrie half-closed her eyes to block the memory of Kin's taunting expression. She reasoned that a goblin was not the same as a Sagewyn seer and Kin was following a hunch without really knowing for sure.

"Condy?"

"Hmm?"

"Is there a reason that you've come outside to find me?" Though she couldn't see his mouth, she knew he frowned by the way his straight, dark eyebrows bent in toward the top of his nose.

"I'm not sure of how to say it . . . what I want to ask you. I'm . . . well, I'm not sure if you'll tell me the truth or if you'll just tell me what I want to hear to make me feel good so I'll help you hide and escape from your king's justice."

"I have never manipulated you, Condy. How can you even suggest that?"

"You're so comfortable being a pampered lord. I see it in the way you play the part of a priest. You're so at ease when others defer to you. I've worked in kitchens my whole life, so I naturally fall into the role of a servant. I've lied for you. I've lied to everyone who is important to me. I wonder if you appreciate me. You haven't given me anything back."

"I don't understand. What do you want, a bouquet of primroses?" He opened his eyes, which were startlingly clean and clear compared to the bloody mess that was the bottom half of his face.

"I want you to be honest with me."

"Oh God," he moaned with a playful exaggeration, his last attempt to lighten the mood. "Oh no, oh please, not that."

"Stop it." Condrie made a fist and was tempted to pop him in the nose and start it bleeding again. "I'm serious."

"Why are you so serious all the time? If I keep secrets from you, don't be offended. It's for your own good. If you're interrogated, the less you know—"

"I understand that! I've been interrogated already." A dark lump formed in the center of her chest that became harder and heavier with each word coming out of her mouth.

"Then what do you want from me?"

"Tell me what they already know. Tell me. . . ."

Condrie peered straight into the pure glass circles that were his eyes. Their gazes locked, and neither of them could look away. It almost felt like sorcery. He seemed to know what her words would be before she asked. He frowned to brace himself.

"Did you really do it?" she asked. "Did you kill them?"

"You want the story? What happened that night?" His calm, clear voice blended with the cawing of crows passing overhead to find their rooftop nests.

Condrie nodded.

Wegdell inhaled deeply, snorting with a nose congested with blood, to prepare himself to speak.

"There were five of us in the flock: five terrible firebirds in bondage to the king's will. We swooped down in blazing fury upon any who opposed him. We helped the oh-so-majestic King Davarche to drive the Athel out of the Northern Bay Islands. We drove the Southlanders out of their vast forests. We smashed the temples of goddess worshippers in the fertile Clichard valleys. We enforced the laws of the throne of Xol and made his kingdom a fearful place to be."

Condrie crossed her arms. As hideous as his words were, she had known all of this for a long time. What he'd said so far wasn't so shocking, though he made it seem like a revelation. She couldn't help staring at his shirt where his tattoo was hidden beneath layers of wool and linen, and she clearly imagined him doing such things.

"You were following orders," she said.

He continued, "My brother was the one who stood up and said, 'I can't do this anymore.' Yigs had the moral fiber to see that what we were doing was wrong, that the orders we followed were wrong. We weren't beyond the laws of men just because we had the power to soar on fiery wings higher than any eagles can go. We didn't deserve to be their lords."

Condrie thought, *What a fine man his brother must have been.*

"We didn't listen to him at first. We were too busy enjoying the party. Oh God, what a delightful party the king provided for us! Fine foods, sparkling jewelry, luxurious accommodations, delightful entertainments . . . but my brother kept his head. Yigs kept talking, and talking, and gradually some of the others started to listen. So did I. The king was getting drunk on his power. Despite all the territory we had helped him conquer, it wasn't enough for him. He craved more."

"What more is left that is not under his flag?" she asked.

"Davarche has eyes on these meadows of yours. That baron who owns the wheat fields where we worked the harvest? He's living on borrowed time. By the new year's day dawning, if the Council of Barons don't sign a treaty of allegiance to King Davarche, the knights camped in their guestrooms—on the pretext of hunting me—will receive orders to rise up and slay them all."

"How horrible," she gasped.

Wegdell shrugged. "King Davarche is not a patient man. He'll fly into a rage at anyone who questions his ruthless tactics, including his own son. The crown prince of Xol is a pampered, soft-hearted fop—according to his father—and a great disappointment. My brother said, 'What sort of kingdom have we helped to build if a compassionate man is reviled as a failure?' Clearly, things had gone too far."

His voice was hypnotic as if he were singing a prayer. Condrie hardly dared to breathe for fear of breaking the rhythm.

"We made a suicide pact," he said.

"By the holies!"

"Yes, my brother convinced us that just retrieving our tail feathers and escaping the king's bondage was not a strong enough statement. Davarche needed to understand how passionately we opposed his policies, that we were willing to . . . to . . ."

"To die on principle?" Condrie finished for him, when he was silent for too long.

"Yes." Wegdell's voice sounded dry. He cleared his throat.

When he hesitated to continue, Condrie held her breath. She waited so long that her own pulse throbbed in her ears and her chest began to hurt. She felt dizzy and weak like the caterpillar clinging sideways to the juniper branch.

"My brother hoped that our spectacular deaths would inspire the other Sagewyn and the un-folk of the provinces to rise up against the king and ignite a revolution."

"It didn't work," she said.

"No." Wegdell lowered his head. "God, I miss him. My brother was a better person than I."

"I know you do. I'm sorry for your loss."

He sniffed wetly and spat out a mouthful of bloody phlegm. "I shouldn't have agreed to it. The whole idea was stupid! A useless waste of precious life. God, I wish I had never gone down to the vault in the first place!"

"The vault?" she repeated. "You admit that you went to the king's vault to get back your tail feather?"

"Yes, everyone knows that I seduced a chambermaid to swipe the king's keys. She testified at my trial, so I hear."

Condrie sat up a little straighter. "So, what happened next?"

"I was a coward. At that last moment, I did not wish for any of us to die. I tried to break the box open, to take back possession of our own tail feathers and set us all free. I tried, and I couldn't. It was made of some mysterious metal that even a firebird could not burn through. God! Damnit! I can melt a blacksmith's anvil down to a puddle of slag, but I couldn't get into the king's strongbox. We couldn't fly away with it off the castle's grounds, either, for it is hell's own magic that holds it within Davarche's possession."

"You could have surrendered," Condrie said.

"My brother . . ." he said. "When the alarm sounded and knights were rushing up the stairs to the tower, Yigs looked me in the eye. He said, 'If you wish us to surrender, just say the word, Brother. I admire your loyalty to the flock and to me, but I know that your convictions are not as strong as mine. I cannot ask you to give up your life if you are not fully committed to my ideas. Together, we will endure whatever punishment the king metes out for this demonstration of resistance. I love you.'" Wegdell sucked in a deep shuddering breath. "I swear by the god of fire that I honestly believed my own feather was in that box when I hurled it into the moat. At that moment, I was ready to die."

"But your feather wasn't in the box." Condrie said it as a statement, not a question.

"No, it wasn't. When the box hit the water and the others' feathers were snuffed out, they . . . they. . . ." Wegdell lowered his head.

"They died?" she asked.

He nodded.

"Would the king have kept yours apart so as not to have all his eggs in one basket?"

"No, he wouldn't have."

"Are you sure?"

"Yes. My feather had to have been very close by, or else I could not have transformed at the same time as the others."

She asked, "How close?"

"A stone's throw or less."

"So whoever got to the box before you must have known about the suicide pact. What do you think happened? Who else knew how to get into the vault and how to open it? Was it a key lock or a padlock? Why wouldn't they remove all the feathers instead of just yours? Why would someone linger nearby with it to watch the rest of your flock die around you?"

The moonlit twinkle on his cheek, she saw, was a tear. Was it real?

"You must have some ideas about what really happened. Talk to me, Weg. Talk to me!" She was close to shouting.

He stood up. "It's getting late. We should head back to the tavern."

Condrie skipped after his heels. "Do you think it was Gerrawgon's wife who wished to save you from this suicide pact? She seems enamored of you."

"She claims she didn't," he said softly. "I asked."

"Do you believe her?"

"Yes." The wistful tone of his voice was the same as many a drunken man crying into his gin for a lady love. Condrie recalled the blue-haired wife of the Sagewyn lord saying, *Wegsemze is utterly gorgeous,* and the melodic lust in that woman's voice had been quite plain.

"How long have you been having an affair with her?"

"What's that? What? Oh, don't be so crude. I wouldn't call it an 'affair,' necessarily. She's a bog blythe, like a kind of water nymph, and I'm a firebird. By rights, we shouldn't be in the same room together. Physically, we can't do anything more than kiss, and even that hurts me greatly. I don't understand it, myself, why I feel the urge to keep doing it."

"Can she use her water powers to subdue you when you're in your firebird form?"

"Of course—yes, water quenches fire," he said.

"So you enjoy the sensation of being quenched?"

Wegdell did not answer.

"Or do you enjoy the idea that a beautiful woman can dominate you when you're in all your flaming glory? Is it the pain of kissing her that gives the passion a thrill? Some men like it, you know, to be bound and flagellated."

Wegdell made a thoughtful *hmmph* as he considered this.

"What I don't understand is how you have kept it a secret from Gerrawgon. Doesn't an immortal Lord of Dreams know everything that goes on around him?"

Wegdell chuckled into the bloody cloth muffling his face. "Gerrie is a thousand and two hundred years old, which misleads him into thinking that he's smarter than everyone else. Time doesn't make a man smarter, and he's too arrogant to concede being fooled by a fledgling like me."

"Do you think it was Gerrawgon who pulled a trick? He's enraged that you're making a cuckold of him?"

"If he wanted to punish me for seducing his wife, he would have let me go through with the suicide pact. Or, if he did hate me so much, he would have removed all of the others' feathers but mine."

"What's wrong with you?" she shouted. "Why aren't you trying harder to figure out what really happened?"

Wegdell hunched forward as he walked at a faster pace, reflexively hiding from her words as if she were pummeling him with her fists. "Why won't you let it go?"

"Because I have sacrificed so much to help you! We all have. Ma Kielsing's tavern may never be the same as it was before. The gals who fled from that night may never come back. You may not have your fiery wings anymore, but you're still swooping over and leaving a path of destruction."

Wegdell turned his face to her, not watching where he walked. His expression was startlingly furious. "I ruined *your* life? How dare you! Haven't I told you, at every opportunity, to get yourself away from me? You knew the risks from the first hour we met. I gave you a choice, again and again, and you chose to be with me."

"Choice? What choice?" She hopped along faster and faster to stay eye to eye with his long-legged strides. "You toyed with my sympathies. I told you of my . . . my . . . unhappy marriage on the first day. You knew that I had never known the love of a tender man, and you preyed upon my lonely desires. You smiled your pretty smile. You blinked your pretty eyes. How could I ever have a choice to do anything but what you asked?"

"Your mother, as you call her, taught you better."

"I thought she did, but I never expected to feel this way. My sensibility turns to pudding when I look at you. And you know it, don't you? *Don't you?*"

He stared down at her with harsh unblinking eyes.

"You just admitted to me that you seduced a chambermaid to swipe the king's keys. Kin told me, and I didn't want to believe him, but I'm wondering now. You're not really a man. You don't have a man's feelings and desires. Can you even pretend to feel affection for a 'stone' like me?"

"What do you wish me to say?" he asked.

"The truth! For once in your life, damn you, tell me the truth of what's in your heart."

"You should know." His voice descended to the lowest tone she had ever heard from him. It was an inhuman growl.

"That's the problem. I don't know. I need you to tell me if you're the least grateful for everything I've done for you . . . what we've *all* done for you! Tell me, are you a cold-hearted bird of prey, or are you a man?"

Wegdell stepped aside to put a space between them. "I've been too goddamned long in human skin."

"That's no answer," she cried. "What does that mean?"

From across the street, pottery crashed to the ground.

Amber stared at them from the back steps of the tavern's kitchen. She held an empty wicker tray. Scattered at her feet were the shards of twenty broken soup bowls. The bucket and rag nearby would have been for wiping the bowls clean.

"Oh God," he said at the expression on Amber's face.

"I . . . I . . . I. . . ." Condrie couldn't form a word beyond that first pronoun, so she clamped her mouth shut.

Ma Kielsing emerged from the back door. "What happened, girl? Did you fall?"

Amber dropped the wicker tray as well. She just stood there, unmoving, her jaw dropped, her eyes wide.

The stout woman turned her gaze to notice Condrie first and then Wegdell. Her cheeks hardened into the severe frown reserved for drunks who ran up a tab without paying, who started fist-fights that broke furniture, and who abused the barmaids.

"You . . . it's you!"

Wegdell bolted sideways and ran. He swooped into the darkness of shadows. In a blink, he was lost to sight.

Ma Kielsing hoisted her long skirts and bolted after him. She ga-humphed a few steps, got as far as where Condrie stood in the middle of the street, and stopped.

Hot tears burned on her chilled cheeks. "I'm . . . s-s-s-sor-sorry."

"You don't owe apologies to me," she said. "You're not the first of my girls to get seduced by a pretty face. Just tell me, are you pregnant?"

Condrie shook her head with a shiver.

"If he comes back, would you hide him again?"

"No."

"Good girl. You've learned your lesson." Ma Kielsing stroked the side of her head, a soft touch that Condrie barely felt through the thickness of her woolly cap.

Condrie raised the apron to wipe the wetness off her face but stopped short. The fabric was soaked from his bloody nose. Tears continued to dribble out of her eyes. Not tears of despair, but anger at how she had been manipulated into giving him assistance. *What a fool I've been. Maybe he did murder them all. Maybe everything he just told me is an elaborate lie. Maybe he wanted to be rid of his self-righteous brother and his oh-so-ethical flock so he'd be free to do whatever he wanted.*

*

As Condrie and Ma Kielsing stood together in the dark street, snow flurries began to fall. The icy flakes pelted her cheeks, lightly stinging her skin as if moths were trying to bite. Glitters swirled on the night breeze. They sparkled silver in the moonlight and gold in the lamplight; the same snowflakes from the same cloud turned to opposites depending on where they happened to fall.

"Let's get inside," Ma Kielsing said, "before we freeze."

Condrie's feet were sluggish walking the rest of the way back to the tavern's door. Amber had gone inside. The upstairs rooms showed light through the linen tarps where glass windows used to be. *Right now, she's telling them all what happened*, Condrie thought, her shivering jaw unable to form words. *They're all going to hate me.*

"In a few days," Ma Kielsing said, walking to force Condrie's numb feet along, "we'll put the first batch of mash into the still. I'm letting the word be known around town that we're having our grand re-opening by the week's end."

"So-s-s-s-so . . . soon?"

Ma Kielsing avoided the kitchen door. She turned away from the rear of the building and guided Condrie around the corner of the porch's overhang. In front of the tavern, a placard was permanently nailed to a post displaying a ring of flowers around the silhouette of a drinking glass. Boards of the porch were sturdy and solid. Two overlapping panels of weathered wood showed the crackling of the years but were otherwise unchanged. *How many men have passed in and out of these doors?* Condrie wondered. Too many to count; too many to remember.

The front doors easily slid apart on rollers in grooves, overlapping the matching left and right panels of the outer walls. It was dark within the parlor, darker than a hole in the ground.

"I haven't been in here since . . . oh, since that night." Ma Kielsing ventured inside. Her arm around Condrie's waist guided her inside as well.

Her eyes quickly adjusted to the dim. Floor cushions were tossed about. Divans that had been against the wall were overturned. Tables were toppled. Shards of glass and pottery lay everywhere like autumn leaves. Mirrored glass behind the bar was cracked into a spider-web pattern. Shelves were empty where rows of bottles used to glitter in the candlelight. Mice scampered away along the baseboards of the walls. Silence dampened the room that had once buzzed with conversation and song.

"There's a lot of work to be done," Ma Kielsing said in a hushed, almost reverent whisper. "Thankfully, the smoke and flame didn't reach here. All the damage was in the rear and up to the roof's eaves at the back. Some sweeping . . . some patting out the cushions . . . some mouse traps. . . . It won't take long to put this right."

Condrie picked up the shard of a broken bowl. Its rim still had the gritty residue of salt from the roasted almonds it had once held.

Overhead, the ceiling's beams creaked with the movement of dozens of feet. Voices hummed through the boards. Rising in volume, they buzzed like hornets in a box. She imagined Amber's face twisted with distress and rage as she relayed the news. *Him! It was him! He was among us all the time!* Condrie's gut clenched in dread of facing them; her legs trembled at the urge to run. How easy it would be to run into the streets, as Wegdell had done, and never be seen again.

"It's going to be like it was before," Ma Kielsing said wistfully as she stroked her palm over the bar. "The customers will return. When the snow piles high, what else is there to do?"

Footsteps thump-thump-thumped rapidly down the stairs. Her last chance to run away had passed; it was too late to escape into the night. Condrie's feet froze in place in the middle of the empty parlor. She turned to the curtains of the connecting door and held still, uncertain if she was ready to face them but certain she had no choice.

Violet carried a tin box lantern into the dark room. A faint glow shined to the underside of her chin and cheekbones. "She's in here!"

More and more of them poured in, shuffling around the debris and the toppled furniture. They all carried some sort of light—glass lanterns, tin lanterns, candlesticks, and oiled wicks in clay cups. The glowing group dispelled the darkness, pushing the shadows into the corners. Condrie's eyes rolled left and right, scanning over two dozen unique faces who were all strangers not so long ago. She knew them all. She knew their names and their heritage, their artisan skills and their former occupations. She knew what they had lost, how far they had traveled, and what they hoped to regain. She knew the color of their hearts; she knew each of their life stories. Yet, in the light of flickering wicks, they were all the same color of beige.

"What are you?" asked Silver, the gray-haired storyteller, coming to the front.

"What girl could appear to be so tender and sincere?" added Willow Leaf, the hunched old man by her side.

"Liar," said Auburn with a clenched jaw.

"Betrayer," Indigo-in-Water's deep voice boomed.

"He was among us?" Slate waved his free hand away from the candlestick in his left. "You let us trek off into the wild and try to track him for bounty, when all the time you knew?"

"You knew," said Tawny and Ruddy in unison.

"We never had a chance of finding him," Olive cried out in a shrill squeal.

"A Sagewyn lurked among us like a spy," said Cyan as Teal and Raven nodded along with him.

"Why?" Ginger blinked back tears.

Tears leaked out of Condrie's eyes. *I'm sorry!* she wanted to scream. Words gagged in the back of her throat, and her tongue curled up into the roof of her mouth. Everything blurred. Coronas shined around each tiny spot of flame in each person's hand, the bright circles overlapping and blending into a web of liquid light.

Ma Kielsing stepped forward to come in between her and the group. She put her fists to her stout hips and stood against the wall of angry, confused faces. "Back off, the lot of you! Nobody attacks one of my girls. Not under my roof, they don't."

"We're not going to hurt her," said Indigo-in-Water grimly. "It isn't our way to do harm."

Amber came alongside the storyteller's elbow. The youngest girl of the group, the one closest to her own age, the eyes that mirrored her own eyes looked at Condrie with hollow sadness. "We don't understand the color of your heart."

Willow Leaf held empty clam shells in the palm of his hand. "We ran out of pigment powders. I have no colors to paint what I wish to say."

Violet came forward to speak for them all. "He came to us in deception. The Sagewyn abused us again without ever lifting a finger. Do you understand? To be a holy man on pilgrimage among us is not a role to play on stage. It is a sacred thing. He made a mockery of what little we still possess after all that was taken from us . . . after what *he* took from us and destroyed."

"And you knew," Slate added.

"Liar . . . liar . . . liar . . ." several voices murmured in a droning chorus.

Condrie leaned against the matron's strength and balance as Ma Kielsing put an arm around her shoulders. Every part of her shivered down to the soles of her feet. It seemed that tears bubbled up from the core of her gut.

More and more tears poured down her face, and she could not imagine ever being able to stop.

"Are ye done having your say?" Ma Kielsing demanded of them all.

"No." Taupe stepped apart from the group. "I . . . I have something to tell."

"There is nothing more to be said." Violet announced it with an air of finality. "She is no longer welcome among us. We have called her Blank—white and innocent—but now we shall call her Air that is colorless and unseen."

"Blame *him*!" Taupe cried. "Don't blame her for being manipulated by an unholy creature."

"Her deception is unforgivable, Brother," said Tawny.

"Who are you to say what is forgivable and what is not?" Taupe demanded. "Listen to me, all of you! Condy is not the only one who has deceived you."

Condrie gulped. *Don't. . . . No. . . .* Her jaw flexed, but the words did not come.

"I've lied," Taupe said. "Yes, I have! I've lied to you all for years. Since I was a small child, there has been something wrong with my eyes. I don't see colors. I can't tell the difference between red or green or orange or blue! Everything in my sight is brown."

Slowly the group rotated to the left and gazed at him, standing apart. Taupe hung his head in shame.

His brother patted him on the shoulder. "I wish you had told us sooner. I'm glad you told us now."

His sister Sienna slipped between the elbows and shoulders to emerge at his side. She put her glass lantern on the floor to free up both arms for embracing him. Taupe crouched over his sister. His eyes closed. His gaunt cheek snuggled into her brown hair.

Willow Leaf said, "This changes nothing for her. Do you understand? Your lie hurt only yourself. Her lies have hurt us all."

"I forgive her," Taupe said, raising his face out of his sister's hair. He looked straight at Condrie, his dark eyes glimmering like two almonds. "I forgive you."

"Th-th-thanks," she managed to choke out.

"You're the only one among us who does." Violet turned on her heel, her bare feet squeaking on the floorboards. The others turned away as a group. One by one, they filed out of the connecting door and ascended the stairwell. Taupe lingered at the rear and, gazing back over his shoulder, was the last to go.

"Hmmph," grunted Ma Kielsing. "A bunch of sanctimonious vagrants."

"They . . . th-they're right. I lied."

"Shrug 'em off, Condy. Nobody died. It's clear you're sorry. We gave 'em a home for the winter and jobs besides, and this is how they show their gratitude? Sweep 'em out of your head."

Ma Kielsing guided Condrie through the curtained archway and down the short, narrow hall. The pleated curtain that covered the stairwell's arch still wavered from all those bodies who had recently passed through. Upstairs had suddenly become a forbidden realm of anger and bitterness where Condrie was no longer welcome.

The kitchen, as always, was the warmest place in the entire tavern. Smoldering logs on the hearth tingled against her chilled cheeks. *How do I go on from here?* she wondered. *How do I carry the burden of mistakes I've made and the pain I've caused?*

She used a clean dish rag to wipe her tears. Staring into the brightness of the hearth, her aching eyes finally dried. A bucket on the stones held a mash of juniper berries soaking in the tail-ends of alcohol preserved from a past distilling. The familiar pungent scent of leathery fruit, yeast, coriander, anise, and cinnamon wafted up to her congested nose.

Ma Kielsing moved about at the far side of the kitchen. The sounds of sliding-open wall panels and unfolding blankets were the familiar sounds of home. For years, Condrie had slept alone in the cubby in the back of the kitchen. She remembered many nights of feeling warm and content snuggling among the piles of wooly blankets and down-stuffed comforters. To gaze back now at the stout woman punching the pillow to fluff it into shape, Condrie wondered if she would ever sleep as soundly again as she had before.

"They've no right to judge you," Ma Kielsing said. "Trust me, there's not a woman alive who hasn't been stupid for a man."

*

In the wee dark hours before dawn, Condrie awoke to the sound of someone shuffling about the kitchen. *Wegdell?* She sat up in bed. Blankets wadded around her like a cocoon.

"Just me," said Kin.

He perched on the hearth, as he often did, squatting on his heels with knees drawn up under his chin. His ragged clothes stank from the filth of the streets. The fire's deep orange glowed on part of his face. Now she noticed the tips of pointed ears under the greasy locks of his shaggy hair. *Of course he's a hobgoblin. Why didn't I see it before?*

"I'm tired," she said.

"Sorry."

"Why are you here?"

Kin rubbed his pug nose with the back of his hand. "I heard them yelling at you. I saw you cry. I don't like to see you cry, Condy."

She hugged the thick blankets to her chest. "I'm not crying now. I just want to sleep. Take a persimmon and please go."

"Just wanted to say, don't cry over what the Athel folk said." Kin rocked back and forth on his heels like a blackbird clinging to a branch in the wind. "You don't belong with them."

"They're good people," she said.

"Yeah, but you're not one of them. Why'd you let 'em name you something different? At least when *he* was in disguise, he always knew who he was. He lied to *them*, but he never lied to himself inside his own head. Even in human skin, he's a firebird through and through, and that's all he'll ever know how to be."

Condrie furrowed her brows at Kin's halting, lilting tone. She had never heard him speak humbly or kindly without a cackle of sarcasm.

She asked, "What else do you know about him?"

"Nothin'. I stay away from his sort." Kin turned his face away from the fire's glow. He stopped rocking. He held utterly still.

"Ever since the first day, you've been convinced of his guilt. Do you know it for sure? Did he really intend to slaughter them all?"

Kin shrugged. "I wasn't there. I just know what I heard."

"From the tree goblins?"

"Yeah, and they're just repeating what they heard from the un-folk in the river."

"Folk *in* the river?" she repeated, not sure if she had heard his words correctly. Kin's uneven brown teeth gave him a slight lisp.

"Yeah. Y'know, the water nymphs heard it from the glow bugs and such. He did what was done. It doesn't matter why. It doesn't matter what's true."

"It matters to me," she said. "You've been dogging him in the streets."

"Sometimes."

"Did you see where he ran away to last night?"

"Nope." Kin's eyes hardened into two black dots. "He's gone away, and that's the best. You're better without him."

She blinked and Kin slipped out of sight. Once more, she was alone in the kitchen. Her gaze wandered to the shutters of the bolted window, where he had dropped through and begged for help on that first night. His blue eyes sparkled clearly in her memory.

*

At dusk on opening night, the parlor was still empty. Remmie wore her best gown washed clean to almost white, cinched at the waist by a satin cord, gauzy sleeves hanging in long points to the floor. Niarr wore a similar blue gown that starkly offset her raven-black hair. Condrie used a step-stool along the walls to light the glass lanterns ensconced on brass hooks. Ma Kielsing herself stood behind the bar, wiping in circles a spot that was already clean.

The rugmaker and the chandler entered first. Both men paused at the doorway. Their eyes rolled around, widening, as if assessing the price of the furniture and lighting fixtures.

"Welcome, fine sirs!" Niarr squared her shoulders and put on her best charming smile.

"I heard," said the rugmaker, "you fixed the damage and cooked up some more gin?"

"Yes, sir." Ma Kielsing hurriedly put aside her wiping rag. "How would you like it? Straight shots or with a mix of lemon water?"

"Straight," said the rugmaker.

"Gin an' bitters," said the chandler.

"Comin' right up!" Ma Kielsing squeaked a cork out of a bottle. Gin gurgled into glasses.

Condrie in the corner held her breath as she watched both men drink. Two gulps, and their faces turned up into smiles.

"By th' spirits, what a fire!" the chandler exclaimed.

Niarr laughed in her low, sultry way as she leaned against the bar along with them. Remmie, standing under the glow of the chandelier, clapped her hands in rhythm and began to sing a riverman's song: "*Don't come ye th' mornin', not yet . . . not yet. Cause when comes th' mornin', I forget . . . forget. My buddies, my ladies, my wine, and my song . . . when come ye th' mornin', you all will be gone.*"

More shopkeepers strolled inside. Their faces brightened in the lamplight. Their cheeks rosy from the cold turned rosy with smiles. The cooper and the cobbler with their gravelly voices joined in singing the refrain, "*Do-o-o-on't come ye th' mornin', not yet . . . not yet!*"

Glasses clinked on the bar. Corks popped. Gin dribbled forth. Niarr laughed in a high-pitched, girlish giggle.

The Lord High Sheriff slipped his arm around Remmie's waist. He stepped a quick circle, bringing her with him in a twirl. "Oh, my sweet buttercup, did ye miss me?"

"Every day." Remmie turned her cheek as he bent in to kiss her. She playfully pushed at his chest and nudged him toward the bar.

"Your usual, Sheriff?" Ma Kielsing reached under the bar for a special ceramic jug.

"Oh, you still have it?"

"They didn't smash everything." Ma poured the mint-green liquid into a glass and topped it off with a jigger of gin.

The Lord High Sheriff tilted his head back. He downed it all in one gulp. Laughing heartily, he pounded the glass back to the bar. "You've come back to life, ol' girl. Blessed be!"

Condrie withdrew to the curtains of the connecting doorway. She lingered with her back to the archway's beam. Her hands fussed with her apron, for there was not much else for her to do at the moment. Later, there would be work to tote the empty glasses away and mop up the spills, but for now, all she could do was stand and watch. She breathed the kaleidoscope of scents, of liquor and lemons, of men and women. Burning candle wax dispelled the cold outside.

The man named Verdant came up behind the curtain from the back room. He wore an apron as well, his cheeks flushed with the steam of the simmering still. "I tried a sip of it," he said softly. "It tastes horrible. I'd sooner drink lamp oil. How can they enjoy it?"

Condrie shrugged. She had never tasted what the still produced.

"You people in this land are full of doing things that surprise me. I think I could live here in this town until I'm an old man like Willow Leaf and I still wouldn't understand you."

He's talking about my lies and aiding Wegdell in his deception. I failed them; I failed them all. Condrie looked down to the hem of her long skirt.

Metal rattled from the front door. It sounded like a suit of armor—a sound she had come to know. Condrie raised her head in time to see a squad of King Davarche's knights stroll inside. The scales of metal riveted to their leather jerkins twinkled in the candlelight.

"Hello!" Niarr reached out to the squad, her arms wide open as if trying to hug them all from across the room.

Ma Kielsing set out a row of glasses. "Welcome, honorable knights. What'll it be? Straight shots or with a mix of lemon water?"

The knights sidled up to the bar. One with auburn curls clapped the Lord High Sheriff on the shoulder and said, "I hear there's a tonic water of mint."

"Ah, yes." Ma Kielsing reached under the bar for the special jug. "It's a secret recipe that you won't find anywhere else: an herbal decoction taught to me by the priestesses of the goddess temples in the Clichard valleys."

The man named Verdant gripped Condrie's arm from behind. "Nails," he whispered. "They're settling in as if they mean to make this town their home."

If knights are hanging around the town, then they are still looking for Wegdell. Drink up, fellas. You won't find him here.

One of the knights looked across the room and spotted her. Condrie recognized the man with auburn curls as the reeve's friend, a lieutenant named Jeremee. Like the others, he wore a heavy tunic of wool as black as Niarr's hair. Metallic rods and rings ran like silvery snakeskin down the length of the sleeves. Hands bare, his lower arms were sealed in leather bracers. His round cheeks spread wide in a happy demeanor. But then, everyone was happy with a glass of Ma Kielsing's gin in hand.

"There she is," Jeree exclaimed loudly. "The peacock's pet."

"I'm no . . . no . . . no one's pet, sir."

"Oh yes, you are." Jeree sucked down his drink and held out the glass for a refill. "You see, girl, you're the only person that *he* has ever treated kindly in his whole sodded life. My captain feels that he'll come back to you someday. It may take a year, it may take five, but when a dock has felt tender sentiments blossom in his heart when he had none before. . . ."

She thought of Wegdell sitting by the fire and weeping for his dead brother. Rage surged. "He . . . he . . . he's got plenty of t-t-t-tender sentiments!"

The squad of knights laughed. All five round, foreign faces tilted up to the rafters, and with mouths wide open, they guffawed. The Lord High Sheriff joined them, and soon the whole room was roaring with howls and hoots and the barking snorts of drunken men.

Ma Kielsing, with a stern expression, came to the end of the bar. "We don't shriek at our customers, Condy. I didn't think I'd have to tell you that."

"Oh, I don't mind that she's upset." The knight coughed to calm down from his fit of laughter. "She's young and innocent. That conniving peacock, he's done it to her good. I've seen it before."

Condrie stepped toward the knight. "Wh-wh-what do you know? You d-d-d-don't know him."

Jeremee told her, "Oh, I know him, pet. I know him better than you do. You see, I've been his personal guard for going on nine years now."

"N-n-nine years?" Condrie tilted her head, curiously, thinking of how often Wegdell had been in plain sight of these knights while harvesting the baron's wheat fields. "Why . . . why d-d-don't you . . . you . . . know his, uh, face?"

Jeremee frowned. "Why are you stammering?"

Niarr beside him leaned over his sleeve. "It gets worse when she's upset."

"I see," he said. "It's a sharp question she asks. The truth is, no, I don't know his face as it is now. His looks are different ever since the night of his crime."

"How . . . d-d-d-diff—?"

"You know what sort of Sagewyn he is? Has he told you?"

Condrie nodded slightly, but the knight did not take notice.

He continued, "A firebird, that's what he is."

Ma Kielsing put a hand over her own belly. "A firebird, here in my house!"

By then, every man in the parlor had fallen into silence. They all held their glasses against their chests but did not drink, did not move, did not hardly breathe. All the eyes were on Jeremee.

"I share the feeling, madam," he said. "Of all the different sorts of Sagewyn that serve the king, even the sea sirens and water nymphs, them firebirds are the worst. And of that flock, *he* was the one that I feared the most. When he's in his true form, he is a raptor bird the size of a man, and every feather is on fire. I have watched him, alone, cause blazing destruction that would have taken a whole division of foot soldiers bearing torches. I have watched him, alone, turn entire forests to ashes in a single night."

Condrie looked down, thinking of the Athel people burned out of their homes. *He did it under orders from your king.*

"But you asked about his face?" Jeremee continued. "It changes every time. After he becomes the firebird and turns himself back into a man, his human face is always different. His body stays the same. His hair is always dark, but what changes is his face."

"A handy trick," the Lord High Sheriff remarked softly.

"It was a game to him, playacting to do mischief around the castle. He made a fool of us guards plenty of times by pretending to be a stranger—a beggar at the door, a newly conscripted recruit, a cousin that I never heard of—and mocking us for how long it took us to recognize him in disguise. Trust me, pet, if you've seen him being decent, you've seen him in a performance. He is a raptor bird by nature, callous and ruthless and cruel. He is a traitor to my king and a murderer. I've got to bring him in or die trying."

"He d-d-d-d-didn't do it."

"Stop defending him," Ma Kielsing said. "Don't be a gullible, stupid girl."

Condrie met Jeremee's eyes dead on. Her jaw locked. She stared at him, hard, and wordlessly challenged him.

"I was the guard on duty that night." Jeremee tapped his thick fingers on the glass of gin. "I saw everything that he did. Pet, I hate to break your heart, but he did murder them."

"No."

"I saw it all happen with my own eyes."

Condrie kept shaking her head. *No, no, he's wrong.*

"Go on, Lieutenant," said Ma Kielsing. "Tell her what happened. It's important that she hears the truth of what sort of fellow she's been infatuated with."

Jeremee gulped until his glass was empty. He took a deep, shuddering breath and began his tale. "All of the firebirds gathered in the highest guard tower overlooking the castle's moat. They told me a lie and ordered me to stand guard at a distance. I took a position halfway down the open stairs where I could still see what they were doing but—God help me—I was too far away to intervene. I complied with their request because his brother, the reasonable one, said they were going to do some magical ceremony that we 'stones' weren't worthy to witness. That's what they call us, you know, the people who aren't hell's damned monsters: stones."

Ma Kielsing refilled his glass and spilled a few drops of gin onto the counter. Jeremee contemplated the glass but did not lift it to drink.

"They all flared up into their glory, as they call it, and that's when I knew something was wrong. They shouldn't be able to do that except by the king's command."

Condrie rubbed her fingers together. "The f-f-f-feathers in . . . in the b-b-b-box?"

"Yeah." Jeremee narrowed his eyes and looked around the room at the wondering audience. "He told you that?"

"Mmm-hmm."

"Well, that's a surprise. He doesn't like us 'stones' to know about that, but yeah, it's true. King Davarche had a tail feather plucked off each one of those unholy creatures. He kept the feathers in a magic strongbox in a secret vault that I don't rank high enough to know about. They're stuck in human form unless the feathers are near."

"I've heard legends of such things," Niarr added.

"So, when they erupted blazing wings, I thought at first they were on an assigned mission from the king. Then it struck me: no, those peckers were trying to make a break for freedom."

Jeremee stopped talking long enough to drain his glass. He wiped his mouth on the back of his hand.

"Did you . . . you. . . ." Condrie wriggled her hands as if she could grab the right words out of midair.

The blacksmith, still wearing his leather apron, finished for her, "Did you sound the alarm, Jeree?"

"Damn right, I did. I clanged that bell as hard as I could and brought everyone in boots a-running. But what could we do? You can't get near them firebirds or you burn. You can't shoot them with arrows or cast spears at them; whatever comes at them turns to cinders. Swords melt. All of them in a group like that, the heat of them started to crack the bricks."

"Why didn't they fly away?" the ferryman asked.

"I could tell they wanted to. One of them held the strongbox that contained their tail feathers. He pecked at the lock but couldn't get it open. You see, that's how my king held them bound to his will. That box has a magic charm that makes it an impossible task to remove it out of the king's possession. In other words, even hell's own monsters could not steal it off the castle's grounds. If they couldn't get that damned box open, they couldn't get their own tail feathers back, and they could never be free. I watched them go mad with fury. I don't know what that magic box is made of, but even solid iron should have melted in the heat they gave off. It held secure no matter what they did to it."

Condrie blinked at tears, imagining how desperate Wegdell must have been to save his brother and his friends from their suicide pact.

"By then, the alarm had roused the other Sagewyn—the water nymphs and silverfish who could subdue the firebirds when us mortal guards stood helpless."

"Oh no," she breathed.

"He had a choice to back down and surrender. Remember that, pet. He had a choice. At that moment, he threw the box over the battlements. I watched it splash into the moat, and oh, what a gush of steam you never saw! They all started up screeching. God, the sound of it, I'll never forget. Four of the five dissolved into cinders and ashes. All but one, the one who threw the box into the water. You see, pet, that means his own tail feather was never in the box in the first place."

He honest-to-God thought it was, Condrie wanted to say.

Jeremee's voice broke from emotion in a way Condrie had never expected of a man who wore a sword with his drinking flask. A fellow knight clapped him on the armored shoulder.

"It came out later that he had bribed and seduced his way down into the secret vault earlier that day. Obviously, he took out his own tail feather and left the others bound. That pecking at the padlock was all a performance. He lured them up there with false promises and lies. He destroyed his own flock and turned back into a man. It was dark, and he had his back to me, so I didn't see his new face. But after nine years of guarding him, I don't need to see his face. He yelled something like, 'God, look what I have done,' and I knew his voice. It was him, pet. It was him."

Condrie trembled, wanting to cry *no*, but she could not force her choked-up throat to make a sound.

"My squad and I rushed up the stairs to the tower. I ordered Weg to stand down, and he jumped. . . . He jumped off the castle's wall and dove into the moat. We all thought he drowned, at first, because firebirds can't swim. Then we saw him crawl out of the mud and run for it. He ran and kept running, and he's running still."

Condrie lowered her head. Closing her eyes, she let the tears leak down her cheeks. *He's innocent. I still believe it.*

The Lord High Sheriff leaned onto his elbow on the bar. "So, if he's in human form and you don't know his face, how will you catch him? He could be any one of the men standing right here in this room."

All the men's heads and caps nodded, looking left and right at each other.

"You've all known each other all your lives," Jeree said. "He'd be a stranger in town."

The cobbler pointed to the curtained archway behind Condrie. "Like them Athel folk who are staying upstairs."

Jeremee tilted his head to his bulky shoulder in a sort of shrug. "Not likely. They're all too quiet and modest. That firebird—oh, he's not a quiet fellow."

The wood joiner snapped his fingers. "I read the proclamation. He's got a tattoo on his chest. Is that right? Wouldn't it change like his face?"

"Nope." Jeremee took a swig of the last of his gin. "The ink is deep in his skin. His face changes, but that sunburst design will always—"

The rugmaker dropped his glass. It cracked on the floorboards and leaked its contents into a glimmering puddle. "Confound me! Is that who you've been talkin' about? The fugitive murderer on the proclamation tacked to the message post in market square is the same firebird you're chasing?"

The chandler elbowed him. "Of course! Who else did you think they was after?"

"I've seen him!"

Condrie gulped a breath.

Jeremee stood taller. "Where?"

"He was working for me, delivering rugs. I thought it was strange he didn't seem to feel cold outside. I gave him a cap and scarf. I thought he was being prideful to resist my generosity. I had to force it on him like a stubborn, spoiled child! I saw a bit of his chest under his shirt when I tucked the scarf around his neck. The tattoo . . . by th' spirits, he had a sunburst tattoo."

Jeremee grabbed the rugmaker's coat sleeve. "Where is he now?"

"I don't know, sir! I don't know. He failed to show up for work the last few days, but I let it slide. His debt was paid in full."

"Debt? What debt?"

Ma Kielsing traded silent glances with Remmie and Niarr. They held utterly silent, eyes cast down so as not to give a clue.

The rugmaker pointed to the curtained archway. "All them folk, the Athel, they needed rugs and blankets because all the beds upstairs got ruined."

Condrie began to shiver. She wanted to scream, *Stop talking!* But she dared not say a word.

Jeremee frowned in confusion. His fellow knights huddled around the rugmaker, all looking at his face from different angles.

"Why would he want to help them?" Jeree asked, slowly enunciating each word.

"He was one of them Athel folk," the rugmaker said. "A priest."

"Shit!" Jeremee blasted. "That monster has gall. After everything he's done to those poor people, to impersonate one of their holy men."

The knights burst apart and all together started for the curtained archway.

"Stop!" Ma Kielsing yelled. "He's not here. He took off a few days ago without a word."

Jeremee narrowed his gray eyes. "Why?"

"I recognized him," she said while wiping a rag over the spilled gin on the bar. "I didn't know it was him. None of us knew. He changed his appearance since that first night. The moment I got a good look at him right in the eye, well, I slammed the door on his face!"

Remmie and Niarr nodded along. "That's right, that's right, she did."

Ma Kielsing draped her fingers around the neck of a gin bottle. She held the bottle tenderly as if it were the greatest and most fragile treasure in all the world. "He's not here, Lieutenant.

The knight slowly turned in place to focus his grim frown on Condrie. "But you're still defending him."

Ma Kielsing countered, "Why are you looking at my girl like that? Do you think she's got him tucked in her apron pocket?"

"I d-d-don't know where he is," Condrie said. "That's . . . uh, that's the truth."

Jeremee came around the end of the bar. He put a heavy hand onto Condrie's shoulder. "You are under arrest, pet."

Niarr and Remmie gasped in unison. The rest of the customers shuffled backward, putting more distance between themselves and where Condrie stood. Some folks at the rear ducked out the front door, returning to the safety and obscurity of the dark, cold night. The Lord High Sheriff turned his face away and took great interest in watching the lanterns flickering at the walls.

Ma Kielsing cried, "Why? She's just a little girl."

"Those are my orders. I must bring her to be examined by My Lord Sagewyn."

Examined. Condrie started to shiver and couldn't make herself stop.

"I'm sorry," Jeremee said.

Ma Kielsing came out from behind the bar to face him. Though she barely topped the upper rim of his breastplate, she had the attitude of someone twice his size. "I'm sorry too, Jeree. You and your comrades are no longer welcome in this establishment."

Another of the footmen started to raise his fist. Jeremee caught him by the wrist.

"So it must be," he said. There was a heavy pause, and then he sounded like a knight once more. "Rest of you men, scatter into the streets of the town. Search every nook and cranny that a man could hide in. Trust me, he won't go far."

"As you command, Lieutenant." The footmen's heavy boots thudded across the floorboards and launched into the darkness.

"Well, pet, don some warm clothes. It's a short ride back to the baron's estate, but it's a damned cold night."

Condrie hesitated, looking to the woman who was the closest thing to a mother she had ever known. Ma Kielsing only burst out sobbing and pressed her apron to her face.

*

A hunting hound trotted behind, following in the horses' hoofprints. The knight Jeremee rode alongside and led Condrie's horse by the reins. Condrie clutched the saddle horn and held on tight, for she had never sat astride a horse before. And such a horse! The grand black steed was larger and heavier than any of the baron's trotters. Broad shoulders and shaggy hooves carried her at a strong pace set by her captor. They spoke very little as their horses plodded along the snow-dusted wagon road.

Why did he not call upon the other knights in the town to come along as escorts? she wondered. *Why did he only take the extra horse and a single hunting hound? Does he not wish to frighten me by surrounding me with a squad of swords and spears? Is this his warped idea of being kind?*

Fear of what lay ahead kept her warm, more than the goat's wool cloak, scarf, and mittens she wore. Yet she shivered at the memory of that other Sagewyn's piercing eyes and the way it had felt to submit to the pressure of his will. Would knowing his name be enough?

Snow began to fall out of the moonlit clouds. The flurries of wet flakes swarmed around them in the darkness like the wings of frozen moths.

"You . . . you know what he's g-g-g-going to . . . to d-d-do to me." Condrie's voice was muffled in the cold open air, and she wasn't sure he heard.

"Yeah, I know."

Jeremee faced forward, not looking at her, his face as expressionless as the horse plodding along the road.

"How can . . . can you do this . . . t-t-t-to me? Does it . . . it . . . m-mean nothing to you that I'm j-j-just a s-s-s-stupid girl? He lied to m-m-me, too."

"It does," he said, "but it can't. My duty to my king and my country will not allow it."

"Your duty?"

"Cooperate, and my lord won't hurt you," he said. "Resist him, and all the spirits of the heavens won't help you."

Soon, the snow ceased cascading out of the sky. The monochrome world divided itself into two parts—dark above and white below—and there was no color anywhere in the frosty trees. Condrie rocked in the saddle to the relentless rhythm of the horse's pace. In that eerie timelessness, devoid of human speech, the horses' snorts and the creak of the saddles droned beneath her tumultuous thoughts.

Cooperate. It sounded so simple. But now, more than before, she couldn't do it. More than Wegdell's life was at stake. She was not the only one who could be accused of harboring a fugitive. If the Sagewyn probed her memories, would he see how the Athel people had revered him as a holy man? If she resisted and failed to illuminate a trail, then could any one of the Athel be seized and violated by the eyes of that heartless Lord of Dreams? As Wegdell had explained before, the Sagewyn walked like a spider in the web of passions that connected all of the people around him. *They are angry and bitter at his deception; they would hand him over without a qualm.*

A man stepped across the road and blocked their way. The horses bobbed their heavy heads as they pulled up short.

Bundled in a shabby cloak with his head swathed in knitted scarves, Condrie couldn't see much of him. The man hunched over with bent knees, his body burdened under the weight of two sacks on his left shoulder. She assumed it was grain heading for the baron's mill.

"Move aside," Jeremee said. "In the name of the King of Xol."

"Aye, sir-ee," the man mumbled with utmost humility. He made a couple of labored steps to the mounds of fresh snow at the side of the road. As he turned to let the horses pass, Condrie saw harvest tools—a sickle and a flail—thrust into his belt.

Jeremee tugged the reins of Condrie's horse, and they started forward.

Condrie turned to look backward over her shoulder. Something about the farmer had struck her as odd, and it took a moment to form the thought. *Why does he need a sickle and a flail in the winter? What's in his sack must be already cut and threshed, ready for the mill. Why carry tools he doesn't need? It only weighs down his belt.*

They passed him, and the farmer dropped his sacks to the snowbank. She saw that he was not wearing gloves.

It's him! He's come for me! Condrie opened her mouth but said nothing.

He pulled the flail from his belt and grasped one of the rods, the other swinging free by the short leather thong that connected them. Straightening from the slouch, he rose to a full head and shoulders taller than the average farmer.

Two hops brought him to the rump of the knight's horse. Wegdell swung the flail overhead. It crashed onto Jeremee's shoulder.

The knight grunted, either from pain or surprise. But he didn't fall from the saddle.

The hunting hound barked. Paws braced wide, the hound placed itself in front of Condrie and kept barking.

Wegdell pulled back his arm for another swing of the flail. By then, Jeremee whirled his horse about. The stallion's teeth clacked against the bit as it strained to bite him.

"Pox-laced cock, ya are," Jeremee bellowed, putting special emphasis on the condescending pronoun. "Have ya ox dung for yer senses, Highwayman, to rob one of King Davarche's knights?"

"I'm not robbing you, Jeree." Wegdell grinned brightly through the threads of his knitted scarf. "I'm rescuing her."

"Well, a-swyver me sideways," Jeremee said. "I can hardly believe it. Lord Wegsemze is trying to rescue someone?"

Wegdell twirled the flail in midair like a wagon wheel with a single spoke. "Let her go, and I won't hurt you."

Condrie gripped her saddle horn, awaiting the knight's response.

"You are under arrest, my lord."

"Where's your squad to help you enforce that, Jeree?"

"Don't need one."

"It's you and me," Wegdell said, twirling the flail.

"So it is."

"Well, are you going to stay up there or come down and fight me like an honorable man?"

Instead of dismounting, Jeremee put two fingers in his mouth and blew a loud whistle. The hunting hound leaped forward with a snarl.

"Char!" Wegdell swung the flail and connected with a thud in the hound's ribs, but it did not slow the animal down. The hound leaped up and chomped onto his arm. Crying out in pain, he dropped the flail.

"Weg!" Condrie cried.

The knight drew his broadsword while he slid from the saddle. When he landed on both feet, he had his blade ready. "Back, back," he commanded, and the growling hound backed away.

Left-handed, Wegdell yanked out the sickle from his belt just in time to block the knight's overhead chop. Cheap iron rang against steel, farm tools against the king's finest. The two men went at each other with a ferocity Condrie had only seen in starving mongrels fighting over food scraps in alleyways. Equally strong arms swung and bashed but couldn't get the upper hand of the other.

Condrie saw a crossbow in the knight's saddle. She slid off her own horse and started to cross the few steps between them. The hound saw her and barked.

Jeremee glanced aside to the barking hound. In that moment, Wegdell swung his sickle and gashed into the knight's thigh. He sliced the burlap trousers at just the spot where there was a gap between the segments of his armor pieces. Jeremee grunted as he staggered. Blood dripped into the snow.

The hound lunged and nipped at Wegdell's leg from behind. He yelped in pain and wildly swung the sickle. The hound nimbly dodged.

"Yah! Go!" the knight hollered to encourage the hound.

The hound snapped again at his other leg. Wegdell danced backward to try and get away from the large animal.

Jeremee swung his broadsword at Wegdell's head. Condrie shrieked.

The flat of the blade impacted the side of his head. Wegdell staggered. Jeremee rushed in and pounded his gloved fist into the same spot at Wegdell's temple—two, three, four hard blows of the steel-studded leather knuckles.

Wegdell hunched over as he had with the sacks of grain on his shoulders. Wavering briefly, he fell face forward into the snow.

"Oh, Weg!" Condrie started toward him.

"Stay back, pet," said the knight, panting heavily. He leaned to favor his bleeding leg. He poised the tip of his broadsword between Wegdell's shoulder blades. "One more step, and you force me to kill him."

"Goddamned bird dog," Wegdell mumbled into his arms.

Jeremee leaned down to tease, "No fun being a 'stone,' is it, my lord? Should have thought of that before you murdered your flock."

*

Wegdell looked woozy when Jeremee hauled him onto his feet. The knight bound his arms behind him. A rope at the waist connected him to the knight's saddle horn.

They continued as they had before. Jeremee set the pace and led her gelding by the reins. They went slowly, for horses, but Wegdell still had to walk lively to keep up and not be dragged the whole way. The hunting hound trotted just behind his heels, snarling and ready to nip if he should slow down.

"Just curious," the knight said. "Where did you go after you left the gin joint?"

"I didn't leave. I perched on the roof. I made a nest of hay bales by the chimney stack."

Jeremee laughed. It was the first time Condrie had heard this man laugh, and it was a pleasant, friendly voice. Only this time, she couldn't share his mood. "Right above our heads! And lo, my squad is scurrying around this night looking for footprints in the snow."

"Let her go," Wegdell said.

"What did you say?"

"Let her go, Jeree. You've got me."

"Damn. Never expected to hear selflessness from you. Still keeping up pretenses, eh?" The knight turned to look at Condrie, and she saw true compassion in the sag of his pale cheeks. "Is that how you keep your hooks in this girl?"

Her legs ached from straddling the horse's broad saddle. But her complaints faded when she looked back to the tall man with blood on his face struggling to keep up with the horse.

"He could ride double, behind me," Condrie said.

"Prisoners walk."

"But have you no kindness at all? He's hurt."

"I'm hurt," Jeremee said, pointing to the bandage wrapped around his thigh.

"But—"

"Not another word, girl," said the knight.

"Save your breath, Condy." Wegdell panted a couple of times before continuing. "Jeremee hates me. He's hated me for years. I should count my blessings that he didn't kill me back there and call it an accident."

"Not that I wasn't tempted, but it woulda looked too deliberate. Everybody knows what a shitty fighter you are in human skin, and my orders are to bring you in alive if at all possible."

Condrie asked over her shoulder, "How did you know to come after me?"

"I was watching from the rooftop," Wegdell said. "I heard the singing, and I was glad that things were getting back to normal for you. Then I heard your mother wailing, 'My girl! My girl!' when they hauled you out the front door. I knew I had to do something to repay you for all you've done for me. I set off, following the road, and here I am."

Jeremee growled, "How touching. Such self-sacrifice and heroism. Too bad it's all such a crock of pigs' dung."

"It is not," Condrie exclaimed. "Why else would he risk recapture to come all the way out here and rescue me?"

"Because he knew that my lord would use you to find him, no matter where he hid. From the passion in your voice, your bond is even stronger now than it was before. May the spirits help you, girl. It's only a fool who loves him."

"You're wrong," she said. "Weg knew I wouldn't betray him, even under your lord's interrogation. He taught me a secret."

Jeremee laughed more bitterly. "Sagewyn never share their secrets."

"Shows you how much he's changed. He told me—"

"My lord's true name? Yeah, I know. I've heard the reports. Don't get cocky, girl." Jeremee gave Wegdell's rope a little tug to make him stumble, but he recovered well. "The mysteries of Sagewyn are nothing for the likes of us 'stones' to play with. If you continue to resist my lord, he will inflict a head injury upon you. I've seen it before. So when you get reduced to a drooling idiot unable to remember your own name, I hope you keep enough of your senses to blame him for promising that a mousey little girl could fight a man who is over a thousand years old and can walk into your dreams."

"I am not a mousey little girl," she said.

"Uh-huh."

"My legs hurt where your damned bird dog bit me," Wegdell piped up. "Can we stop and rest? My toes are cold. "

"You're lying. Your toes are never cold."

Wegdell countered, "Maybe I've been in human form too long."

"That's crap."

"You can't claim to understand everything about me, Jeree."

"Nine years guarding you, I think I got it."

"You could guard me for nine hundred years and not begin to understand me."

"Ha!" Jeremee huffed. "You haughty peacock."

"You lump . . . you stone."

"Don't antagonize him," Condrie said hurriedly, thinking she had to stop a fight. Neither man seemed to be escalating their verbal conflict. She concluded that this was their habitual way of conversing, by snapping at each other. "Weg, show him what kind of man you are."

"I know what kind of man he is. It's you that needs the education, girl."
The knight's horse blubbered its lips so loudly that Jeremee had to pause for a
moment. "Why don't you ask your hero about who he assaulted to get those
clothes for that disguise?"

Wegdell said, "I borrowed it from a workman's trunk. I didn't hurt
anyone."

"I'll see that fellow gets his clothes back when I've delivered you to my
lord."

*

As they approached Baron Fordon's estate, Condrie squinted into the dark
to seek out the manor house that she knew was up ahead. Silvery moonlight
illuminated the frost-dusted pine trees and the snow's fleece. The mill pond
was a perfect circle covered in ice, rimmed by the straight rods of hyssk reeds
and spindly thorn bushes. Not so long ago, threshers had pounded flails
against stacks of wheat on this very spot.

Jeremee's horse crossed the stone bridge spanning the creek. Wegdell's
boots slipped and skidded, but he managed to stay on his feet. Condrie,
riding behind them, wondered if the lieutenant might drag him the rest of
the way uphill if he fell.

The hound ran ahead. More hounds barked at their approach.

A gateway straddled the wagon road. Condrie tilted her head to assess
the fortifications. Iron bars dusted with frost curved a high arch over the
gate. A chevron-shaped shield displayed the emblem of this baron's
household: a ring of juniper flowers and a thresher's flail. *Does he think this
wall is a protection against the legions of the King of Xol?* she wondered sadly.
*If he has already welcomed foreign lords into his home as guests, I may as well be
in Davarche's kingdom through no assent of my own.*

Beyond the gateway was a square courtyard. A circular fountain at the
center was frozen over into a mirror of black glass. Jeremee led the way
around the curve of the road. Gabled windows at the front of the house had
honeycomb panes of iron grillwork with hundreds of lead glass circles; the
bluish-amber glow was the only source of color in all of the gray and white
world.

The horses perked up their heads in sensing the light and warmth of the carriage house. The quicker pace tugged at the rope. Wegdell slipped. He fell hard, twisted to one side.

"Ugh," he grunted and did not make an effort to get up.

"Are you hurt?" she asked.

"He's not fragile, girl," said Jeremee gazing down from his high saddle.

A foot soldier hopped out of the carriage house. By his youthful face, Condrie judged he was barely old enough to sit a horse. He wore the black wool jerkin and heavy boots of a soldier, but no plates of armor were riveted to his uniform. A leather glove covered only his left hand; she assumed he must have taken a glove off to eat his supper.

"Sir Jeremee," the young man cried. "You have returned alone from town?"

"Yes. I need word sent to my squad to call off the search. I bring our lord good news. Take my horses, Squire."

"As you say, sir." The foot soldier grasped the stallion's bridle. As Jeremee dismounted, the youth looked to Wegdell and widened his eyes.

"Oh yes, Squire," Jeremee said. "That's *him*."

"Him?"

"He assaulted me on the road."

"Excellently well done, sir." The squire tilted his head curiously. "He doesn't look so fearsome."

When she peeled herself off the saddle and brought her legs together, her thighs burned after so many hours. Condrie clenched her teeth against crying out. She swayed on her weak legs, still feeling the rhythm of the mighty animal that was no longer beneath her. Faltering, she forced her stiff body to move to follow the two men inside.

Jeremee grabbed a fistful of Wegdell's woolen jacket. He hoisted him to his feet and dragged him up the steps of the porch more roughly than necessary.

She wrapped the cloak around her body, but that left her feet cold in the snow. Flat leather shoes were made for walking around town, and her hose were too thin to keep her ankles warm. Condrie ascended the broad stone steps, feeling as if no one would notice if she were to tuck up her skirts and run all the way back to town.

In the foyer, a handful of knights loitered. Candlelight flickered in their glass goblets. Odors of brandywine and gin mixed with the stink of horses and wet wool uniforms. Air was trapped within octagonal walls.

"By the king's blood," one lieutenant exclaimed. "What've you got there, Jeree?"

"Him."

The knights with wet hair gawked at the prisoner. Wegdell shuffled over the terra cotta tiles. Blood smeared his handsome face. Arms were bound behind his back.

"Where is our lord?" Jeremee asked.

"Uh. . . ." Their faces turned away to the interior of the manor house. "The baron's daughter is giving a performance."

Music seeped from a connecting arch on the ground floor. Bell-like strings tapped an unfamiliar tune, unlike anything Condrie had ever heard before. It was not a rousing drinking song, a riverboat ditty, a thresher's chant, or a jig. Condrie listened closely, hoping to hear a pattern, but it sounded as if the harpist was striking the strings at random.

The mistress began to sing. Ma Kielsing had once described a good singer's voice as ocean waves, withdrawing and swelling and curling to crash decisively onto the shore. The baron's daughter had a voice more like a storm at high sea without purpose or direction.

"Well, don't just stand there, man!" Jeremee tightened his grip on the ropes that bound Wegdell's arms. "Go notify our lord that I've caught him."

"Uh, we should report to Captain Leera first. She's running late getting dressed, but I expect she should be down presently. It's proper that she should inform—"

"Protocol? You're going to make me stand here on protocol?" Jeremee shifted his weight to favor his injured leg. The bandage around his thigh had a broad stain of deep red.

Wegdell slumped forward and groaned. Condrie wondered if the home's warmth, after so long in the snow, was a shock to his human skin.

Two figures emerged at the top of the staircase. "Well, well, is this why the hounds are barking?"

The Sagewyn named Gerrawgon, the Lord of Dreams, descended the blocky steps of slate tiles jutting out of the wattle-and-daub walls. His blue-haired wife flowed gracefully down the stairs at his side. Against the earthen colors of the background, their clothes were a stark contrast: finery of vivid satins and velvets, of mismatched solids and broad stripes, of colors as vivid as a field of spring wildflowers. Gemstones of all kinds—garnets, topaz, emeralds, and sapphires—glittered on earrings, brooches, necklaces, and bracelets.

Lord Gerrawgon descended more quickly ahead of his wife. The lady stayed in the background, hesitant to reach the foot of the stairs.

Face to face, both men were the same height, but Gerrawgon had twice the girth. His velvets and furs commanded more of the floor space than Jeremee and Wegdell standing together. Yet his plump cheeks made his eyes seem small. Condrie braced herself for the inevitable gloating.

Instead, the Sagewyn asked, "How did he come to be abused?"

"He attacked me on the road, my lord, and tried to kill me. I defended myself."

Captain Leera descended from the second floor. Her black wool jerkin was brushed smooth; her cinnamon hair was washed clean; her gorget, breastplate, riveted shoulder plates, and steel bracers shined, reflecting the candlelight. As she slipped past the Sagewyn's wife and descended to the ground floor, she said, "I think there's a commendation in this for you, Jeree. Well done."

"I am honored, Captain. I relinquish the prisoner into your custody."

"Of course, Lieutenant. Go and tend to your injuries. The kitchen staff will give you anything you need."

"Thank you, Captain."

Wegdell pouted in a childish way that Condrie had never seen him behave. "He let his filthy bird dog bite me. Then he made me walk the whole way while *she* rode a horse."

Gerrawgon whirled around, outraged, and called to Jeremee, who was limping the long hallway toward the kitchen. "Is this true? You made a Sagewyn walk for hours through the snow while this larva rode a horse?"

"My lord, with all respect," Jeremee began after a sideways glance to his captain, "if I had allowed him anywhere near a saddle, knowing his equestrian skills, you wouldn't have him here right now."

"His clothing stinks," Gerrawgon seethed.

The lady spoke over her shoulder to her husband's ear but carefully avoided looking at Wegdell directly. "We can't take him to the prince in this condition. It will offend His Highness's eyes."

Jeremee halted. "His . . . His Highness is here?"

The knights standing in a semi-circle behind Wegdell gestured with their brandy goblets. Music continued from the partly open doorway down the hall. The baron's daughter squealed to reach for a high note.

"He arrived at dusk," Gerrawgon said, more to Wegdell than the astonished lieutenant in the corridor. "The musical performance is a prelude to supper. They'll be serving squab."

Condrie blinked at all of them, trying to read their expressions, trying to guess what they would say next. Where, she wondered, was the gloating, the threats, the domination? Why were the Sagewyn not treating him like an accused murderer?

"I'd prefer to have you bathed and dressed properly . . ." Gerrawgon's voice trailed off, lost in thought.

Captain Leera spoke up to fill the silence. "The prince will want to see him at once."

"I'd prefer to have you bathed and dressed presentably to appear before His Highness. . . ." Gerrawgon's voice trailed off, lost in thought.

In the midst of raven-colored coats, Wegdell hung his head. They gripped his upper arms from either side and escorted him down the hallway. She wondered if he would look back for her and try to communicate something. But he just watched his own feet plod across the ornate rugs that softened the heels of the knights' boots.

"Enjoy your last bird bath," the captain grumbled under her breath.

"Presumptive, Captain?" the Sagewyn's lady asked. "Perhaps the prince will show mercy."

"Mercy?" Rage flared in the captain's eyes. "Did *he* show mercy to the others that he slaughtered? To his own brother, a better man than he could ever hope to be?"

Lord Gerrawgon raised a hand, signaling silence. The captain humbly lowered her eyes. He spoke aside to Condrie, "Lord Wegsemze's brother voiced intentions to be the captain's betrothed."

"Betrothed?" Condrie repeated.

"That is, if he could persuade the king to grant permission."

Captain Leera said, "It was not a childish lust, as you've been feeling for him the last few months. No, ours was the purest sort of spiritual love that troubadours celebrate in song. Are you beginning to understand, girl, the depravity of his crime? He robbed the world of a truly noble soul. There can be no mercy for such a sin! I hope that the prince upholds the king's judgment, and Weg will pay the ultimate price."

Lord Gerrawgon added, "Are you also hoping to get the honor of wielding the axe?"

"Yes! Yes, I am."

Condrie broke out into uncontrollable sobbing. She raised her ice-cold apron to muffle her voice, choking on tears.

The front door blew open in a rush of snowy wind. "Captain, there are some people insisting to see the kitchen girl."

"What people, Lieutenant?"

"They claim to be family and friends. . . ."

Ma Kielsing's bold voice exclaimed, "There she is!"

Condrie turned to greet the on-rushing group of women. She flung herself at Ma Kielsing's solid strength and clung to it as if a strong gust of wind would blow her away.

"Oh, my poor little girl, my girl," Ma Kielsing blubbered.

Condrie became aware of more than two hands stroking her back, more than one pair of lips kissing her head. She could not count or see because she snuggled her face into her mother's neck and blocked out the world. She smelled juniper berries and the musk of wool blankets and knew that some Athel women had come too.

Dimly, she was aware of a knight angrily saying, "Here, I told you to wait in the—"

Lord Gerrawgon ordered, "Allow them the indulgence, Lieutenant. After all, we've caught our quarry. I have no more use for this little larva."

*

When Condrie came before the Prince of Xol, she was not as nervous as she expected to be. Even the knights in armor were as familiar as well as the folk of the village . . . all except for the female captain whom Wegdell had been conspicuously silent about. Now Condrie knew why. He hadn't wanted her to know that Captain Leera Vilbyss had been betrothed to his brother—practically his sister-in-law. *More lies. More deception.*

She found the courage to stand without her legs quivering in the grand reception hall of the baron's manor house. The atrium soared to a vaulted ceiling three stories high to create a breathtaking open space unbroken from the ground floor to the rafters of the roof. She felt dizzy gazing up at the ribbed crossbeams as high above her as the boughs of a sycamore tree. Fluted columns were hewn from solid trunks of pine and gave the feeling of walking a forest path. Jasmine vines grew out of planter boxes and spiraled around the columns, their white flowers a pungent and pleasing scent.

At one end of the chamber was the lord's banquet table. Except no feast was being served at the moment. The table's dark planks were barren, devoid of platters or bowls. Several people sat at the table. Condrie counted eight noblemen in high-backed chairs turned to face out to the room. Her eyes roved over their velvet finery, their jeweled necklaces and rings. She wondered which of them was Baron Fordon, which of them were his vassals in attendance, and which of them was the Prince of Xol.

One fellow stood up at the end of the table. He held a parchment. He looked sideways for an imperceptible nod of permission from the others, cleared his throat, and began to recite from the paper in his hands.

"Condrie, widow of Mister Sagmus ulb Annalis, daughter of . . . oh, it's blank here. Would you help us fill in your father's name later?" He cleared his throat again. "The charges against you are as follows. Concealing and harboring a fugitive from a capital crime. Giving false account to duly authorized officers of Davarche, the First King of Xol. Resisting interrogation by a lord of the Sagewyn and assault upon his person."

Assault? Condrie thought. *By calling his name to break myself out of his grasp, did I assault him?*

"I have here . . ." the scribe fumbled through some papers, ". . . several petitions on your behalf. Baron Jonvil of Rivertown Manor, Lieutenant Jeremee born of Goodman Aigrue, and Captain Leera born to the House of Vilbyss have all attested to your youth, inexperience, and vulnerability to the cunning manipulations of Lord Wegsemze the Sagewyn. Our lord Baron

Fordon and the Crown Prince of Xol have both reviewed these petitions carefully. Do you have anything to say in your own defense?"

Condrie raised her head at the prompt. Only one of the lords, a slender, youthful man, was looking down and fiddling with his jeweled rings. He had the air of someone who was bored and wished he could be somewhere else. He had a massive mane of black curls that seemed too much of a load for his lithe body to hold.

"I . . . I . . . I . . . always b-b-b-believed—"

The scribe interrupted, "Could you speak more loudly, please? We cannot hear you."

Condrie took a breath and raised her voice as if to shout across the bustling marketplace in town. "I . . . I. . . ."

Ma Kielsing put an arm around Condrie's waist, holding her warmly. "My girl has a frailty that causes her tongue to tangle. May I speak on her behalf? As I understand from observing the situation, she naively believed that he was innocent and wrongly accused of murdering those people. That's why she helped him evade what she wrongly thought to be persecution. With all respect, considering that the Council of Barons has not formally assented to pledge allegiance to the King of Xol, it means that Condrie was not under obligation to obey His Majesty's knights at the time of her giving hospitality and refuge to a stranger in need."

The scribe sat down and started writing notes in a ledger.

"Let me state for the record," said a portly, older man that Condrie assumed to be Baron Fordon. "This woman named Ma Kielsing is known to me. Her reputation as a fair and sensible businesswoman is renowned across the territory. I respectfully propose that His Highness accept her testimony and, furthermore, show leniency to this love-addled girl. I plead with you, sir, to grant her clemency from all charges."

The prince stood up but didn't seem much taller than he had been sitting down. He had weak posture, a man who had spent more time reclining in chairs than standing on his own two feet. Condrie wondered how old he was, for she was unfamiliar with the royal family. Twenty-five, perhaps.

"The Lord Prince who standeth before thee . . ." he began in a pipey voice that Condrie could barely hear. She mused, *No one dares ask him to speak more loudly, do they?* ". . . doth acknowledge from firsthand witness the skill of Lord Wegsemze's persuasive charms and stipulates that a puerile and naive girl such as thee would be deluded by his manipulations."

Condrie frowned and looked to her mother for a translation. "He believes you," Ma Kielsing whispered.

"My august personage doth magnanimously sympathize with thy tender heart's victimization. Nevertheless, the Lord Prince who standeth before thee cannot condone such disrespectful behaviors as thou hast demonstrated toward duly appointed officers of His Majestic Existence, my father Davarche the Peacemaker, the Bringer of Light, the Founder of the Kingdom of Xol—may the dynasty reign in peace and prosperity for a thousand upon ten thousand years."

"Please fo-fo-forgive me." Condrie sank to her knees on the hard tile floor. "I was a s-s-s-s-stupid girl."

Ma Kielsing and all the other women in the group joined her in sinking to their knees as well.

The prince waved his hand in a slow, sweeping gesture. His fingers twinkled with dark gems over rosy pink gloves. "If thou but makest reparation in a tangible form, thy offenses shall be forgiven, thy transgressions expunged. The sum of fifty silver coins . . ."

Ma Kielsing nodded firmly. Condrie could see in her eyes the tallying of the tavern's coffers.

". . . is to be provided to Lord Madrein here as a duly authorized deputy treasurer of the king. If thou art unable to pay this sum, thou shalt be required to provide six months of domestic service at the castle of the king."

Her mother announced, "We are able to pay the sum, my lord."

The scribes noted this and said, "Well, what are you still standing there for? You're dismissed. Go."

Condrie bowed and then spun about to hug her.

"It's over, girl," Ma Kielsing said.

The women around her smiled and clapped her back. As a group, they turned to leave.

More knights entered the grand hall. Condrie's glee melted away. She knew before she saw him that the next prisoner was being brought for judgment.

Her mother pulled her aside. Knights tromped past with that grim man in their midst. Slouching like before, head down, he looked at no one and nothing but his own feet. Wegdell was more filthy than she remembered, as no one had allowed him to change out of his blood-spattered shirt.

"Let's go, girl."

Condrie resisted the pull. "I want to hear, Ma. I want to know what they're going to do to him."

The baron himself stood up for Wegdell, something he had not done for her. He recited from a parchment scroll mounted on shiny brass rods. "Lord Wegsemze the Sagewyn, the charges against you are as follows. Mass murder of four Sagewyn, including your own brother, with malice aforethought. Treason against your lord and king, Davarche the Peacemaker. Disobeying a royal order of execution. And evading the implementation of your sentence which was decided after a fair trial and royal judgment."

"Fair trial?" Condrie whispered under her breath. "He wasn't even there to face his accusers."

The baron lifted more sheets of parchment off the table. "In addition, I have statements here from Captain Leera, born to the House of Vilbyss, and her squadron of knights. You have incurred the following charges. An act of arson which resulted in extensive damages to a reputable place of commerce in the Riverfront Town."

Condrie thought, *No, they can't mean to blame him for the fire at the tavern.*

"Physical assault upon numerous officers in the performance of their duty to the king. Assault upon the Lord of Dreams, both in the physical realm and in the realm of spirits while evading pursuit. And adultery."

Wegdell raised his head at that last one.

The baron sat down.

The Prince of Xol leaned a hand on the table to address Wegdell directly. "Weg, my friend, you understand that the reading of these charges is a perfunctory exercise. You have already been tried and condemned. My father has signed your death warrant. It's embossed in gold and sealed with wax. As much as I wish to extend the hand of mercy, there is nothing in my authority to save you now."

Wegdell merely nodded, looking down at the floor.

"We shall require the hours of this night," the prince told him, "to bless and purify your executioner."

Wegdell snapped his head to the left, to stare at the captain with the cinnamon hair. Leera had washed and brushed her locks with care, in contrast with her black wool jerkin. She nodded, very slightly, holding in what must have been immense glee. Condrie saw a twinge of a painful frown before he dropped his head forward.

"Come the dawn of the morrow, you shall be brought to a consecrated place. There, your head shall be separated from your body. Your remains shall be cast into a bonfire, reduced to ash, and scattered to the winds of winter without ceremony of burial. So is the judgment of your lord and king. So shall it be."

Condrie felt chills at the way he was standing, his head bent and his neck so white and clean and exposed. It was as if he awaited the axe at this moment.

A whimper squeaked out of her throat that, in the utter silence, echoed everywhere. Ma Kielsing hugged her. Everybody heard it and turned around. Even Wegdell looked at her. She only had a glimpse of his moist blue eyes before the knights dragged him away with his hands bound behind his back.

*

The sleeping pads in the guestroom weren't soft, but the room was warm with a stone fireplace. The women gathered around: Ma Kielsing, Niarr, Violet, and Amber. They dined on cheese, dark bread, and flagons of ale. Condrie begged off, saying she was exhausted, and lay down. Pretending to sleep, she listened to their conversation without interest and could only think of how he had looked so lost and alone.

Ma Kielsing gently patted her Condrie's head. "Snowstorm be damned. We'll get you out of here and on the road home tomorrow."

Amber said, "I'm staying to watch."

"Oh!" Niarr gasped. "How could you? Even though I hadn't met him before, I don't think I could stomach it."

"You haven't seen what I've seen," the Athel girl replied. Small and thin and dark, she resembled a strip of rawhide shriveled in the sun. "What can be done to human flesh? A beheading is nothing to me."

"Poor child," said Ma Kielsing. "He hurt you, too?"

"In his mind, a priest—a holy man—was just a disguise. To us, what he has done is an unforgivable sacrilege."

"That's a Sagewyn," Niarr said. "They think they're gods in human form. He probably knew exactly what he was doing to you people. That's what made it so effective a disguise for him. And he didn't care how it would hurt you."

Violet added, "He seemed so sincere. So kind. It's hard to believe you can fake those kinds of feelings."

Niarr laughed loudly in a few bursts. Then she sucked up her breath so she could talk. "He's a good whore."

Condrie rolled onto her back. "All S-S-Sagewyn are . . . whores to that k-k-k-king."

Ma Kielsing laughed more quietly. "They just don't know it."

The Athel girl clamped a hand over her mouth, but her round, dark eyes—which were big in her thin face—seemed to smile.

Condrie explained, "They m-m-made a suicide p-p-pact. They wanted . . . they wanted . . . out."

Ma Kielsing stroked her forehead, smoothing the stray locks of hair off Condrie's face. "Is that what he told you, sweetie?"

"I know, I know, I know, it could be a . . . a lie, Ma."

"Could be?" Niarr echoed.

"Or, if it's true. . . ."

The other women in the room groaned in unison.

Condrie sat up in bed to speak loudly against the drone of the chorus. "If it's t-t-t-true, it means . . . it means someone else . . . p-p-plo- . . . p-p-p-plo- . . ."

"Plotted to . . . ?" Niarr began.

"Plotted to make it g-g-g-go wrong!" Condrie finished, gasping with the effort.

Ma Kielsing nodded, quietly watching her. "Go on."

"So . . . so he'd be the . . . the only one s-s-s-s-standing."

"Who would do such a thing?" Niarr asked. "Who would gain anything from slaughtering a bunch of Sagewyn and leaving one to take the blame?"

Condrie started counting on her fingers, naming the suspects one by one in her mind. The Lord of Dreams Gerrawgon. His wife, the blue-haired bog blythe. Another of the legion of Sagewyn who served King Davarche. Someone in the king's court. The prince or one of the land barons. The king himself?

Violet put her hand over Condrie's hand. "It isn't your responsibility to help him."

Ma Kielsing agreed, "Let him go, sweetie."

Condrie shook her head, looking down. Her brown hair hung in thin, weak strings with raggy ends. Once, her hair had been touched by him and turned to gold. "I . . . I . . . want to see him, Ma."

"No."

"P-p-p-please? We argued. I need to . . . to say goodbye."

Ma Kielsing pulled Condrie into a tight hug and smothered out the world. "Dear girl, I know how you feel. Angry words give birth to regrets. When he dies, you won't have a chance to make peace. If you don't make peace, you'll carry sorrow for the rest of your life. You've enough sorrow to bear already for one so young."

"He may haunt you," Violet added. "The ghost of a Sagewyn—who knows what it can do? I agree, you need to make peace with him."

"But," her mother said, "how could we arrange it? He's not allowed visitors."

Niarr said, "Maybe I could talk to Jeremee." Aside, to the other two women, she explained, "He used to be my regular customer until Mama got angry at him for arresting Condy."

Ma Kielsing let go of Condrie. "Tell Jeremee that he can reestablish credit at my house in exchange for a small favor."

Smiling bright, turning on the glow already, Niarr got up and headed for her basket of cosmetics. "Can't let him see me like this."

*

Niarr led the way downstairs and continued down on the way to the wine cellar. Condrie dogged her heels, and the other women followed close behind. Going down the narrow stairwell felt, to Condrie, like being swallowed by a giant stone snake. The only light in the world came from Niarr holding a candlestick on a brass saucer. Its flame flickered as they hurried down the creaky stairs. Shadows danced on the cold stone walls.

The stairs ended at a wooden door. A large man stood guard in the shadows.

Jeremee whispered, "You can say goodbye, but make it quick. I'm risking my commission for this."

"I'll make it up to you," Niarr said in her best bedroom voice, and she kissed him. The knight closed his eyes to relish the tenderness on his face, the only part of his armor-clad body that was soft.

"Later," Ma Kielsing urged.

Not by choice, but by time constraint, he pulled back and hissed, "Hurry!"

Condrie went first, unafraid, to the bolted oak door. A tiny hinged flap was at a man's eye level, too high for Condrie to peep through without going up on her toes. Jeremee opened the flap with his fingertips and called inside, "You. Hey, Weg. You've got a visitor."

Jeremee unhooked a brass hoop from his belt that held several rod-like keys as large as kitchen tongs. He twisted one into an iron padlock and hauled open the huge, solid door.

Condrie cringed at the prospect of going into that dark place. Like the root cellar under the floor of her own kitchen, she wondered if the baron's wine cellar might be haunted. In a way, she mused, it was—by a Sagewyn. By habit, she clutched the blue clay bell around her neck, the sound of which was supposed to chase off angry ghosts and evil spirits.

She stepped inside, into the chilly air that bore the faint aroma of oak barrels and fermented fruit. A single glass lantern illuminated the space where he sat on the floor.

Wegdell rose to his feet as the women entered. He looked as unkempt as he had in the hall of judgment, but his demeanor was as calm as a host welcoming an invited guest.

"Condy, my dear girl, what are you doing here?"

"I wanted to say goodbye, and—"

"Stop!" Her mother held out an arm as a barrier between them. "Stop right there. Where did you learn your manners, sir?"

Niarr quipped, "From lordship school?"

"What?" His pleasantness dimmed. Condrie saw the fierceness in his blue eyes now and the proud carriage of his tall body. He loomed a full head and chest over her stout mother, but that didn't daunt her in the least.

Ma Kielsing continued, "After the hell you've put my girl through these past months, the first words out of your mouth should be an expression of sincere and humble gratitude for saving your sodded carcass."

"Even my clients say thanks," Niarr remarked. "And I don't risk my life for them."

Condrie sighed. The last thing she wanted was for this to dissolve into a group debate. "Mama, Niarr—everyone, could I speak with him alone, please?"

"Sorry, girl, but I don't think that would be wise."

His eyes snapped left and right, as if deciding which one to take on first. "I'll have you know, I do deeply appreciate everything that Condy has done for me."

Ma Kielsing put her hands on her hips. "'Appreciate'? I appreciate a fine pair of shoes. You owe her a damned sight more than your appreciation."

Condrie sighed. "Mama, please."

Her eyes met Wegdell's, and they had a moment of understanding.

"I regret that we argued," he said.

"So do I."

"What you asked me to say. . . . What's in my heart is not easy for me to say. No one in my life—firebird or human folk—has ever asked me to say it."

"I know."

Wegdell spoke more gently, never looking away, staring into Condrie's eyes as if there were only the two of them in the world. Her heart thumped and pattered, and she could hardly breathe.

"The apology that I owe you," he said, "is for being so rude and insulting. It is not an easy thing for a bird of prey to admit that he is capable of human sentiments. I got angry that you asked. I wanted to push you away, so I hurt you—deeply. I'm sorry."

Ma Kielsing grunted her reluctant approval. Niarr, the echo, murmured, "Damn, he's good."

Wegdell snapped his attention to her. "I'm not trying to be 'good.' I'm being sincere. It's not easy, so could I have a little quiet, please? Thank you."

Condrie never looked away from him. Stray locks of straight black hair crossed his brow. Flecks of dirt clung to his cheek. A few days' worth of stubble roughened his jaw. How much his noble appearance had decayed from the first night she saw him, but his eyes had not changed.

"You accused me of being more of a cold-hearted bird of prey than a man. I am ashamed to admit, yes, it's true. I do manipulate people who view this human skin as attractive. It's how I've learned to behave. As a fire bird, I soared above and never looked back at the destruction I had caused. Until I met you, it was never important to me that I made girls weep."

Condrie laid a hand to his warm cheek. "I know. I know."

The other women breathed softly, transfixed by his words.

"I've told you secrets that I've never told to anyone else. I was trying to behave better, as my brother would have done. Yigs was the better one. . . . He was modest and thoughtful and kind. I wish you could have known him. Every day, I aspire to be more like him, and I fail."

He rested his hand over Condrie's hand that still lay on his cheek. He stared at her so intently, without blinking, that her eyes hurt to hold his gaze.

"Isn't there anything else we can do?" Condrie asked.

Wegdell grinned that wide, sparkling grin that had taken her breath away the first day. "Don't risk yourself any further for my sake. I'm sorry that I've been clinging to you when saving my life should not be your responsibility. I'm resigned to my fate now. Whether it's justice or not . . . whether the truth of my innocence is discovered or not . . . it no longer matters. This ending is the best outcome for which I could ever hope. At last, I shall be unbound from the king's will."

Tears bubbled up to her eyes. "How can you be so calm? Aren't you afraid?"

"I shall be at peace. I won't be the king's tool of war anymore. My powers won't be used to hurt anyone ever again. It's what my brother wanted."

With trembling fingers, Condrie untied the leather thong around her neck. She gave him the blue clay bell. He received it tenderly and stroked the glazed side. "Tenmarkian blue," he murmured.

"No," she said. "The clay bell keeps away angry ghosts and evil spirits."

"I'll have no use for it after tomorrow." He tried to hand it back, but she pressed his hands into his chest where she knew the sunburst tattoo lay. Condrie inhaled the smell of him. Although his clothes reeked from the scent of his human form, it was *his* odor, his body, like the garlic and other spices she put into stew, pungent and yet compelling.

"Go home, Condy," he softly said. "Don't stay to watch. The only way I'll have the courage to get through this is if I know you're not watching."

His hands gently pushed her off, and Condrie slowly backed away from him. Her mother's stout but stronger body embraced her. "Come, girl. Let's go home."

Niarr paused to say to him, "You've got a seed of decency in you. Too bad there's no time to have it blossom."

"Thank you. And take good care of her."

"We will."

Condrie's feet grew heavier and heavier. At the threshold of the door, she stopped. "Mama, I . . . I . . . I want to stay a little more. Just one night. Just *this* night. He shouldn't be alone."

Ma Kielsing turned her face away, looking outward to the dim stone corridor. The bright candle that Niarr held cast a flickering orange glow on her mother's pale cheeks.

"I'm not sure if I agree with letting you stay, but I understand you wanting to give comfort and solace to a condemned man."

"Thank you, Mama. I'll see you in the morning."

The women filed out to be swallowed into the shadows. They murmured thanks to Jeremee for risking a reprimand from his superior officers. Their hushed voices slowly faded as the women once more journeyed up through the darkness.

*

"You're not planning to spend the entire night with me, are you?"

Condrie turned to face him. One glass lantern, hanging on a hook, turned his face and the nearby wine barrels to varying hues of green. Everything beyond his arm's reach was darkness.

"Don't you want someone to comfort you?"

"Well, of course I appreciate it," he said. "The night's going to be very long and boring, waiting for . . . uh, for the dawn."

"Boring?" Condrie took a step toward him. She studied his face—the eyes that she knew so well. "Why aren't you more distraught? I saw more panic in your eyes the first night we met."

He turned his back on the lamp and all his face went into shadows. "Perhaps I've made peace with my fate."

"Tell me the truth," she said. "Tell me the real reason why you don't want me spending this night with you, and I'll go back upstairs."

"It breaks my heart to see you saddened and to know that I am the cause of it."

Condrie stepped closer to him. "I don't believe you. I think you've got a secret plan."

Wegdell nodded slowly. "I see. You assume that I'm planning an escape?"

"Yes."

"Are you sure you're not a Sagewyn too? Because . . ." he suddenly grinned, his teeth catching a glint of light in the darkness, ". . . you're absolutely right."

That smile . . . Condrie's hand balled into a fist. She extended her arm to its full length, straight up, to pop him in the nose.

"Ow!" Wegdell grabbed his face as he stepped back. "What did you do that for?"

"You liar," she shouted. "I felt sorry for you spending your last night alone, and you just want me out of the way!"

He dabbed his hand to his nose and checked his fingertips for blood. "Calm down."

"Shut your damned lying mouth! Everything you say is a trick, and I'm the one who always pays the price."

The blue clay bell she had given him was on his neck. Tenmarkian blue. It had no real value; it was a cheap trinket purchased off a merchant's pushcart. Yet she felt a surge of rage at her past self for giving away her only lucky charm. She dove for it with both hands, clutching it as if were the finest diamond. She tugged on the string, forcing him to bend down. "Give me that back. Give it back!"

"Stop pulling so hard, and I can untie the knot. All right?" He raised his arms to fiddle with the thong at the back of his neck. The whole time, she tugged and tugged.

The string came loose. Condrie lost her grip on it. The clay bell crashed onto the stone floor. She went absolutely still, staring at the fragments. Glazed blue on the outside, the ceramic was a pebbly gray on the inside.

"Oh, what a shame," he said.

Condrie whirled about to shout at him, "Don't say it if you don't mean it!"

"I do."

"No, you don't. People are just stones to you, like pegs on a Gish board." Condrie flapped her hands in the air as if she were manipulating the pegs of a nobleman's game. "All that sweet stuff you said to me just now—was any of it true? It's not that you don't want me to watch you die, but you don't want me to see...." *Your escape.*

Wegdell rushed forward and put his fingers across her mouth. "Quiet."

Condrie twisted free. "Don't tell me to be quiet."

He got fierce as she'd never seen him before. Wegdell tugged her, stumbling and skipping, over to the wall behind the racks of wine barrels. He pressed her against the stone and bent down to her height to talk straight into her face.

"That door is solid oak, true, but voices carry. Please, please be quiet."

Condrie's lower lip trembled. "What do I do now? It's fine for you to escape, but I'm the one who pays the price. He'll interrogate me again. That man . . . I don't think I can stomach his touch again."

"I wouldn't let Gerrie hurt you again. I owe you that much."

"I don't believe you."

Wegdell straightened his back on the inhale. He got very tall and aloof. He took a moment to scratch his head vigorously, and then he issued a noble-sounding command.

"Sit down."

"I don't feel like sitting down, my lord."

"I know," he said, continuing to scratch his scalp. "That's why you need to sit down."

Condrie felt incredibly weary under his cold, steady stare. Her burst of anger faded, and the long ordeal of the past few days weighed upon her. She cooperated, folding her legs into her skirts. She settled cross-legged on the floor.

Wegdell sank down to sit on his heels beside her. "Please calm down. Your situation is not as bleak as you think." Then he stopped again to scratch his head, just behind the ear, digging down deep into the scalp until she was sure he would draw blood.

"I guess so," she agreed. "It could be worse."

"That's right."

"I could have hair lice."

"Exactly." Wegdell's other hand went to the nape of his neck and scrubbed. ". . . What did you say?"

She reached up and clamped her hands onto his head. Gentle pressure coaxed him into looking down and exposing the nape of his neck. She dug her fingers into his thick hair and pried the strands open to the roots. There was enough glow from the lantern for her to see the nits: a neat cluster of granular white jewels close to the scalp. She pinched one and slowly drew it out like a tiny pearl bead on a string. Cupping her palm underneath, she opened her fingers for him to see.

"Oh char," he moaned. "They gave me that filthy blanket."

Condrie flicked the nit to the floor.

"As I was saying. . . ." He put a hand on her knee, and she was too weary to push it off. "I am truly grateful for everything you have done for me, and I am truly sorry for everything that you've suffered because of me. In my planning, I have given a great deal of thought to your welfare."

"Have you, now?"

"I'm the one they want. The king has no use for a plain human girl. No harm will come to you or the tavern wenches after I've gone."

"How can you say that? What about *him*? He'll use me to find you, like before."

"No, he won't," Wegdell said through his grin. "I'm taking *her* with me."

"Have you gone completely daft?"

"She's a bog blythe, remember? Immy can obscure my location if we're together, even if he tries to seek me out. Water is her element. She distorts things from view. Have you ever viewed a straight stick seem to bend if put into a jar of water?"

"Are you sure she'll run away with you? Has she said she loves you?"

Wegdell shook his head while he scratched. "I never asked about love. Even though she enjoys kissing me, I knew 'love' would never be enough to get her to betray her lord and husband. I needed to invent a more compelling motivation to ply her into treason."

"What lies did you tell her?"

He paused for effect, or perhaps he was genuinely reluctant to say it. "I promised Immy her most secret desire: her freedom. I said that, when I was in the king's secret vault getting the box, I also saw the object that the king holds to keep her in bondage to him."

"Did you?"

"No, but I'm reasonably sure it's most likely to be there. Where else would he keep it? It's a small vial of pond water from the pond where she originated. If I have more time, I'm sure I can find it among all the things cluttering his vault."

Condrie asked, "And if you fail to keep your promise?"

He got real grim. "Then I have no doubt she'll go into a rage and kill me in the most agonizing way possible. Firebirds aren't meant to drown."

*

The hours of the night wore on. He taught her to play a game of squares on the floor with hay and pebbles. When she got bored of him winning every round, he found a basket of corks on a top shelf. "These could be pegs," he said. "I could improvise a Gish board. Have you ever played Eights-of-Gish?"

"No," she said. "I never bothered to learn tabletop games, just as you've never learned to make a loaf of bread or churn butter or pluck a roastin' pheasant—"

Wegdell held up a hand to request a pause. "I don't eat poultry. It's a matter of principle, you understand."

"You know what I mean to say." Condrie folded her arms. "I'm tired of playing only the games that you know. It puts me at a disadvantage, and it's not fun."

Wegdell put aside the box of wine corks. "Perhaps we could pass the time doing something else that you'd enjoy more. What would you like to do?"

A quiet moment passed between them. She smiled faintly to imagine the Sagewyn's lady walking in on them kissing, for a change, when she would be coming to rescue him. Would she get into a jealous rage, stomp off in a huff, get spiteful, and leave him to die? Condrie licked her dry lips and looked away to the racks of wine barrels.

Wegdell scratched his head. "Surely you know some games," he said, breaking the silence. "Teach me one of yours."

Condrie thought about it for a moment. She had not played very many games except for dice and coin toss, and they did not have any on hand. Then she thought about her pick-pocketing friend Kin, who knew an endless number of riddles. She was never sure if he had heard them in the streets or was clever enough to make them up himself.

"What gets full without eating?" she asked.

"The moon."

"What sort of bird has no bones?"

"The lily flower called Bird-of-Dawn," he said.

"How can you hold an oak tree in the palm of your hand?"

"Acorn."

Condrie clenched her jaw. "This isn't fun either."

"I'm sorry, love, but I was trained in witty banter by the jesters of the king's court. They tell riddles in stanzas of rhyming, metered verse."

"Oh."

The lantern was running low on oil by this time, and the wine cellar was becoming darker. Condrie stared at the shadowy corners, hearing scuttle sounds that she hoped were just mice and cockroaches. She pulled her knees up to her chest and looked to the shards of the broken clay bell on the floor. *Only babies are afraid of wicked spirits and shadow wraiths,* she told herself. *There's nothing in the dark that isn't in the light.*

"Sing to me," she said. "Everyone says you have a good voice. I'd like to hear it."

"Surely I've sung for you before?" he asked.

"No," she said. "Never."

"My apologies. What would you like to hear?"

"A funny ballad that will make me laugh. I haven't laughed in so long. Sing me something like what you sang for the caravans."

He scratched his head vigorously as he thought about it. "How about 'The Barleyman, the Toad, and the Straw Cap'? It's got lots of verses, and you can join in at the refrain."

Condrie hugged her knees close to her chest. "I'll try, but I don't sing very well."

"Nonsense, it's easy." He cleared his throat and straightened his shoulders. "I'll teach you."

Before he could start, the flap in the door smacked open. Condrie flinched. The knight outside called, "On your feet, Weg. You've got a visitor."

He didn't get up. "There's no one I want to see."

The iron door opened with a heavy creak. A pair of knights entered carrying tin box lanterns. Light glistened brightly on their armor pieces, and their polished leather boots shined like black glass. Between them walked a woman who was a column of fine velvets twinkling with jewels, the gold-embroidered hem trailing on the floor, the hood of her cloak shrouding her head.

Her gown was a vivid hue of lavender—not purple, not mauve, not lilac—the color of apologies in the silent language of the Athel. Condrie glanced to him, wondering if he noticed it too.

"Why have you come here, Immy?" he demanded with an undertone of curiosity.

"I wanted to see you one last time." The noblewoman's voice was faint, weak, and full of emotion that sounded too good to be fake. Her own guts began to congeal. Clearly this was not the first step in the rescue.

"Well, now you've seen me. Go back to your darling husband. Goodbye, Immy."

"Oh, Weg." She pressed a lace-edged handkerchief to her face. "I hate to see you like this. I wish I could do something to help you."

Wegdell lowered his head, humble, yet still not devastated as he should be if he understood what she was saying. Condrie wanted to poke his ribs and insist, *Listen, you bird brain. This isn't the rescue! She just said she can't help you.*

"Your sympathy is appreciated, Immy," he said. "But alas, my fate is sealed by the hand of the king himself. At sundown, I meet my destiny."

"You're so brave," she responded. "It isn't right that a diamond should be shattered into dust by a stone."

He nodded, still humble.

"I wish I knew what to do," the Sagewyn's wife said. "Gerrie suspects that I might try to do something sentimental and foolish, like this pet of yours has done. I'm being watched every moment."

"I understand," he said calmly.

Condrie could not hold her silence any longer. "No, I don't think you do. Can't you hear what she's saying? She's being watched every moment. Get it? She's being watched!"

Wegdell's blue eyes flared wide. He leaped to his feet. At his sudden movement, the knights drew their broadswords. Three sharp steel blades aimed at his belly, and he halted.

"Forgive me," the noblewoman pleaded. "I am very fond of you. I shall miss you terribly."

"Immy?" Now his voice cracked with emotion. Condrie shuddered.

The woman turned, and her trailing gown swept dirty hay around the floor. Cockroaches scurried away from the disturbance.

The noblewoman moaned sobs into her velvet gloves. She exited, weeping. The two knights turned to follow her.

"Immy!" Wegdell's shout echoed between the wine barrels. He rushed at the door as they hauled it closed. When it slammed into the frame, he collapsed against it and pounded on the thick boards with his fists.

Condrie sat still to watch him rail and rage against the door. After he'd shouted himself hoarse, he began to cry into his arms. He moaned in a high voice that sounded like a loon over a moonlit lake. The lantern, running out of oil, rapidly died down. The flicker struggled to survive at the tip of the wick.

Condrie came to him slowly and settled down next to him. He huddled into his knees with his face tucked into his bent arm.

Wordlessly, she rested her cheek on his shoulder. His arm reached to go around her. She snuggled up under his wing. Where their bodies connected was warm.

His voice broke the silence. "I'm afraid to die."

"You won't be alone," she promised as tears leaked onto her cheeks.

Wegdell kissed the top of her head. "I love you."

"You don't have to say that."

"I want to say it because I don't think I have really loved anyone until this moment."

Condrie held her breath, wondering if she should believe him this time. She thought of her friend Kin, who always gushed, 'You're my best friend in the world,' whenever she did something to help him. Then again, Kin had never faced execution. Perhaps this time, Wegdell was sincere. Perhaps he wanted to die without regrets.

*

Before long, the flap in the door slid open again. "You there, Weg, stand up and get back from the door."

"And if I refuse?" he grunted, not moving from where he sat huddled against the planks. "What'll you do, kill me?"

The man's voice outside said, "We're here to take her back upstairs. Captain's orders. You don't deserve a woman's comforting arms."

Wegdell removed his arm from her. Condrie felt the cold air rush back around her.

"No," she said. "I'm not leaving."

He stood up and strolled away to the far side of the wine rack. "Open it up, my good man. I won't make a move."

The iron hinges cranked open. Several knights entered, bearing spears and halberds. The lieutenant, wielding a drawn sword, had wheat-blond hair and the square-jawed features of a forester. Condrie recognized him as one of the spies who had labored in the wheat fields at Baron Jonvil's grist mill.

Condrie leaped to her feet and stood between the king's knights and the condemned man. "Please don't take me away. Please let me stay with him."

The blond knight blasted back at her, "Are you stupid? We're being good to you! You're not under arrest. You're free to go. Can you get that idea into the mush that fills your head? You're free! Go back upstairs and sleep in a real bed with the Madam and her gaggle of whores. Go, you pox'ed twat, before I lose my patience."

Wegdell took a step forward. "Foul-mouthed, vulgar clod. I demand you apologize to the lady."

The knight blinked, genuinely confused. "What lady?"

Condrie whirled about to face the blue eyes that sparkled with indignation. "Don't antagonize them, please. Don't make it any worse for yourself."

"How can it be any worse?" A wild desperation sparkled in his eyes.

The spear carriers leveled their halberds, the serrated, curved blades poised at the ready.

"We have orders not to kill you," said the lieutenant, slowly waving his sword back and forth. "That's a job for the executioner. But we can break your knees and drag you to the chopping block."

Wegdell spread his arms wide. "I'd like you to try."

Condrie grabbed his sleeve and cried at his shoulder. "Stop it, stop it!"

"Get behind me, Condy, and stay out of the way," he said.

"No!"

"I mean it." He flexed his long fingers. "I'm starting to feel something strange and familiar that I haven't felt in a long time. I don't understand. It's not possible."

Wegdell stiffened his shoulders where he stood. His eyes squeezed shut. His mouth opened wide, but he snorted up a sharp breath only through his nose. From his expression, holding his breath, he could almost be in pain.

"Are you all right?" She wondered if the other Sagewyn were doing something to him. "What's wrong?"

"Oh . . . oh, god of fire." He panted hard, speaking with effort. "It feels so good. So good."

Condrie let go of his sleeve. His body was even warmer than usual, like a roast of meat fresh off the grill.

The lieutenant raised his sword as he stepped toward her. "Cover me," he said to the spear carriers. "If he makes a move to attack me, stab the whore and say it was an accident."

"Get . . . behind. . . ." In the cold air of the cellar, a steamy mist rose off his bare skin. Soon, the heat grew to that of standing by a fireplace hearth.

Condrie took a step back. *Impossible*, she thought. *Is he starting to transform into a firebird? Was Immy able to help him after all?*

The lieutenant sheathed his broadsword. From his belt, he raised a miniature crossbow not much larger than a slingshot. In a quick click and a twist of the wrist, he loaded an iron bolt. "Stand down, Weg, or else—to rubbish with my orders—this goes between your eyes."

Condrie backed away. She watched him breathing hard and fast as if he were running uphill. His skin flushed to the scarlet hue of a man suffering from a fever. Mouth open, eyes squinted, his chest heaved with the effort.

"I said, stand down!" the lieutenant cried. "This is your final warning."

Each pale finger came alight like the wicks of candles. Flames spread over Wegdell's hands, becoming fiery gloves of orange and red. He flexed his wrists and the wisps of fire were like glowing feathers.

"Shit!" the lieutenant hollered. "Sound the alarm! Hurry!"

Two of the spear carriers rushed back out the door. Their shouts were muffled in the stairwell. Two remained, holding up their halberd blades on either side of their commanding officer.

The lieutenant squeezed the trigger of his little crossbow. The iron bolt launched.

Wegdell tilted his head aside. The bolt scratched his cheek as it whizzed by. The iron point clinked off the stone wall.

"Keep her nearby," the lieutenant ordered as he scrambled to reload his little crossbow. "He won't go up to full flare if she's next to him."

Condrie faced the serrated crescent blades of the long spears. She felt the rising heat at her side, and for once in her life, she did not feel afraid.

"Do it," she said. "Go."

Wegdell raised his fiery hands high overhead. He stretched high and tall, as if reaching to touch the crossbeams of the ceiling. His eyes rolled up and his eyelids fluttered. He craned back his long neck. The knot in his throat, which every man had, thinned away into nothing.

His flaming gloves turned to yellow-white. Fire dribbled down his arms. Fire poured over his shoulders. Sheets of fiery satin unrolled around his skin. His face and his human body dissolved under the feathery brightness. Condrie squinted as if looking at the noonday sun. *He's beautiful*, she thought as the heat grew.

He swept open his arms—no, his wings—and heat flooded the cellar with a rushing boom. Hot wind pushed her away. Stronger than the gust of a summer storm, the blast of heat lifted her off her feet. Condrie was thrown backward, falling sideways, and yet she felt oddly safe.

She tumbled to the brick floor. She rolled over a couple of times, like a log going downhill, until she bashed into the wall and came to a stop.

Ears ringing, she sat up and blinked to focus through the golden haze of rippling hot air.

The knights sprawled on the floor. When they did not move, she could not be sure if they were knocked senseless or dead.

Wegdell was still the same height that he had been as a man, only now he had the spindly legs and body of a crane the color of molten gold. His scarlet head, with a long, thin beak, sprouted plumes of white-hot fire. A peacock's tail of red and orange erupted out of the small of his back. The tail laid a thick swag of rippling fiery feathers that dragged at least three stick-lengths behind him.

"Run!" she cried, shouting over the crackle of fiery heat that filled the cellar. "What are you waiting for? Go!"

He looked at her and cocked his head. Though he had the face of a crane, she felt that she still knew him. He folded back his wings. He lowered his shining beak. His eye was a black dot in a fiery yellow iris. Yet strangely, it was still his eye.

"Do you understand me? You need to hurry!"

The longer he stayed, the hotter the air became. Even through her layers of skirts, she felt the stone floor becoming as hot as a bread oven. Wine simmered in the barrels and hissed fragrant steam. The fringe of her wool shawl sparkled, and she patted at herself to keep the threads from igniting.

"You . . . you're hurting me." Condrie's cheeks tingled and started to ache. "Please go."

His glowing talons stepped gingerly over the knights' bodies. He bowed his head to duck through the door. He strutted up the stairwell, his long, fiery tail sizzling up the stairs behind him.

Condrie got up to her shaking feet. She licked her chapped lips. The cellar was dim and dark without him, but the bricks were still hot.

She slowly approached the knights sprawled on the floor. She hoisted her skirts up to her knees but could not bring herself to step over them. As brutally as they had behaved, they were just simple soldiers following their lords' and their king's orders.

Sinking to her knees, Condrie touched the neck of the blond lieutenant. She felt a pulse. He breathed.

"Praises be," she whispered.

A spear carrier groaned. The other one flexed his hands.

"I've been telling you all along," Condrie said to the lieutenant's fluttering eyelids, "he's not a murderer."

From the doorway spoke a velvety, cruel voice. "Obviously he's not a murderer, you little larva."

Condrie looked up to see Lord Gerrawgon the Sagewyn standing there in all his pompous finery. He was a dizzying patchwork of brightly colored stripes and solids, velvets and satins in clashing hues of pink, orange, purple, and green. Jewels glimmered on multiple ear studs, nose rings, necklaces, finger rings, and a double row of buttons.

Upstairs, the whole house thundered with commotion. Boots thumped, running to and fro. Men shouted. Furniture crashed. Glass shattered. Women screamed.

Yet Condrie, fixed on staring into the cold gray eyes of that Lord of Dreams, could not find the strength to rise from her knees.

"You believe in his innocence?" Condrie asked, breathless.

The Sagewyn chuckled. "I don't need to 'believe' in him. I have forced him to relive that night in his dreams half a dozen times in the last few months. I have witnessed those events again and again, but I still do not understand."

"Understand what?" Condrie asked.

He carried an iron pomander hanging from a chain, like an incense burner that a Clichard priestess would use. Contained within was something that glowed bright reddish gold. *Wegdell's tail feather!*

"I don't understand who removed *this* from the king's strongbox before Weg sneaked down to the vault to steal it. Who else knew of their idiotic suicide pact? Who would have loved him enough to save *his* life, and let all the other firebirds destroy themselves? Who has been hiding it all this time, and where? More importantly, who slipped a note under my bedtime brandywine, informing me of where to find *this* stashed in a bread oven?"

Condrie shook her head with amazement. "I don't know."

"Obviously you don't know," he said with a haughty snort. "But you're not as stupid as you pretend to be. I'll have you know that I've walked this earth for over a thousand years, and I have learned to assess people's talents. You, little larva, are smarter than my wife. You're clearly smarter than Weg. I daresay you're smarter than most of those clods running around upstairs."

Condrie looked up to the ceiling. The commotion overhead had gone silent. Utterly silent.

"Ah." The lord also rolled his eyes upward. "That would be my lovely Immeirelda coming to the rescue of all those fumbling, incompetent jack-boots. How many wooden arrows did they waste shooting at him, I wonder?"

Condrie gulped. "You trust Immy?"

The Sagewyn smiled, which made his over-fed cheeks seem even more plump. "I don't need to trust my wife. I own her."

*

The Sagewyn lord gripped her by the elbow and forced her to hurry up the stairs. On the way, Condrie could not help staring at the iron pomander that he held. It squeaked as it swung on its chain, and a thin line of smoke trailed behind them. *Weg's tail feather!* If only she could get it back into the hands of its rightful owner, he would be truly free.

Condrie's flat shoes squished into a soggy, flooded carpet. Every surface in the parlor was scorched black. Pinewood paneling had warped away from the brick walls. Shreds of what were once tapestries dangled from brass rods.

Furniture had shattered, reduced to piles of fire logs. Lumps of molten glass were all that remained of lanterns. Oak shutters were cracked off their hinges, and window panes were blasted out of their iron grillwork. Snowflakes blew inside to swirl on the lingering smoke. But it was the smell that gouged into her gut and nearly made her retch. The stench of rancid pond water smothered the odor of charred wood and stone.

"Well done, my dear."

The Sagewyn released his grip on Condrie's arm. He stroked the shoulders of the lady who stood in the center of the ruined room.

Her velvet gown was drenched, ruining forever the luxurious fabric's furry nap. Her long blue hair, also dripping wet, hung in soggy strings to either side of her face.

"I washed them all outside." Immeirelda's voice sounded congested. She sniffed wetly.

"Well done, my dear. Well done." Gerrawgon looked aside to check the flagpole jammed through the door handles. "You even managed to bar the door."

"As you instructed, my lord husband," she said.

A nude man kneeled at the center of the blackened rug. He had his back to her and faced the cold stone fireplace. From the harvest time and all those weeks of watching him from behind as he swung a sickle, she recognized those shoulders. She knew the pale tone of his skin, the curve of that long spine, and the shape of those lean ribs.

"Weg?"

"I'm sorry," he said hoarsely. "I failed."

She removed her woolen shawl and draped it around his naked shoulders. "Gerrie's got your tail feather. He's holding it in his hands, right here."

"I know. I can feel it." He flexed his fingers. "But if I try to transform, she'll quench me again."

Wegdell looked up at her standing beside him. She gasped at how his face had changed. Though she had been told by Jeremee, it still startled her. The face of a stranger was pasted onto the body she knew so well. His cheekbones were higher, his jaw was more narrow, and his nose had extended and broadened. Even his ears were a different shape. Yet his eyes had not changed. Those were same blue eyes that had pleaded with her, *Help me*, on the first day he dropped into her kitchen.

From outside the room, a knight's heavy fist pounded on the door. "Open up, in the name of the king!"

Gerrawgon called out, "I have everything quite well managed, Lieutenant. Tell your men to stand down and withdraw. I am going to conduct an interrogation, and I do not wish to be disturbed."

"Are you sure about that, sir?" It was Jeremee's voice.

"You have your orders, Lieutenant!"

"As you say, sir. So shall it be."

Gerrawgon hooked the iron pomander's chain on a half-melted torch sconce nailed into the wall. "By the bones, look what you've done to this place! You've ruined every stick of very fine furniture. I was of a mind to be a gracious host and allow you to recline on a cushioned divan while I did my walk-in. . . ."

"Oh no, not again." Wegdell groaned. "I'd rather face the axe."

Condrie held his bare elbow as he got to his feet. The wool shawl slipped off his naked shoulders. He caught the shawl and held it to cover the front of his lower half.

"Listen to him." Condrie looked up to his height, for though his face had changed, he was just as tall as before. "He believes in your innocence. He wants to find out who the real murderer is just as much as we do."

"Why? Why help me?"

The Sagewyn sauntered back to him. "Because, you dim-witted peacock, there is a lying, scheming traitor running loose in the king's castle who has eluded *my* perception. I cannot allow that affront to stand."

Condrie pointed to the iron pomander hanging on the hook at the far side of the room. "Someone's been keeping it hidden somewhere all this time. Today, he put a note under Gerrie's brandywine, telling him to find it in a bread oven."

Wegdell looked to the blue-haired lady. She shook her head, saying, "If I ever had it, I surely would have found some way to deliver it to *you*, not my husband."

The cuckold Sagewyn glanced back over his shoulder at her. His frown made her cringe and back away.

"By the bones," said Gerrawgon, returning his attention to Wegdell. "Think about it, man! My duty should have been to deliver this dreadful thing to My Lord Prince for immediate transport to the king's vault. Why am I walking around with it, hmm? Why would I bring it within ten stick-lengths of the wine cellar's door if I weren't testing if this fiery feather belonged to you? And if I knew it was yours, why would I give you an opportunity to make all this damned mess in the hour before your execution?"

"He makes sense," Condrie said.

The icy light at the broken windows began to turn pink. The Sagewyn glanced aside briefly. "It will be sunrise soon. We must proceed with all haste."

"Wait," Condrie said. "Can't you tell them to delay the execution? Can't you explain why you believe he's innocent?"

"No, I cannot. I have no evidence or testimony that will refute a single word in the trial record. Neither I nor the lord prince has the authority to countermand the king's sealed order."

"Then. . . ." Condrie's mouth hung open. Words would not come.

"Yes, the execution is still on schedule. The captain is almost finished with her purification ritual, and the blacksmith is sharpening the axe."

Wegdell said, "I'll wager she plans to miss my neck deliberately on the first swing and chop off an ear. She hates me."

Condrie gave a shaky nod, recalling the woman captain's passionate grief at the death of Wegdell's brother, her betrothed. She took a deep breath to clear her mind of the distracting detail.

She said, "It seems like a strange idea, but I think we should trust him."

"I will never trust *him*," he said. "But I trust you, Condy."

"Her?" Immy cried out. "You trust this greasy little larva?"

"Yes," he said, turning on the lady. "And, as long as we're speaking honestly, I *don't* enjoy the sensation of being quenched. I do not enjoy it and I never have . . . not one little bit."

"Oh!" The lady dashed across the room. She stood by the smashed window and, weeping into her hands, let the moth-like snowflakes swirl around her.

Gerrawgon extended his hand like a gracious host. "Would you be comfortable sitting at the hearth side?"

"Always."

Wegdell strolled to the fireplace of densely packed river stones that dominated most of the wall. Granite chunks of blue, white, and gray were glazed with a layer of black soot. Warmth still radiated from the stones.

"You too, larva," said the lord.

Condrie folded her arms. "I have a name."

"I'm quite aware of that." The lord pointed to the hearth. "Sit beside him, please."

"Let her go, Gerrie." Wegdell pulled up his feet and crossed his bare legs. The wool shawl covered his lap, but not much else.

"Sit."

Condrie obeyed. She settled onto the hearth stones and patted her apron smooth over her layers of skirts.

The Sagewyn put his right hand against Wegdell's cheek. He leaned in close to the man's nose and peered deeply into his blue eyes. "Ah, yes, just as I expected. When you've freshly transformed into the form of a man, you are weakened. You're as pliable as I've ever seen you be."

"Just do it already and get it over with."

"Mmm-mmm," the Sagewyn hummed a droning tone from low in his throat.

Wegdell's caramel skin went pale as a corpse. His lips turned purple. His eyes rolled up in his head.

With his right hand still on Wegdell's cheek, Gerrawgon reached his left hand to Condrie.

"You . . . you. . . ." The lord spoke with some effort, his eyes half-closed and rambling in a singsong as if talking in his sleep. "You resisted before, and it was . . . it was unpleasant for you. If you calm yourself and allow me. . . . Don't fight. . . ."

"I understand," she said. "I'm ready."

Condrie squinted and watched through her eyelashes as he descended from his height. He put the tip of his nose near hers and held it. This close, she couldn't focus properly, and his eyes appeared to merge into one at the center of his forehead.

She cringed away, but he held her. On reflex, she pressed her hands against his chest, but he still held her. She bent her knees, trying to slide down off the hearth to get away, but he wouldn't let go. The harder it was to breathe, the stronger her dizziness became. She squinted her eyes shut. The room spun around like riding a sled on an icy pond. In a haze of purplish and green sparkles, her vision went pure white.

*

Condrie opened her mouth for a big inhale. Only then was she aware of standing knee-deep in white mist.

Overhead, the sky was black and cloudless. Yet there were no stars or even a moon. Only blackness overhead and white mist below. *White*, she thought. Blank. Ready to receive color.

A tentacle grabbed Condrie's ankle. She screamed as it dragged her down. She clutched at the mists, but there was nothing to hook her fingers into. Helpless to resist, she was pulled by the tentacle into a warm pond.

Algae made the water as thick as baked pudding. She gagged on the slime. Blindly, she paddled with her arms against the downward drag of the tentacle.

Someone from above grabbed her wrists. Her rescuer hauled with such strength that Condrie feared she might rip in half. She kicked at the tentacle with her free leg. It did not let go.

Sand came underneath her belly. Condrie felt herself dragged over the coarse grains. Her face burst from the water, and she drew in a deep breath.

Her rescuer's hands continued to pull, dragging her up out of the tepid water and onto the pebbly sand. Condrie clawed at the grit, desperately searching for something solid to hold. At the same time, she kicked, trying to loosen the black tentacle off her ankle. Solid as a riverboat's tether, the grip on her leg was too strong to shake.

"Calm yourself, little larva. It's a dream landscape. You're not actually at risk of drowning."

"Gerrawgon?" she cried out.

The lord Sagewyn merely smiled, still holding her wrists. She hardly recognized him without all his jewelry. He wore plain, flat shoes, brown leggings, and a loose-fitting linen shirt. "I like it when you say my name in welcome. It feels good."

Condrie looked down to her feet for a view of the tentacle clutching her ankle. Instead, she saw a man's hand.

Gerrawgon still worked to drag her farther up the sands and away from the water. Along with her, a man's shoulder, a head of sloppily cropped black hair, and gradually the rest of his body emerged from the water. He was nude and so covered in algae and sticky ocean mud that he looked like a sea monster himself.

Condrie smiled with relief. "Weg, it's you."

The lord dropped her wrists. He clapped his hands clean of the slime. "By the bones, must you always do this? You always start in the wrong spot!"

Wegdell raised his head from where he lay facedown in the sand. He opened his mouth to speak, and greenish tar gurgled out in thick globs.

She asked, "Where are we?"

The sound of her voice became a rushing wind that blew away the fog. Now she could see that she lay on a bank of pebbly sand. The waters were not a pond after all, but a channel that gouged a wide circle around a high stone wall. The embankment on the opposite shore was part of the wall's foundation.

Condrie looked up the wall's height. At the top were square blocks of stone that formed a pattern of jagged teeth. Beyond the wall, she could see the tips of conical towers.

Gerrawgon squatted down on his heels. "He always starts at the end, after they're all dead. This is the point when he has jumped into the castle's moat. From here, he runs. It's no use to start here, I always say, and we waste time and effort about how to get back to the beginning."

Wegdell groaned through the mush in his mouth, "I don't want to be here. I don't want to do this."

She stroked his hair. "I'm with you. Don't be afraid."

He sat up and wiped the muck off his face with both hands. His features had returned to the face that she had known when they first met. "This is absolutely the last time I'll go through this again."

"One way or another," said the lord.

"Take me back to the beginning. Show me what happened." Condrie took hold of his hand.

The whole world dissolved into a storm of wind and light and colors mixing, tumbling, and swirling upside-down. Condrie kept her eyes open for watching it all spin by. She held her breath. Her blood quickened. Her heart plunged into her gut. In a rush of fevered intensity, it all came to a stop.

"Ah," she grunted as ordinary shapes solidified around her.

She stood at his side. Gerrawgon stood by his opposite shoulder. They were atop the castle's wall on a broad walkway that ran the whole length with slanted, shingled roofs to one side and the tooth-like crenellation to the other. Exactly in the middle. At either end of the walkway lay a cylindrical tower, so from here Condrie had a clear view into both of the arched doorways.

"What now?" Condrie asked.

"Shhhh." The Sagewyn leaned closer to Wegdell's shoulder. "They're late. They promised. . . ."

"They're late," Wegdell repeated, looking off to the tower at Condrie's side. "They promised to be here by sundown."

"My lord!" a guard called.

Condrie looked past Gerrawgon to the other tower, and two knights of Xol emerged from the arched doorway. One was Jeremee and one was the blond forester.

Wegdell hurriedly tucked a slim iron box under his cloak. "As you were, lieutenant."

"My lord," Jeremee said, "with all respect, I was not informed that you would be requiring service this evening."

"I don't."

"Then, if I may ask, sir," Jeremee hooked a hand in his belt, a little nearer to the hilt of his broadsword, "what are you doing out here?"

"It's none of your concern, Jeree."

"Now, sir, if I may say so, you're putting me in a very awkward position. It's my duty to—"

Wegdell turned on him. "It's your duty to obey your lords. Must I report you to your captain?"

Jeremee shared a worried glance with the other knight. "No, sir."

Three nobles emerged from the opposite tower, a lord and two ladies. Condrie perked up at the sight of them approaching, for by their luxurious fashion and haughty mannerisms, they had to be Sagewyn. *Is that his brother?* she wondered.

Gerrawgon stepped back to be out of the way of their approach. He quietly said to her, "That is most definitely *not* his brother. It's Lord Thydrick and his two pecking hens, Lady Waemaria and Lady Semmarie. They were hatched from a different clutch of eggs."

"Weg, darling!" The two ladies hooked their arms around his, one on either side. Wegdell smiled brightly to the left and to the right. Condrie noticed he was struggling to conceal the box under his cloak while the ladies cuddled up to his sides.

"Lieutenant, uh, what's your name?" Lord Thydrick said. "Oh, never mind. We require you and your squad to vacate that guard tower immediately."

"With all respect," Jeremee said, "that's a highly irregular request, sir. May I ask why?"

Wegdell rolled his eyes but had no answer.

Lord Thydrick said, "We intend to perform a Sagewyn ritual that you 'stones' are not worthy to witness."

"Understood, sir, and I'm all too happy to comply." Jeremee paused to draw a breath. "Do have a signed clearance from the watch commander?"

"Oh God," Wegdell whispered.

The pair of ladies giggled. "Silly lump! Why do you disobey your lord?"

"My deepest apologies, and I beg your leniency, but I'm trying to avoid any misunderstandings that might get me and my comrades flogged for dereliction of duty and abandoning our post. Now, I'll require either a signed clearance from the watch commander or an explanation of this Sagewyn ritual and why it's so urgent that you—"

Lord Thydrick grabbed Wegdell's face in both hands. He dove in and smashed their mouths together. The two men closed their eyes and held the kiss for a good long count before they broke apart.

"Ugh," the other knight grunted. "I thought you only did your rutting when you were in bird form."

Lord Thydrick shrugged. "We're curious to play human."

"Want to watch, Jeree?" Wegdell asked teasingly.

"No, sir."

Condrie smiled to herself. Jeremee had left out this detail from the version he told in the kitchen. *What else did he leave out?*

"I don't want to watch any of this nonsense," Jeremee continued. "But I don't see how I can leave my post without. . . ."

One more Sagewyn lord emerged from the doorway in the opposite tower. *His brother.* Condrie knew him at once, without a doubt. He was dark-haired, tall, lithe, and handsome in an unassuming way. Although he dressed in similar finery, he walked with the somber stride of a penitent.

Jeremee bowed to his approach. "Lord Yigzemsei, good evening, sir."

"Lieutenant, my flock requires use of the tower." He offered a folded parchment sealed with a blob of black wax. "I have spoken to the watch commander and obtained his seal of approval. Your squad is dismissed for the night."

"Yes, sir." Jeremee tapped the shoulder of the knight at his side. "Come on."

Jeremee raised his arm to catch the attention of the other knights at the top of the tower. "Withdraw from your post, men. Return to the barracks and sign out. We're off duty for the night."

"Yes, sir, Lieutenant!" Hooting their exuberance, the knights trotted down the stairwell. They smiled to wave their thanks and then descended an open-air ramp leading down and away.

Wegdell and the others bowed their heads, waiting and listening for the boots to go away down the stairs.

"Did you get it?" his brother asked softly.

Opening one side of his cloak, Wegdell displayed the slender iron box. "Are you sure about this, Yigs? It's not too late. I can put it back."

His brother laid a gentle hand on Weg's shoulder. Thydrick and the two women followed his example until they were all touching him.

"His agents have pursued us and trapped us once before. He will find the means to pursue us and trap us once again, even if we fly free, unless we take the ultimate step to guarantee that we are forever out of his reach. Do you understand, Weg? What we do here tonight is not just for our sake, but for the sake of all those bound to this tyrant's will, and for the sake of all the innocents we have caused to be slaughtered, and for the sake of all the innocents whom we may save from being slaughtered in generations to come. When the other Sagewyn witness the price we are willing to pay, they will be inspired to rise up and resist the king's domination. Though we won't be here to see it come to fruition, we are sowing the seeds of a revolution that will transform the world."

Wegdell turned aside and spoke blindly to the open air. "Please, Gerrie, make it stop now. I don't want to do this again. Please don't make me do this again."

Condrie blinked at the tears streaming down her cheeks.

At her side, Gerrawgon snorted in disdain. "Idealistic dolt."

Lord Yigzemsei led the way along the full length of the castle's curtain wall. He entered the archway at the base of the guard tower first. Wegdell followed on his heels. After him came the others in pecking order.

Condrie entered the stairwell after the last of the ladies, and Gerrawgon brought up the rear.

"How close does it need to be?" Condrie asked over her shoulder.

"Eh?"

"His tail feather," she added. "In the parlor, you said something about coming within ten stick-lengths of the wine cellar's door. Is that how close he needs to be to his own tail feather before he can transform into a firebird?"

"It has actually measured out to be thirteen sticks, give or take a nibbet or two. Why?"

Condrie emerged to the top of the guard tower. A shingled cone formed a canopy over the open space. From here, she had a broad panoramic view of the moon glinting on the black waters of Lake Ward.

While the others gathered as a group at the center, she went to the edge of the crenellation. She looked down to the walkway below and judged the distance. To her eyes, it seemed about the same as looking down from the second story of the tavern. "This tower is . . . what, eight or nine stick-lengths high?"

"Nine and a half to the walkway," Gerrawgon said. "But it's a full twenty stick-lengths to the ground level. I see what you're thinking."

"Do you?"

The Sagewyn leaned his belly against the blocky turret. He pointed to the ramp that led to a landing and broad stairs. "I've examined this question myself. Jeremee and Baines are there on the stairs, just beyond the line of sight, spying on this bunch of idiots. I have interrogated both of those men and a dozen of the other boots who will come running along later. I've viewed them and reviewed them witnessing this scene from a dozen different angles."

Golden firelight erupted behind them as bright as the noonday sun crashing into the ground. Condrie glanced over her shoulder, and for a moment went breathless at the sight. All of them had transformed into fiery cranes. Their bodies were gold. Their long, slender necks and small heads were a vivid scarlet. Plumes of white heat spiked off their foreheads. Their wings spread wide open, touching end to end in a circle like festival banners set ablaze. Their tails extended outward as spokes of a fiery wheel.

"But it has to be nearby," Condrie insisted, raising her voice to be heard over the thunderous roar of feathery flames, "or he wouldn't be able to do that. Am I right?"

Gerrawgon pointed to the shingled rooftops that ran along the length of the walkway. "If someone had crawled into the attic of the chapel or the bath chamber, I have not found them yet. I have made a thorough search of these rafters by both human soldiers and shadow wraiths, and *it* was never stashed there."

"Are you certain of that? Perhaps someone moved it later."

Gerrawgon nodded. "It would leave a sulfurous odor that the wraiths would know."

Condrie frowned at how real everything seemed to be. Her hands felt the gritty texture of the stone. She felt the heat of fiery feathers prickling her cheeks. She smelled the burning wood of sword racks crumbling into cinders. Bricks gave off the scent of chalky smoke.

"In this dream, are we really here, or are we only seeing what he remembers?"

"I am the master of this landscape," he said. "I am constructing it, moment by moment, from the memories of all those whom I have interrogated in regards to the events of this night."

"Did you interrogate Captain Leera, too?"

He shook his head. "It wasn't necessary. I checked the watch commander's duty roster. She was assigned to sentry at the—"

One of the firebirds shrieked at the others. Although she could not understand their language, Condrie understood what Weg was saying to them. *We don't have to die. We can fly away. We can be free.* He pecked at the iron box with his shining gold beak. He pecked and pecked but could not get it open.

"The time is growing short," Gerrawgon said. "Both in here and in the real world. The hour of his execution draws near. What do you see, girl? What do you see that I have overlooked?"

"I don't know." Condrie balled up her fists.

The tallest and most serene of the firebirds bobbed his head rapidly a few times. Then he leaned down and nuzzled his beak alongside Wegdell's, quietly convincing him to stop uselessly pecking at the box.

Lord Yigzemsei cooed softly like a turtledove. Condrie recalled what Wegdell had told her once, and in the dream, it was easy to remember every word: *I cannot ask you to give up your life if you are not fully committed to my ideas.*

"We're out of time," Gerrawgon said.

"No, no," she cried. "Make it start again. Let me see it again!"

"You failed." Gerrawgon leaned an elbow on the turret. He slouched back to watch.

It was indeed Wegdell who grasped the iron box in his beak. Condrie looked straight into the dark dot of his fiery eye, and she knew it to be him. The other four cooed their approval. They gently waved their wings and encouraged him to fulfill their suicide pact.

He whipped his long neck and hurled the box into the open air.

Brass bells clanged. Men shouted. Torches flared up. Boots thumped up the stairwell.

The iron box splashed into the moat below. A column of steam erupted out of the water.

Four of the firebirds screeched an ear-splitting howl. The chorus of agony was as lightning ripping open the night sky. Condrie pressed her hands to her ears, but she could not block it out. She screamed along with them but could not hear herself.

Fiery plumage darkened, turning black from the outside. Cold blackness ate away into their centers. Screams faded into echoes. Their elegant bodies turned into charred remnants, holding their crane-like shape for just a moment before they crumbled into piles of ashes. Feathery cinders sprinkled away and scattered on the night's wind.

The last firebird standing folded back his wings. His brightness diminished, changing colors from yellow to dull beige. His fiery tail vanished. Wings became arms. Talons became feet. Plumage flattened down into a veneer of human skin. Once more, it was the man she knew as Wegdell standing naked with his back to the stairwell.

The knights of Xol rushed up the stairs with their swords drawn. They reached the top just in time to hear him speak. "Oh God, forgive me. What have I done?"

Jeremee shouted, "You're under arrest, Weg. Don't move."

Instead, he took two steps and leaped over the edge. The squad of knights shouted oaths as they rushed forward, too late to stop him.

Condrie turned away in despair.

Gerrawgon clapped his hands clean. "Well, that's the end. I must say, I'm disappointed. I had hopes that you would—"

"Wait." Condrie spotted one more black uniform in the stairwell. The glow of torches in the hands of Jeremee's squad made just enough light for her to see locks of cinnamon hair.

Gerrawgon held up his hand, and all movement stopped. The guards were in mid-step, turning to begin pursuit. Jeremee's mouth hung open in the middle of shouting orders. Even the fire of their torches stayed frozen.

"Captain Leera is here," she said, pointing to the woman knight in the stairwell.

"Ah, well, someone must have seen her from the corner of his eye and thought nothing of it. Good work, larva, though it's a meaningless revelation."

"Is it? You said she was assigned to sentry duty somewhere else in the castle."

"Yes," Gerrawgon said with a sigh. "But when the alarm bells rang out general quarters, every able-bodied man and woman—on duty or not—jumped into the fray. It means that she arrived on the scene in time to see her paramour reduced to cinders. She has made no secret of the fact. This very moment is the reason that she publicly vowed revenge upon the brother-killer who murdered the one true love of her life."

Condrie leaned over the turret and gazed out at the stony labyrinth of the castle's towers and walls.

"Where exactly was she assigned to sentry duty?" she asked.

Gerrawgon tapped his fingertips on the turret to think for a moment. "Uh, according to the duty roster, she was assigned to the third level arsenal chamber. The quartermaster was doing an inventory of the ordnance and was working on his reports until a late hour."

"And where is that, exactly?"

He pointed casually back over his shoulder. "The arsenal tower, of course, just past the upper bailey tower."

"And we are . . . where?"

"Isn't it obvious? That's the moat right there. We're in the lower bailey tower near the gatehouse."

Condrie thought of her pickpocket friend Kin, who used to brag about how quickly he could scamper through the alleyways of the town to avoid pursuit or to pursue a target.

"How long would it take someone to run . . ." Condrie pointed to the farthest tower at the opposite end of the stony labyrinth, ". . . from all the way over there to all the way over here?"

Gerrawgon frowned. "Let me think."

She began to smile. "Jeree rang the alarm bell after Weg tossed the box into the moat. They screamed, and then. . . . How long . . . ?"

Gerrawgon stood up straight. He gazed outward with her to the array of towers and walls and stairs.

"Too long," he said.

"It's her!" Condrie cried with glee. "She did it."

He coughed a sharp laugh. "By the bones! In all my thousand and two hundred years of walking this earth, that is the most illogical, nonsensical, fantastically stupid deduction that I have ever heard. She loved his brother, not him. Even if she knew of the suicide pact in advance, why would she save Weg's life and not her lover's?"

Condrie shrugged. "I don't know. Let's ask her."

*

The castle scene blurred and faded. In a blink, it was replaced rudely with the stink of the scorched parlor. Condrie sat on the hearth, where she had been before the dream began. A massive headache wrapped around her skull and squeezed so hard that she feared she might faint of it.

Wegdell, at her side, clutched his head and cried out a loud groan.

Gerrawgon staggered away, hugging his own belly. "By the . . . !"

His wife rushed to his side. "Did the larva hurt you, my darling?"

All he could do was shake his head weakly before he dropped to his knees and spat out a stream of vomit.

"What happened?" Wegdell sounded groggy like a man waking up after a drunken binge.

Feeling nauseous because she hadn't eaten anything in hours, Condrie closed her eyes to wait for her stomach to settle. "He strained himself doing it to both of us."

"Both of us? So I wasn't imagining. You really were in there."

"Mmm-hmm."

"You saw . . . ?" Wegdell groaned in coughing spasms of dry heaves.

Condrie's eyes popped open. "Yes! Yes, I saw. . . ."

Lady Immeirelda pulled away the flagpole that was blocking the door handle. She flung open the parlor's double doors and shouted into the corridor. "Guards! Guards, come! The prisoner has assaulted my lord! Take him. Take him now."

"Oh God." Condrie grasped his bare forearm. "Turn into a firebird again. Hurry!"

"I . . . can't," Wegdell said groggily. "It's too soon after. . . ." His limp hand made a grab for a fireplace poker. The iron rod fell out of his reach and clattered to the hearth bricks.

"No, no," Condrie cried, but the whirlwind of steel-plated black uniforms did not listen. She slapped weakly at their padded shoulders. "He's innocent! He's innocent!"

The knights pushed her aside. In a rattle of spears and chains, they dragged Wegdell away.

The dawn's light shined through the broken window. The night's darkness had turned to a vivid shade of red. *Red. The color of war and blood.*

Condrie regained her balance and dogged after them as they dragged Wegdell out the parlor's door. "Listen to me! He's innocent! I saw it. I saw it all."

A spear carrier shoved her, hard. Condrie stumbled backward into a framework of charred furniture. Until now, it had held its shape, but it collapsed into a heap of gritty gray ashes when she landed on it.

She banged her head on the floor. Underneath the soggy, scorched carpet was solid stone. Her ears rang. For a moment, she saw glittering sparkles of purple and green.

"Help me carry my lord," Immy commanded. "He needs to rest in bed after this exertion."

"As you say, my lady."

Condrie weakly raised herself to her elbow. The room still seemed to be lolling to and fro like a ferryman's raft on a stormy river. She watched sideways as a pair of knights lifted Lord Gerrawgon—by his shoulders and by his feet—to carry him out of the room.

Immy walked alongside, keeping her hand pressed to the sleeping man's cheek. "My lord, my lord."

Condrie recalled his words, *I don't need to trust my wife. I own her.*

She went to her knees. Hoisting her long skirts, she strained to get herself back up on her feet. Nausea still raged at her gut. She took a few deep breaths to hold it down and clear her head.

By then, everyone had gone.

No.

Heavy boots clumped on the stairs as the knights carried Gerrawgon up to a bed chamber.

No.

Condrie forced her sluggish feet to move. She trudged across the soggy carpet and passed through the scorched door frame. The hallway was dim, its sconces not lit. She braced a hand to the wall as she pushed herself along.

A foyer opened up at the base of the staircase. The wheel-shaped chandelier and its thick candlesticks gave off a gentle golden light. Archways opened off the foyer, leading to other hallways and other areas of the baron's manor house: the dining room, the library, the children's playroom, and the kitchen. All of the archways were dark and silent. The whole house seemed deserted.

Condrie clutched her belly as she realized where everyone had gone. *To watch him be executed.*

Each new shuddering breath gave her strength. She hurried to the front door.

A few spare boots were left behind on the straw mats. Condrie grabbed the first pair that came to hand and shoved her feet—flat shoes and all—down into the tube of leather. From a peg, she snatched a knitted scarf and wool cap. Throwing someone's cloak around her shoulders, she launched outside into the snow.

The wagon road had been trampled, leaving a clear trail to the east. Snowflakes were falling and soon would fill in the prints of the horses' hooves and the men's boots. Dawn's colors were behind her back, and all the landscape ahead lingered in a dim indigo-gray.

Firelight twinkled in the distance atop a hill. Condrie recalled the Prince of Xol proclaiming the sentence of execution: *You shall be brought to a consecrated place.* The only consecrated ground nearby would be the baron's family cemetery.

Condrie lifted her skirts up out of the freshly fallen snow. She tucked the bulk into her apron strings as best she could. Hands free, she raised her fists to her ribs and set off to run.

Each step plunged into the fresh powder. Snow was ankle-deep and continued to fall. She breathed hard, huffing hot through the knitted wool that wrapped her face.

Snow deepened as the road inclined uphill. She was not so much running as she was hopping from step to step. Lungs burning, she scolded herself for being so weak. It was not so far; she had run farther many times to chase Kin through the alleyways of the town. Yet after a short time, it felt as if she had been running for hours.

The road curved a leisurely course ascending to the top of the hill. Condrie went off the trail, cutting straight through the spindly beech and snow-glazed pine trees.

She dodged around tree stumps that were half buried in mounds of icy whiteness. Her boots crunched into black twigs. Her head brushed a low-hanging branch of pine, weighed down by the lumps of snow that clung to its needles, and wet slush exploded over her shoulders. She shook it off and kept going.

Firelight was her beacon at the top of the hill.

Condrie came to a low stone wall. She sat on it, swung her legs over, and emerged on the other side. Headstones protruded from the snow as if broken chunks of the moon had fallen to earth.

"Pardon me," she whispered, in case the ghosts of the dead lords buried there had noticed her intrusion.

She hurried along the narrow path between the headstones. Warmth beckoned.

A circle of bonfires—blazing logs as high as haystacks—illuminated a cleared space. Snowflakes melted in midair before they ever reached the ground.

Condrie rushed into the circle of fire. She shuddered to painfully inhale warm air into her chilled lungs.

Black horses and black uniforms stood all around. The knights of Xol were standing at attention, a living wall of grim faces. Spears in a row held erect like slats of a fence. Condrie dashed through a gap and into the center of them. Baron Fordon, dressed in furs and jewels, sat there as a witness. The prince himself was not present.

Wegdell knelt at a stump of a birch tree, a cylinder of white wood. Naked, his arms were bound at his back.

A foot soldier at one side of him had a grip on his hair and was pressing him down, down, to lay his cheek on the chopping block.

Captain Leera stood at his left side. Axe in her hands, she wore a bleached linen shift that covered all but her face and hands in a shapeless cone of white.

Black gloved hands grabbed Condrie, holding her back. There was nothing else she could do.

"*She* killed them!" Condrie called out. "She did it."

Captain Leera hesitated to raise the axe. A twinkle of emotion passed over her eyes—too many emotions for Condrie to try and guess. Surprise? Rage? Guilt? Love? Hate?

"I was just in a dream with Lord Gerrawgon and I saw everything that happened that night. I saw you, Captain. I know what you did."

"You're lying," Leera scoffed. "This is a last desperate attempt to spare his sodded life."

"The duty roster from that night says you were on sentry at the arsenal tower because somebody was doing an inventory of something, but you weren't really there, were you?"

Leera tensed her grip on the axe handle.

One of the officers standing near the baron's chair spoke up. "I was on sentry duty at the arsenal tower that night. Leera . . . you weren't there. What's she saying? I don't understand."

Gloved hands loosened their grip on Condrie's arms. Now she had their attention. Condrie fixed her stare on the woman knight and spoke as if there were only the two of them in all the world.

"You went down to the king's secret vault earlier that day, before Wegdell got there. You knew about their suicide pact. You didn't care about the others dying, you just wanted to save Yigs, your lover. When you took a feather out of the strongbox, you . . . you made a mistake. You thought you were getting your lover's tail feather, but instead you took Weg's."

"Idiot whore," Captain Leera cried. "I don't make life-and-death mistakes!"

Condrie's eyes widened as she realized the only other possible explanation. "Yigs went into the vault with you?"

"Oh my God," Wegdell whispered, his cheek still on the chopping block.

Leera slouched as if someone had punched her in the gut. Her lower lip trembled. "He promised we would run away together. He said it was the only way he could be free. I was going to resign my commission to become his wife."

Condrie held her breath, listening. No one in the circle of bonfires made a move except for Baron Fordon, who stood up out of his chair.

"Yigs knew the combination to the padlock on the king's strongbox," Leera said.

"Oh God," Wegdell gasped.

"He pointed out to me which feather to take," Leera continued, her voice losing its strength with every word that came out of her mouth. "He instructed me in how to handle it with tongs, how to put it in the pomander. He told me to stash it away while he went to break the news to his flock of our intended elopement. At the same time, I was to compose a letter of resignation to my commanding officer."

"Where did you stash it?" Condrie asked.

"In the stairwell of that damned guard tower," Leera said, her voice sinking into a lower, quiet range. "Behind a loose brick."

Murmurs and hushing whispers of coarse oaths rushed around the crowd of observers. Yet they all just stood there, watching and listening.

"He lied to you," Condrie said.

"Yes."

Condrie kept going, unable to stop the flow of words tumbling out of her mouth. "You didn't know that he'd made a suicide pact with his flock. He never intended to run away with you."

"He said that he ... that we. ..." The captain's voice broke, and she could not finish her thought out loud.

"Perhaps Yigs really did love you," Condrie said gently. "But his love for you was outweighed by his passion for resisting the king."

Wegdell raised himself up off the chopping block at last. No one made a move to stop him. He came upright on his knees, and his eyes were also moist with tears.

Condrie turned to speak directly to him. "Your brother said it to your face, and you didn't understand. He said, 'I cannot ask you to give up your life if you are not fully committed to my ideas.' Yigs planned it all from the beginning. He intended for *you* to be the last one standing. When he said that the flock's suicide would inspire other Sagewyn to rise up against the king and ignite a revolution, he didn't mean Gerrie or Immy or some shadow wraiths. He meant you, Weg. He meant to inspire you, not with his words, but with the sacrifice of his life."

Once more, Condrie turned back to Leera. "He expected that you would return Weg's tail feather to him after it was all over. If you were already willing to resign your commission, perhaps he hoped that your commitment to that uniform could be broken. He might have dreamed of you two becoming friends out of mutual loss and partners in the new cause. He didn't plan on your grief turning into rage and hate."

Leera's arms began to tremble. She tightened her grip on the axe.

Baron Fordon proclaimed, "As lord of this land, I rescind my permission for King Davarche's justice to be carried out on *my* property. I order this execution to be halted immediately."

"No!" Leera screamed.

She swung the axe. Condrie gasped.

Wegdell crouched and rolled out of the way. The blade swooped through the air.

Black uniforms swarmed in to surround her, grabbing her arms to hold her back from trying again.

"It should have been *you* to die, not him! It should've been you!"

*

They returned to the baron's manor house by the east wing. Torches held by the mounted knights illuminated the dark, weathered stones overgrown with vines and the slats of shuttered windows.

A chilling wind nipped at Condrie's right cheek, but she did not care. She slid down off the rump of Lieutenant Jeremee's horse; the knight dismounted after her.

"Be gentle with him," she said.

Hands in black leather gloves surrounded Wegdell. They caught him as he tumbled weakly out of the saddle. Barefoot in the snow, he was nude except for a cloak that someone had tossed around him. Head bowed down, he wobbled, still groggy on his feet.

"I got you." Jeremee hooked Wegdell's arm across his own shoulders and used his stout body as a bracing support.

"Where is she?" Wegdell's head lolled left and right.

"I'm here." Condrie, following on the baron's heels, walked just ahead of him and Jeremee.

Baron Fordon entered the east-wing door, a smaller, less ornate version of the portico at the main entrance. He cast off his cloaks and furs to the floor of the mudroom. A house servant dropped to the baron's feet and worked quickly at removing his wet boots.

Knights entered in his wake. They paused in the mudroom long enough to stomp their boots on straw mats and shake off the clumps of white slush that clung to their shoulders.

"My lord, my lord!" The valet, in a housecoat of indigo wool trimmed with gray cord, opened his arms to greet the baron. "It is a disaster. It is a catastrophe!"

"What are you saying, man?" the baron asked.

"The parlor, sir—it has been ruined by fire. . . . Oh!" The valet stepped back, giving room for the knights to help Wegdell stagger inside the foyer. "That's him!"

"Yes, yes, that's him." The baron waved his valet aside. "I have ordered a stay of execution. New information has come to light. I must speak with the prince at once."

"But sir," the valet insisted. "The parlor . . . !"

"Carpets and curtains are not my concern right now. I'll appreciate you to heat up a carafe of brandy. I need a drink!"

"As you say sir," said the valet, bowing away.

Condrie removed the cloak and boots she had borrowed. No one seemed to mind, though, if she kept the knitted scarf looped around her neck and shoulders.

The baron led the way up the free-standing curved stairway that spiraled to fill the open space of the foyer. Condrie followed behind the knights that followed him. A headache still throbbed and rang dizziness in her ears. She held up her long skirts, which were heavy, cold, and soggy with melting snow. Her aching legs cried out for rest, but she forced herself to move, to keep going, just a few more steps, just a few more. She glanced back over her shoulder to the curve of the stairs below. Wegdell leaned heavily on Lieutenant Jeremee while gripping the bannister and pulling himself up, step by painful step. The cloak sagged off his left shoulder, exposing part of his naked chest. The sunburst tattoo—the mark of the king—was still there.

Baron Fordon took broad strides along the rug in the upstairs hallway. Wall sconces lit the way. Floorboards creaked under the weight of knights who sorted themselves into a two-by-two formation.

Condrie glanced into the open doorway of the first guestroom.

Gerrawgon the Sagewyn lay on a luxurious canopy bed with a high mattress and enough blankets to keep a dozen orphans warm. He was propped up against white pillows. Warmth beckoned, and she paused on the threshold to view the brightly lit scene within.

His blue-haired wife sat beside him on the mattress. She held a bowl of soup and offered a spoon to his lips.

The Lord of Dreams noticed her just then and looked straight at Condrie. Even from across the room, his eyes seemed to pierce into her like needles.

"Ah, there you are. On your feet, are you? How resilient. I still have a howling wolf of a headache."

Condrie gestured over her shoulder at Wegdell, leaning on the knight's shoulder as he staggered by. "I was right! It *was* Leera. His brother. . . ."

Gerrawgon held up a hand to request her silence. "I'll read the reports later."

Dipping her knees in a curtsey, Condrie hurried to catch up with the others.

Up ahead, women's voices spoke loudly and urgently all at once. Their words jumbled and tumbled over each other. Yet despite the chaos of the cacophony, Condrie recognized each of their familiar tones. She heard snippets of phrases.

Ma Kielsing pleaded, "Where is my dau- . . . ?"

Niarr cried, ". . . done with her?"

The baron approached a pair of double doors that were open to a much larger, south-facing guestroom. "Prince Naiirengé, I beseech Your Highness to hear me."

Knights held Wegdell up at the threshold. Head bowed, shoulders slumped, he groaned from the effort of staying on his feet.

"What is the meaning of this?" the prince demanded from within.

"I halted the execution."

"You had no authority!"

"I have *every* authority," the baron said. "With all due respect, sir, I must remind you that until I sign a treaty with your father, I am the lord of this land and you are a guest in my house."

A long, quiet moment passed when the only sounds in all the world were the knights' breathing and the fireplace's crackling. Condrie held her breath, wondering what his reaction would be, for surely no one but his own father had ever spoken to the Prince of Xol with such command.

The prince asked, "You had a good reason, I trust?"

"Yes, sir, I did."

The captain of the guard spoke up. "It was a scheme of Captain Leera, Your Highness. She's under arrest. It's a long story, sir. I'll compose a full and detailed report within the hour."

"Very good, Captain."

The captain of the guard made a bow, saluted with a clenched fist, and then withdrew into the hallway.

Wegdell clamped his arm across his belly. "Apologies, sir, but I'm feeling quite unwell."

"Yes, yes, please come inside."

Lieutenant Jeremee alone helped Wegdell stagger into the room. The rest of the uniforms, following their captain's lead, retreated back down the hallway.

Condrie breathed a sigh of relief when they had gone; at last, not to be surrounded by a bullish herd of black uniforms and swords and spears. *It's over. It's done.* All of her strength drained out of her frozen feet, and at that moment, she could hardly keep her eyes open.

The baron gave one last shallow bow, hardly more than a tilt of his head. "If you'll excuse me, sir?"

"Yes, Fordon. We shall hold a lengthy discussion in the morning after I have read my captain's report."

Condrie stepped aside to allow the baron to emerge from the room. He passed her without a glance. The last she saw of him was from behind, strolling away into the dim.

The prince raised his high-pitched voice to a commanding volume. "Lord Wegsemze, you may recline upon my bed. A suitable guestroom shall be prepared for you forthwith."

"Thanks, sir."

Condrie slipped past the guards' elbows. Unnoticed, she popped into the prince's bed chamber and darted toward her mother.

"There she is!" Ma Kielsing rushed to embrace her. "My girl, my girl," she said, with such genuine jubilation that Condrie believed nothing in the world would hurt her as long as she clung to that firm block of flesh.

Niarr gathered near to stroke her soft hands over her back. Condrie began to shiver, just now realizing how she was chilled to the bone.

"You should get out of these wet clothes," her mother said sternly, "before you catch your death of the cold!"

Jeremee helped Wegdell walk sluggishly across the rugs to the ornate canopy bed. The lieutenant steadied his elbow as Wegdell put one foot on the stepstool and then heaved and rolled the man's long legs onto the high mattress. The prince's own chambermaid, wearing a loose-fitting satin housecoat, rushed over to arrange the blankets neatly over the reclining man.

"Mama," Condrie said, "it's just as I've been telling everybody all along. He didn't do it. He didn't! And now, I've proved it."

Ma Kielsing gently stroked her cheek. "All that matters is that *you* aren't being persecuted anymore."

"No, it's over." Condrie grinned.

Snapping fingers turned all of their attention to the thin-boned man in layers of black and rouge velvets. Prince Naiirengé gave them a stern frown. "No one hath thee persecuted," he said, though his pipey voice failed to give the proper force to his words. "Justice has been served."

"Yes, of course," Ma Kielsing said with a soothing tone, as she would assuage a complaining customer. "I beg Your Highness's pardon for my thoughtless choice of words. We are grateful for your wisdom and mercy."

The prince waved her off and turned himself around to the wine cart.

Condrie looked to the fireside, where a dining table was heaped with platters of food. There was enough of a feast to satisfy everyone in the room, and yet there was only a single chair at the table. Condrie gaped at the stack of ball-sized yeast buns, wedges of winter melon and blueberries in cream, fillets of grilled whitefish, cubes of peppered meat on skewers, curls of bacon, snow peas, carrots cut into flower blossoms, pickled cabbage, a cup of barley soup, and a wheel of cheese. Grains of salt filled a silver dish. *Was the prince enjoying his supper as Weg was getting beheaded? What cold-hearted tyrant is this?* She clamped her trembling jaw shut, grinding her teeth, and hoped that Gerrawgon truly was incapacitated. If the Sagewyn were to interrogate her now, he would see the outrage burning within her, and all of their sacrifice would be for nothing.

The prince poured apple brandy from a decanter of crackled green glass. He filled two goblets—one was for himself, and one he carried to the bedside.

Wegdell said, "Thanks," and drained the goblet in a few deep gulps. He lay in his element as a Sagewyn lord once again in ultimate comfort and luxury.

"It's a curiously refreshing vintage that this area produces," the prince remarked, sipping from his own goblet. "I should take a barrel or two when I return to my father's court."

"Actually, sir," Wegdell began, "you may find the baron's wine cellar to be in somewhat of a shambles. I, uh, put up a struggle when they came to take me to the chopping block."

The prince laughed softly and looked at him, eye to eye, like a friend. "Kicked up a fuss, did you?"

Wegdell looked into his prince's eyes, and his casual smile dropped flat. He went utterly still. Condrie took a sharp breath; even with a new face, she knew his expression of surprise. *What is it?* she wondered. *What does he see? What is he thinking?*

The prince continued in a casual, chatty tone. "I shall review the captain's report as soon as it is ready for my eyes. Based upon what I expect to be exculpatory testimony, I shall compose a letter of pleading to my father that he should convene a retrial that will exonerate you of all blame."

"Uh-huh," Wegdell grunted, still staring into the prince's eyes.

Lieutenant Jeremee said, "I'll testify for you too, sir."

"Oh . . . uh, thanks, Jeree."

"Shall I refill your brandy?" the prince offered.

"No, no, thanks." Wegdell handed back the empty goblet. "I don't feel well, you understand, after all that's happened."

"Of course. You need to rest." The prince strolled back to his dining table. He took a seat, spread the napkin on his lap, and continued eating.

Ma Kielsing bent her knees in a curtsey. "Again, may I speak for all of us when I say how deeply we appreciate your mercy and compassion, Your Highness. I offer my most heartfelt apology for raising my voice earlier out of desperate concern for my girl and beg for your oh-most-generous forgiveness."

The prince shrugged, not looking up from his feast.

"Then, with our eternal gratitude, may we be excused?"

"Yes, go." The prince drizzled honey in long, liquid strings onto a bit of bread.

The women withdrew into the hallway. Condrie dallied behind, lingering on the threshold, not sure of where to go.

"Condy?" he called out across the broad room. "Not going to leave me without a proper kiss goodbye, are you?"

A blush burned her cheeks. She licked her lips. "Uh. . . ."

Niarr chuckled from the hallway. "Oh, go on. What are you waiting for?"

Condrie forced her chilled feet to move across the room. She clenched her teeth to hold back from screaming, *I don't understand what you really want! What is happening?*

His blue eyes twinkled brightly in the firelight. "I want to thank you, dear woman, for your courage and commitment to digging out the truth. I owe you my life."

"I, uh . . . you're welcome." She leaned into the bed frame. The mattresses were stacked higher than her waistline.

He raised himself upright and blankets fell away from his naked chest. Bending toward her, he cupped her face in his warm palms. Condrie held her breath and closed her eyes. She braced herself, gripping his bare wrists and wondering what would happen next.

His lips connected with hers and held still. She shivered down to her cold shoes. Startling in its brevity, but so soft, so tender, it was just as she imagined a real kiss would be. All too soon, he peeled his mouth away but kept his face near, breathing hotly against her tingling cheeks.

"He's not the prince." Wegdell whispered so softly that even she could hardly hear it. "It's an imposter."

Condrie's eyes snapped open wide.

"Shh, no, no, don't cry." Wegdell smiled and stroked his thumb against her cheek as if wiping away tears that were not there. "I'm fine now. Everything's fine. Don't worry about me anymore. I just need to rest for a bit, and I'm sure that I'll be feeling like my old self again very soon."

He let go of her cheeks then and briefly wriggled his fingers in midair. It was the same gesture he had made in the wine cellar just before transforming into a firebird.

His tail feather! Condrie inhaled a shuddering gasp to recall that the iron pomander was most likely forgotten, still hanging on the wall hook where Gerrawgon had put it. The parlor was in the west wing of the manor house, which meant the pomander—and his fiery feather—was out of reach.

"Go on, now." Wegdell leaned back against the pile of satin pillows. "Go with your mother. A new day has dawned. Go . . . go home."

Condrie backed away, shivering, and hoped they all assumed it was because her skirts were soggy with melted snow. She looked sideways at the prince and then quickly averted her eyes. *How is he sure it's an imposter? When did he figure it out? Just now?*

"So, how was it?" Niarr hooked her arm around Condrie's elbow.

"I . . . I, uh. . . ." Her feet were numb. Her mind was a storm of wild and tumbling thoughts that swirled around one image: the iron pomander ball.

"Oh dear," said Ma Kielsing. "I figured as much. It's the Sagewyn's magic—it must be. As long as he's around, it untangles your tongue. Isn't that right, sweetie? Is that why you've been so attracted to him?"

Niarr chuckled deeply. "One of the reasons, eh?"

Condrie looked back into the room. Wegdell was settling into the nest of blankets and pillows. He tucked his face into his bent arm.

Lieutenant Jeremee loitered at the foot of the canopy bed. He hooked a thumb in his sword belt and slouched against the bedpost. Standing guard, but not on guard.

"Go off, Jeree," Wegdell mumbled into the pillow. "Go get some breakfast and dry your socks."

The lieutenant asked the prince, "Does Your Highness require my service?"

"Dismissed."

Jeremee bowed, made a saluting gesture with his fist, and removed himself into the hallway. Yet he lingered just outside the door. He looked down at his feet and frowned in thought. A candle in a wall scone flickered a soft amber glow above his head.

Does he suspect something's wrong? Did he see Weg's reaction as I did? He knows him better than I do. He's been his guard for nine years.

Ma Kielsing kissed her forehead. "I know what you need, sweetie. Dry clothes and a hot breakfast in bed."

Condrie half-closed her eyes and imagined the layout of the manor house in her mind. The last place she needed to be was a room in the guest quarters. Somehow, she had to get closer to the west wing of the house.

"K-k-k-kitchen...."

"Yes, exactly what I was thinking," her mother said. "We shall ask the kitchen servants if they'll lend you some clothes while these dry by the fire."

They strolled deeper into the dim corridors of the baron's manor house. Tapestries hung at intervals on the wood paneling, and ceramic urns on pedestals decorated the spaces in between. They passed the door of the baron's bed chamber just as servants brought him a tray of food and a wine carafe wrapped in a towel.

Does he know the prince is an imposter? Condrie wondered. *Who could have engineered such a scheme? What does it mean?*

Descending by the servants' stairs, they arrived at the rear of the kitchen. A large fireplace blazed, its logs piled high like a bonfire framed in stone. Condrie inhaled warm air with a shudder.

Violet and Amber were there with sleeves rolled up, helping to scrape clean the loaf pans and skillets. The Athel girl spotted them first and dropped her scrub brush.

Violet smiled with an iron skillet in one hand and a spatula in the other. "Praises be."

Condrie nodded gratefully, but her thoughts continued to howl and storm. *I have to get out of here. I have to go the parlor. I have to get it back to him!*

Ma Kielsing led her to the fireplace. Servants—men and women—gathered around and all began talking at once. Gossip had already reached them. The servants excitedly told the events of the aborted execution and the captain's disgrace.

"They're plum sodded daft," said the kitchen master, a burly bearded man with corn-blond hair and small blue eyes. "The lot of them—Sagewyn and blackcoats alike—as nutty as loons."

Condrie rolled her eyes as a thought came to mind. Her heart thumped as she braced herself for telling a lie to the woman who had never lied to her. "Oh, M-m-mama, I d-dropped my b-b-bell . . . in the . . . in the . . ."

"In the wine cellar?" Niarr asked.

Condrie nodded.

"It's just a cheap trinket," her mother said. "You can buy another one."

"N-n-n-no, that . . . that one. . . ." Condrie backed away to an open doorway where darkness beckoned.

Before anyone could say something to stop her, Condrie whirled about and broke into a run. She held up her soggy skirts, and her cold shoes slapped on the dark floorboards. She dashed along the corridors as fast as she could force her aching, chilled legs to go. She passed slow-moving servants going in the opposite direction and ignored them when they called after her.

She reached the foyer of the west wing. Her shoes squeaked as she spun on her heels.

The burned husk of a door was still wide open. Morning light shined pale on the broken window at the far side of the room. What remained of furniture was in various hues of blue and gray and white. In the cold air, the stench of charcoal and pond water was not as repugnant as before.

One tiny spot of color twinkled. A faint glimmer of orange shined within an iron ball.

"What are you doing here, pet?" Lieutenant Jeremee's strong voice broke the stillness.

Condrie did not look back to the doorway, where he stood. She hurried to the far wall, to where the iron pomander still hung on its hook. She reached up as high as she could and grabbed the chain. She jumped in place to shake it loose.

"Damn me, that's *his*!" Jeremee braced his feet where he stood, blocking the exit. "Don't be stupid, girl. It's one thing to prove him innocent of murder. It's a whole other thing to—"

She ran for the broken window.

Jeremee barked, "Shit!" and lumbered toward her.

Condrie got there first. She sat herself on the window sill, swung her legs over, and launched outside into the snow.

Each step plunged as high as her calves. Her flat shoes were trowels scooping up freshly fallen powder. She huffed and panted with every hopping step.

"Don't do this!" Jeremee shouted from the window, but his voice blew away on the cold night wind.

She managed to turn the corner of the house, to the south side, where the snow was not so deep. She ducked under a lattice awning of jasmine and wisteria fronds. Beneath the snow was grass, not flagstones, so unafraid to slip and fall, she dug in her feet and ran faster.

She plugged to a stop just short of the southwest corner of the house. She looked up to the second-story windows, counting off her best guess of where the prince's bed chamber might be.

Am I close enough? Am I within thirteen stick-lengths?

The pomander got warmer. Condrie held it by its chain, but even at arm's length, it radiated the heat of a blazing bonfire. The iron itself began to change color from black to a deep blood red. She smiled. Her chapped lips stung, but she kept smiling.

The second-story window glowed from within, brighter and brighter. Yellow turned to white.

Fire blossomed out of that upstairs room. Window shutters blew apart into kindling sticks. Shards of glass panes crackled. Twisted rods of grillwork sprinkled into the air. Fiery tongues lapped at the air as thick smoke billowed up to the sky.

The firebird launched from within. The window's frame and part of the wall smashed outward, and its broken remnants tumbled into the hedges.

His fiery wings spread wide, and the rush of air boomed in the sky. Condrie squinted at the brightness of him, as if part of the noonday sun had swooped down close to the earth.

Wegdell the firebird glided in a circle above her. Each golden feather of his sleek body shimmered of its own light. His broad wings flared to full extension, the fringe feathers spreading like outstretched fingers. His wings tilted to and fro as he banked around the curve. Condrie craned her head back to watch the long, flaming tail draw a broad ring of reddish gold against the drab sky. When she blinked, she could still see its shape burned into her eyelids.

Condrie twirled the chain. She cranked her whole arm to swing the iron ball, and with all her strength, she released it upward.

His talons snatched the pomander in midair.

"Go!" she cried, but with the rumbling rush of his fiery wings curdling the air, she could hardly hear herself. "Go, be free!"

He swooped down for one more pass. She saw the dark dot of his pupil at the center of his fiery eye. Heat prickled her cheeks. Steam wafted out of her clothes.

Then he pumped his mighty wings and undulated his crane-like neck. Each stroke whooshed like a storm's gusts. His passing shook clumps of snow from the treetops.

Standing still, Condrie watched that bit of glowing flame soar to the sky. It got smaller and smaller until it was no larger than a candlewick. Clouds drifted over the lingering crescent moon, and she lost sight of him altogether.

Lieutenant Jeremee came to stand beside her. He joined her in studying the sky. "Well, I can't say I blame the pecker."

"Am I . . . am I . . . under . . ."

"Under arrest?" he finished. "For what?"

Condrie pointed to the sky.

"Oh, surely you didn't have a hand in that? Aren't you in the kitchen right now with the tavern wenches, getting a change of dry clothes and a hot breakfast?" Jeremee walked backward as he said this, backing away, heading for the corner of the house.

Already the hordes of black uniforms were rushing in from the northwest side. They called out to him. Jeremee turned to greet them.

Condrie slipped into a side door—a servant's entrance—and made her way back to the kitchen.

*

Later that morning, Condrie departed the manor with Ma Kielsing and the other women. They huddled into the carriage sleigh in which they had arrived with blankets, flasks of hot tea, and a kettle of smoldering coals to keep them warm on the journey home.

It almost felt like being in the Sagewyn's dream landscape, as if the hours had turned backward and she was reliving a previous day. Once before, they had said their goodbyes to Baron Fordon and thanked him for his hospitality. Once before, the burly spinster had climbed up to her driver's seat and gathered the reins of the carriage horses. This time, it was really happening; they were really going home. Wegdell was free. The culprit was in chains. Baron Fordon was not happy about the damage to his home, but the Prince of Xol vowed to finance all repairs.

What does it mean? she wondered. *The prince is an imposter? Are his personal servants aware of it? Does Gerrawgon know, or perhaps is he the grand architect of this scheme?* Condrie hugged herself within the heavy blankets that swaddled her. She did not speak as the carriage lurched into motion. *The intrigues of the court of a foreign king. . . . Why should any of it be my concern? Why can't I stop worrying about it?* She half-closed her weary eyes, listening to the jingle of the harness bells and the swish of the sleigh's blades on the slushy, wet snow.

At nightfall, they stopped at Third Town.

Condrie shuddered, not from cold, as they entered the front door of the Boar's Head Tavern. She looked aside to the blazing fireplace and remembered Wegdell taking a sponge bath on that very rug.

"A room for the night, please," said Ma Kielsing to the innkeeper.

"How many?"

"There's six of us," she said.

The innkeeper squinted his shaggy eyebrows. "I only see five."

"The other person in our group is Baron Jonvil's wagon driver," she said.

"Say, don't I know you? You're the Madam of the Rivertown tavern?"

"Yes, I am," she said proudly.

The innkeeper continued frowning. "Well, if your sixth is a prick here for getting a-swyvered, then I'll have to charge you the double rate."

Ma Kielsing put a hand on her hip. "I said, it's our coach driver who is tending to the horses at the moment."

"Coach driver, eh? How are you paying him to court you around the landscape?"

Ma Kielsing reached into a leather pouch at her belt. She brought out a pair of pewter coins stamped with the emblem of Baron Jonvil's house. "The same way I'm paying you, my good man: in my lord's good currency."

"Knights of Xol pay me in silver."

Niarr put a hand on her mother's sleeve. "Don't haggle with this boor, Mama. Let's go sleep in the alehouse as we did on the way up."

"No, we deserve a warm meal and a comfortable bed." Ma Kielsing reached into her pouch for another coin, a whiter metal, pale in the amber light of candlesticks. It was stamped with the sign of a bull's head, the emblem of King Davarche of Xol.

The innkeeper smiled. "Upstairs, fourth door to the left. Bedrolls, blankets, and candles are in the closet."

"Thank you," said Ma Kielsing.

Condrie inhaled the scent of a meaty broth simmering in a large cauldron at the fire. Her stomach gurgled.

Violet slipped her thin arm around Condrie's waist. "Come, Girl. Let's have supper."

The women crossed the long, open room. At the fireplace, they filled bowls with a hearty stew. They broke off chunks of bread from a large loaf and each took a small green apple from a hanging basket.

Condrie sat on the floor with the others. They slurped the stew and crunched into the apples. Soon, the wagon driver came to join them. Food filled their mouths, and so they did very little talking.

*

In the morning, Condrie awoke first. She lay snuggled in a bundle of several layers of warm blankets on the floor. A soft straw mat ran underneath the entire length of her body. Her head rested on a pillow stuffed with bean husks. The warmth of women's bodies all around took the chill out of the air. The room was still dark, but her eyes—once opened—would not close again. All the others breathed deeply in their exhaustion; Niarr, especially, was rarely known to rise before mid-afternoon. *They deserve to rest*, she thought, *after all they've suffered because of me.*

Condrie tiptoed out of the nest of sleeping women. The scent of yeast bread wafted up the stairs. She descended into the brightness of the ground-level room.

Windows had goats' vellum instead of glass window panes, but the papery skin let in enough of the morning's glow to turn everything into varying hues of amber. The fireplace blazed high. Customers sat cross-legged on the floor, some on stools, and heartily slurped at soup bowls.

Condrie went to the fireplace to fill her own bowl with dumplings and onion soup. She swirled the ladle to be sure there was no chicken in it.

A knight of Xol entered the front door. A squire at his side caught the man's cloak and cap as he tossed them off. "Bring me breakfast! Sausage and boiled eggs and a loaf of bread. Hurry, man! I carry a message for the king, and I need to be on my way!"

The knight took a seat at one of the few tables in the room. He stretched out his legs, flexing his knees. The sword's scabbard touched the floor.

"Here you are, sir." The innkeeper himself brought a platter to the table.

"And a tankard of hot cider," the knight demanded. "It's damned cold out there, and I have a long way to ride this day."

The innkeeper brought a pewter mug with wisps of steam at the rim. "If I may ask, sir, what is such urgent news that it brings such a fine gentleman as yourself out on the road in such weather?"

Condrie stayed by the fireplace at the opposite end of the long room. She sipped at her soup while she kept her eyes fixed upon the knight. All of the other travelers, sitting cross-legged on the floor, kept their heads down as if they hoped to be invisible.

"You shall hear the tale soon enough," said the knight, while cramming eggs and sausage into his mouth. "But you'll hear it first from me. You know the fugitive Sagewyn who was due to be executed at Fordonhold? Well, he's off free. He didn't do it! My own captain Leera Vilbyss confessed to the crime."

"A captain of the king's guard!" the innkeeper exclaimed.

"Yeah, it's high treason, what she did. You'll see her coming along in a few days, in chains, with the prince's entourage. I'm riding ahead to bring the news to His Majesty."

"But I don't understand," said the innkeeper. "Why would she do such a thing?"

The knight gulped his hot cider and then burst out laughing. "Love! She was in love with one of the dead Sagewyn and got all jelly in the head."

"Love, eh?" The innkeeper hooked his thumbs in the waistband of his burlap apron. "Women do nutty things for love. Like *that* one."

The knight looked across the room, to where the innkeeper had gestured with a tock of his head. Condrie caught his fixed stare and cringed when he smiled recognition.

"Hey there, you."

Condrie nodded a polite hello from across the room.

"Hope you learned your lesson, eh? That one. . . . He's a cold-hearted peacock, that one is. We all tried to tell you, didn't we? You didn't listen. You would've jumped into a bonfire for his sake, and what thanks do you get? He flew off and left you. Now that the bird's out of his cage, you'll never see him again."

Condrie's lower lip trembled. She latched onto the soup bowl so they would not see.

The knight laughed at her and returned to eating his breakfast. Condrie stared at him, hoping he would finish soon and leave.

One of the travelers sitting on the floor looked up at her just then. Their eyes met. His face was not familiar—a narrow brow, broad cheeks, a round chin, and a pert nose. Yet his eyes sparkled a brilliant blue.

Condrie choked on a sliver of onion in the soup. *It's him!*

Wegdell quickly looked down, but not quickly enough. In the pause, he slouched his shoulders and Condrie knew that he was aware of being recognized. She held her breath, wondering what he would do, how they could find a private place away from all these strangers to meet and talk.

He got to his feet. He left his soup bowl and tankard on the floor.

"Say, you, who do you think is going to pick up your dish?"

Wegdell flicked a coin into the air. The innkeeper deftly snatched it into his fist.

Not saying a word, Wegdell strolled quickly to the door. From a row of wall pegs, he took a cloak and a cap. No gloves. No scarf. No boots. He stepped outside into a gray and white snowy world.

Condrie gripped her bowl tightly and resisted the urge to go running after him. *He's free. He doesn't need me anymore.*

*

The carriage sleigh continued southward, following the curves of the river. Condrie rested her head on her mother's shoulder. *Not long now*, she told herself. *We'll be home soon, and everything will go back to the way it was before I ever met him.* Tears leaked out onto her cheeks. She wiped her cold hand over her face.

"I'm going to miss you all," said Amber. "It's a rare and special gift when the colors of strangers blend into a new hue."

"I feel the same." Violet put her arm around the Athel girl. "But what's all this about missing us? I'm staying at Baron Jonvil's manor at least until the spring, when I've promised to plant his tulip bulbs. And you . . . your people are staying to sow the fields, aren't you?"

"I'm not sure," Amber said. "I'm coming up to the age when I should marry, but I haven't made a promise to anyone among our people. They're all fine men, but. . . ."

"But?" Niarr prompted with a knowing lilt in her voice.

"Sometimes I look at the other men—the foresters and the townsmen and even the knights of Xol—and I feel so confused." Amber wiped back stray locks of hair from her face. "I don't know what to do."

Niarr said, "You could come and work with us for a while. Try them all out and see which sort of man is your best match."

The girl looked across to the opposite bench. "Is that what you're doing?"

For the first time, Condrie saw her blush. "Jeree asked me to marry him."

Condrie, pressed in between them on the bench, felt the older woman take in a sharp breath. "And what did you say?"

Niarr smiled sweetly. "I said I needed to ask your permission."

Ma Kielsing reached across Condrie's lap to take hold of Niarr's hand. "You don't need to wait for my permission, Girl. You know my first rule: no woman works in my house if she does not wish to be there. If your heart's desire is to become the wife of a knight of Xol, then his wife you shall be."

"Oh, Mama, thank you!"

*

By nightfall, they arrived at Baron Jonvil's estate. The coach driver waited for them all to disembark, and then she jingled the reins one more time and drove the sleigh a short distance around the manor to the carriage house in the back.

They all hugged goodbye under the shelter of the main door's portico. Then, like snowflakes blowing on the wind, they broke apart and went their separate ways. Amber strolled down the hedge path to the servants' quarters, where the Athel people were waiting for her to return. Violet went to the gardening hut between the smokehouse and the blacksmith's shed.

Niarr went to the parlor, which at this hour was vacant. She put a new log on the fire, reclined on the divan, and said, "I'll wait here for Jeree. He said he would come for me soon."

Ma Kielsing put her arm around Condrie, and together they ascended the stairs to one of the guestrooms. Only a few days had passed, and yet it felt like years—a lifetime—since Condrie had been employed in the kitchen of this house.

"Can't we push through the night, Mama? Can't we make it home to our own bed?"

"Whichever bed we are in, we make it our own."

*

Condrie lay awake in the dark as her mother quickly fell asleep. She stared up at the slats supporting the canopy over the bed. Her thoughts were a storm of half-formed dreams and imaginings of the future. Niarr—a humble wife. Violet—a docile caretaker of the baron's herb garden. Amber—scantily wrapped in a bed sheet. And herself as an older woman—counting coins and keeping a ledger of the tavern's accounts.

Light shined under the door. Someone softly knocked.

Niarr? Has Jeremee arrived to sweep you away? Condrie slipped out of the warm bed. She wrapped a wool shawl around her shoulders on the way to the door.

But when she opened it, no one was there. In the hallway was a glowing lantern, a sprig of dried lavender, and a carriage whip. Her brow furrowed in confusion. *Who could have dropped it?*

Looking down the hall, she listened for any sound of movement. A few doors away, Baron Jonvil snored loudly enough to be heard through his bedroom door.

The glowing lantern shined up through her hands. "Oh God," she whispered.

Picking up the lantern, Condrie hurried along the corridor. *It can't be.* Her feet pattered quickly over the hardwood floor. *Why would he be here?* At last, she arrived at the coachman's cloak room.

She slid aside the door panel, and there he was. This face was the new face she had seen at the roadside inn. But those eyes, twinkling in the light of the lantern she held—those eyes were the same.

His strong hands gripped her shoulders and pulled her inside. He slid the door panel shut. Together they huddled among the fur cloaks and fur-lined woolen capes.

"Why are you here?" she asked softly.

"I'm not here to beg you for help," he said. "I swear by the god of fire, I would not come near you if it weren't critical for me to warn you."

Condrie folded her arms. "Warn me about what?"

"Don't say anything about what I told you the last time we spoke."

"You mean when you pretended to kiss me goodbye so you could whisper a secret message into my ear?"

He put a warm hand to her cheek. Condrie turned her head away.

"Oh," he sighed, "don't be like that."

"Like what?" Condrie rotated around and faced the rack of woven scarves.

"I love you."

She gulped. "Don't say it."

"It's because I love you that I left. There's intrigue going on in the king's court, and I don't want to put you in danger. I've put you in enough danger already just by telling you. I'm sorry."

Slowly, she came around to him again. She raised her chin to look up at his face.

"Did you think the imposter would kill you if he knew that you spotted him?"

"Yes, I panicked. I'm sorry. I shouldn't have involved you. I should have held my tongue and found another way to break free."

Condrie rested a hand on his chest and felt the beating of his heart. "You're afraid of this imposter?"

"Yes."

"Is he in cahoots with Gerrie?"

"I'm not sure. I can't be sure of anything. I don't know who to trust."

She slipped her hand up to rest against his neck. "I'm glad you didn't kill him, though. That would've caused more trouble."

He licked his lips in a quick, darting motion. "Condy. . . ."

"You'll figure out this puzzle, and I won't say a thing until the truth comes to light."

"Condy, listen to me. I tried to kill him. God, I tried."

"What are you saying?" Her hand slipped away from his neck.

"The imposter who is impersonating the prince? He is not a man. He is not a Sagewyn of any type that I have ever seen. When I looked deep into the back of his eyes, I did not see flesh and blood. I saw . . ." he wagged his head, ". . .I saw stone."

Condrie put her hand to her own chest. "Stone?"

"More like a bluish-green jade or an unpolished peridot, I think. It was only a glance, but it was enough to see that he's not . . . alive. Condy, I went up to full flare. I reduced every stick of furniture in that room to ashes in a flash. I burned off all his clothes, too, and he just stood there, naked and confused. I couldn't even singe his hair!"

Condrie looked away from him to clear her thoughts. "Why would someone do such a thing?"

"That's an easy question to answer. Whoever created this abomination has control of a puppet who is destined to inherit the throne of the mightiest kingdom in the world."

"Does he mean to assassinate the king?" she asked.

"Most probably, when the time suits him . . . or them. God, I don't know who or how many people are involved in this conspiracy. It could be a single person. It could be a legion. The imposter is flawless to all eyes but mine. Even his own wife could be fooled."

"The prince has a wife?"

"Yes, certainly. He has a princess, a son, and two daughters."

"How old is the youngest child?"

"She's in her second year," Wegdell said. "Why?"

"That means the stone puppet replaced the prince less than three years ago."

Wegdell sat down on a stool. Now they were eye to eye. "It could have happened while I was still there. Yigs and I could have bowed to him and said good morning every day without really looking at him. I have the eyes of an eagle, but I never bothered to look at him. How could I be so stupid?"

She said, "Or the switch could have happened at some point after *that* night."

"I suppose, in all the commotion of hunting me . . . there would be opportunities when the prince made his journey up from the castle at Lake Ward to meet with the Council of Barons at Fordonhold. My God, it could be that Baron Fordon is behind it. We were in his household, after all."

Condrie frowned to think of what a mess it was. How could she be sure of whether to sympathize with the plotters or do everything in her power to foil their scheme? "Do you think the real prince is dead?"

He shrugged. "I don't know."

"Think! Do you think there's any hope that this magic needs the real prince to stay alive?"

"I don't know," he said again. "But if the real prince is breathing air anywhere in this world, I know of only one sure way to find him. I need to summon a shadow wraith."

"A wraith?" she gasped.

Wegdell stood up from the stool and moved for the door. "Once they get the scent of a target, there is not a man alive who can elude one."

He slid open the door panel. Condrie followed him into the dark hallway. Her eyes rolled left and right, wondering what sort of unholy spirits lurked unseen in the shadows. She whispered, "How do you summon one of those things?"

He lowered his head. If not for the lantern she held, she would have lost sight of him altogether.

"I'm sorry to involve you again, but . . . well, there's a few things I'll need from the kitchen. Go back to bed. I'll manage."

"Tell me," she said matter-of-factly. "What do you need?"

"An iron cauldron, a handful of soil, a flask of clean water, a kindling stick of oak or cedar, and. . . ."

When he paused too long, she asked, "And what?"

"A blood sacrifice," he answered in a breathy whisper.

*

So, it seems we're not going down into the root cellar. Isn't that where all the dark creatures of the underworld should be lurking? Condrie followed him out of the kitchen and into the narrow stairwell that only the servants used. She cradled the iron cauldron like a newborn babe in her arms. Inside it, she carried the soil, the flask of water, and the kindling stick from the wood pile. Wegdell carried one of the butler's cage traps, and inside it wriggled a large brown rat.

He led her upstairs to the second floor. He strolled down a connecting corridor leading to the north side of the house. The rat in the cage squealed and hissed so loudly that Condrie feared the pest would wake everyone in the house.

"Can't you do something to make it quiet?" she whispered.

"Not much farther," he answered.

Wegdell reached up to the ceiling for an iron ring. He pulled down a rack of wooden stairs on a chain.

"The attic?" she asked.

"After you, love."

Condrie balanced the cauldron on her hip so she could hold up her skirts with the other hand. She ascended the narrow stairs and emerged in a dim, moonlit space. A glass-paned window let the colors of the night shine through. The air was cool and blue.

"Are you sure you know how to do this?" she asked.

"Yes." The roof beams slanted so sharply that Wegdell had to crouch over. "You see, wraiths are simple creatures. I think of them in the same way as I think of hummingbirds and butterflies. If you have a garden of blooming flowers, they will come."

Condrie knelt to set the cauldron down. Wegdell settled cross-legged on the floor, facing her, with the pot in between them. He uncorked the flask and dribbled the water into the soil. He stirred it with the stick until the mud was a creamy paste.

Next, he set the caged rat on top of the rim. He leaned over it and, with the tender care of a master cook, sang a low droning note into the cauldron. His voice echoed in the little iron pot as if he were singing into a deep well. Her gut vibrated. Her ears rang. The rat held still.

When he stopped singing, she looked around the room at the locked trunks, dusty rocking chairs, children's toys, and harp. The shadows were still just shadows; nothing had moved.

"It didn't wo—" Condrie turned back to him, and words gagged in her throat.

At his side crouched a man, but not a man. He had a thin pale face and eyes drained of all color. His lips were gray. He wore a black cowl and black clothes, so all that showed of him was his face.

"Hello, Weg," he said. His voice had a light, boyish tone.

"Thank you for coming, Sele. I need to find someone." Wegdell gestured to the caged rat. "I brought you a gift."

"It's a bit small." The wraith's colorless eyes roved in Condrie's direction. She balled up her fists but held her ground. "We were, uh, in a rush."

"It's important, Sele, so if you could consider this an advance payment? As a favor to me?"

"For you, Weg," said the wraith as he took hold of the cage. "Who do you wish to find?"

"Prince Naiirengé."

The wraith grinned, and in the moonlight, all of his teeth were blue. "He's at Fordonhold, negotiating a treaty with the Council of Barons. You didn't need to summon *me* to learn that."

"It's not really him. That one's an imposter masquerading as the prince."

"Oh, now that's interesting!" The wraith opened the cage trap. He snatched out the rat and, with a quick twist of his hands, snapped its neck. Then he held the animal's head close to his mouth. Eyes closed, the wraith inhaled the rat's last gasp.

Condrie crossed her arms, but somehow, she did not feel afraid. She marveled at herself for sitting here in the presence of a nightmarish creature, and all the frightening stories she had ever heard since childhood faded away in her mind. She had witnessed it sucking out the soul of a poor, innocent animal and licking his lips to savor the taste of the death. Even so, she did not fear for her own safety.

Wegdell continued, "I'm not sure if the real prince is alive or not. If not, then I owe you a fat coney. If he is, and if he's being held captive somewhere, that'll give me the answer as to who is behind this scheme. I'll buy you a whole rabbit hutch to suck down if you lead me to him."

"Lambs," said the wraith, pursing his thin, pale lips. "If I find the prince alive, I want a dozen spring lambs."

"Deal."

The wraith somersaulted backward into the shadows. Condrie felt a prickle on her neck that caused her to blink, and when she opened her eyes again, he was gone.

He said, "I'm sorry that was unpleasant. Thank you for your help."

She picked up the cauldron and started back for the hatch in the floor. "No, actually, it was not so bad at all. He's quite polite."

"All wraiths were ordinary men at one time in their lives. Some of them can still remember being human." He remained where he sat, looking to the moonlit window.

"Aren't you coming?" she asked.

"No, you go back to bed. Get some sleep. I'll wait here for him."

Condrie put down her foot to the first step. "If you get the answer that the prince is alive somewhere, will you come and wake me?"

"Of course, love."

"Promise? You won't leave without telling me?"

"You have my word."

*

Condrie awoke in bed to the touch of a gentle hand on her shoulder. The fingers were cool. Not him.

"You must be exhausted, sweetie," said her mother. "I brought you a little breakfast."

"Is it . . . is it . . . m-m-morning?" Condrie sat up, and wool blankets fell away into her lap. The bed's curtains were drawn aside. Golden sunlight shined through the slats of the window shutters. Cool air seeped into the thin weave of her linen shift.

"Very much so." Her mother, fully dressed, sat on the mattress to offer a flask of cider, a yeast roll, a wedge of cheese, and an apple.

Condrie chewed the cold food slowly. *He didn't keep his promise. He left without me.*

"It's a clear day," her mother said. "Not a cloud for as far as a hawk can see. Hardly a puff of wind to speak of. So there's no need to hurry. When you feel ready, we'll walk home."

"Thank you, Mama." She drank a little cider; it was sweet and bitter at the same time. "Is Niarr still w-w-w-waiting . . . ?"

Ma Kielsing looked down at her own hands. "The lieutenant arrived just before dawn. He proposed marriage to her by getting down on bended knee with his whole squad as witnesses."

"I m-m-missed it?"

"So did I, sweetie."

A commotion of voices drummed past the door. Rapidly moving shoes rattled the floorboards of the hallway. Condrie frowned curiously; it sounded like dozens of people hurrying about.

"Mama, what's—?"

"Don't give it a thought."

As soon as her mother had said this, Condrie recognized the unique sound of heavy black boots stomping up and down a household's stairs. *He proposed marriage with his whole squad as witnesses!* Then she recalled the messenger at the roadside tavern from a few days before. He had advised the innkeeper that Captain Leera Vilbyss was being transported in chains to the king's court along with the prince's entourage

"Mama, who . . . who . . . ?"

Knuckles rapped at the door.

Baron Jonvil himself flung it open and breezed inside. He was informally dressed in a housecoat, silk hose, and flat shoes. His shaggy hair was in disarray, and locks fell across his forehead. Large brown eyes seemed ready to pop out of his small face.

"Praises be, Kiels, you're still here." His usually calm voice had a tinge of desperation.

Ma Kielsing stood up politely to greet him. "Yes, sir, I want to offer thanks for your most generous intercession on my girl's behalf."

The baron glanced to the bed and then back to the standing woman. "My daughter is having a fit of shyness and has locked herself in her room. She refuses to serve as hostess for our guests. She wishes for me to say that she is ill with a fever or some such nonsense. By the stars, if only I had remarried!"

Ma Kielsing approached him slowly, as one would approach an injured dog. "Can your aunt come?"

"Yes, yes, I've already sent word to the temple in Gorm Valley, but it's going to take at least a week for her to get here. Whatever shall I do *now*, today? My guests must be properly received and settled into their accommodations. Oh yes, my steward can welcome them at the door, but . . . Kiels, I need you!"

She put a hand on his sleeve. "Of course, Jon."

"Why is this happening to me? Why do they need to come here? How much damage can there be at Fordonhold, after all? Some fireplace got out of hand and ruined a few carpets, and now the Council of Barons and the Prince of Xol himself are bringing their summit *here*?"

Condrie rose out of bed.

"A whole division of knights is taking over my servants' barracks. Their horses are crowding into my stables. They have a prisoner in chains! They're stowing her in my wine cellar as we speak. What is my house now, a jail?"

Condrie pulled her one-piece gown over her head. She tightened up the lacing strings that sealed the front seam of the bodice.

"Please calm yourself, Jon," said Ma Kielsing.

Baron Jonvil paced back and forth to the shuttered window. He flexed his hands in and out of fists. "How can I calm myself, Kiels? I've got a prince and all his retinue, a quorum of barons and all their entourage, and a pair of Sagewyn here! Did you hear me? Mystical creatures with magical powers are under my roof. My liege lords are all assembled here, in my house, to negotiate a treaty with the Kingdom of Xol. The success or failure of this summit—no, the entire fate of the world is in my hands. By the stars, what do I know of etiquette and courtly manners? If I should happen to offend anyone, the negotiations may fail, and it will lead to a war of conquest. My wheat fields will go up in flames. My home will be reduced to rubble. And it will all be my fault if I don't draw a proper seating arrangement at supper!"

Ma Kielsing took hold of his face. She looked him sternly in the eye. "I'm here, Jon."

"Praises be. I'm so lost."

"Listen, now, I have served the likes of these, and I know their habits very well. Be assured that I shall properly welcome all your guests as if I were the lady of the house."

Baron Jonvil took a deep shuddering breath. "Thank you, Kiels. Bless you."

"You'll owe me six silver coins for every day that I'm here."

Condrie turned away from the baron's shocked expression so he would not see her smile. That was more than the house steward earned in a month. She made her hands busy with tucking her hair up into her linen cap.

"Six?" the baron repeated. "In silver? Per day?"

"Yes," she said. "And if you wish me to provide you with private bed service, the fee is double."

The baron stepped out of her hands. "No, I'm sure I won't be in the mood for that. I'll thank you to just provide assistance to my steward for the guest accommodations and supper arrangements. The girl here . . . she'll work in the kitchen?"

"Of course, she'd be glad to," said Ma Kielsing with a broad smile. "For twenty copper squares a day."

Condrie tied her apron around her waist. "Mama. . . ."

"Fifteen?" the baron asked.

Her mother glanced over her shoulder and let Condrie decide. *I was going to say twelve out of sympathy.* "Fi-fi-fifteen is fair."

*

Condrie rolled up her sleeves and kept her head down. She focused on chopping onions, slicing carrots, peeling squash and scooping out the seeds. She whipped egg whites into stiff peaks. She shredded cheese. She said not a word to anyone as the jumble of servants squabbled all around her. Pots of water splashed and spilled. Oil sizzled. Bread burned. Meringue went flat. Blue spotted pigeons got loose and, with clipped wings flapping, they ran across the kitchen floor.

All the while, as she worked up a sweat at the chopping table, she wondered if he were still hiding in the attic.

"What is that horrid smell?" Gerrawgon the Sagewyn strolled into the kitchen.

The master cook was in the middle of rubbing a paste of mustard, honey, peppercorns, and dried sage over a pork rump roast. He dropped to his knees, bowing to the lord. Everyone else in the kitchen prostrated their hands and foreheads to the floor. Condrie joined them and was glad for the opportunity to tuck her face into her sleeves.

Gerrawgon sniffed deeply, inhaling the scent of the numerous bubbling cauldrons. "It's not the fish heads or the duck livers or the pork intestines."

"Shall I . . . ?" The master cook gulped his nervousness before he continued. "If there is an odor that offends you, sir, shall I make Your Lordship a pomander of lemon rind and cloves?"

"I know this stink." Gerrawgon strolled away from the fireplace. He came nearer and nearer to where Condrie knelt, curled in prostration.

"Whatever offends you, sir," the cook said. "I shall remove it immediately."

Gerrawgon stood just behind her feet. He sniffed the air again. "I know it now. It's a shadow wraith."

"What!" the cook cried.

"How odd," the Sagewyn continued in a calm, thoughtful tone. "I don't see a mourning wreath. No one has died in this household recently, have they?"

"Uh, no . . . no, sir," the cook said. "Not for many years."

Gerrawgon strolled away to the main door. "Well, perhaps it's all this slaughter of livestock that brought the damned wretch sniffing around. Never mind. Carry on, my good man. And don't over-boil the fish."

When he had gone, everyone in the kitchen rose shakily to their feet. "Circle o' blood," the cook swore, clutching his apron as the cauldrons bubbled over and the bacon sizzled to blackened strips.

Condrie was the first to coolly resume her task: shelling green peas out of their pods. "The ba-ba-bacon. . . ."

"Damn!"

Condrie looked around at all of the servants shaken by a fever of terror. *It's not right that one person should have such an influence—even if he is a thousand years old! I solved the mystery when he couldn't bother to think it through. What thanks do I get? To stand here shelling peapods.* She looked down at her wrinkled fingertips. *What am I even doing here, in this kitchen? After all the adventures I've survived and all the fantastic things I've seen, is this my reward? Fifteen copper squares a day? Is this what my life is destined to be?*

A tall, lean fellow passed behind her. He carried a sack of flour on his broad shoulders. He paused at Condrie's back and leaned down close to her ear.

"I owe someone a dozen lambs," he whispered.

The real prince is alive! Condrie dropped her handful of pea pods. She whirled about on her heels.

Wegdell dumped the flour sack on a table where two women rocked back and forth, kneading loaves in clouds of white dust. He did not look back. He kept walking across the kitchen on his way to the delivery door at the rear.

She hurried after him.

"Hey, you," the cook called. "Where are you going?"

"Fi-fi-fi-firewood."

Condrie leaped out the back door. Her flat shoes slipped on the icy slush, and she put out her arms to catch her balance.

There he was, on the footpath heading for the stables. She tucked up her long skirts and sprinted after him.

At the rosemary hedges, he turned and caught her in his hands. "It seems we're always saying goodbye."

"Take me with you!" She panted in gusts of thick white fog.

"I can't."

"Oh." Condrie raised her eyes and admired the blue sky, free of clouds. The crisp, cool air had limitless possibilities. "You're going to fly?"

"Actually, no. Wraiths can't fly, and he's the only one who can sniff out the trail. I'm going to borrow a horse."

She brought her hopeful smile back to him. "Then you *can* take me with you."

"It's most likely going to be dangerous. He's found a trail leading south and followed it for a while before he turned around to come and get me. Do you understand what I'm saying? The trail leads south."

"Into the heartland of the Kingdom of Xol?"

"Yes."

"So it isn't a work of treachery from one of our barons. It's a plot hatched in the court of the king?"

"Appears that way." He took a step backward, and she kept with him. "Please, go back to the kitchen."

She gripped his sleeve. "I won't. I can't. I tell you, I'll go utterly mad if you make me go back! If I have to shell one more pea pod, I swear I'll start screaming and I won't be able to stop!"

He shook his head, averting his eyes. "I understand how you feel, but I can't have you risking your life to rescue a man who is not your prince."

"What if I *want* to risk my life to rescue someone?" Shivering, she leaned in closer to him. His body was as warm as a fire brick. "Shouldn't it be my choice?"

He looked aside to the footpath leading to the stables. Underneath the snow-coated chestnut tree, a shadowy black figure lurked.

"He's impatient to leave now," he said. "I can't wait for you to get dressed and pack a bag."

"You'll keep me warm, won't you?"

He looked back to her, and their eyes met, and he could not look away.

*

Condrie sat astride a saddle. Wegdell rode behind her on the horse's rump. His arms reached around her to hold the reins. Her legs rested on top of his that were fixed into the stirrups. His full-circle wool cloak wrapped around them both. The black horse galloped along the snowy road that Condrie had walked so many times before. That oak tree . . . that pond . . . that cluster of hyssk reeds bent sideways with the weight of snow. . . . Faster and faster, the landscape turned into a blur. *Is this like flying?* she wondered.

The horse galloped over the bridge. Condrie looked aside to where she had often lingered at the stone railing to watch the currents flow into the river. Creek waters gurgled around lumps of frosted rock. It passed in a blink.

Rooftops of the town surged into view. How strange it all looked to her, though she had called this place home for the last ten years. Those stucco walls and dark wooden fences all crammed together in the dish of a broad valley. She knew every craftsman's shop and imagined them going about their daily chores. Every day, the same drudgery. Until now, she had never wondered how people could endure such a monotonous life.

Wegdell turned the horse away from the town. She felt the subtle shift of his body and did her best to follow along, leaning when he leaned slightly to the left or to the right. Bending forward into the horse's pumping neck caused the mighty beast to go even faster. Faster! Its broad, shaggy hooves padded noiselessly in the powdery snow.

They galloped on the frontage road that followed the shore of the river. It would have taken most of the day for her to walk this far, but the sun was still high in the clear blue sky.

"Faster, faster!" she called out with delight.

"Hmmph," he grunted with his cheek snuggled into her hair.

The horse stretched forth its broad neck and pumped its thick legs harder. Rooftops and stucco walls whizzed by the corners of her eyes. Cool air stung her cheeks, and she did not worry about frostbite. The firebird was at her back.

Merchants' wagons and artisans' pushcarts were slow-moving obstacles on the road. Condrie sucked up her breath as they swooped full-speed into the midst of them.

"Watch out!" she cried.

He did not slow down. He guided the horse deftly, weaving among them like a hummingbird among the flowers.

"Hey!" men shouted. Apple baskets toppled. Caged pigeons flapped. Children screamed. Voices faded in the wake of the galloping horse's tail.

Stop, stop, she wanted to say, but her jaw clenched too tightly to speak. Her hands gripped the saddle's pommel.

An ale maker's wagon rushed into view. Condrie held her breath. Her eyes widened, and in that moment, she was certain they would either leap the wagon or crash head first into the barrels.

Wegdell dodged it—just barely—but smacked a pole off someone's shoulder. A bucket shattered. Clumps of half-frozen dung pelted them like black snowballs.

"Char!"

She laughed.

He reined in the speed and brought the galloping horse down to a loping gait. By the time they reached the riverside wharf, the horse was trotting and Condrie was bouncing on the saddle.

"Whoa, whoa," he said, bringing the mighty beast to a stop.

The horse dropped its nose to the ground. It snorted and huffed in clouds of foggy breath. Sweat droplets glistened on its black hair.

Wegdell sprang off the rump. Condrie, alone in the saddle, shivered at the grip of icy air. He reached up to catch her as she slid off. She landed on the ground and snuggled up under his warm cloak once more.

"Was that fun?" he asked.

"Oh God, yes! Is that how it feels to fly?"

"Not at all."

He flicked a bronze coin through the air to a ferryman loitering by a fence. "Take care of this horse, my good man, and be sure he's returned to the nearest knight of Xol."

"Yes, sir."

Wegdell sharply looked aside. She followed his gaze. A shadow slipped around the corner of the dock house.

"I should like to hire a boat," he said to the dock master.

"Of course, my good man." He puffed on a pipe. The dock master had a beard of thick whiskers. Nothing of his face showed except for his squinting gray eyes. "Whither ye bound?"

"South."

"How far?"

"Until I say stop."

The dock master turned his scrutiny to her. Although she was under the wing of his cloak, anyone could clearly see that she only wore a house gown, an apron, a linen cap, and flat shoes. His narrow eyes rolled to the side and took a survey of the grand black steed with its elegant tooled saddle of Xolian leather.

Condrie's mind buzzed with all sorts of possible explanations for their peculiar appearance. Each lie was more ridiculous than the last. Perhaps she was escaping from the abuses of a cruel husband. Perhaps he was being pressured by his family to marry a woman he did not love and was running away with her. Perhaps he was a lord from the Kingdom of Xol and had come north to purchase a bride.

"Two silver coins up front," Wegdell said to the dock master. "Three more when I get to my destination."

The dock master put out his hand. Wegdell put a pair of coins into his knit glove.

"I have just the boat for you, sir."

*

A lone ferryman piloted a broad skiff with a long oar affixed to the rear. A large crate occupied much of the boat's center. They reclined together on bench seats at the prow. Condrie snuggled under his warm cloak. She rested her head on his chest and listened to his heartbeat, steady, slow, and deep like the waters of the river swishing beneath them.

She watched the sunset through the drooping boughs of snow-crusted trees lining the river. Always the white land was in motion, ever changing. Whatever she had known for the last ten years was passing away. Dark waters flowed between frosty riverbanks that, in the evening's fiery colors, looked like a meringue of strawberry cream. *Could this be my life? New colors. New sights. New people. Not only for this day, but for all the years ahead?*

Soon the sky darkened to a deep shade of indigo. The moon shined like a silver coin. Stars reflected in the dark, flowing waters of the river, and the sparkles made it seem as if the boat floated across the heavens.

She fell asleep with his chest as her pillow. She dreamed of lying beside a fiery yellow crane, embraced in his wings of burning feathers. She was not harmed, for she had become a bird herself, with flaming plumage of scarlet and orange.

By morning, the boat pulled into the docks of a small village. The ferryman swapped places with a man whom he greeted as a friend. Wegdell gave a couple of square bronze coins to a villager and received a basket of apples, some walnuts in a kerchief, and skewers of grilled trout.

"How much farther south, sir?" the replacement ferryman asked. He took hold of the long oar at the rear of the skiff.

"Until I say stop."

Condrie glimpsed a wisp of a shadow darting through the frosted bushes at the shoreline. *The wraith.* Wegdell kept watching the riverbank with his keen eyes narrowed. She also wondered how much farther they would go; before long, they would reach the borders of the Kingdom of Xol.

The boat meandered onward, southward, leisurely following the currents that flowed out of the northern mountains. Spruce and pine trees became sparse. Barren fruit trees and broadleaf flowering trees grew out of the snowy meadows. Young stags chewed at tree bark. Sparrows and jays and swallows filled the clear air with fluttering wings.

"My mother must be wondering what happened to me by now."

He stroked the top of her head. "It's not too late. I can drop you at the next village. I'll give you coins to hire a ride back home."

Condrie tugged the edge of his cloak more tightly under her chin. "I am home."

He pecked a kiss on her forehead.

"But can we buy a sheet of paper at the next village? I'll write her a letter."

His arm tightened around her. "Perhaps it's best if we wait to write letters until we've done what we're going to do."

"Oh . . . I see." She looked to the shoreline and, in a blink, caught the wisp of a shadow slipping between the tree trunks.

"Perhaps you're forgetting that we may be going into danger."

"No, I'm not," she said.

"It's so wonderful to have you sleeping in my arms," he continued, talking on top of her without missing a beat. "But we can't afford to get too comfortable nesting in this boat. We don't know what lies ahead."

"Can't you send *him* to—"

"He's a tracker, not a soldier. He will lead us to our target, but he will not approach it. You need to understand that once we reach our destination, the wraith can't help us."

*

The river broadened, opening to the afternoon sky and curving southwest. The snow was not so deep here, and in scattered patches, the darker ground showed through. Trees had two colors in mirror image: a dusting of frost covered the northern sides of their trunks and boughs, and the opposite sides were dry and free of whiteness.

"How much farther, sir?" the ferryman asked.

"Keep going until I say so."

At sunset, the boat pulled into a dock at a fishing village. Wegdell bought a couple of pastries filled with a pepper-and-onion meat hash. Condrie chewed slowly on the unfamiliar spices.

She looked at the villagers, who were taller than most of the people in her town. They had light brown or cinnamon-colored hair and covered their heads with round, flat caps instead of hoods or cowls. Men and women alike wore the same sort of wraparound robe belted at the waist. Baggy trousers tucked into ankle-high boots with sagging cuffs.

Children tossed a ball between themselves. They laughed, speaking in the dialect that Condrie had only heard from burly riverboat merchants, and their little voices were like the twittering of sparrows.

"Things are so different here," she said.

"Last chance to change your mind and go home, Condy." He gulped from a jug and then offered the spout to her. She shared a drink of his barley beer.

"I can't go back." She spoke softly, for him only. "I have to discover who . . . where . . . how . . . I can't know if *it's* a good thing or a bad thing until we reach the end of the road."

"Very well." He climbed back into the boat. "Let's pray that when we reach the end of the road, it won't be too late."

*

By nightfall on the second day, the skiff glided into the archway of a massive stone bridge. Condrie turned her head left and right to marvel at the full length of it. Blocks of granite fit together into a seamless span, a log of stone supported on massive pillars. Birds nested in the watery tunnel. Water gurgled, lapping against the columns.

Colossal statues stood sentinel beyond the bridge at the river's bend. The statues were not of people or animals, but a mixture of both. They had legs with hawks' feet, hands with claws, slender necks and vipers' heads, spike horns, scaly whiskers, and bat-like wings outstretched to either side. Their inhuman faces snarled in fearsome expressions. Their stony hands were open and reaching toward the river as if to seize whoever passed beneath them. Each talon matched the size of the boat in which they rode. She couldn't help but cringe closer to Wegdell's elbow.

"Those are the burned ones," he said. "The ancient gods, the architects of the world, who are worshiped by King Davarche and his court."

"They're hideous."

"It means we've crossed the border. We have entered the kingdom."

The ferryman steered toward the eastern riverbank. A wharf extended out from the rocky shore. Fires blazed in iron braziers. Torches marked the corners of the dock. Other boats were moored there, some larger and some smaller than the skiff in which they rode. Knights in black uniforms loitered at the dockside, leaning on their spears like farmers leaning on their rakes.

"Keep going into the lake," Wegdell said to the ferryman.

"I can't do that, sir. I need to pull in and be inspected first."

Wegdell offered a handful of silver coins. "I said, keep going."

The ferryman let up his grip on the oar. "Circle o' blood, if you wanted to be smuggled into th' kingdom, you shoulda said so at the start. I know some creeks . . . but now they've a-seed us."

Condrie sat up straight. "We've nothing to hide."

"How's that again?" Wegdell asked.

She finger-combed his black hair off his forehead. "You are the . . . the bastard son of Baron Jonvil, and you're curious about the kingdom that your father is planning to sign allegiance to. You've come down here to see the place for yourself."

The ferryman groaned. "That's terrible."

Condrie crossed her arms as the boat glided closer and closer to the dock. "Well, do you have a better story?"

Wegdell pinched the bridge of his nose. "Let me think."

"Say you're comin' to apply for a job," the ferryman said hurriedly. "Ye heard the castle's full of opportunity and you're a . . . a . . . what skills you got? What trade can you do? Wood joiner? Stone mason? Ale brewer?"

"He can sing," Condrie said.

"Oh, filth," the ferryman swore. "Pay me now."

A broad smile brightened Wegdell's face. "Have no worries, my good man."

The skiff pulled into the dock. Knights in black uniforms reached down to grab the rope and secure it to a post. Wegdell stood up tall at the prow, one foot perched on the plank where he had been sitting. He raised both of his hands in greeting.

"Good evening, my fine sirs." Wegdell's foreign accent dropped away. To Condrie's ears, he pronounced each word as plainly and clearly as a baron himself. "My name is Cobyn the Bateman's son, and I am a servant of Baron Jonvil of Rivertown Manor. I come from the hinterlands of the North bearing happy tidings to you."

"What tidings could ya bring to me, bumpkin?" The lieutenant hooked a thumb in his sword belt.

"It's about a friend of yours: Lieutenant Jeremee, born of Goodman Aigrue. He has proposed marriage to a fine woman."

"Jeree? That whore-monger? Getting married?" The knights burst into a chorus of hearty guffaws.

"It's true!" Wegdell put an arm around Condrie's shoulders. "This woman is her sister. We're coming to bring the news to his honorable father. So, my good sir, if you could be so kind as to give us a pass, we'll be on our way."

One of the knights—a woman with blonde hair—cocked her eyebrow. "On yer way to where, exactly?"

Wegdell kept smiling. "Jeree said that his home is a town on the east shore of Lake Ward, a place called, uh, Khro-buggis-fog-zin?"

"Khrobugh'iszn," the woman knight corrected.

"Yes, that's it! Oh, these foreign words. . . . I'm told that from the marketplace fountain, I go past the cooper's shop, three streets down, take a left at the ditch, and look for the silversmith's shop between the tea house and the tailor."

The first lieutenant nodded along. "Yeah, that's Jeree's father's house all right."

Another knight handed Condrie a wafer of reddish cedar. Burned into the wood was the emblem of a bull's head and the intricate lettering of High Classical Xol. She recognized a few numerals and guessed that it indicated this day's date.

"Thank you, good sirs." Wegdell gave them a deep, flourishing bow that rocked the boat.

The ferryman pushed off from the dock. He let out a sigh. Behind them, the knights remarked to each other, "I hope we get invited to the wedding. What woman would agree to marry him? That's something I'd pay to see!"

"How much farther, sir?" the ferryman asked.

"Until I say stop."

*

The river emptied into Lake Ward, an expanse of calm waters as broad as any meadowlands that Condrie had ever seen. Her eyes widened to try and take it all in. If only the night were not so dark, nor the waning moon so pale; she would have liked to see more colors. A small island was a dark spot at the center of shimmering, glassy waters. Snow-dusted trees in the distance were all the hint she could see of the lake's edges. At the far eastern shore, she saw dimly the blocky shapes of what she assumed were rocky cliffs.

"This is as far as I go, sir." The ferryman pulled into a pebbly shore. He hopped out of the boat and gestured for the two of them to do the same.

Wegdell looked off to the trees. A man's pale face lurked in the hollows of branches.

"I didn't say stop."

"You're not paying me enough, sir." The ferryman pointed to the eastern shore. "You tricked the coats into giving you a pass over the border, but whatever wicked business brings you to Xolhold Castle, it's your business alone."

Xolhold Castle! She squinted again to the eastern shore and the pale stones faintly outlined by moonlight. Now she recognized the evenly measured shapes of the round towers and square walls of the labyrinth that she had only seen before in a dream.

"Go steal a boat from town. I shake you off my shoes."

"Too much to ask for you to wait here for us?" Wegdell climbed out of the skiff. He grimaced when his boots plunged calf-deep into the water.

"Quite right, sir." The ferryman accepted coins into his hand. "I'm turning around from here. May the goddess watch over you."

"Thank you for taking us this far," Condrie said to the man.

Wegdell lifted her up in his arms to carry her to dry land. He set her feet down on cold grass.

Together they watched the ferryman push off from shore. The oar lapped softly in the calm waters.

Condrie rubbed her arms, but though she felt cool, it was nowhere near the bite of freezing air. The trees had no snow. The grass had no frost. Breathing produced only a faint puff of vapor. It seemed that in the span of days, they had glided ahead through the seasons and winter was already turning into spring. She recalled what he had told her once: *The only thing about the king's domain that is mild is the weather.*

"It's not far now," the wraith whispered behind his back.

Wegdell looked across his shoulder. "How can that be, Sele? We're practically at the old bull's doorstep."

"I smell him," the wraith said. "I smell him nearby. He is very near . . . very near."

"Lead the way."

Condrie followed them, not into the woods, but along the lake's shore. Her shoes crunched softly on the pebbled grass. They walked for a while but did not seem to be getting anywhere. More pine and fir and sycamore trees, more juniper and fern bushes, more moss-covered rocks passed by, but they only seemed to be circling around the lake.

A fisherman's home came into view—one of the first at the edge of the unpronounceable town. One small rowboat was hung up sideways on a post.

The wraith crouched over to sniff at the ground. "Here. The last place he put foot on land is here."

Wegdell put his hands on his hips. "How can that be? Is he in this house?"

"No." The wraith raised his nose to sniff at the lake's waters. "There."

"Oh God, is he in the castle?"

"No, the island." The wraith inhaled deeply. "Yes, I'm sure of it. He's on that island."

Wegdell threw his hands up to the air, his cloak flaring out like dark wings. "Char!"

She asked, "What's wrong?"

He whirled about and pointed his whole arm at the lake. "The Isle of Xettzin has a flower garden that is the prince's favorite place to be. He tenderly cares for orchids and amaryllis under a tent of silk mesh. He catches butterflies on his fingertips. He writes poetry when the plum blossoms come into bloom."

"I don't understand," Condrie said.

"I've been an idiot! I see . . . but I don't *think* about what I see. This whole time, I assumed that an impersonator would be a part of some treasonous scheme. I never considered that the opposite could be true. Oh God! During the war, the king used men dressed up as decoys of himself in battle. It seems that, for his own son, he's come up with something a bit better."

"A decoy," she repeated. "Of course! Why send your real flesh-and-blood son and heir into unknown territory? If the barons were foolish enough to take him hostage or assassinate him, they would gain nothing. An enchanted puppet would act as a trustworthy representative in an unknown situation. He can't be bribed. He can't be coerced. It's a brilliant idea, if that's what is really happening here."

"Of course that's what's happening." Wegdell kicked into the pebbly soil. "Let the puppet do all the work, and Naiins sits safely at home with his feet dry and warm by a fire."

The wraith said, "You still owe me a dozen spring lambs. I did what you asked."

"Yes, yes, Sele, I promise. Find me in the spring, and I'll gladly pay you then."

The wraith's colorless eyes turned to Condrie. "I'll find *her*."

Condrie blinked, and the shadow was gone.

Wegdell sat down on a log. He put his elbows on his knees and pressed his hands over his face. "I'm sorry I hauled you all the way down here for no good reason. I'm sorry I'm such an idiot."

Condrie stayed on her feet. It felt good to stand after so many hours of sitting in the boat.

"It doesn't have to be a wasted day," she said. "You know, there's still a death warrant and a bounty on your head. The puppet promised to write a letter to his father . . . er, the king, to ask for a new trial for you. But that won't happen until after the summit with the Council of Barons and after all the celebration and feasting and such. It could be another month or two before he returns here. Until then, you're still a wanted fugitive."

He looked up at her. "What are you suggesting?"

"Let's talk to the real prince tonight. He feels friendly toward you, doesn't he? Let's tell him what happened with Leera and the feathers and ask *him* to appeal to his father in the morning. You might have a signed pardon in your hands by lunchtime tomorrow."

Wegdell slowly rose to his feet. "Have I told you how wonderful you are?"

*

When they reached the island at the center of Lake Ward, he dragged the rowboat up to a hedge of thorny bushes. Condrie went ahead to the latch of a gateway in the high wooden fence. The garden door swung outward quietly on well-oiled iron hinges. *Oh yes, someone is living here.*

Wegdell picked up a glass lantern that was hanging off the handle of a wheelbarrow. He reached in to pinch the wick. Fire sprang off his fingertips and set the lantern aglow.

A footpath of hard-packed sand threaded between all sorts of ferns and shrubbery. Condrie regarded the dim leaves as she strolled along and wondered what sorts of flowers might bloom in the spring. Thorns snagged on her apron, and she knew them to be roses.

Water trickled from a fountain's spout into a pond. A willow tree drooped its fronds near the surface. Gentle fish swam in circles around the tall stalks of lilies. All the colors were gray.

"Even in the dark, it's beautiful here," she said. "I never imagined there could be such a place in King Davarche's domain."

Wegdell said nothing. He walked ahead of her, carrying the lantern to the door of a thatched cottage. It was a simple abode with stucco walls and a straw roof. It looked more like a woodcutter's home than a place fit for a prince.

The door had no lock. Wegdell flipped the latch and pushed inward.

Condrie entered with him into a cozy little room. At one side, a fireplace was dying down to a dull orange glow. At the other side, a man slept on a simple cot. She knew his face at once—the same narrow cheekbones and pointed chin. A knitted nightcap was halfway falling off his thick black hair.

"Char," Wegdell swore. He set the lantern on a square tea table that had a single stool.

She went to put another log on the fire.

Wegdell rapped his knuckles on the headboard of the bed. "Your Highness, sir?"

The prince sat up, startled. "Prithee, who disturbeth me?"

He genuflected down on one knee. He looked the prince straight in the eye. "It's me, sir, Wegsemze."

The prince seized his hand. "Ah, so it is. Dear friend, how wonderful it is to see you!"

"The feeling is reciprocated, sir."

The prince looked across the room to Condrie at the fireplace. "You there, are you Lady Waemaria or Lady Semmarie?"

She whirled around. "Um, neither. They're both dead."

"Dead?" the prince gasped.

"My God," Wegdell said. "Hasn't anyone told you?"

The prince shifted around on the cot's narrow mattress. He leaned up, sitting against the wall. "I don't like to hear about what happens out there. It's all so terrible."

"Yes, much of it is." Wegdell settled down to sit cross-legged on the floor. Even sitting, the level of his head was not much lower than the prince in bed slouched against the wall. "How long have you been hiding away in this garden, Your Highness?"

"A year and a half."

Wegdell tilted his head. "So, back at the start of summertime, you were in here with your posies and your butterflies. No one told you about the tragedy?"

"You have my belated condolences. I'm sincerely sorry that the ladies are dead. Do you mourn them? You must have loved them, in your own sort of way. Did you?"

Wegdell looked down at his lap. "They were in my flock. I was mating with them; I wasn't in love with them."

The prince gazed across the room and made eye contact with Condrie. "What about this one? Is she your new mate?"

"Sir, if I may?" Wegdell raised his face. "I need to tell you what happened on the night that my flock died."

"Is it not only the ladies?"

"No, Your Highness, it's Lord Thydrick and my brother, too. All of them . . . all of them are gone. You see, it began as—"

The prince closed his eyes. "Don't."

"But sir—"

"No, no, no, I don't want to hear anything about people dying. So much sorrow. So much blood . . . so much blood. I cannot bear the thought of it."

Wegdell rose up to his knees. "But sir, you need to understand what happened if I'm to beg a favor of you."

"No!" The prince drew up his knees into his chest. "I cannot grant anyone any favors."

Wegdell got to his feet. He loomed over the slender young man on the cot. "I am wrongly accused of their murders! The king has signed my death warrant. I need you to—"

"Stop, stop." The prince put his hands over his ears.

"Damnit, by God, have you no spine at all?"

Condrie hurried over to take hold of Wegdell's sleeve. "Take a step back. You won't get anywhere by shouting at him."

He stomped away. He took a stand by the fireplace and gripped the rough-hewn timber that served as a mantle.

"Please don't be angry," the prince said quietly. "Don't be angry. Don't be angry. Don't be angry."

Condrie settled beside him on the narrow cot. The frame squeaked. She laid her gentle hand on his head, although she doubted he could feel her touch through the knitted nightcap and his thick curly hair.

"What color are your roses?" she asked.

He blinked at her, and his eyes were soft and moist. "What is it thou askest me?"

"Tell me about your roses."

His brows crinkled in curiosity as he kept his eyes fixed on hers. "I have yellow ones and red ones and white ones. I cross-pollinate them and make blended colors. Red and yellow make orange. Red and white make pink. I keep a logbook to try and predict a pattern in the results. Sometimes they're dappled. Sometimes a pair of pink roses produces white again. Those are my favorite—the ones taken from pink that come out white."

"White," she said with a smile. "Blank, empty, ready to be painted."

The prince touched her hand. "Thou art a firebird *not*."

She shrugged. "I'm just a woman."

He pulled his hand away. "Weg, you should not be here. My father will be very angry. Please don't make him angry."

While staring into the growing fire, he spoke over his shoulder. "I know about the puppet . . . the doll . . . whatever you call that abomination you sent to negotiate with the Council of Barons."

"It's the blue clay of the gods," the prince informed him. "It does my father's bidding, and I am grateful for it."

"My God, man, are you so afraid to speak up to your own father—"

"Yes!" the prince cried. "It's a fool who isn't afraid of him. For my whole life, I have felt nothing but terror of that man. He has felt nothing but contempt for me. Do you think I don't hear how the lords at court mock me behind their hands? Do you think I am unaware that my father has toyed with the idea of quietly assassinating me or locking me in some forgotten hole in his dungeon? As soon as I managed to produce a grandson for him, I knew my days were numbered."

Condrie blinked at tears welling up in her eyes. Until now, she had reviled her own father as the wickedest man in the world for selling her into marriage with the landlord to pay off a debt. Yet even in the darkest days of her life, she had never feared that her father—or her husband—might actually murder her.

"Gerrie told me of this legendary clay that he had heard rumor of a few hundred years ago. He helped my father find it and instructed him in how to sculpt it in my image. The puppet is animated by a lock of my hair that I donated with my blessing."

"With your blessing?" Wegdell sneered back at him. "You abandoned your own family by choice? You hide yourself away in this butterfly garden with your pink roses and rainbow fish while you let a walking statue be a father to your children and a husband to your wife?"

"He is a better prince, husband, and father than I could ever be. He is proud and fearless without being greedy or ambitious. He is obedient without being meek. He is everything that I am not. My father is pleased with him, and I am allowed to live."

Condrie's jaw shuddered. Tears leaked freely down her cheeks.

Looking at her, the prince began to smile. "Thou weepest for my sake? What a gift thou hast given to me. Not a soul has wept for my sake in all of my life."

"I don't weep for your sake," she said, deliberately omitting any sort of honorific. "I weep for the sake of your son, for the future of this kingdom, and for all of us in this world."

The prince pressed his hand to her shoulder, nudging her to stand up. "Weg, you should leave me now. You're not supposed to be here. No one is supposed to know I'm here."

*

Outside the garden wall, he stopped and stood very still. "God, I am so tempted to go up to full flare right now. I want to reduce this whole place to ashes."

"Please don't." Condrie looked up at him. Turned away from the moonlight, his face was all darkness. "You'll only frighten him worse and lose any chance to ever coax him out of hiding."

He took broad, quick steps toward the rowboat. She hurried to keep up with him.

"I wanted so much to perform a grand, heroic rescue. I wanted to do something that would have made my brother proud."

"Yigs would be proud of you," she said. "As I am."

He held her arm, like a gentleman would, and helped her step into the rowboat.

"Where should I go now?" He waded knee-deep to push the rowboat into the water. Its hull scraped over the pebbly sand. "How can I start a revolution if I can't even convince one timid man to get up out of his comfortable bed?"

She gazed across the lake to the southwestern shore. Moonlight illuminated the jagged rooftops of the town. A few windows still glimmered as faint dots of orange amid the bluish-black landscape.

"Let's find a tavern," she said, "and get a room for the night."

"Or what's left of the night." He climbed into the boat, took the seat facing her, and picked up the oars.

Condrie looked beyond the town at the shadows between the trees. She thought of the wraith that came when summoned and disappeared when the task was done. The oars lapped loudly in the deep, dark waters. She thought of the Sagewyn's wife. *Gerrawgon had said, "I don't need to trust her. I own her."*

She said, "What if you don't need to start with convincing *men* to get up out of their beds? What if you follow your brother's example and start with the Sagewyn?"

"Start . . . how? Tell me more of what you're thinking." He rocked slowly forward and back, flexing his arms to pull the oars. The rowboat glided slowly, silently across the lake.

"This king is so powerful and terrifying because he has mystical creatures like you to enforce his will. Am I right?"

"Yes."

"What if he were just a man . . . just a greedy, mean-tempered man without Sagewyn to serve his every cruel whim?"

"Actually, the king is a very pleasant and congenial fellow," Wegdell said. "If he considers you a friend, that is."

"You know what I'm trying to say!"

He shined a teasing smile. "Yes, love, I know."

"What if you were to keep your promise to Immy and find the vial of her native pond water? I think she'd like to be free of her husband."

He flexed his knees and dug in the oars a little deeper. "Perhaps."

"What if you keep going? What if you track down the un-folk, the weird, the shunned, and the damned before the king's hunter-trappers get to them? What if you help them to hide? What if you make a sanctuary someplace far away, so if the king wants to hold onto his dominion of the world, he's going to need to work for it?"

"With brute force, you mean, and legions of highly disciplined troops?" He checked over his shoulder to aim for the town's wharf.

"Troops are just people like Jeree," she said.

"Hmm, a bit naïve, but mostly true."

"It won't be easy," she said. "It will take some time. If we manage to hide them all the way you've been hiding, we could keep them out of his reach. Even more, we could start rumors that there are no such things as firebirds and water nymphs and wraiths in the shadows. In a generation or two, people might come to believe that they're just silly stories and stop hunting them altogether."

He pulled the oars a few more times before he drew them in and held still.

"I like this," he said. "I like this idea of being the protector and guardian of all the un-folk of the world."

The rowboat glided smoothly up to the pier. Condrie reached up to loop the rope over an iron post.

"It may not be the revolution your brother imagined, but it's a start."

Wegdell gripped a pier and held the rowboat steady while she climbed out first. Condrie stood waiting for him to ascend the ladder and join her on the dock.

"It will be dangerous," he said, coming to stand next to her.

Condrie smiled thinly. "I've been in danger since the first day I met you. By now, I'm getting used to the feeling."

"Then you have no hesitation to abandon any chance you still have for an ordinary home life? You would be willing to continue living as we have done the past few days?"

"I'm not afraid." Condrie pressed close to his side. She waited for him to put his arm around her.

Instead, he started walking forward. He set the pace with broad, slow strides. His boots clump-clumped heavily on the wooden pier.

She walked alongside him, her shorter legs working hard to keep up with his unhurried pace. The air's chill seeped through her linen sleeves and into her skin. As she walked, she rubbed her arms.

"You're cold." He glanced down to her from the corners of his eyes. "I'm sorry that I keep forgetting."

"We'll be indoors soon."

Wegdell slipped off his cloak and draped it over her shoulders. His warmth, held in the wool's linen lining, became her own. The hem that had barely reached his ankles dragged on the pier behind her.

She asked, "Have you been to this town before? From what you said to the guards at the border, I'm assuming you know your way around the streets?"

"You should be in charge of this." He handed over his bag of coins.

"By the way, where did you get this money?" she asked. "You didn't steal it, did you?"

He stopped.

Condrie went on a few steps before she realized he was not with her. She turned around to face him.

He bowed his head as if ashamed and began to breathe more heavily.

"I shouldn't have asked. It's not important." The coin bag was too heavy for her to strap to her belt, so she just held it against her belly.

Flexing his shoulders, he extended his arms and stiffened his fingers. His breaths came harder now, huffing loudly as if he had been running for hours. Warm air wafted into her chilled cheeks, and then she knew. *He's transforming.*

"Why are you doing this!" she cried. "Where are you going without me? You're not going to do something rash at the castle, are you?"

"I've told you all along that you should stay away from me, but I apologize for not explaining why we shouldn't be together."

"What are you saying?"

"Did you . . . ever stop to wonder"—he spoke in halting gasps, his voice thickening to a hoarse squawk—"why Gerrie . . . always called you a larva?"

As she reached for him, Wegdell's hands erupted in flames. The yellow-white brightness startled her. She jumped back.

"Don't do this!

Back arched, neck craned back, he opened his mouth as if to gulp the cold moonlight. He raised his arms straight overhead. Fire dribbled down off his hands. He released a loud groan as his neck elongated and his jaw lengthened into a golden beak. Flames poured over his shoulders. Clothes dissolved into sparkling cinders that sprinkled around his feet. Condrie squinted as she strained to keep watching his human skin unraveling, turning into feathers. His legs shrank into spindly legs. His toes warped into talons.

"Please stop it! Stop it!"

Wegdell cawed a shrill cry from his fiery golden beak. The resonance pierced her skull like a fife blown into her ear. She winced. Her eyes squinted shut so hard that sparkles of green and purple filled her sight.

His caw echoed deeper and deeper inside her. It banged and throbbed. Her thoughts cracked. Memories unraveled. The boat on the river and being cocooned in the warmth of his arms . . . the curtained bed in the baron's manor house . . . the secure bricks of the wine cellar . . . the comfort of the tavern's kitchen with all its windows shuttered . . . enclosed . . . safe . . . *larva*.

Memories continued to dance through her mind. Once more, she relived the funeral of her elderly husband and the scorn of the townsfolk. *Husband-killer . . . barren womb. . . .* She recalled gripping the widow's veil tightly under her chin and not saying a word in response.

Tumbling backward over the years of her life, the scenes that she had thought long forgotten resurfaced in her mind. Her father counted a handful of coins as he avoided looking into her eyes. *Cain't keep you no more . . . cain't feed ya . . . marriage is th' best place for ya. . . .* The cottage where she spent her childhood years swelled up larger and larger in her memories. The same tabletop was once unreachable to her fingertips. The ladles and spatulas hanging on hooks by the fireplace were once too large to handle.

She had toddled on unsteady feet. Before that, she had crawled on her belly. Before that, she had been carried in a swaddling blanket.

Earlier and earlier, the storm of her thoughts continued to blow in reverse until she came to a memory seen through a blueish haze. She felt smaller than she ever had, no larger than a barnyard hen being carried in someone's arms. A woman . . . a weeping woman carried her toward a man. . .

.

Her father was in his younger years, when his hair was still dark and his shoulders were not bent.

"It's a girl," said the midwife.

"She's so small."

"Yeah, that she is. Came too early. Pray she survives till morn, tho' I won't lie to ya. She may not."

Her father received Condrie into his arms. His fingertips touched her cheek, and Condrie felt an impulse to purse her lips and turn toward it. Hunger cramped her belly. Air scratched her newly inflated lungs. She cried, and it sounded like a cricket's chirp.

"My wife?"

"Spirits bless us, but she's got th' childbed fever. Ya should say goodbye now."

"No . . . no. . . ." He moved closer to the wall of mud and straw.

A woman lay on the dirt floor. Coarse blankets covered all but her face and one arm. Reddish-orange curls were limp with sweat. Her eyes were closed. Her hand was purplish blue and the color slowly wicked upward staining her brown skin to violet.

"Ya shouldn't bring th' baby near," said the midwife. "Did ya hear? It's th' childbed fever. Do ya wanna lose 'em both?"

"Go away. Get out!"

The midwife withdrew. "Spirits bless this place. Mercy on the mother. Mercy on the child."

Her father sank to his knees beside the woman on the floor. "My love, my love. What've I done to ya? How stupid o' me! That a simple clod can keep to wife such a wondrous one as ye."

Her eyelids fluttered and strained to open. "Husband?"

"Yeah! I'm here. I got yer baby girl. She's a beaut. Look! Look, can ya see her?"

The woman's irises were as black as the pupils and filled the entire hollow of her eyelids. "My sweet."

"Don't leave me, my love. What'll I do without ya? How will I raise a daughter all by meself?"

"I am not leaving you," the woman whispered. "I will always be with you. Every time you take a breath . . . every time the spring winds stir the flowering trees . . . every flap of a bird's wings. . . ."

"No, no, no!"

The woman smiled as she closed her eyes. "Do not weep for me. It is as it should be."

"No."

"I have been too long in human skin."

She stopped breathing, and yet the rushing sound of a sigh grew louder. Air brushed over Condrie's cheeks.

The woman's brown skin faded to gray. Then a hue of purplish indigo seeped up from her forearms to her shoulder, filled up the gray skin on her neck, and spread over her face. The features of her face dissolved. Her nose flattened. Her lips melted together. Her skin crinkled like a dried persimmon. Her chest deflated, and the blanket that covered her body went flat to the ground.

A pause hushed the small room.

"Oh no, no, spirits of th' air and earth, please let me keep her a little longer." Her father hugged little baby Condrie close to his chest, a tiny bundle swaddled in a coarse linen kerchief.

The blanket pulsed and rippled. It swelled upward into a dome. Then it burst.

Moths swarmed out from the blanket. A thousand fluttering wings of all different kinds—orange and black, blue and yellow, spotted white and gray. They swirled in a tornado of little wings, sprinkling colored dust in a living vine that coiled around the sunbeams. They swarmed upward in an unraveling column of colored wings, upward to the thatched roof, upward out the little hole at the peak of the ceiling where the cooking fire's smoke would go. Upward and beyond, they went streaming out into the freedom of the clear blue sky.

Condrie's thoughts whirled like the rush of opening a door to the winter's winds. Inhaling the cold night and the memory of a long-forgotten day, her mind streaked back to the present.

Once more, she stood on the pier at Lake Ward, looking into the clear, cold yellow eyes of the firebird.

"All along, you always knew?" She raised her voice to shout into the rippling heat veil that surrounded him. "You knew! I am . . . I am only half a girl, and I am half a Sagewyn too?"

Wegdell tilted his beak and bobbed his head slightly.

"I'm a Sagewyn too," she said again. "A rare type, I think. I was born of a type of moth, was I?"

A rush of hot wind caused her to blink. When she opened her eyes again, he had already turned about. Heat became a wall of crackling air pushing her away. At that moment, she knew he was leaving and would not be back. Never again would she hear his human voice or see his latest new face. Wings spread wide, he skipped a few sizzling steps and leaped off the pier.

The firebird jumped beak-first into the soft breezes that drifted over the lake's still waters. Wings pumped to climb through the currents of the air, higher and higher. She rotated in place to watch him glide a circle that spiraled ever upward. She watched his fiery wings shrink smaller and smaller. At last, he plunged into clouds and disappeared from her view. She kept standing there for a while, looking up at the pale moon in the empty sky. She waited to feel an urge to cry, but felt nothing but serenity.

"There's no such things as firebirds," she whispered. "There's no such thing."

The bag of coins weighed on her hand. Drawing in a breath, Condrie turned away from the end of the pier. Her cloak flared wide as she quickly walked back toward the beginning. Her footsteps grew faster and faster. Her feet became lighter and lighter. The bag of coins dropped to thud on the planks.

Her body burst free of its human skin. A swarm of white moths fluttered out of the empty woolen cloak. Thousands and thousands of moths' pale wings shined with flakes of moon dust swirling up into the night sky.

THE END

Don't miss out!

Visit the website below and you can sign up to receive emails whenever Denise Tanaka publishes a new book. There's no charge and no obligation.

https://books2read.com/r/B-A-UPKD-DCON

BOOKS 2 READ

Connecting independent readers to independent writers.

About the Author

Denise Tanaka has a lifelong passion for writing stories of magical beings and faraway worlds. Her father inspired a love of art with his landscape paintings, portraits, and photography. Her mother inspired a love of books by reading aloud *The Gingerbread Man* and *Mrs. Tittlemouse*, so from a very young age Denise believed that cookies run away and mice can talk.

Read more at sasorizabooks.com.